SLOCUM

Other novels by Alfred Dennis

Chiricahua
Lone Eagle
Elkhorn Divide
Brant's Fort
Catamount
The Mustangers
Rover
Sandigras Canyon
Yellowstone Brigade
Shawnee Trail
Fort Reno
Yuma
Ride the Rough String
Trail to Medicine Mound
Arapaho Lance: Crow Killer Series - Book 1
Lance Bearer: Crow Killer Series - Book 2
Track of the Grizzly: Crow Killer Series - Book 3
Bear Claw: Crow Killer Series - Book 4

To see more books by Alfred Dennis visit
www.alfreddennis.com

SLOCUM

by

Alfred Dennis

Walnut Creek Publishing
Tuskahoma, Oklahoma

Slocum

This novel is a work of fiction. Names, characters, places, and incidents are
either the product of the author's imagination or are used fictitiously. Any
resemblance to actual events, locales, organizations, or persons, living or dead, is
entirely coincidental and beyond the intent of either the author or the publisher.

ISBN: 978-1-942869-33-7
First Edition, Paperback
Published 2020 by Walnut Creek Publishing
Library of Congress Control Number: 2020909945

Books may be purchased in quantity and/or special sales by contacting
the publisher;
Walnut Creek Publishing
PO Box 820
Talihina, OK 74571
www.wc-books.com

Front cover
Photograph of author's father, Asa (A.C. Dennis) & Buck.
"Great cowboy and great cowdog."

This book is dedicated to
my two sons, Carl and Kevin,
taken from this earth far too early in life.
Rest in peace my sons.
You are both truly missed and never forgotten

Forward

Eighteen seventy, the Civil War was over as the last shot of the bloody war had been fired. Soldiers, thieves, killers, Comanche and Comancheros, along with the few honest settlers were the ones living on the edge of the wild Texas frontier. Along the sparsely populated Brazos and Bosque Rivers, the land was flat and overrun with the wily, unpredictable Texas Longhorns. The hardy longhorn cattle, running wild and unfettered during the war, had multiplied several times over. There was always danger lurking whenever a rider rode out alone, leaving his home ranch, venturing out into the vast lands of northern Texas.

Reed Slocum's uncle, Wes Slocum, had been severely hurt when he was working cattle which put the upcoming cattle drive to Sedalia, Missouri in jeopardy. Wes Slocum, owner of the huge Bar S Ranch, was busted up badly, close to dying, and unable to lead the herd north. The Bar S Ranch had a note coming due by the first of the year, a note now held by his onetime friend and owner of the Rafter J Ranch, Rail Johnson. After Wes Slocum's brother, Watt, had killed Freckles Johnson, Rail Johnson's brother, in a fit of rage over his wife, the two ranchers had become bitter enemies. Now, Johnson held the note and would foreclose on the Bar S in revenge for his brother's death.

Watt Slocum, the younger brother, was a huge man, standing well over six feet and weighing in over two hundred thirty pounds. A giant man for the times, and he had a temper to match his size. Watt Slocum had been sent away and left the Bar S after he had killed Freckles Johnson with his bare hands. Now, Wes needed him back. The Bar S needed him back. Watt Slocum was the only man Wes could depend on to get the herd to Sedalia.

The big man had to be found which would be no easy task, as he had been away from the Bar S for fifteen years. The round-up and branding could be handled by Emmet Tabor, the ramrod of the outfit. However, the herd had to have a strong, hard man with special gifts to head them safely to Missouri. Watt Slocum was that man; a killer of men, but a leader of men as well. Wes Slocum knew his brother was hunting wolves in Colorado territory. He had been spotted several times around Amarillo and the small town of Dade.

The hurt man had to send someone after his brother, someone who wouldn't get himself killed before he could explain to the wolfer what he was sent after him for. Watt Slocum had become a hard man, one who had killed and whipped many a man with his bare hands, all across Texas. He was a man who would shoot first and ask questions later.

Looking up from the bed, Wes stared at the tall young man he had raised. He knew his nephew, Reed Slocum, was the only one he could send after his brother. The only one Watt Slocum wouldn't shoot once he knew who the youngster was. The boy was young, but could he handle such a difficult, long journey and bring Watt Slocum back to the ranch in time?

Wes knew he could get the lad killed, but he had no choice. He either sends him after his brother or loses the ranch. Only one man could get the Bar S cattle to Sedalia and that man was Watt Slocum. Miles and miles of prairie, the Llano Estacado, snakes, killers, Comanches and the dreaded Comancheros waited out there for the young Slocum. Would the youngster have the nerve and ability to get the job done?

CHAPTER 1

Dust and plowed dirt drifted in a haze over the corral as the wild, range cattle milled about the log pole enclosure. Shaking their long, sharp horns and bawling in fear and rage, the rangy cows pawed the ground and threatened to charge the working cowboys. Two hog-tied calves, on the ground, bawled out in pain as the red-hot branding iron bit into their hides. A grizzled, older man worked the fire, keeping the irons red-hot while two muggers waited as the wranglers on horseback dragged struggling calves to the hot fire.

"Watch that old mossy horn cow, boss." One of the mounted riders called out. "She's really stirred up and on the warpath."

"I got my eye on her, Emmet." A big man flanked the struggling calf powerfully on its side, he nodded for the branding iron.

Releasing the calf, Wes Slocum motioned for another calf, then grinned over at the young man beside him. A brindle calf was dragged to the fire by his hind legs and held fast as two men, one young and one older, took hold of it and removed the hemp rope.

"We're doing pretty good, Uncle Wes." The tall, light-headed young man flanked the bawling calf and held it for the hot iron. "We should finish this bunch by midday."

"We should alright, but we've still got plenty more to brand." The older man nodded. "Now, get yourself a good grip, this calf is stout."

Both men and animals smelled the stench of burning hair as the hot air carried the acrid smoke across the dusty corral, causing the mother cows to shake their heads in fury. Maddened by the noise of their helpless calves bawling from the searing pain of the iron, the older cows would charge man or horse. Dragging another calf to the fire, the second mounted rider, engrossed with the struggling calf, momentarily took his eyes from the mother cows. He didn't notice the mossy horn cow charge toward the fire where her calf was being thrown on its side. With all the noise from the bawling cattle and the thick dust, he didn't see the enraged cow before she hooked him, gutting his horse and knocking him from the saddle. Racing past the down and kicking horse, the cow charged the fire where her calf lay struggling. The rangy cow lunged at the larger man, who at the last moment tried to avoid her deadly, bloody horns.

Knocked face first into the dirt, the big man didn't see the swinging rope that encircled the cow's horns. The rope jerked taught dragging the cow away at the last moment, preventing her from goring him worse.

"You hurt bad, Uncle Wes?" The younger man hovered over the gasping man anxiously.

Trying to regain his wind, the big rancher rolled around on the dusty ground. Looking down worriedly while kneeling beside the hurt man, Reed Slocum tried to watch the herd as he attempted to raise his uncle into a sitting position.

"Don't lift him, boy." A tall, thin rider swung down easily from his saddle. "Just let him lie there and catch his wind."

"I think she missed him with her horns." The younger man examined the torn shirt. "Leastways, I don't see any blood."

"Maybe so, but he took a terrible shot. He could be hurt inside… a rib or something." The tall rider knelt beside the groaning man. "You leave him be now, and skedaddle for the doc."

"Yes, sir." The younger Slocum nodded. "You'll see to him then?"

"I'll get him into the house." Emmett Tabor studied the young man. "Take my animal and ride, boy."

"Yes, sir. I'm gone."

"Ride hard. Don't spare the leather, Reed." Tabor laid his hand on the rasping man's chest. "I fear he may be hurt pretty bad inside."

"I'll hurry, Emmett." The younger man raced for the huge bay horse.

Tabor looked at the gored horse. "One of your boys put him out of his misery."

Several cowhands lounged along the porch railing as a high-stepping bay pulled the doctor's buggy to a stop in front of the rambling ranch house. Stepping down stiffly, the grey-haired doctor cast a dubious glance at the worried riders as he started through the door.

"You want us to take care of your horse, Doc?" A small bowlegged rider called through the open door.

"You leave him be, Joe Casper." The grouchy voice answered from inside the door. "If I want him tended to, I'll do it myself."

"Sure is a friendly cuss, ain't he?" Another cowhand laughed.

"No, Ned. He ain't friendly." The redheaded Casper spoke up. "What he is… he's the best sawbones in the country."

"Sure he is. Trouble is, he's the only sawbones around these parts." Another cowhand spat. "That's what you mean, ain't it?"

"Don't matter what I mean, Howe." The redhead shook his head. "He's the best we got."

"Why, cause he patched you back together after that roan broke your leg last year?"

"Now that's the plain truth, me and how many others?" Casper shook his head as the small doctor disappeared through the door.

Doc Samuel Boudean approached the bed where the big man lay on his back with his eyes closed. He could see the chest slowly rising and dropping, and he could hear a raspy rattle as the hurt man drew in air. Easing his stethoscope out of the worn black bag, he was about to bend over the injured rancher when the blue eyes snapped open wide, locking onto the doctor's face.

"Good to see you, Sam." The voice was low, coming out in a hoarse whisper. "Hate the boy had to get you out of your bed so early."

"Smart aleck." Boudean shook his head. "Well, Mister Wes Slocum, peers you have gotten yourself in a real fix this time."

"Yeah, peers I have this time for sure." The sweaty, brown hair nodded slowly.

"Lie quiet now and let me have a listen." For several minutes the doctor examined the hurt man, then slowly shook his head.

"Bad, Doc?"

Boudean glanced over to where Reed Slocum and Emmet Tabor,

the ranch foreman, stood back against the far wall. "Wes, you're hurt bad and this time it's serious."

"Well, spit it out Sam. How bad is it?" The words slurred painfully.

Boudean looked over at the two men again, then rubbed his chin. "You've got some broken ribs and one of them punched a hole through your lung."

"What else?" Slocum coughed slightly. "Shucks, I've been busted up pretty bad before, but my insides feel like they've been ridden hard and put up wet this go 'round."

"Can't say for sure, but hopefully your spleen and liver aren't damaged." Boudean rubbed his chin. "You sure took a blow alright."

"Am I a goner or can you pull me through?" The rancher swallowed. "Just lay it out plain, Doc, and don't hold nothing back."

"The ribs and lung should heal, providing you don't get any infections." The little doctor shook his head. "The rest will take a few days to work out. We'll just have to wait and see."

"A few days?" Slocum's glazed eyes looked up at the doctor. "What's a few mean, Sam?"

"Let's get you fixed up, then we'll worry about the rest."

"I need to know Doc, now." Slocum glared up at Boudean. "I ain't got the time to tiptoe around this one."

"Wes, at the very least, you'll be in this bed for several weeks."

"Are you crazy, you old windbag? I can't lay here that long." Wes Slocum swore. "Can't you hear me?"

"You'll stay put Wes, that is, if you want to pull through this wreck." Boudean frowned down at the rancher. "You get out of that bed any sooner and you're as good as dead. Take that from this old windbag."

"Don't get your feathers ruffled, I've called you worse." Slocum looked over at Reed and Tabor. "But, this time I can't stay in bed. I've got a herd to drive north."

"You've got men that can handle the roundup and drive." The doctor pulled out a roll of white cloth. "I'll send out a woman from town to nurse you while they're gone."

"You'll play the devil doing that."

"I've never known of you fearing the women, Mister Slocum." Boudean shook his head. "What's one more?"

"Wrap me up, Sam, and then get out." Wes growled. "And don't you be sending any female out here to wet nurse me."

"You'll be needing a cook."

"Henry will do my cooking." Slocum snapped.

"You talking about old Henry, your old barn sweeper? Why he barely can feed your horses." Boudean laughed. "Probably poison you to boot."

Only the sound of gritting teeth was heard in the room as the doctor wrapped the broken ribs and pulled the cloth tight to secure it. Closing his medical bag, Boudean straightened and looked down at his patient. Removing his glasses and rubbing his chin thoughtfully, the doctor placed a bottle of pills on the nightstand, then picked up his coat.

"For once in your life you better listen to me, Wes Slocum, or you could get an infection that'll kill you." Boudean looked at the other two men. "Young man, you want your uncle to die? Well then, you just let him get out of that bed before I say so."

"He's the boss here, Doc." Tabor straightened. "He sure don't take kindly to us telling him what to do."

"Well, Emmet, he may be the boss around here, but I'm telling you, he'll be doing his bossing from this bed, for many weeks to come, or from the graveyard." Boudean shook his finger.

"Get out, Sam." The injured man spoke up. "And no woman."

"You've got such a sweet personality, Wes." Boudean shook his head. "It's made you one of my favorite patients, ever since you were whelped."

"Yeah, and you don't help it none." Slocum cussed in pain. "You sure ain't no saint to be around yourself, you old reprobate."

"I'll be back tomorrow." The old doctor rubbed his chin again and clucked his tongue lightly. "Those pills are for pain, use them."

"No woman, you hear me, Sam?"

"Did you say something, Wes?"

"Dang your miserable old hide, Sam Boudean. Get out!"

The younger Slocum and Tabor moved closer to the bed as the door closed behind the frowning doctor. Both men looked down at the rancher and waited for him to speak first. Slocum hesitated several minutes, holding his words before turning his eyes to look up at them.

"We've got ourselves into a real pickle this time, boys." The dark head nodded. "This is really bad."

"Is it that bad, boss?" Tabor asked.

"Worse, I ain't spoke of it. Weren't anyone's concern. The Bar S has a note against it, due at the bank sometime next spring." Slocum studied the two figures. "That's why I've been riding you boys so hard to finish the round-up, quick as we can."

"We'll make out alright, Wes." Tabor leaned over the bed. "What's your orders?"

"Emmett, you and the boys continue with the gather and branding." Slocum coughed slightly. "Get them cows ready for the trail, then we'll go from there."

"Ok, boss. How much time we got before we need to be driving north?"

"Maybe a month, month and a half, not one day more." Slocum grimaced in pain. "We've got to reach Sedalia ahead of the others. To get the highest market for our steers, we've got to get there first."

"We'll need another thirty horses for the remuda." Tabor slapped the weathered hat against his side. "At least thirty."

"I've already made arrangements for them." Slocum seemed to smile. "That's one little item our opponents don't know about yet. Charlie Snooks sold me the horses."

"Our opponents, by that you're meaning Rail Johnson?"

"Yep, the one and only. He wants this ranch, has for years, and he'll do anything to stop this drive." Wes frowned. "Worse, he's the one holding the note I signed."

"Thought you said the bank held it?"

"At first the bank did."

"What happened?"

"When Dirk Barnaby at the bank took over, the old horse thief sold my note to Johnson, who holds the papers now." Wes nodded slowly. "Rail's got himself a bulldog grip on the Bar S okay. And boys, if he has his way, he'll choke the life out this ranch."

"That sure sounds kinda sticky, boss." Tabor slapped his leg. "Rail Johnson is a polecat. Is it legal?"

"I reckon it's legal, but don't matter in the long run." Slocum nodded. "I signed the paper and gave my word, and a man is only as good as his word."

Tabor grinned. "Well, at least you can't blame that old, mossy horn, brindle cow on him."

"Don't know about that. He might have told her to get me out of the way."

"Boss?"

"Get to it, Emmett, times a wasting. Give the boys the lowdown." Slocum looked over at his nephew. "You wait here a minute, Reed. I'll have words with you."

"Yes, sir."

"Emmett, tell the boys there'll be a bonus for each of them if they stick with me, and we make it to Sedalia in time."

"They won't hang you out to dry. You know that." Tabor stopped and turned at the door. "Boss, weren't you and Rail Johnson pretty close at one time?"

Frowning, the big rancher nodded, then motioned Tabor from the room. "At one time, we were like brothers."

"What happened?"

"Watt Slocum. It happened before your time."

"Your brother?"

"Yes, my brother."

Both men waited until they heard the Bar S Riders move off the porch before speaking.

"Boy, I've got a rough job waiting for you. I hate to give you the task, but the simple fact is, you are the only one that can get this job done."

"Yes, sir."

"I know you're young, but even so, I also know you've always been steady when the going gets rough."

"Tell me what it is you want." The youngster waved off the words of praise. "I can handle it."

Slocum stared up at the ceiling for several minutes, then turned his piercing blue eyes on the youth. "I s'pect old Doc Sam was telling the truth. I won't be leaving this bed for some time. I can feel my bones playing with one another, just grinding away every time I take a breath."

"You were pretty rough on the doctor."

"Nah, just our way of going at each other." Wes smiled slightly. "He don't take offense, nor do I."

"Uncle, what are you asking of me?"

"You're still young and you've never had a chance to lead a long drive or handle men." Wes looked up at the tall young man. "But, you're like your pa. You've got the makings."

"I ain't that young, turned nineteen last week." Reed shrugged. "Anyhow, you've got Emmett."

"Emmett is a good man sure enough, but he's a cowman not a gunfighter. He's sure not strong enough to buck Rail Johnson and his Rafter J killers."

"That's being kinda hard on him isn't it, Uncle?" Reed looked down at the hurting man. "He's rode with you for ten or twelve years now. He's always got the job done."

"Just the truth, lad… just the truth." Wes looked out the window. "You know, out here, we have to own up to the bare facts. You want Emmett Tabor dead, boy? I'm telling you, he's no match for Rail Johnson or his riders."

"What are you wanting me to do?" Reed studied the pain-racked face. "You figure I'm a match for Johnson's bunch?"

"I don't want you fighting Johnson, lad. You're still kinda green behind the ears." Slocum grimaced. "I've got another job for you."

"Well?"

"Now, don't get yourself all het up. I know you've tangled with your share of men and held your own with most of them." Slocum grimaced. "You got sand, boy, but that's not what I need right now."

"Spit it out, Uncle Wes." Reed shook his head. "Tell me what you want."

"There's only one man I know who can get this herd through. Only one man I can trust the life of this ranch with." Slocum wiped his mouth. "Lord, how I hate to send for him. The words go sour on my tongue."

"Who are you talking about?"

Slocum looked up into the tall youth's eyes. "Never in this lifetime would I have thought it."

"Who?" Reed Slocum was becoming frustrated with his uncle's stalling.

"My brother, Watt Slocum." The injured man swore. "Meanest, cold-hearted man that ever drew a breath."

Reed had never heard the name mentioned. He didn't even know his uncle had a brother until Tabor had said the word brother. "You've never spoken of him."

"I ran him off the Bar S fifteen years ago and forbid his name to be used in my earshot." Slocum frowned. "I'd fire anybody who mentioned his name. Matter of fact, I have."

"I thought you said he was a bad man. How did you run him off?"

"He's bad, sure enough, clean through." Slocum hesitated. "But, one thing our pa taught us as kids, family don't fight family."

"Just like that?" Reed was curious. "You told your own brother to leave and he did?"

"He's younger than me by a couple years. I told him to ride, he rode out, and I haven't seen him since."

"Didn't your pa leave this ranch to both of you?"

"He did, Watt's part will be here when he straightens his head out." Wes scowled. "Providing he ever does."

"What did he do that was so bad you had to run your own blood off the ranch?"

"It was a long time ago, boy. Best just to let it be."

"No, I want to hear it. If I'm going after him, I deserve to know." Reed shook his head stubbornly. "And it sure sounds like that's where I'm heading."

"I don't like it, but I've got to send you after him."

"Alright, but first you tell me, what did he do, Uncle Wes?"

"Beat a man to death out there in the bunkhouse with his bare hands." Wes closed his eyes. "He was Rail Johnson's brother, Freckles Johnson. Now, you've heard it. Are you satisfied?"

Nodding his head, Reed looked out the window. "I guess you learn something new every day."

"I'm short of riders, lad. I know it'll be hard, but I need you to take this ride." Wes looked over at Reed. "I won't order you, I'm asking. If we don't get Watt back here, we're liable to lose the ranch and our home."

"I'm a grown man, Uncle." The youngster tapped his pistol. "Every day, I do a man's work. Emmett made sure I know how to use a gun and my fists."

"I want you to find Watt Slocum and give him a message from me."

"Where would I look? You said you haven't seen him in years."

"No, I haven't seen him, but I've kept tabs of his whereabouts and some of his escapades." Wes shook his head. "Anybody in five hundred miles 'round about these parts, knows and fears Watt Slocum."

"Okay, where you figure he is?"

"Old Henry was told by a grub line rider couple weeks back that he was seen wolf hunting, up around Dade, Colorado."

"A wolfer!" Reed shook his head. "I've heard Emmett and the boys say they are the lowest form of bounty hunters. They say they use strychnine poison to kill the wolves."

"Some do, I reckon. Up north, after the last bad winter, the wolves moved in and seemed to multiply overnight, eating everything in their path, alive or dead."

"So they called in the wolf hunters for the bounty?"

"Wolves are smart and deadly. It takes a killer to hunt down a killer." Wes looked out the window. "Yes, they're about the wiliest creatures the good Lord ever created."

"And this brother of yours, my uncle, is a killer?"

"That he is, Reed. He's meaner than a starving rattlesnake." Slocum moved his head. "Don't you ever think different, boy. My brother is bad clear through."

Reed shook his head. "That's pretty mean."

"Watt is up there somewhere. I'm asking you to ride up there and bring him back." Wes nodded. "I sure wouldn't say anything to him about bounty hunting for wolves though."

"And if he doesn't want to come?"

"Bring him." Wes waved his hand. "Get money from my desk and ride."

"Colorado is a far piece to ride." The youngster shrugged. "I thought you needed these cattle on the trail quick?"

"I do, but we've still got pert near two thousand head to round up and trail brand."

"Yes, sir." Reed nodded. "That'll take some time alright."

"We've got the jump on the other ranches." Wes smiled. "They don't know yet we're gathering our cattle."

Reed knew the ranches were flung far and wide across the open plains. Most ranch houses could be as far as fifty miles apart. Only a rider accidentally passing by, where the herds were being gathered, could spread the word so they probably hadn't been discovered yet.

"I reckon we've been lucky so far." Reed nodded down at the hurt man. "When do you want me to leave?"

"Soon as you can saddle a horse." Wes moaned. "We've no time to lose."

"I'll saddle up."

"It'll take at least a month or more to finish the gather and branding." Wes looked at his young nephew. "Riding hard, you should reach Amarillo in a couple weeks or less."

"Locating him may not be easy. That's a lot of country to cover."

"I'll guarantee, if'n he's in a hundred mile circle, people will know of him."

"He must be a rough one."

"You just make sure he knows who you are before you ride up on him." Wes looked at the younger man. "You scared, boy?"

"No, sir. It's just that I ain't never been farther away from the ranch than the railhead last year on that one trip to Amarillo."

"I know I'm asking a lot, but I know Watt, and he'd probably kill anyone else I send after him." Wes moved painfully in the bed. "When you find him, remember to make sure you identify yourself to him quick. It would be healthier for you."

"Thanks a lot, Uncle." Reed looked across the bed and shook his head. "Is he really all that bad?"

"Clean to the bone and back." The hurt man seemed to be recollecting on his past. "He's walking death, son, with a knife, gun or his bare fists."

"He sounds kinda spooky."

"Don't know about spooky, but he's a big man, powerful and cat quick." Wes swore. "You watch him, Reed. He's cold and he don't back water from any living soul. You remember that when you face him."

"And after I find him, providing I do, what then?" Reed shrugged.

"Cut across the panhandle and catch up to the herd at Doan's Crossing on the Red River." Slocum rolled his head on his pillows. "It's down around Wichita Falls. My brother will know the way."

"I'll do my best." Reed looked at the heaving chest. "You figure Emmett can point the cattle to this Doan's Crossing okay?"

"Johnson won't try anything as long as the herd's still in Texas." Slocum groaned. "He doesn't want any trouble with the rangers."

"Alright, Uncle, I'll do my best."

"I need better than your best, Reed. I'm depending on you." The big man nodded. "Be on the alert, besides Watt Slocum, there's a whole country with plenty of Indians and bad men out there to give you trouble."

"Watt Slocum, so he's my uncle too?"

Wes turned his head. "Yeah, boy. I reckon he is, for what it's worth."

"Well then, I'll gather my gear and head north." Reed turned for the door. "How far you reckon Amarillo is?"

"Riding hard, I figure it'll take you ten or eleven days, maybe less." Wes held out his hand. "Load up a packhorse with supplies and sleeping gear."

"Sounds like it's a long ride." Reed took the extended hand.

"You rode to Amarillo last year with Emmett." Wes tried to smile. "You can do it again."

"Yes, sir." Reed nodded. "I had fun. All I remember was the sea of grass out on the plains and that small fight with the Comancheros."

"Well, it ain't moved any." Slocum groaned. "You'll find my brother somewhere north of Amarillo."

"Yeah, I sorta remember Amarillo." Reed grinned. "Emmet showed me the saloons and such."

"When you get there, ask around. They'll put you on the right trail north." Wes nodded weakly. "Don't trust anybody and don't make friends. Keep to yourself, and be alert and distrustful of every rider you meet."

"Yes, sir."

"And remember, the Comancheros are still out there just waiting for a stray to ride into their hands."

"I'll remember." Reed's mind flashed back to the fight they had with the small band of Comancheros on their way to Amarillo. They were a tough bunch of killers, riffraff, and completely fearless.

"Send Emmet back in." Wes nodded. "And Reed, if you're jumped, you shoot first and ask questions second."

"Yes, sir."

"And don't turn your back on anyone or anything." Wes winced. "Don't trust anyone or anything. You hear?"

"Yes, sir." Reed nodded. "I heard you the first time, Uncle."

Tabor eased through the door and crossed softly to the bed. "I'm here, Wes."

The pain-wracked eyes blinked open. "I didn't want to do it, Emmet, but I had to send the boy north to find my brother."

"To head the drive?"

"No… offense, Emmet. I need a hard man to make sure we beat Rail Johnson." The rancher turned his head slightly. "If we don't get these cattle to market, we lose everything. All of us."

"I understand, no offense taken."

"I'm sending Reed. What do you think of his chances?"

"Well boss, he's young, but the boy has a level head and more grit than most seasoned men." Emmet looked over at the bed. "We've raised him pretty rough. He's been through an awful lot for his short years."

"Will grit be enough, Emmet?"

"Like I said, Wes, he's young." Tabor looked out the window. "But if I was in a tough spot, he's the one I'd want siding me."

"Why?"

"I told you, he has grit. He's faster with that forty-four on his side than anyone I've ever seen." Emmet smiled. "And I've not yet seen the man that can whip him in a stand up fistfight, except maybe Watt Slocum himself."

"I wish I could believe that."

"You remember that big Swede that worked for the Diamond C Ranch?"

"I do, all three hundred pounds of him, all muscle." Wes nodded. "He's one giant of a man and tough as rawhide."

"Well, Reed whipped him in town a couple months back." Emmet laughed. "He wouldn't let any of us tell you about it."

"Was that why he was limping around here for a week or better?"

"Yep, it was nip and tuck there for a while, but believe it or not, the boy finally got it done." Emmet chuckled with the recollection. "That Swede is one tough customer. The next day they said his face was as black as the ace of spades."

"I'd have liked to have seen that fight." Wes nodded. "Hard to believe the kid whipped that big ox, Slos Hangren."

"He did, but you wouldn't have liked to watch it." Emmet frowned. "I didn't. Reed was brutal. He beat that man something awful. When he gets mad, he's mean like your brother, maybe meaner."

"That's hard to believe anyone is as mean as my brother."

"Boss, do you recall the gun slick that worked for us a couple months to earn traveling money?"

"You mean Bodie Paul?" Wes nodded. "I remember him."

"That's him, he taught Reed every trick with a six-gun he knew and he knew a lot of them." Tabor grinned. "No, sir, that boy will do just fine. I wouldn't want to be in the boots of the man that crosses him."

"I must have missed something. I didn't know he knew that much about guns."

"Don't worry boss, he knows." Tabor nodded. "Like I said, he's faster than any man I ever seen with a six-gun, and I've seen them all; Paul, Longley, and Wes Hardin."

"But, just not as deadly."

"Not yet, but like you said, he's young yet." Emmet smiled. "He's kinda like your brother, stir him up, and he's hard and unforgiving. I'm afraid he'll learn to be deadly real quick."

CHAPTER 2

Reed Slocum had just turned nineteen. He was big for his age, and like his uncles, his frame promised great strength and physical size with full maturity. The Slocum family had originally emigrated from south of Scotland, and every generation was blessed with an imposing carriage and bearing. Reed Slocum was the product of strong men, but he was young and hadn't learned the hard lessons of life the prairies and badlands could teach. He had fought his fair share of bunkhouse fistfights or with the town's toughs, and so far, he had held his own with all of them.

Now, he would be riding through dangerous land, chocked full of every riffraff imaginable, which was far removed from the friendly fistfights in town. Comanches, Comancheros, outlaws, ex-soldiers, wild animals, and rattlesnakes that could strike the length of their body and kill with one bite. Every type of killer roamed or crawled on these prairies. Most of the lowlife men riding these lands would steal the money from their dead momma's eyes.

The injured rancher never wanted to send his nephew on the long ride to the north through the dangerous country that was inhabited by dangers of every kind. Nevertheless, he had no choice as he was short of riders, but that was not his only reason. Anyone approaching Watt Slocum, trying to persuade him to return to the Bar S, could get killed real sudden like. They would be dead before they had time to explain Wes Slocum's reasons for requesting Watt's return. He knew his nephew Reed wasn't in any danger from Watt. Wes knew his brother wouldn't harm the young man, that is once he knew who he was.

He hated the thought of asking his brother's help for any reason, but this time he had little choice. He remembered his brother, standing well over six feet and thick as a pickaxe handle. Long, thick brown hair framed a broad forehead that held wide, deep-set blue eyes. Every time Wes looked into his brother's eyes, he remembered his father telling him stories of the olden-time great warriors of the Scots. He knew Watt Slocum was a throwback to those larger than life warriors. The man was huge, but his hair-triggered temper was even bigger. Wes remembered the night his brother had beaten Freckles Johnson to death, for his part in his wife's death. Freckles' remark about the dead woman was the final straw that broke Watt, causing him to attack the man in a rage. The remark was bad, but not enough to kill a man over words. The killing had happened so fast, Freckles was dead before anyone could stop him. Almost fifteen years had passed since he had seen Watt and he wondered if he had changed. Remembering the way Freckles' neck had snapped under the power of his brother's powerful hands, he doubted he had.

As Reed passed through lands, where herds of buffalo still roamed, the vast stretches of grass with broad plains stretching farther than an eye could see kept him in awe. Acres and acres of open prairie spread across the landscape like an ocean of rich untouched grass. The vastness of this land was enough to take the breath from any new traveler. The wind-blown and fledgling town of Amarillo, Texas was just a small sleepy cow town lying deep in the grassy plains of the land known by the Comanche as the Llano Estacado. The huge Grand Canyon of Texas, known locally as Palo Duro Canyon, lay just a few miles to the south of Amarillo. Comanches, Comancheros, buffalo hunters, and all kinds of rough men roamed this vast land looking for any defenseless travelers they could find. Many were fugitives from the law, some running from the Texas Rangers and some from the U.S. Calvary. A dangerous hunting ground, land seeped in blood, marked the land the younger Slocum had passed across as he neared the dusty town. Traveling steadily, he had taken several days of hard riding and luck to make the ride north. Now, the small trail he followed had finally brought him to the small hamlet on the plains.

Somehow, Reed Slocum had safely traversed the grassy plains avoiding several bands of Indians, plus a few other unsavory looking characters. As the saying went, luck had ridden on his shoulder, keeping him from harm's way. Several times, he had spotted small specks that turned out to be mounted riders far off in the tall waving grass, but sometimes it was just a small herd of buffalo. Staying low in the saddle, making sure he wasn't detected, Reed waited until the riders had passed unaware of his presence. He was riding a deep-chested, long-legged bay with plenty of speed, but the animal had traveled many a mile and was trail weary. He didn't know if the horse would be able to outdistance fresher horses if he was discovered out on the flat lands. Occasionally, he had nervously touched the forty-four on his side just to reassure himself the gun was there.

Following a well-beaten game trail, his eyes nervously scoured the deep grass lining the path. Finally, the trail led out onto a rutted wagon road. Reining in the horses, he studied the horizon where he had detected several spirals of smoke that had to be the smoking chimneys of the distant town of Amarillo. The trail weary, tired geldings trotted down the road, pricking their ears as the town's outskirts and several nearby horses tied to hitch racks came into sight. Just past midmorning, he reined the horses up, taking in the many horses and wagons lining the dusty road. Reed kicked the tired geldings on into town. His sharp eyes counted two general stores, three saloons, two livery stables, and a smattering of other businesses along the rutted street that led through the main artery of the settlement. Cattle pens stood close to the west end of town causing the smell of cattle to drift over the small settlement.

Not suited for farming, the land around Amarillo had been covered with vast herds of buffalo for centuries, but now, longhorn cattle also grazed and fattened on the tall grass. The town had grown considerably since his last trip north. He had ridden here just last year with Emmett Tabor to purchase a blooded bull for his uncle. On their return to the Bar S, the Comancheros had tried to steal the bull which caused a shoot-out with the bloodthirsty riders. Luckily for them, the Comancheros had been discovered by Reed in time to fight off the raiders. Reed, Emmet Tabor, and Joe Casper had been alerted, sending a swarm of bullets into the charging riders driving them off. It had been a hot contest for a few minutes, but finally the raiders had retreated leaving two of their dead behind in the grass.

Dismounting tiredly in front of the nearest livery, Reed nodded as an old man rose from where he had been reclining against a rough wall. He knew the old hostler had been watching him closely from far off as he rode into town and approached the stable.

"They've been ridden hard. Grain them and give 'em a good rub down." Reed studied the man. "How much?"

"Four bits a day." The old hostler spat a stream of tobacco. "In advance."

"Alright." Reed reached into his pocket and handed over a dollar. "I'm looking for a man."

"Do I know you, young man?"

"I doubt it, old-timer, less you been south along the Brazos Flats."

"Nope, ain't been that far south, but you do remind me of someone." The old one scratched his whiskered chin. "It'll come to me."

"You didn't ask who I was looking for."

"Alright, youngster, you got my curiosity up. Tell me, what man would that be?"

"Watt Slocum." Reed knew he had spoken the wrong name by the look that came over the hostler's face.

"Watt Slocum." The old hostler swallowed hard. "Some around here say it may not be healthy to find that one, young fella."

"That'll be my problem. You know him?"

"Yeah, to my regret, I know him." The old man reached out his hand. "Here, take your money back, boy, and find another place to stable them."

"You took my money, old man." Reed's voice hardened as his hand rested lightly on the pistol butt on his side. "Now, you take my horses and you better treat them like you would your mother. Very gently."

Swallowing nervously, the old man looked into the hard eyes of the youngster, then took the extended reins. "One night is all."

"I gave you a dollar that pays for two nights." Reed could sense the fear emitting from the man. "What are you so scared of?"

"Nothing." The old one started inside with the horses. "A word of advice, mister, if'n I was you, I wouldn't be tossing that name around. It ain't healthy, and some around here might just take offense."

"Why?"

"I ain't saying no more." The old hostler stopped and looked across the street. "Figure, I done shot my mouth off too much already."

"I ain't heard you say a thing yet, old-timer."

"Boy, the name Slocum is pure poison around these parts." The hostler nodded. "Mister Watt Slocum has run roughshod or killed over half the men in this town... no, half this country."

"He's a rough one, huh?"

"That's putting it mildly." The old man swallowed hard. "That one is meaner than a two-headed rattlesnake."

"I ain't never seen a double headed rattler."

"You meet up with Watt Slocum and you'll find your snake." The old man looked at Reed. "Take my advice, boy, and go back to wherever you came from, quick!"

"Surely he can't be that rough."

"Coldest man I ever met." The gray head nodded. "He'll kill a man for looking at him too long. No, sir, for myself, I hope I don't meet up with him again, ever."

"Alright then, tell me, where can I get a good meal?"

"Dora's boardinghouse, right over there." The old man pointed. "I sure wouldn't swear how good it'll be today, but I can guarantee it'll sure stick to your ribs."

The hostler rubbed his chin as he watched the tall youngster cross over to the eatery. There was something about this one that seemed familiar, he just couldn't put his finger on it. Even as young as the boy was, the old hostler could feel the hardness in him. The cold blue eyes never flinched as he looked squarely at him. No, sir, his instincts told him this one was already a rough hand. He knew most Texans were a tough bunch of men. Ask anyone who had witnessed a crew of cowhands when they hit a trail town. He wondered why he was hunting Watt Slocum. Could he be some kind of lawman looking for the gunman? No, the old hostler knew the lad was still too young to be toting the badge of a lawman, but there was something else about the tall youngster that seemed to tickle his mind.

Entering a warm room that smelled of baked bread, Reed removed his hat and sat down at a table covered with a clean checkered tablecloth. Taking the chair with his back against the wall, he remembered Emmet's many warnings that he should always sit looking at the door with his back guarded. He also remembered his uncle's last words of warning for him to be alert and trust no one. The way the hostler acted at the mention of Watt Slocum's name made him curious. There seemed to be no doubt, his uncle wasn't a well-thought-of man in these parts. Maybe, he shouldn't be so quick to toss the name Slocum around, at least in public.

"Beans, fried bread, and pork is what's on the stove, young man. We can fry you up some eggs and side meat if you prefer?"

A middle-aged, good-looking woman surprised him, interrupting his thoughts. So much for being alert.

"The beans will do fine, ma'am." Reed looked up at her.

Straightening, the woman's eyes opened wide in shock as she looked at Reed's face. "Coffee?"

"Just water will do."

"Suit yourself." The woman smiled. "Be back in a jiffy."

Reed studied the few locals finishing their coffee, then turned his attention to the steaming plate of food set before him. As he ate, he could feel eyes studying him curiously. He was young and having frequented few towns in his life, he was unfamiliar with the town's people. He hadn't learned yet that locals were always curious about strangers. The staring eyes of the men darted away quickly when he caught them looking. Finishing his meal, he watched as the woman moved toward his table.

"You be wanting some pie, young feller?"

"No, ma'am. I'm full as a tick." Reed shook his head. "That was a mighty tasty meal."

"Thank you." The woman studied his face curiously. "Compliments are always appreciated by the cook."

"Something wrong?"

"No, it's just… you remind me of somebody."

"I've heard that already once today." Reed picked up his hat. "How much do I owe you?"

"Two bits will bail you out." The woman smiled. "What's your name?"

"Reed."

"Reed what? Most folks carry a last name."

"Just Reed will do for now."

"Are you running from something, Reed?"

"You're mighty curious." Reed looked around the room at the listening men. "No, I ain't running, but I am looking for someone."

"That would be Watt Slocum wouldn't it?"

"News sure seems to spread fast around these parts."

She laughed lightly. "Just a woman's natural curiosity and intuition is all."

"You're right, ma'am. I am looking for Watt Slocum and I need to find him fast." Reed laid a quarter on the table.

"A day's ride west of here, there's a town called Dade, just a wide spot in the road mind you." The woman whispered looking over at the other customers. "If'n I was you which I'm not, I'd ride over there and take a look see."

"I'm a thanking you, ma'am." He turned for the door. His uncle had mentioned that Watt might be in the town of Dade.

"You're a polite youngster. Ride soft, Mister Reed Slocum, and mind your backsides."

"So you know my whole name?" Reed smiled. "Now I'm curious, how?"

"I'd bet my life on it. Yes, you're a Slocum for sure." The woman shrugged her shoulders. "You're a dead ringer for Watt fifteen years back."

"What else." He could feel the woman wanted to say more.

"Nothing, it's just I've heard Watt speak of you and his brother Wes Slocum many times when he was let's say, a little under the weather."

"You mean drunk."

"I was trying to be polite." Dora smiled. "Fact is, Watt does like his makings."

"Peers like my uncle isn't very popular in these parts."

"Your uncle?" She smiled. "That's a curious way of putting a face on him. Fact is, he ain't."

"Why?"

"He's whipped every man that stood up to him around here. Even killed a few, that's why." The woman picked up the money. "Even the law doesn't fool with him, unless they're forced into it that is."

"You know him well?"

"I know him well enough." She grinned. "Meanest, cold-blooded galoot I ever met, but there's one thing about him."

"What would that be, ma'am?" Reed was curious.

"He's all man that one is." She smiled thoughtfully. "He stands six foot four, packing around two hundred forty pounds of solid muscle."

Blushing, Reed quickly headed for the door. "Yes, ma'am."

The old hostler didn't bother to move or look up as Reed neared the door of the stable. "You be wanting your horses?"

"Nope, we're all trail weary." Reed looked over where two men stood leaning against the stable wall. "Reckon I'll bed down in one of your stalls for the night. That is if that's okay with you?"

"Cost you two bits extra." The hostler nodded. "But, you're already paid up."

"You know, somehow I already had that figured out."

"You, be gone come daybreak." The old man leaned back in his chair. "Early daybreak. You know, it's healthier riding in the cool of the morning."

Reed nodded and looked over at the two loafers. "You folks around here sure make a stranger feel mighty welcome."

"You heard the old man, sonny, daylight." One of the men straightened slowly and glared at the tall youngster. "That means first light."

"Yeah, I heard him, mister." Reed took in the low hanging pistol on the man's side. "But, you see I'm kinda a late sleeper."

"You're lucky, boy, that he's letting you light your tail here for the night." The other man grinned. "We don't normally allow East Texas trash to stay long in our little town."

"I didn't know you two boys were letting me do anything." Reed smiled coldly and pointed at the hostler. "I thought this stable belonged to him."

"For a kid, you've sure got yourself a smart mouth on you."

"I doubt you two would have the sense to know whether my mouth is smart or not." Reed turned, squaring off toward the two men.

As the two men straightened, the old hostler stepped between the men. "I told him he could stay till morning, boys. Let's let it go at that and not have any trouble here."

"Alright, Mister Pike, but we better not see or smell him around here come daylight." The two men turned and swaggered away laughing. "That means be gone by break of day, sonny."

"That's Jake and Tom Burden, both bad actors, boy." Pike smiled slightly as he watched the two men walk casually away. "They're two good reasons for you to be gone before daylight, like they said."

"I'm a bad actor myself, old man." Reed turned for the stable doorway. "You tell them that."

"You've been warned, youngster." The old man nodded. "You've been warned."

"I'm going inside and I'm gonna get me some sleep." Reed glared down at the hostler. "You let anybody slip in and disturb my sleep, you may just find out how bad."

"I reckon I can keep an eye out for you."

"You better."

"I had you figured right."

"You had what figured right?" Reed hesitated.

"Just that you're some kind of kin to Watt Slocum, ain't you?"

"Does it show that bad?"

"Yes, sir. The family resemblance is pretty strong."

"Alright, old man, he's my uncle."

"Uncle!" The old man spat, then returned to his seat mumbling to himself. "I reckon that's just what we need around here, another Slocum."

Sunlight flowed into the long hallway of the stables waking Reed up from his exhausted sleep. Even though the livery smelled strongly of horses, wet horse blankets, and hay, he had slept soundly. Brushing loose straw from his clothes, he walked outside to find the old man sitting in the same spot, leaning back against the stable wall.

"Good morning, Mister Pike." Reed had heard the two men call the old man Pike.

Removing the smoking pipe from his grizzled face, the hostler looked up at the tall youth. "Sleep well?"

"Yes, sir. I was downright tired."

"One good thing about being young, you can sleep the peacefulness of a baby." The old man chuckled. "These old bones of mine ache so much they keep me awake no matter how tired I am. I fall asleep real sound, then they'll go to talking to me and wake me back up."

"Losing sleep will make an old man of you quick."

"Already has."

"Believe I'll cross over and get me a bite to eat before I ride out."

"It's past daylight, youngster."

"So I noticed, but I'm a growing boy and I aim to eat." Reed looked at the rising sun and smiled slightly.

"You've been warned. I'll feed your animals and have them saddled when you return." Pike shook his head. "If you return that is."

"Will that cost another two bits?"

"How'd you guess?"

"Just a lucky guesser I reckon." Reed smiled. "You got any law around this town?"

"We got us a part-time marshal sometimes."

"What's a part-time marshal?"

"Well." The old man rubbed his chin. "He's part-time here and part-time fishing."

"You mean when there's trouble a brewing, he goes fishing?"

"Son, you are a good guesser. Now, you be careful over there." The old man looked nervously over at the café. "Those two Burden boys are dangerous when they're on the prod."

"And, I'm guessing those two are always on the prod."

"You guessed right again, and the marshal heard about you being in town and went fishing." Pike grinned.

"Now, I wouldn't have guessed that at all, but it figures." Reed laughed lightly. "Yes, Mister Pike, it surely figures."

"I reckon you'll be riding out after you eat?" The woman placed steaming coffee in front of Reed.

"A nice lady gave me a good tip. I aim to go take a look see."

"The lady is gonna give you another." The woman smiled down at him. "Be careful when you walk out the door."

Reed looked out the window for the two men that had been at the livery. He didn't see any signs of the ones that had given him the friendly warning to leave town. "Well, thank you, ma'am."

"Tell Watt he's been missed."

"I'll do that, ma'am. But, who do I say is doing the telling?"

"The name is Dora, Dora Camp."

"Yes, ma'am, Miss Dora." Reed smiled. "I'll be sure to tell him just that, providing I find him that is."

"I have a hunch you'll catch up to him alright." Dora looked out the window. "Watch your back, Reed Slocum."

Finishing his breakfast, Reed left money on the table and pushed through the doorway into the early morning sun. The woman had been right, Jake and Tom Burden stood outside on the boardwalk watching the café door. Both men straightened as he cleared the building. Like the old hostler had said, they were on the prod, he just didn't know why. He didn't even know them.

"You're running a little late, boy." The taller of the two spoke. "It's way past sunup from where I stand."

Reed looked up at the rising sun, then turned his full attention on them. He stood on the walkway, less than twenty feet from the pair. The way they stood and the look out of their eyes, he could tell they were ready for him to make a move.

"I didn't know there was any hurry, boys."

"You were told daylight, that's two hours ago." Tom Burden spat a stream of tobacco. "Way past leaving time."

"Well, I never was one to be on time."

Jake Burden glared at the youth. "Well, boy, we're fixing to show you the error of your ways and how to keep from running late."

"Tell me, loudmouth, just how are you planning on doing that?"

"You choose it, boy, guns, knives, or fists?"

Dora Camp stepped out into the morning sun. "Jake, you and Tom leave him be."

"No, ma'am, he was told to clear out before daylight."

"You boys had better pay heed to the lady, sounds like good advice to me." Reed loosened the thong on his forty-four.

"You're scaring us, boy." The two men separated slightly and seemed to brace themselves. "We're just shaking in our boots."

Reed studied the two men. He felt the taller brother, Tom Burden, would be the faster and more dangerous of the pair. Bodie Paul had taught him all about the forty-four and the fast draw, but never in his life had he expected to be in a situation like this. Bracing himself, he waited, staring coldly into the eyes of the two men.

"You better be scared, boys." The old hostler spoke up from where he stood watching. "You shoot this young man and you'll have Watt Slocum on your trail before he hits the ground."

"What's this one to Watt Slocum, old man?"

"I figure a nephew." Pike grinned. "Ain't quite sure, but you boys can see the resemblance, can't you?"

Nervously, the men looked at each other then back at Reed. "Maybe we'll let you off this time, sonny. Get on your horse and ride."

"Nope." The word came out like the hiss of a rope as it swung through the air. "You call it, old man."

"Now, wait a minute, boy." Tom Burden held up his hand. "We were just funning."

"I ain't, Mister Burden." Reed's voice hardened. "You wanted this dance, now start the music."

"On the count of three." The old man could see the fear in the men's faces. Not so much fear of the youngster they faced, but they did fear his uncle. They had started this little show not knowing the kid was kin to Watt Slocum. Both men knew full well what the consequences of killing a Slocum would be.

Turning, both men quickly walked away from the watching crowd. Relaxing his shoulders, Reed touched his hat to the woman, then turned toward the stable.

"Thanks, Mister Pike." He looked down at the old man walking beside him. "Is that gonna cost me another two bits?"

"Don't thank me, young 'un. Those two skunks are cowards and bullies, but they're mean." The hostler looked up and down the street. "You be careful, they're back shooters. They may just be lying someplace ahead on the trail waiting on you."

"I'll be careful."

As Reed mounted the bay, the hostler sauntered back out to where he sat the horse and smiled up at him. Taking a dally around his saddle horn with the lead rope, Reed looked down and shook hands with the old hostler.

"The trail to Dade is that way." The old one pointed out the trail leading west. "Dora told me to get you on the right road."

Touching his hat, Reed nodded. "Thanks again."

"Watch your backsides out there, Reed Slocum." The old man grinned. In the short time the youngster had been in town, he had kinda grown to like the lad. "I know them two. I'll bet my bottom dollar they'll be waiting for you out there somewhere."

Only a wave came in response as the rider kicked his horses into a short ground-eating lope to the west. The lady shopkeeper had said Dade was just a day's ride west of Amarillo. Reed knew that could mean ten to twenty miles, depending on how you were mounted. Most towns were ten or so miles apart, making it easier for the ranchers and what dirt farmers there were out there to get to town for supplies and get back home before dark to do their chores. He remembered, she had also said the small town was just a wide spot on the trail west. Also, she had added, a lot of rough prairie scum hung out in the lone saloon the town afforded, and Watt Slocum was a regular visitor to Dade, that is when he wasn't out wolfing.

Reed was curious, since his arrival in Amarillo, not one person except for Dora Camp had voiced one good word about Watt Slocum. At the mere mention of the name, most seemed scared and hadn't waited around to voice any opinion at all. He felt the confrontation with the two men this morning had only stopped with the mention of his uncle's name. Shaking his head, he took in the deep swells of the prairie as the grass swayed with the slight breeze. This was a dangerous land. The tall grass could hide an army and he wouldn't even know they were watching him. Reed smiled as he wondered who he should watch for closer, the two Burden brothers or Watt Slocum.

Slowing the horses to a walk, he took in a long breath, then uncorked his canteen and took a long pull on the water. He wondered how the roundup was coming along, and how his uncle Wes was doing. Replacing the cork, the youngster kicked the horses into a slow trot. He was eager to find Watt Slocum and get headed for the crossing on the Red River, wherever that was. He had been out over a week. If his luck held, his uncle would be in Dade and they could start back by morning. Reed was well aware this was a dangerous and wild country. Nevertheless, he was enjoying the peaceful ride and the fresh sweet aromatic smell of the wild flowers that grew everywhere across the prairie.

CHAPTER 3

Reed heard the shot and tried to grab the saddle horn, but his horse whirled sideways, slinging him onto his back into the tall grass bordering the narrow road. Rolling as he slammed hard against the ground, he crawled deeper into the shelter of the grass as running horses approached. Reaching automatically for the forty-four, he found his holster empty. The thong holding the pistol had broken from the impact of his fall, letting the weapon drop somewhere in the heavy foliage. Defenseless, he had to conceal himself quickly in the thick grass. There was no time to look for his weapon.

"Did you get him, Tom?" Jake Burden studied the bent grass, then looked over at the two horses standing quietly alongside the road.

"Don't know how bad, but I hit him alright." Tom nodded. "I saw the dust fly from his coat when the bullet hit."

"We gonna search him out?"

"He's a dead man, Jake. We got his horses and gear." Tom looked about nervously. "He's a goner for sure. Ain't no use us wasting our time on him."

"Yeah, and if we go in after him, he might just get off a final shot before he gives up the ghost." Jake laughed. "No sense us taking a chance."

"Let's ride." The two men caught Reed's two horses and headed down the road toward Dade. "I've built me up a mighty thirst."

Jake cussed. "Me too, brother. Gunplay always makes me thirsty."

"If Mister Slocum is still alive, he'll bleed out quick." Tom kicked his horse. "We did good. We made us a pretty good haul today."

Jake looked over at the horses. "They'll bring enough to keep us in drinking whiskey for six months or more."

Reed stood up slowly as the sound of the horse's hoofbeats became faint in the distance. Searching the grass for his hat and pistol, he finally found them and stepped out onto the dusty road. Shaking his head to clear the cobwebs, he quickly wiped off his pistol, then made sure the gun was in working order and the barrel wasn't clogged with dirt. The brothers had made a bad mistake in not making sure he was dead. He knew exactly who they were and where they were heading. Even though he was young, his long legs couldn't carry him as fast as a horse, but the tracks in the sandy ground would lead him straight to them. Watt Slocum was temporarily forgotten as the Slocum temper was aflame. For now, Reed's temper redirected his quest as he focused on the Burden brothers.

A half day and full night of hard walking finally brought Reed to the outskirts of a small ramshackle bunch of buildings that had a small sign that read Dade, Colorado. Somewhere behind him, he had crossed into Colorado Territory without realizing it. The miles walking with only small amounts of wild onions, a few wild roots, and the little water he had found left him tired, hungry, and thirsty. However, his rough state hadn't slacked his thirst for revenge against the brothers. Luckily, his money was safe in his jacket pocket, not in his saddlebags on the lost horses.

Bending over a long water trough, the dusty, tired youngster removed his hat and doused his head into the refreshing water. Shaking the water from his long light brown hair and replacing his hat, he looked around for an eating place or general store. Either would do. He just needed food to return his strength. Being young, with strong recuperative powers, all he needed was some nourishment and rest to make him good as new. Although, his feet were sore from the long walk causing him to have a slight limp. Cowmen wore high-heeled boots made for riding, not walking. Reed hadn't noticed the bullet hole in his coat until he checked to see that his money pouch was intact. He had been lucky, Burden's rifle ball only missed him by an inch. He could see how the shooter had figured he had hit his target. Reed looked about the buildings if the brothers were still in Dade, they would keep until after he ate.

Looking around the general store as he stepped into the cool interior, Reed noticed only the lone clerk at the counter. The mercantile smelled of harness leather, coal oil, and different odors he was familiar with from the stores back on the Brazos Flats. Walking to the cracker barrel, he helped himself to a handful of stale crackers and moldy cheese.

The old storekeeper behind the counter took in the dusty clothes and haggard appearance of the young man, as he pulled down his spectacles. "Hope you can pay for them crackers, young feller."

"I can pay." Reed nodded slowly. "You got anything else around here, a little tastier and not so stale?"

"In the back on the stove." The old man motioned to a curtain. "If'n you can pay, help yourself."

Reed dropped a dollar on the counter, then pushed through the curtains concealing a small kitchen. Stopping suddenly as a young woman turned from the cast iron stove, he quickly removed his hat.

"Sorry, ma'am, the storekeeper out front said I could get a meal back here."

"Sit down." The girl took in the tall unkempt young man. "My father sometimes forgets this is a store, not a restaurant."

"Well, ma'am, I'd be thankful for anything." Reed pulled out a chair. "I'm mighty hungry."

The girl smiled. "Yes, I could see that, the way you chewed up those stale crackers."

"You were watching when I entered?"

"I was watching." Pointing up at a small bell attached to a string over the door, she nodded. "Lets me know when we have customers."

"We'll, ma'am, if you have a restaurant in this town, I'll go there."

"You've already paid, and besides, we don't have an eatery in this dust bowl of a town." The white teeth of the girl showed when she smiled. "What's your name, mister?"

"Reed Slocum."

"Slocum?" The girl stiffened. "You related to Watt Slocum by any chance?"

Reed shook his head. Maybe he shouldn't have given his name. "Yessum, I'm his nephew. If that's a problem, I'll move on."

"No, Mister Reed Slocum, there's no problem. Sit yourself down and I'll feed you." The girl smiled. "Any kin of Watt Slocum is welcome here."

"Yes, ma'am." Reed was shocked at her words.

"What are you doing here?"

Reed looked over the cornbread, fried potatoes, and beans she placed before him. "My uncle, Wes, sent me after Watt to bring him home."

"Thought they didn't see eye-to-eye?" The girl sat down across from the hungry youngster. "I've been told they were on the outs."

"Their problems will have to be put aside." Reed took a drink of water. "We need to push a herd north to Missouri, and he's needed."

"You've come a long way across dangerous lands." She watched as he chewed hungrily. "I didn't see anyone ride in with you."

"No, I came alone. Uncle Wes couldn't spare any men to ride with me."

"You look awfully young to be riding these plains all by yourself." The girl smiled. "These are dangerous lands out here."

"I reckon I'm young alright." Reed nodded. "But, like I said, I'm the only one my uncle could spare from the round-up."

"I see." She nodded. "Or, are you the only one he dared send?"

"How do you know my uncle and family problems so well?" Reed looked across the table at the beautiful girl.

"Watt Slocum and his woman are regulars around this town when he isn't out wolfing." She laughed. "He has a fondness for let's say spirits."

"Woman?"

"Yes, he has a woman. Helps him skin and keeps his camp." She studied him closely. He was indeed a handsome young man. "You know cooks, washes, stuff like that."

"He has a wife?"

"Not exactly, but I wouldn't say anything about that, were I you." She laughed. "He lives with several Kiowa men and women."

"Handy."

"Yes, it is. They're a good team, seems like." She studied his face as he ate. "Every one of them are good hunters and skinners."

"You like her?" Reed looked across at the girl. "His woman I mean."

"Hardly know her."

"What?"

"She's not exactly civilized in some ways." The girl laughed. "Like I said, she's full-blood Kiowa. Stays away from what we call civilization most of the time."

"You haven't told me your name."

"Lee Hargrove, and that's my pa, Harvey, out front."

"Well, Miss Hargrove, what do you mean civilized?"

"You'll just have to meet her." The blue eyes seemed to twinkle as she laughed again. "I'll let you make up your own mind."

"Are they in Dade now?"

"Not that I know of. They usually camp down along the creek west of here when they're in town." Lee refilled his glass. "If they were close by, I believe Bannock or Watt would have been in for shells."

"And just where would this camp be?"

"Take the west trail about a mile from town." Lee nodded with her chin. "It'll lead you to their camp. You can't miss it."

"You wouldn't know two men known as Jake and Tom would you?"

"The Burdens? You sure do know some interesting characters, Mister Slocum."

"Seems like I'm getting acquainted alright."

"So, they're why you walked into town." She looked down at his dusty clothes and boots. "Limping like a sore-footed mule."

"You don't miss much, Miss Hargrove."

"I try to keep my eyes open." Lee smiled lightly. "Let me guess, they stole your horses and put you afoot?"

"Reckon they did for a fact." Reed finished his food. "Now, how'd you know?"

"Just a guess, but they have been known to have sticky fingers with other people's property." Lee nodded. "Real sticky fingers."

"They're in town?"

"Over at the saloon. Been holed up there all day drinking." Lee shrugged. "I guess they took a pretty good haul from you?"

"My horses and gear would give them enough money to stay drunk for quite a spell around here."

"I'm sorry they robbed you." Lee nodded. "But, you're right. Those fine-blooded horses of yours will bring them a pretty good bit of spirits."

"Thank you, ma'am." Reed smiled. "I'm figuring it'll be the Burdens who will be sorry for their misdeeds."

"You can get your horses back and ride out without them knowing you're here."

"My horses?" Reed looked curiously at the girl. "You know my horses?"

"Long-legged bay and a blaze-faced sorrel toting a packsaddle."

"That's them." Reed was surprised at the girl. "Missy, you've got a good eye. You sure don't miss much."

"They're across the street at the livery." Lee gathered his dishes. "Mister Foster, the owner, knows the Burdens and he'll let you have your horses back."

"The brothers seem pretty sure of themselves."

The blond hair bobbed up and down. "Well, they've got away with rustling and killing around here for years. They're bad men, Mister Slocum. You be real careful approaching that pair of snakes. They haven't been bested or defanged yet."

"I heard they were cowards." Reed stood up. "I know they're back shooters."

"Cowards they might be, but it hasn't been proven yet." Lee frowned. "The graveyard down the street is plumb full of men that called them horse thieves."

"Why hasn't the law done something about them?"

Shrugging, she looked up at the tall man as he stood up. "Look around, Reed Slocum, there's no law here. Sometimes, the Texas Rangers pass through Amarillo, but they're not interested in two small-time horse thieves, and the Colorado Territory is out of their jurisdiction."

Thanking the girl, Reed pushed through the curtain and continued to the front door. Looking up and down, what most people would call a one-horse town, he started through the door when he felt a hand touch his arm.

"You don't have to fight them, Reed."

"Where I come from, ma'am, only a coward would let someone shoot at you, steal your horses, and make you like it."

"Then you be careful, Reed Slocum." She looked out the door. "You get yourself killed and Watt will probably kill the Burdens himself."

"So, you're not worried about me, but my uncle." Reed studied the pretty face. "I doubt he'd get involved. My uncle doesn't even know me."

"You're right and wrong, Mister Slocum." She stepped past him. "I don't want him in trouble and I don't want you hurt either."

"I'm curious, Miss Hargrove, tell me why you don't dislike my uncle like everyone else does?"

The girl looked up into his blue eyes. "You know you're the spitting image of your uncle. To answer your question, Watt Slocum had always treated me and my dad very kindly." Lee looked into the street. "For all his toughness, he's a real gentleman."

"I see." Reed touched his hat and stepped out onto the porch. "Be seeing you, Lee Hargrove."

"You be careful, Mister Slocum."

An easy grin came across the sun-tanned face. "Why, ma'am, careful, that's my middle name."

"I'll bet." She watched him walk down the street, then mumbled. "I hope to see you real soon, Reed Slocum."

Walking to the livery, Reed found his horses and saddles just as the girl had said he would. As he was looking over the corral poles, a heavyset man walked up to him.

"You looking to buy a horse?" The fat one took in the dusty clothes. "I saw you walk into town a few minutes ago."

"I'm looking for two horses, mister." Reed studied the heavyset man. "You, Mister Foster, the owner of this place?"

The stable man looked nervously at the two horses Reed was eyeing. The Burdens had brought the horses into the stable late last night. The stable man well knew the brother's reputation and they were known for stealing horses. He had thought it odd when the two brothers led the horses in and told him to stable them so late. He had noticed the stirrups of the bay saddle horse as he unsaddled him. Whoever rode the animal was long-legged, much taller than the short-legged Burden brothers. He knew their legs could never reach the stirrups on the bay's saddle. He also knew he had never seen the Bar S brand locally around Dade.

"Yes, sir. I'm Foster." The big man nodded. "You see them here?"

"Yes, sir. Right there, see that Bar S brand on their hip?" Reed nodded at the horses. "They're mine or at least they were until the Burdens relieved me of them yesterday."

"I see it." The stable man dropped his eyes. He already knew the horse's home range wasn't close to Dade. "What brand is it?"

"Slocum, the Bar S." Reed looked hard at the man. "The Bar S is down around the Brazos River country."

"The Burdens left them here. They claim them." Blood drained from the man's face at the mention of the name. "I'm afraid, young man, you'll have to take that up with them."

"I aim to, mister. You can count on it." Reed frowned and moved closer toward the man. "Where are they?"

"They're over at the saloon getting drunk right now." Foster was scared, sweat beaded on his face. "That's their second home when they're in Dade."

"Mister stable man, I want you to go over and tell them the man who owns the horses and the man they ambushed east of here, is waiting right here for them."

"No, sir. Not me. I don't want to get involved with them two." The fat man took a step back and raised his hand. "No, sir. They're pure poison when they are riled."

Reed turned on the man. "You became involved when you stabled my horses without asking questions."

"I was minding my own business, it's a lot healthier." The man shrugged. "I didn't know they were stolen."

"Maybe it is and maybe you didn't, but now get over there before I become riled." Reed turned on the scared hostler. "If you want to get real unhealthy all of a sudden, you just keep standing where you are."

"Honest, mister. I had no idea." The stable man pleaded. "We ain't got any law here."

"Get."

"They might kill me if I tell them what you said." The man pleaded. "Please, mister."

"I aim to kill you in one second if you don't get your fat tail over to that saloon." Reed touched the butt of the forty-four. "And that second just passed."

Cussing, as he moved away, the fat man seemed to drag his feet, taking his time as he crossed the dusty street. Reed checked the loads in his pistol and dropped it back softly into the well-oiled holster. Ever since he had been big enough to thumb back the forty-four's hammer, Emmet Tabor taught him all he knew about the weapon. When Bodie Paul had hired on for the Bar S, his real education with the horse pistol had begun. Paul was a gunfighter, hiring on at the Slocum Ranch just long enough to build himself up a stake to travel on. While he worked for the Bar S, Tabor put Reed to work with Paul purposely to learn the forty-four inside and out. Emmet Tabor had secretly supplied the gunfighter with all the forty-four shells he needed for their work. Wes Slocum hadn't liked Reed hanging around with the gunfighter and learning to be a gun slick. Still, he knew every Texan wanting to survive in this harsh land had to learn how to use the six gun. Every time cowhands rode from the ranch and went out on the Texas plains, they knew they might have to contend with Indians, rustlers, bad men, and wild animals that inhabited the land and threatened their lives.

Reed had never drawn the weapon against a man, but he had faced raiding Comanche warriors, a few Comancheros, and wild animals several times. Working daily with the forty-four, Paul and Tabor had been amazed as they watched the young Slocum become faster and deadlier with the forty-four than any man they had ever seen pull a gun. The youngster was a natural with the pistol as his hand speed and wrist strength was unbelievable. He could fire the powerful weapon at targets, seventy-five feet away, without a miss. Even the vaunted, Wild Bill Hickok, would be a match for the youngster. The difference between the two would come down to; Hickok was a killer and experienced gunfighter, while Reed Slocum wasn't, and that would be all the difference Hickok would need against an untried youngster.

Separating several steps as they stopped in front of the livery, Tom Burden grinned broadly as they faced Reed.

"Heard you were just dying to see us again." Burden laughed insolently. "We thought we had seen the last of you."

"Well, as you boys can see for yourselves, you ain't."

"So, what now, boy?" Jake Burden chimed in. "You're causing us to miss out on our drinking."

"You two sober now?"

"Why do you ask?" Tom laughed. "You a doctor or something?"

"I'm taking you two in for horse stealing and attempted murder." Reed nodded.

"Is that so, sonny?" Jake laughed. "We ain't even got a jail in this dump of a town."

"No law dogs here either, boy." Tom chimed in. "No badge toters here either. Nope, just you and us."

"And you're calling us out?" Jake asked. "If you are, your old uncle Watt sure can't blame us for defending ourselves."

"That's true, mister." Reed watched the two men's eyes. "Horse stealing and attempted murder is a hanging offense. I don't reckon I'll be needing a jail or a badge toter as you say. I just want to be sure you two are sober before I kill you."

"Mighty big talk for a whelp still wet behind the ears." Tom Burden cussed. "Your uncle ain't here to help you now."

"He wasn't in Amarillo yesterday either when you boys ate crow." Reed knew today was a different day. The brothers had been drinking and the whiskey was talking so Watt Slocum never entered their foggy brains. "You're both yellow."

"Can you prove we're horse thieves?" Jake grinned, moving his hand closer to the pistol butt on his side. "And tell us, who did we try to murder?"

"Proof's standing right back there in the corral." Reed nodded over his shoulder. "You brought them in and claimed them as your own."

"You man enough to take us, boy?" Jake laughed sarcastically. "Like my brother says, your bad uncle ain't here right now to help you."

"I reckon that's to be seen, ain't it?" Reed stiffened. "Now, drop those belts."

"Don't think we can do that, Mister Slocum." Tom crouched, ready to draw. "Nope, you're gonna have to take them."

"It's your choice." Reed smiled easily. "Live or die, like I said, your choice."

Only the widening of their eyes gave the two brothers away as they clawed for their pistols. Blank expressions of surprise and pain came across the bearded faces as Reed's forty-four roared twice, dropping the two men onto the sandy street. Tom Burden rolled to his side trying to raise his weapon, but again the forty-four roared and bucked, finishing the man.

"Saddle my horses." Reed spoke to the stunned liveryman who was staring blankly at the dead men. "Now."

"You killed them both."

"Yep, I believe you. That's the mortal truth, they are dead." Reed looked down at the two dead brothers. "A forty-four slug has a nasty way of tearing a man's insides out."

The chunky hostler removed his hat, wiping his face. "But, they're dead."

"They called the play, not me."

"Yes, but them Burdens were fast, yet neither one got off a shot."

"I reckon they weren't that fast." Reed looked up as a buckskin clad Indian stopped briefly, stared down at the two bodies, then kicked his horse into a hard lope out of town. "Who was that?"

"He's just an old Kiowa that hangs around town looking for handouts." The liveryman shook his head again as he turned. "We've got a few of them here, down on their luck and hungry."

Reed had looked hard at the Indian, and one thing was for sure, the dark face didn't have the looks of a man down on his luck or a beggar. The man looked strong and proud as he had briefly looked into Reed's face. No, he would bet his last dollar the Indian, whoever he was, sure wasn't an everyday loafer or beggar. Reed had seen the mighty Comanche down in Texas that rode with Quanah Parker. No, sir, that Indian had the fierce look of the Comanche warriors and he was proud.

Reed looked over at the general store where Hargrove and his daughter stood watching. He noticed how she hung onto her father's arm, fear freezing her face. Several bystanders smiled and nodded as he turned back to the livery.

"They won't say it, but they're glad you killed them two sidewinders and I am too." The stable man quit shaking and cinched up the packsaddle.

"They've caused a lot of trouble, have they?"

"A lot of trouble is an understatement." The man stepped back from the animal. "They've been known to steal a man's horse here in town in broad daylight with him watching."

"Why doesn't this town have a town marshal?"

"A marshal?" The man shook his head. "Shucks, mister, this town can hardly afford to catch a cold, much less pay for a marshal."

"I can see that." Reed nodded. "Well, you witnessed what happened, it was a fair fight."

"Don't worry about it, young feller." The fat man looked to where a wagon was picking up the bodies. "We all seen it. Sides, no one really cares in this country."

"I know you seen it, but will you say that at the right time?"

"If needed, we will for a fact." The hostler nodded. "No, we'll just plant them in the cemetery along with some they've sent to their maker, and that'll be the end of it."

"The end of it? Life seems to be mighty cheap out here." Reed shook his head.

"Yes, sir, that's the only thing that's cheap in these parts."

Reed mounted the bay and turned toward the trail Lee Hargrove had told him about. His hands were shaking from the shooting and the adrenaline coursing through his body. He had tried to hide them from the stable man, and hopefully he had succeeded. The shooting had happened so quickly, he hadn't had time to think, only react. He wasn't ashamed of shooting the two men that tried to kill him, but he was so keyed up he couldn't keep his hands from trembling. Catching movement from the corner of his eye as he turned, Reed noticed the girl waving at him from the store's porch. Reining in at the store, he dismounted.

"You're not hurt?"

"No, I'm okay."

"I was watching." She wrung her hands nervously. "It happened so fast that I didn't have time to be scared for you."

"I'm okay."

"I'm thankful, but I'm sorry you had to kill them." Lee's shoulders trembled slightly. "They were bad men, but to die so young."

"They made the first move. Dying was their choice." Reed shrugged. "If I hadn't shot first, I could be lying out there on the ground myself."

"I know that."

"They didn't give me much choice."

"How many men have you killed?"

"Just these two and I didn't want to kill this time." He stared at her. "I'm not a killer, Miss Hargrove, until now."

"I know, I could hear you and them talking."

"You think less of me now?"

"No, Reed, I don't." She looked away. "It's just that."

"What?"

"You did kill them purposely." She straightened her small shoulders. "I watched as you sent Mister Foster after them."

"Yes, I sent him for the brothers." He turned back to the horses. "Good-bye, Miss Hargrove."

"Good-bye, Mister Slocum."

"Tell me, Miss Hargrove." Reed settled in the saddle. "If Uncle Watt isn't where you said he camps, where should I look for him?"

"Last I heard he was working the Grant Range about twenty miles west." Lee looked into his eyes. "Ride careful out there, at least until your uncle knows who you are and what you want."

"Thank you. If he were to get past me, would you tell him I'm here and what I'm here for?"

"I'll do that." The girl looked over at the bay horse and the young man. She smiled. He was indeed very handsome. Still, she couldn't get the thought of him killing the Burdens out of her thoughts. "But, he'll know all about you before the day's out."

"How's that?"

"The Kiowa that rode by you was the brother of Nakima, the Indian wife of Watt Slocum." She had seen the Kiowa warrior, Bannock, ride out of town at a high lope. "Spies, Mister Slocum, spies."

"Spies?" Reed was curious. "I thought spies were only white."

"Just follow Bannock's trail and he'll lead you right to your uncle."

"Thanks, Miss Lee."

As Reed located and looked about the abandoned campsite, he could tell it had been vacant a long time. By the looks of the cold, blackened campfire, Watt Slocum hadn't camped on this site in several weeks. Kicking the horse, he rode on along the west road that was barely a trail. Now, his only hope of finding the wolf hunter's camp was to head west to locate Grant Range where Lee Hargrove had told him to look.

He pondered his situation. How long did he dare waste riding the trail west in hopes of finding his uncle? Uncle Wes had made it plain. Watt was needed to lead the Bar S herd north to Sedalia. Absently flicking at flies on the horse's neck with his split reins, Reed contemplated his choices. He could head back to the Bar S and help with the trail herd, but that was not what his uncle Wes had sent him to do. Kicking the horses into a slow trot, he started west down the trail. He would ride another twenty miles to the range Lee Hargrove had told him of, in hopes of locating the big hunter. Another few days wouldn't matter. He would try to pick up the Kiowa's trail as Lee Hargrove had suggested as he rode from Dade.

CHAPTER 4

After riding through the grassy plains, the ground slowly turned into rougher country. Now, the land was lined with lightly timbered ridges, covering the sloping hills. The air was beginning to thin and cool as Reed climbed along the flower-lined trail. A small river slowly drifted by the path he was following. Not familiar with the country, Reed had no way of knowing the small creek's name or if it had one.

Lee had told him to ride a full day west and that would put him on the Grant Range where Watt Slocum hunted the marauding wolves. Along the trail, Reed spotted rib cages and gleaming bones of the dead cattle that had perished from the previous winter during the brutally cold blizzards. Now, the scavenging wolves had multiplied and with the dead carcasses gnawed bare, the hungry killers had started taking down newborn calves and weakened older cattle.

The stockmen, in desperation after losing hundreds of animals, had posted a bounty and called in the wolf hunters to try to eradicate the problem. Reed had heard his entire young life as the riders on the Bar S talked about wolf hunters being the lowest of the low. Cruel and quarrelsome, most wolf hunters were best avoided and left alone if a man liked living. Using a skinning knife to make a living, they had no qualms about using their sharp blades on a man. Now, he was searching out his uncle, a hide hunter.

Watering his horses at a shallow crossing, he stood by them as they swigged down the clear creek water greedily. Spotting fresh tracks leading into the water, Reed studied the far bank closely. Smaller timber lined the creek bank, but it wasn't thick enough to hide an enemy, if one was lurking ahead. Reed thought of the Indian that had ridden out of Dade, and perhaps the tracks were his. The horse wasn't shod, but that didn't mean a lot because some of the ranches didn't shoe their horses. If a horse went lame, the riders would just turn him out and grab another from the huge remudas most ranches kept. Still, some of the ranches kept their favorite horses shod so the rider ahead would most likely be Kiowa or Comanche.

The huge, powerful bulk of a man covered in worn, bloody buck-skins and ankle high moccasins, sat atop a wooden keg, listening intently as the Kiowa warrior excitedly told what he had seen in Dade. In a hurry to tell what he had witnessed, Bannock had completely forgotten about the shells Watt Slocum had sent him after. The bowie knife held in the huge hands whittled steadily on a chunk of wood. The big man had never seen the Kiowa warrior as worked up and excited as he was now.

"Him just a boy. Him look just like you, Tall Pine, when you first came to our people."

"You catch his name?"

"No, but he look for Watt Slocum. I listen in window of store. Hear him ask store woman about Watt Slocum." The warrior shook his head. "Him sound like you, look like you, when you young."

Slocum nodded slowly. The Kiowa people had renamed him Tall Pine because he had killed a huge black bear with only the knife he now held. "You say he killed the Burdens?"

"Me see, young white him kill 'em dead, bang bang." Bannock pointed his finger. "Them meet their ancestors quick. They not even get to shoot at this young one."

"They didn't fire one shot?" The big man looked curiously at the warrior. "Not one got off a single round?"

"These Burdens kill many. Them bad men, everyone fear them." The warrior shook his head. "Not this young one. He brave one, great warrior."

"They were bad men alright, with bad reputations." Watt nodded slowly. "This man you saw must be really fast."

"Them dead, not need reputations now, I think." Bannock shook his head excitedly. "Tall Pine right, this one shoot gun faster than eye can watch."

"So you think he's looking for me, wonder what for?" Watt shrugged.

"Bannock hear brothers speak your name before they get shoot 'em dead."

"Why would he want me?" Watt studied the wood curious. "He's too young to be the law."

"Not know why. Bannock knows him young, but this one thinks the young one very dangerous. He has no fear." Bannock explained.

"You get my shells?"

"No, me forget 'em when gun talking starts."

"And you say he looks like me?"

Bannock nodded, then flattened his hands. "Like two fawns with spots."

"We've got to have shells. Take two warriors and go back to Dade and get them." Watt cut a deep sliver with the knife. "Find out what Lee Hargrove knows."

"Me go quick, Tall Pine. You watch close for this one if he comes here."

"I doubt he'll find me here, old friend, but I'll sure keep a look out."

Motioning for two other warriors standing about the camp, Bannock grabbed a fresh horse from the picket line and swung up on him. "You no forget, my brother, you keep eyes open. Watch like eagle."

"Like a mother hen protecting her chicks." Watt laughed. "I'll keep my eyes peeled."

Bannock frowned from where he sat the horse. "Tall Pine, this not funny. You see plenty quick, I think."

Standing, Watt sheathed the bowie knife and walked to where a handsome Indian woman was working over a stretched deer hide. The woman was tall for a Kiowa, slender as a pole with smooth olive skin and the darkest eyes.

"What is Nakima working on?"

"You need new clothes, my husband."

Watt looked down at his bloodstained hunting shirt. "Reckon you're right about that. This one has seen better days for sure."

"My brother says someone looks for you." Her dark eyes settled on him.

Watt grinned and stroked her coal black hair. "Your brother worries too much."

"Maybe, but maybe my husband does not worry enough." The woman frowned at him worriedly. "You listen to Bannock's warning always. Maybe, you live longer."

Watt could see the woman was worried and her inclinations most of the time came true. "Alright, my lady. I'll worry some if that'll make you happy?"

"It will please me, my husband." The woman held up the doeskin shirt. "If you would just take some things more serious."

"I will, I will." The big man laughed and walked away.

Alerted by the sound of approaching horses, Bannock watched from a hidden wash as Reed guided the horses through a deep-cut trail leading up to a flat plateau. The rider had just crossed a small creek that meandered aimlessly through the hilly country. He recognized the young one coming straight at them. He was the same man that had killed the two brothers the day before in the white man's village called Dade.

"He has the same hair, same stature of Tall Pine, only not as heavy." A young warrior beside Bannock nodded. "Shall we kill him?"

"Maybe he comes after our brother Tall Pine." Another warrior, Lone Bear, spoke up. "We should not let him pass and reach our camp."

Bannock watched as the young rider topped over the pass. The warrior's dark eyes were sharp as the hawk. They studied the strong young face approaching as he listened to the warriors speak. Clutching the Winchester rifle tightly, he tried to decide what Tall Pine would want him to do. It would be easy to kill the young one coming toward them down the trail. Still, his instincts held him back. The rider looked so much like Tall Pine, and it was uncanny. The young man, even sat a horse as Tall Pine did.

"Let us kill him, take his horses, then ride into the white man's town and get Tall Pine's shells." A young warrior declared.

"Do this, Bannock." Lone Bear spoke up. "Then it will be finished."

Bannock shook his head. "No, we not kill this one."

"He comes for our brother." Lone Bear argued, gesturing with his hand. "You said you heard him ask the woman about Tall Pine."

"We not kill." Bannock demanded. "We must capture this rider."

The warrior, Adotte, pointed. "He nears."

"We take him captive, then take him back to Tall Pine." Bannock glared at the other two Kiowa. "Hear me, this one not to be harmed."

Reed watched as his horse's ears flicked forward and his head rose slightly. Nothing showed ahead on the trail, but still he knew the horse had detected something. Probably a deer, or maybe a wild horse or burro was on the trail. Clearing the last dip, Reed suddenly felt himself being knocked from the saddle by something heavy, and then landed on his back. Rolling quickly to his feet, Reed faced three warriors confronting him. Slamming one of the attacking warriors bodily to the ground, he swung a lethal punch, knocking another one backward onto his back. Lunging and fighting off the two warriors attacking him, Reed lost consciousness as a hard blow hit him from behind.

"He is a great warrior for one so young." Bannock looked down at the unconscious Reed. "He is very strong."

"Bah, we had him beaten, maybe." Adotte grinned.

"I would like to see this one wrestle the great Satanta." Lone Bear dusted himself off and laughed. "Perhaps the great Chief Satanta wouldn't brag so much about his wrestling then."

"Bind him. We take the young one to Tall Pine." Bannock shook his head. He knew the warriors wouldn't have beaten the young one if he hadn't stepped in with the rifle. This young one was strong and fearless.

Reed regained consciousness as the horse plodded along the rough trail. Bound and strapped across the back of his horse, his head pounded as if it was fixing to come off from the blow he had received.

Seeing he had come to, Bannock ordered a stop and dismounted beside Reed's horse. "We let you ride like man if you not try to fight us, white one."

"Kinda hard to fight with my hands tied."

"You give 'em word. You no fight, we release your hands."

Reed recognized the warrior speaking as the one from Dade. "You got it."

"You fight us, we kill you this time, maybe." Lone Bear growled.

"You got my word." Reed didn't figure they intended to kill him or they would have already done it.

A quick flick of Lone Bear's knife brought a small trickle of blood from Reed's arm. "You see, white man, we can bleed you."

Reed studied the hard face of the knife bearer glaring over at him. About to lunge forward at the warrior, Reed stopped as Bannock's horse intervened between the two men. Motioning the warrior back, Bannock nodded at Reed's horse.

"You get on horse, white man."

"The name's Reed Slocum."

All three warriors looked closely at the young man as he spoke his name. "Your name is Slocum, white man?"

"That's what I said." Reed frowned. "That's Slocum with an S if any of you can read."

Bannock watched curiously as Reed mounted his horse, then motioned the riders forward. "Come, we go."

Watt Slocum looked up at the commotion made by two camp dogs. He was surprised as Bannock and the others along with a white man rode into his camp. Cursing at the curs that continued to bark and nip at the white's horse, he walked forward, waiting as the warriors reined in and dismounted. Bannock pointed up at Reed and spoke quietly to the big man.

"Him say his name is Slocum." The warrior nodded. "Same as you, Tall Pine."

"Slocum?" The big man looked at Reed with a shocked expression.

Reed gazed down from the gelding at the huge caricature that stood before him. The man was a giant, exactly as the woman, Dora, had described him. At least six foot four and well over two hundred pounds. A long blondish brown beard hung scraggily from the man's face. Long shoulder-length hair, the same color as the beard, hung thickly down his back. Blood smears covered the filthy hunting shirt. There was no doubt, Reed knew he was looking at Watt Slocum himself. The man was the spitting image of Wes Slocum, only much larger.

Stepping closer to where the youngster sat his horse, Slocum noticed the blood covering the sliced sleeve and looked questioningly at Bannock. "Him put up heap fight, Tall Pine."

"Get down, boy."

Dismounting slowly, Reed dropped his reins and turned to where the big man stood. Dried blood showed on his forehead from the blow he had received on his head.

"You Watt Slocum?" He looked the big man in the eye. Both men were the same height, but the older man was much heavier, thicker through the chest.

"I'm Watt Slocum." The voice was deep and hoarse. "Who are you, boy?"

"Reed Slocum."

Shock showed in his face as Watt looked the young man in front of him up and down. "Reed?"

"I guess you're my uncle. I don't reckon we've ever met."

"Uncle?" Watt cleared his throat. "We've met alright, but it was a long time ago."

"Uncle Wes said you were my uncle." Reed looked calmly at the big man. "Did he lie to me?"

"My brother said that?"

"Not exactly in those words. He said you were his brother so that makes you an uncle too, I reckon." Reed stared into the deep-set blue eyes.

"What are you doing here? What do you want?" Watt looked at the young man. "Never mind that for now. Sit down and let my woman clean you up."

Reed looked to where the tall woman waited. "I can clean up my own self."

"Sit down!"

As Nakima worked on Reed's slight cuts, he watched closely as the big man spoke with Bannock and the other warriors. Several times, the warriors looked across at Reed, then dropped their heads. Thanking Nakima, he stood and walked to where the men sat around a small fire.

"Sit down, Mister Reed Slocum." Watt motioned to a seat as Lone Bear offered Reed his knife. "Take it."

Taking the knife, Reed looked curiously at the warrior, then over at Watt. "What's this for?"

"He is offering you the knife, if you wish his blood."

Flipping the knife, Reed buried it in the ground between the warrior's feet. "I don't wish it."

Nodding, Watt smiled slightly. "Why are you here, Mister Slocum?"

"Uncle Wes sent me."

"I figured it was something like that, but tell me why?" Watt glared across at Reed. "What does my brother want?"

"He wants you to return to the Bar S. He needs your help." Reed explained.

"My help?" Watt scoffed. "Now, that's a good one. My dear brother never needed or asked for my help in fifteen years."

"He needs help now. He's hurt bad and could be dead even now as we speak." Reed quickly related to Watt how his brother had been hurt and how bad it was. "He needs you to ramrod the Bar S stock north to Sedalia."

"Missouri?"

"If this herd doesn't get through and the money brought back, Uncle Wes will lose the ranch."

"Now, that would be just terrible, wouldn't it?" Watt shook his head. "I haven't lost anything back down on the Brazos."

"It's your ranch too, Uncle."

"Uncle?" Watt looked at the young man, then changed the subject. "What happened in Dade?"

"You mean the Burden brothers?"

"Bannock told me of the fight. Why did you kill them?"

Reed quickly told what had happened to him and why he had called the Burdens out. Bannock shook his head from time to time as he spoke.

"Him shoot quicker than striking snake." The warrior spoke in Kiowa then hissed. "Maybe even faster."

"Are you a professional gunfighter, boy?"

Reed shook his head. "I'm just a ranch hand."

Watt nodded. "I believe Bannock here. If you're so good with that gun you're carrying, why does Wes need me?"

"Like I said, I'm just a ranch hand. I don't know anything about trailing a herd north to Sedalia." Reed frowned. "That's why he sent me to bring you. We've got to get the herd through, and you know how to handle men."

"That sounds like my brother's troubles."

"You're a Slocum ain't you, Uncle?"

"Never talk on an empty stomach, Reed." Watt looked to where Nakima was beckoning them to eat. "Let's eat, then talk later."

Finishing the meat, the woman had prepared, Watt looked over at the younger man. He tried to remember the youth's age. The last time he had seen the boy was the same night he had killed Freckles Johnson and the night his brother Wes had ordered him from the Bar S.

"Your mother, her name was Rebecca."

Reed nodded. "So I've been told."

"She was beautiful, light blond hair and the bluest of eyes." Watt shook his head slowly. "Yes, she was very beautiful."

"You knew her well?"

"Yes, very well."

"Uncle Wes told me of her. He even has a picture of her hanging in the parlor of the ranch house."

"And your father?"

"He has never mentioned my father."

"I see." Watt looked to where Bannock was sitting. "Take Lone Bear and go after those shells."

Nodding, the warrior stood up easily. "I go."

"We have to pass through Dade on our way south." Reed looked over at Watt. "You won't be needing those shells."

"Are you dead sure that I'm going, boy?"

"I am dead certain, one way or another, you're going alright."

"That simply, huh?" Watt smiled sadly. "Just like that?"

"One way or the other, Uncle Watt." Reed repeated his words. "I gave my word to bring you."

"Don't call me your uncle." Watt shook his head. "And I don't think I'll accommodate you, boy."

Reed studied the big man in front of him and nodded. He doubted his chances of coming out on top in a stand up toe-to-toe swinging match. The man was a full-grown mature man, just too big, but he had no choice. He had promised his uncle, Wes, he would get Watt, so he had to try. How he was going to bring him in, he had no idea. He couldn't up and shoot him. Wounded or dead, he wouldn't be any help on the drive and there were still the Kiowa hunters, lurking around, that worked for the wolf hunter.

Watching as the younger man stood up, Watt held up his hand. "I see what you're thinking, but let's settle this come morning. I'd like to hear about the Bar S and my dear brother before we have our set to."

"Alright." Reed sat back down as Nakima handed him a cup of coffee. "I reckon it can wait one night."

"You're a hardheaded cuss for one so young."

"I was raised hard, and Uncle Wes needs you." Reed nodded. "Like I said, I gave him my word, I'd bring you."

"And your word is your bond, is that it?"

"That's it in a nutshell." Reed nodded. "A man is only as good as his word."

"Well, I hear you, boy." The big hunter smiled slightly. The youngster was surrounded by Kiowa warriors and still demanding that he return with him. Watt had to admire the young one's grit. "We'll finish this conversation come morning."

As Reed sat down to eat, three Kiowa warriors rode from the camp in a hard lope, heading for Dade to pick up the shells Watt needed. Usually, weapons would not be sold to Indians under any circumstances, but Harvey Hargrove, the shopkeeper, knew Bannock hunted and skinned wolves for Watt. Over the last few years, Watt Slocum had become good friends with Hargrove, and Bannock had procured shells for Slocum on many occasions.

Two days later, Bannock and Lone Bear pulled up their lathered horses as daylight broke over the camp where Nakima was preparing breakfast. Both warriors quickly raced excitedly to where Watt sat, holding a hot cup of steaming coffee in his hand.

"You boys got a bear after you or something?" Watt studied the blowing horses. "What's wrong?"

Bannock took a cup of coffee from Nakima, then looked across at the big man. "Much trouble in white man's village. Much trouble."

"What kind of trouble?" Watt straightened.

"Store man, Hargrove, robbed and killed." Bannock looked into the hard blue eyes of the hunter.

"Hargrove was killed?" Watt dumped his dregs onto the ground. "How did it happen?"

"Him dead. Red hair white man and one Indian beat him bad with gun."

"How many whites?"

"Maybe this many." Bannock held up five fingers. "Maybe more."

"Where is Lone Bear?"

"He follow trail of bad men." The warrior gulped down his coffee. "He will leave sign for us to follow."

"Good."

"Bannock knows Tall Pine will want to follow to kill these bad whites." Bannock sipped on the hot coffee. "There is more."

"Why, what else has happened?"

The warrior shook his head. "Something bad. Store man dead. Now, you go after bad men."

"What's wrong, Bannock?"

"Your friend, young Hargrove woman, taken by these bad men."

Watt was shocked at the words. "Lee Hargrove has been taken captive?"

"They take." Bannock shrugged. "Maybe sell or trade to Comancheros."

"We'll have to put off our tussle for a spell, boy." The older Slocum lunged suddenly to his feet. "I won't be going with you now, for sure."

Reed thought of the pretty honey-blond girl who had befriended him when he had ridden into the town of Dade. She was a beautiful girl in looks and manners. She had told him of her friendship with Watt Slocum. Reed knew Watt had to go help the girl, and he didn't blame him. A beautiful woman taken captive by a bunch of thieves and killers, there was no telling what fate lay in store for her. The girl had to be rescued somehow and before the killer's trail vanished. The ranch and the cattle drive would have to wait for now.

Looking at Watt Slocum's hard face, he knew he wouldn't want to be in the outlaw's shoes when he caught up with them. Shouting orders in Kiowa, Watt looked over at Reed. "You coming with us, young fellow?"

"I'll ride with you long enough to get the girl, then we'll head for Doan's Crossing."

"You don't give up, do you?"

"No, sir, but I'll help you get the girl back."

"Then get saddled up, we're riding out." Watt turned for the picket line. "We have no time to lose right now."

Reed saddled his horses and watched as Bannock spoke quietly with Nakima. Two younger warriors stayed behind with the woman as Watt led them in a slow lope from the camp. Bannock, followed by five other warriors, followed the hunter to the east with Reed riding last.

All day, Watt kept the riders traveling hard with just occasional stops to breathe the horses. Normally, Dade was an easy two day ride from where the camp lay, but the big hunter aimed to push hard and reach the town in a little over a day.

Almost noon on the second day, the horses were lathered and jaded as the hunters rode into Dade. Dismounting in front of the mercantile, they were surprised as several townspeople appeared on the boardwalk.

"I'm so glad you're here, Watt." Matt Foster the stable owner walked up. "It was horrible, just horrible."

"Do you know who they were, Matt?"

"I know alright." The stable man nodded. "It was Doak Keeler and his bunch of cutthroats."

"Keeler?" Watt shook his head. "I thought his range was farther east in Kansas."

"It was him. I'd know that ugly face anywhere and a couple of them others riding with him." Foster swore.

"You know where he was headed?"

"All I know for sure is, them devils left here riding west with Lee Hargrove." The man wiped his face. "Poor girl, there's no telling what they'll do to her."

"Why would they take her?"

Foster shook his head. "She tried to help her pa, then shot and killed one of Keeler's men."

"She what?" Reed was shocked. "That sweet little girl actually shot somebody?"

"They were pistol-whipping Hargrove something awful." The man continued. "She grabbed one of their guns and shot."

"If you can furnish us some fresh horses, we'll ride out as soon as we can round up some grub."

"I'll get you some horses." The stable man turned. "I'll make sure and saddle the best I've got."

Reed unsaddled his two horses and turned them into the corral as Watt and Bannock selected from the herd of horses milling about in two lots.

"Pick out a good horse each." Watt pointed out to Bannock the one he wanted. "We'll probably be in for a long, hard ride."

"I wanna talk to you." Reed stepped in front of the big man.

"Alright, boy, make it quick." Watt looked over at Reed. "What is it? We need to be riding."

"I want to put a proposition to you."

"Make it quick, Reed. We've got a long ride ahead of us." Watt took a horse from Bannock. "The girl is in danger."

"This looks like it could be a long trail. I'll go after the girl and you take the Bar S cattle to Sedalia." Reed explained.

"No!"

"Yes." Reed squared off against Watt. "I'll bring the girl back, you have my word on it."

"You're just a pup." The wolf hunter scoffed. "You think you're a match up against Doak Keeler and his bunch of hardened killers?"

"I may be young yet, Mister Slocum, but remember, I took the Burdens and I'll take Keeler and his bunch." Reed touched his pistol butt.

"And if I won't let you do it?"

"Then, we'll settle this right now."

"You ain't concerned about the girl?"

"Yes, I'm concerned. I'm willing to risk my life going after her." Reed stepped back. "But, on a horse or across it, you're going east to help your brother. I gave my word."

"Tell me, Reed Slocum, why should I ride to help my brother after he tossed me off the Bar S?" Watt looked sharply at the young man. "Give me one good reason, just one."

Reed nodded, then smiled. "Because he's your brother. He's family and he needs your help real bad. And most of all, he asked for your help."

"He must be hurt pretty bad to ask my help." Watt flung his saddle on the horse. "Pretty bad."

"Yes, sir, he's hurt real bad. He may not even be alive as we speak." Reed agreed. "All the more reason for you to go drive the herd."

"Before Rebecca was killed there never was a harsh word spoken between us." Watt looked to where Bannock was motioning for him. Turning, he walked to where the two warriors were waiting.

"Tall Pine go help brother as young one asks?" Bannock looked worriedly to where Reed was standing. "We help young one get Lee Hargrove back."

"Why do you want me to do this?" Watt shook his head. "You don't even know my brother."

"If you do not do this thing he asks." The warrior shrugged. "Bannock knows one of you could die this day."

"Young one same as Tall Pine." Lone Bear tapped his head. "Hard head."

"You think he would fight me?" Watt looked at the two Kiowa.

"Him fight." Both men nodded slowly. "You betcha."

Watt studied the hard face of the young man. Lone Bear and Bannock were right, the youngster was ready to fight. If he didn't agree to go help his brother, they would have to settle it right now, one way or the other. He wanted to go after the girl, but he didn't want to fight the boy, he couldn't. If he let Reed go after Keeler, he might be sending him to his death. Watt looked to where Bannock and the others waited with the fresh horses. Speaking to the warriors in their own language, he turned his attention back to Reed.

"Alright, young man, I don't want to fight you." The big man nodded. "It sure won't do the girl or Wes much good, if we go at each other."

"And I don't want to fight with you, but Uncle Wes needs you bad." Reed nodded.

"And you gave your word to bring me?"

"I did, but I didn't figure on this happening."

"You think you can get her back?"

"I'll do my best." Reed shrugged. "That's all I can say."

Watt nodded. "I reckon that's all a man can ask of another."

"If there's any way possible, Mister Slocum, I'll get her back."

"Bannock and Lone Bear will ride with you." Slocum nodded. "I'll take Tolman with me and send the others back to camp."

Reed looked at the two warriors and both looked like they were matured fighters. The scars on their bodies told both had fought many battles in their days. Reed knew he was no tracker. These two were hunters and they would be needed to help track Keeler and the girl.

"I'll need them." Reed nodded. "I ain't never had a reason to track a man before."

"You do now."

"I do at that."

"They're good men. You can trust them with your life." Watt studied the warriors. "I have, many times."

"You give me your word to lead the trail herd north to Sedalia?"

"You have it for what it's worth." The big man reached out his hand. "I'm to meet them at Doan's Trading Post on the Red River?"

Reed nodded. "That's what Uncle Wes said."

"Where's the herd now? How much time do I have?"

Reed knew it had been almost two weeks since he had ridden from the Bar S and headed north. Wes Slocum had said it would take a month or better before the herd would be ready to be trailed north to Bents.

"Can you reach the Red in two weeks?"

"It'll take some doing, but you have my word, I'll wear out some horses."

Reed looked about at the other warriors. "You said you ain't taking these warriors with you?"

"No, just Tolman. I'll send the rest back to the camp until I finish with the drive."

"Tolman?" Reed looked curiously at the young Kiowa. "Isn't he Kiowa?"

"Yes, he's Kiowa alright, but he's also my son."

"Your son, a Kiowa?"

"His mother is Nakima, she's Kiowa and my wife."

"Sorry, I had no idea." Reed apologized. "I didn't know he was your son. He don't talk much."

"You do now, lad." Watt looked to where the dark complexioned young one sat his horse. "The rest will stay here and hunt the wolves."

"That's good. With the Comanche and Kiowa running wild across Texas, I don't think they'd receive a warm welcome down south."

"Who's ramrodding the drive to the Red?"

"Emmet Tabor."

"Don't reckon I know him."

"No, sir, he came after you left the ranch."

"You're going after dangerous men. You take care of yourself, lad." Watt nodded. "I'll see you in three months."

"I'll get her back and I'll stay alive." Reed nodded at the big man.

Only a nod came from the big hunter as he turned and spoke briefly with Bannock and Lone Bear. Checking his cinches, Watt stepped nimbly into the saddle for such a big man. Nodding, he kicked the two geldings back to the east, breaking them into a hard lope. The two Kiowa waved and watched as Slocum and Tolman rode out of sight.

Several of the town's people stood about curiously as the young white and the two Kiowa warriors followed the tracks of Keeler and his men out of town. Passing from sight of Dade's buildings, Reed stayed behind and let Bannock and Lone Bear follow the trail. Reed had listened to tales about the wily Comanche and Kiowa since his youth. He knew these two warriors ahead of him were far better at following a trail than he would ever be.

At first, the tracks showed plainly in the soft dirt of the small rutted trail, making it simple for the warriors to follow. Reed figured Keeler wasn't trying to hide his trail. The outlaw wasn't worried in the least about the people of Dade following him. There weren't enough able-bodied men in the small settlement to put up much of a fight, even if they had a mind to. Keeler's arrogance had caused him to overlook one thing, the outlaw had no way of knowing about Watt Slocum's friendship with the Hargrove's or for that matter the big hunter being anywhere near Dade. The sun was setting as the trio reined in on the bank of a small mountain stream. Cold hardtack and stale crackers taken from the deserted store made up their supper. Reed watched the two warriors as they moved about. They seemed to sniff the air as they moved slowly around the trail, reminding him of two wolves as they studied Keeler's tracks.

CHAPTER 5

Late next morning, Reed sat his horse and watched as Bannock and Lone Bear carefully studied the tracks along the beaten trail where Keeler and his men had made camp for the night. Riding his horse to where the two warriors spoke quietly, as they examined the trail, he looked down at the tracks.

"How far ahead are they?"

"Maybe two sleeps." Bannock studied the tracks and blackened campfire. "Me no think these bad ones know we follow."

"The girl?"

Bannack pointed at a small track in the sandy ground. "Woman place foot there."

"At least she's alive." Reed breathed a sigh of relief.

"Girl still lives, for now." The warrior shook his head.

"You know her well, Bannock?"

The dark face frowned slightly. "I know Lee Hargrove. If she is harmed, these white eye will die slowly, very slowly."

"But, she is a white woman." Reed knew the warrior wasn't just talking. He could feel the hostility in the Kiowa's voice.

"No, she is much more. She is our friend." Lone Bear spoke up. "She show us much respect. She has fed us and given us clothes. No, she is much more than a white woman. We will kill if they harm her."

"If we ride hard, how soon can we catch up with them?"

"We must not let them know we are coming." Lone Bear shrugged. "We must surprise these men before they harm white squaw."

"You think they'd kill the girl?"

"This one, Keeler, would kill. Him very bad man." Bannock nodded slowly. "This one has ridden with the Comanchero."

"No, him worse than Comanchero. Him like lobo wolf." Lone Bear spoke up. "Keeler kill anything in his way, like him killed girl's father."

"How we gonna get her back unharmed?" Reed was young and green when it came to hunting men. He had no idea what Bannock had planned.

"These men not know white man follows their trail yet." Lone Bear looked at Reed. "They not worry about us. We just Kiowa out to raid."

"Keeler, him think like most whites; all Kiowa bad men." Bannock frowned. "They think all Kiowa kill and take what they want."

"Our brother, Tall Pine, teach us to earn white man's money. No have to steal from others." Lone Bear nodded. "We are brothers to Tall Pine. We good Injun."

Reed looked at the two warriors curiously. That was the first good word anyone had ever said about Watt Slocum. He studied the muscular Kiowa. They were dressed in white man's shirts and cotton pants, but both still wore the traditional breechcloth and moccasins. Their leather vests were fringed with hair, silver Conchos covered their broad shoulders, and neither man wore a hat. Bannock had his hair braided, while Lone Bear wore his loose. Both men carried the many shooting Henry Repeater rifles with a bandoleer full of shells, strapped across their chests. Each warrior carried a long skinning knife on his side. Reed had to admit, they were formidable looking men.

Perhaps, they were good Indians as Lone Bear had said, but Reed knew he wouldn't want them on his trail. Watt Slocum might have domesticated them a little, but they still retained the ability to cut a man's throat without him knowing it until his head fell off.

After a hard day's ride, Bannock held up his hand at a small stream and reined in. "We camp here tonight."

Lone Bear led his horse down to the water. "Bad men close now. Maybe, we catch up with new light."

"Why are we turning back south, Doak?" A string bean, hard-looking, redheaded man spoke up from where he was watering his dust covered horse. "Why did you bring the girl along? She's just slowing us down."

"Her old man's dead. Besides, he didn't have anything but that store. She sure ain't gonna bring any ransom money." A younger man spoke up.

"I took her and I'm keeping her for now, and that's that!" Keeler's voice was hard. "Now, see to those fleabag horses of yours and take your eyes off her."

"I know it ain't cause she killed old Toaker." The redhead laughed shrilly. "You never liked that old coot anyway."

"We should keep her." The younger man Waco laughed. "She shoots better than you do, Red."

"You're real funny, Waco." The redhead glared at the younger man. "She wasn't two feet from old Toaker when she cut loose."

"Well, you let her get the gun from you." Waco laughed again. "Poor old Toaker, put under by a mere wisp of a girl."

"Shut up, both of you." Keeler looked across at the men.

Five men, and Lee Hargrove, stood on a knoll overlooking a small mountain stream as they let their tired horses take in air. Dade was five days behind them and still the heavyset outlaw had kept his men moving fast. He had been moving higher into the mountains. Now suddenly, he turned south toward Texas and the tall grass country. He was edgy and something bothered him, but he couldn't put his finger on what it was.

Turning, he looked at the oldest member of the bunch. "Tell me, Bodie, you figure there might be somebody on our trail?"

Leaning tiredly against his saddle, the smaller man looked back down the last steep climb they had just ridden up. "Couldn't say for sure, but I don't know of anyone that brave or foolish back in Dade."

"I can feel something." The outlaw leader followed the small man's gaze. "There's something or someone back there."

"Ah, Keeler you're just being too careful." Waco studied the trail, then shrugged. "We're fixing to start into the Llano. No white man in his right mind would follow us out there."

"Maybe I am careful as you say but what would a young pup like you know of anything." The big man glared at Waco.

Looking over at the tired and disheveled girl, Waco shook his head. "Tell me, Keeler, why did you bring her along?"

"She's insurance, just in case we're followed. Besides, Waco, my boy, she ain't half bad to look at." Keeler grinned over at the girl.

"I doubt she'll be much insurance as you call it." Red Jack laughed. "And it's like Dobie said, ain't nobody back in Dade with the backbone to follow us out here."

Glaring at the redheaded man, Keeler turned to his horse. "I'm running things here, Red Jack, just you remember that."

"I remember, you just remember to not get me killed." The redhead frowned. "My mama wouldn't like that much."

"Shucks, Red Jack, you never had a mama, so I heard." Waco laughed his sarcastic laugh.

"What you hear, could get you killed."

"Not by you." Waco's hand hovered over his pistol. "You've got the slows, Red."

"Alright, knock it off." Keeler stepped between the two men. "I'm gonna send the Comanche back to check our trail."

"You do that, Mister Keeler." Waco grinned. "I'm gonna ride down to that stream and water my animal, feed myself, then turn in."

Motioning to a stocky built Indian, Keeler waited until the man led his bay gelding over to where he stood. Squat and powerfully built, the warrior wore a funny looking derby hat ordained with a hawk's feather sticking through its crown. A long scar ran along the entire left side of the man's swarthy face. The cold black eyes were like pieces of coal when they looked your way. This one had the stoic look of being mean clear through. The others he rode with knew was indeed vicious. As a youth, the warrior had first ridden with the Comancheros, then he had joined up with Keeler to raid and plunder the staked plains. With Keeler and this wild bunch, he didn't have to split the money between so many as he did with the Comancheros. As for Keeler, he wanted the Comanche with him because he was insurance when they ran into hostile Indians, plus he was a great tracker and deadly fighter when needed.

"I wouldn't trust him as far as I could throw him." Bodie whispered as the Indian moved toward them. "He gives me the creeps."

"I wouldn't either, but he's a good man to have on your side in a fight." Keeler looked to where the Comanche stopped. "And, if any of his wild relatives show up, he keeps our hair in place."

Bodie shrugged. "I reckon that's in his favor."

"Hawk, go back and check our back trail. See if anyone follows us."

"How far you want me to follow trail?"

"The horses are done in, they need a rest. Ride back in one day. Come daybreak, we'll mosey on ahead real slow so you can catch up without killing your horse."

"Me go take look." The dark eyes fastened on Bodie Paul. "You no trust Hawk, white man?"

Turning red the small man shrugged. "I trust you, Indian."

"Good." The warrior swung up on his horse. "Hawk good Indian."

Bodie watched as Hawk rode away, out of earshot and mumbled. "Just about as far as I could throw you."

The Comanche grunted as he passed in front of Keeler and Bodie. Nothing else emitted from his hard face, only a cold stare. Kicking his gelding, he slapped the horse with his rifle barrel. The horse and rider seemed to be as one as they loped back down the trail in perfect rhythm.

"Bodie, did you know the Comanche are the greatest horsemen on the plains." Keeler smiled. "But, as you will learn one day, they are a cruel cutthroat bunch, and old Hawk there is worse than most."

Bodie nodded in agreement. "The Indian is something alright. I'd hate to have him after me in the dark."

"To tell you the truth, I'd hate to have him after me in the daylight." Keeler laughed. "That Comanche is real bad medicine."

"Yeah." Bodie nodded. "That Comanche is my age, but when I'm dogged tired, he seems fresh as a daisy."

"Let's ride on down to water. We'll make camp, then let the horses get some rest and grass in them."

Glancing over as one of the men helped the girl on her horse, Bodie nodded. "Sounds good. Maybe we can get a hot meal in us."

Keeler noticed the small man's eyes on the girl. "She's my worry, Bodie, not yours."

"You're the boss, Keeler. Just don't push real hard." The small man grinned. "You're welcome to her."

"You don't like her being here, do you?"

"I learnt a long time ago, women on the trail bring bad luck." Bodie smiled. "I think she's trouble fixing to happen, Mister Keeler."

The trail, Reed and his trackers followed, led off to the west, but then suddenly the tracks turned to the south. Bannock and Lone Bear had no trouble following the rock-strewn, sandy trail as the day passed. Near midafternoon of the third day, Bannock held up his hand and rode into a small spattering of trees and dismounted. Holding his horse's nose, he made sure Reed and Lone Bear followed his lead.

"Riders come this way."

Every eye strained, watching for the oncoming horsemen to ride into view. Expecting the riders to come into sight at any time, Bannock stiffened suddenly as the trail was consumed in complete silence. Not a horse hoof sounded on the trail, not a hint of passing horses hitting against the rocky ground, nothing.

"They wait there." Bannock looked around at Reed. "Whoever riders are, they know we are here."

"Who's out there, Keeler and his bunch?" Reed checked his weapons.

"Me not know, but I think these are not the bad ones that take girl."

Suddenly, several warriors rode out into plain sight and reined in less than fifty yards from where Reed and the warriors sat their horses.

"Kiowa." Bannock raised his arm as the warriors rode their horses toward them at a slow walk. "Say nothing, I will speak."

Reed studied the eight mounted Kiowa sitting their horses before him. He had fought Kiowa and Comanche many times in running fights when they tried to raid their cattle or horse herds. Never had he seen them up close where he could get a good look at the warriors. The Kiowa were taller people, different from the stocky, bowlegged Comanche. Unlike Comanche, they wore every kind of clothing, even white men's hats. Most were bare-chested, wearing only vests. Reed could see bloodstains on the vests, probably taken in a raid from a dead settler. The leader wore a battered, lopsided, black hat that had seen better days.

Bannock spoke with the men in Kiowa and a mixture of hand signals. Several times, the warriors looked at Reed and pointed. He knew, being the only white present, he was the center of their attention. Turning to where Reed sat, Bannock motioned him forward.

"This one, Red Shirt, son of Kiowa Chief Satank." Bannock nodded at the young warrior dressed as his name suggested in a red flannel shirt.

"Him say four white men with one Comanche and one white woman. Maybe, one day ride ahead."

"He see them?"

"Him see plenty good." Bannock shook his head. "He says whites lazy, make camp, sleep. They no see them when they pass."

"Good." Reed nodded slowly. "Is the girl okay?"

Bannock spoke again to the warrior. "Him say girl is good. Him say these whites ride south now to trade her to Comancheros."

"Comancheros!" Reed had heard many bad things about the whites and Mexicans that had strongholds far out on the plains. Comancheros traded guns and whiskey for captive white women and gold.

"Woman not be hurt until she sold." Bannock flattened his hand, quieting Reed. "Comanchero not buy if woman harmed."

"Would these warriors help us get her back?"

"No, this white problem, not his." Bannock shook his head. "We go now. You give this one something for telling us these things."

"Give him what?"

"What you have?"

Reed remembered the small harmonica in his saddlebag, he had been trying to learn to play. Pulling the shiny object out, he blew through it making a musical sound, then handed it to the smiling young warrior.

"Good medicine." Amazed, Red Shirt blew on the harmonica several times and laughed. The young warrior pointed at Reed, then tapped his chest with a closed fist. "You, tall one, are good man like your father."

Lone Bear knew Reed didn't understand what Red Shirt had said. "Young one has made a friend this day."

"Tell young white, the men who have woman are the bad ones that follow a man named Keeler." Red Shirt spoke to Bannock. "These very bad white men, kill whites and many Indians. They steal much horse, gun, money. You maybe waste time and maybe lose your hair. I no think you get white woman back alive."

Raising his hand, Bannock kicked his horse forward. Reed watched the Kiowa closely as he passed by them. Never had he seen such a motley dressed bunch, but the scars showing on their bare chests told they were fighters. Today, luckily Bannock and Lone Bear were with him or things might not have turned out so peaceful.

Hawk sat hidden from view as the two groups spoke for several minutes. He knew Red Shirt, the Kiowa, and he knew Bannock and Lone Bear, the two Kiowa that rode with the white one called Tall Pine. Watching their occasional hand signs, the Comanche knew they were talking about the whites ahead and the girl.

The dark eyes watched the two groups talk several minutes, then turned his gelding and slipped away silently, back to the south to catch up with Keeler. Hawk had studied the young white with Bannock, and this one reminded him of someone, but he couldn't think who it was. Kicking his horse into a harder lope, he hurried back to find Keeler.

Keeler turned in his saddle as he heard the hooves of Hawk's horse pounding up behind them. Reining in, he waited as the Comanche rode his blowing horse beside him.

"Hawk, you sure are in a hurry." Keeler studied the heaving horse. "You're gonna kill that animal."

"Me ride hard to catch up." The warrior pointed his rifle back down the trail behind him. "Keeler right, three riders follow our trail."

"You get close enough to see them?"

"Me see."

"Well, speak man, tell me what you seen." Keeler spoke up frustrated. "Who are they?"

"Three men follow you and come here." Hawk warned. "Two warriors, Bannock and Lone Bear, who hunt wolves with Tall Pine, and one other."

"And the other?"

"Young white."

"White?"

"Young white, tall, look very strong." Hawk nodded. "I think this one is fighter, killer of men."

"Anything else?"

"They speak with Red Shirt, the Kiowa, about this one." Hawk nodded over at Lee. They follow you. They come here for woman."

"Girl, you know who he's speaking of?" Keeler looked at Lee. "Who is this young white man?"

Shaking her head, the tired, disheveled girl lied. She knew the Indian described the young man who had been at the store looking for Watt Slocum. "No, I know of no such person."

"Don't lie to me, girl." Keeler studied her face. "Do you know this youngster? Why is he following you?"

"I don't know him. He's not anyone from Dade." Lee denied.

"Him ride big bay horse with mark on shoulder like this." Hawk drew a Bar S brand in the dirt. "I think this bad omen."

Keeler scoffed at the word. "It's just a brand, a mark, to identify the animal is all."

Bodie looked closely at the drawing, then over at Hawk. "This man you saw, he carrying a big forty-four caliber horse pistol on his hip?"

"You mean like the one you have?" Hawk looked at Bodie's pistol. "It look the same."

Bodie shook his head, knowing most hunters, out on the plains, only carried their long shooting Hawkins or Henry rifles to kill with. The white, the Comanche had described, sounded like Reed Slocum, but what would he be doing this far from the Bar S Ranch? Bodie hadn't seen the young Slocum since riding away from the ranch two years ago. No, it had to be another. Reed Slocum would never be this far away from the Slocum Ranch. He looked at the girl, then back at Keeler. These men he rode with were the meanest bunch of killers he had ever known, and Hawk, the Comanche, was death walking on two feet. Hopefully, it wasn't Reed looking for the girl. He had grown a strong friendship with the youngster in the few months he had worked at the Bar S.

Bodie studied each man carefully. Keeler led the gang; a big cold-blooded killer with no qualms about whom he killed or robbed. Next was Red Jack, the scraggly redhead with the shaggy red beard. The last of the five, besides Bodie and the Comanche, was a youngster with two side guns called Waco. Bodie had never heard his last name, but the name didn't matter. He had seen the young man draw and shoot. He was fast, accurate, and a killer, deadly as Keeler himself. He knew Reed Slocum was too young and inexperienced, and no match for this bunch.

"They ain't worth waiting here for, Keeler." Bodie looked over at the big man. "Let's leave the woman here and ride."

"Leave the woman?" Keeler growled. "Why? What for?"

Bodie shook his head. "If we leave her behind, maybe they won't keep following us. They'll have to take her back to civilization."

Keeler laughed. "You want me to turn loose the good money I'll get for the girl? Then break and run from two Kiowa and a white youngster?"

"Do it, and let's ride." Bodie looked at the man. "We don't need this problem."

"No, I'm keeping the lady here."

"Why are you keeping the girl?" Bodie shook his head. "Let's do as we planned, hit some horse herds or cattle."

"I'm keeping the girl." Keeler frowned. "With that blond hair and beauty, that little gal is gonna bring a good bit from Valdez down south. Lot's more than horses or cattle, and with a lot less work."

"Why worry with her, she's just an extra load on us." Waco spoke up agreeing with Bodie. "I'll shoot her if'n you ain't got the guts to do it."

Pulling his pistol, Keeler pointed the gun at Waco. "You ain't shooting anyone, Waco."

"I was just joshing you, Doak." Waco studied the drawn pistol and the glare from Keeler. "I wouldn't shoot a pretty little thing like her."

"Alright then, but I'm telling you, the Comancheros will pay much gold for her." Keeler holstered the gun, then shook his head. "Big money, she's staying."

"Comancheros, that's a far ride isn't it?" Bodie questioned.

"Not far, just a hoop and a holler." Keeler smiled.

"I don't like it." Bodie argued. "The ones behind will dog us until they catch up."

Keeler looked over at the small man. "I'm ramrodding this outfit and I say she stays. You don't like it, then ride out."

"Suit yourself." Bodie knew he had said all he could. Keeler wanted the girl and he wasn't about to turn her loose.

"I've got me a better idea."

Motioning at the redhead and the Comanche, Keeler waited as they walked over. "Hawk, take the girl's fresher horse. I want you to show Red Jack where you last spotted the white man."

The dark head nodded. "What we do this for?"

Looking at the redhead, Keeler smiled cruelly. "Red, you're always wanting to use that gun of yours, go with Hawk and kill the white."

"What about Bannock and Lone Bear? Them ride with this white man." Hawk looked over at Keeler. "Them both fighters, bad Indians."

"They're probably just tracking for him." Keeler shrugged. "They'll stay clear of the shooting."

"And if they don't?" Red Jack grinned. "Can I gun 'em?"

"They're Slocum's Kiowa. Don't do anything to them unless they try to interfere." The big man shook his head. "We sure don't want trouble with Watt Slocum."

"But, if they interfere?" The redhead's voice slurred in anticipation as he spoke.

Exasperated with the questions, Keeler nodded. "Then kill 'em."

"Keeler." Bodie spoke up. "Let's just ride on and leave them alone."

"Nothing doing. Bannock and Lone Bear can follow an ant's tracks across a dry skillet. They'll stay after us and bring whoever is with them straight to us." Keeler looked at Bodie. "And I sure ain't hankering for them to follow us into Comanchero country."

Hawk nodded coldly. "Valdez will kill them, and maybe us too for letting a white man follow us to his stronghold."

"You better send me, boss." Waco spoke up from where he had been listening.

"Why? Red Jack can handle it."

"Maybe he can, then maybe he can't." The younger man shrugged. "He ain't as fast as I am."

"No, Red Jack will go." Keeler smiled. "He needs the practice."

"I'll ride with Red Jack." Bodie stood up. "He may need some help."

"No, I said Red will handle this. It shouldn't take the whole bunch of y'all to kill one kid."

Bodie watched as the redhead and Hawk disappeared back along the trail they had just traveled. He worried that it might be Reed Slocum following them. He knew Keeler's hair-trigger temper so he said no more about letting the girl go. Still, he hoped it wasn't the youngster. He had grown fond of young Slocum in the months he had worked on the Bar S. He remembered working with the boy and his speed with his gun, but Bodie wasn't sure he was fast enough to go against either Red Jack or Waco. He had watched as Waco had coldly killed two Mexican herders, the man was pure lightning with his forty-four.

Watt Slocum and Tolman reined in at the livery in Amarillo. Tossing the horses' reins at the old hostler, the big man looked around the dusty street. "Feed 'em up good, Mister Pike."

"You gonna be needing them anymore today, Mister Slocum?" The old hostler couldn't look the big man straight in the eye.

"Yes, sir. I'm riding on, soon as we get some grub in us." Watt looked across the street. "We'll give the horses a couple hours rest, then we'll be moving on."

"I'll tend to them." Pike stared hard at Tolman, then dropped his eyes. "Say, Mister Slocum, I reckon you heard that a fella named Reed Slocum was looking for you?"

"I heard." Watt nodded. "What of it?"

"You hear too, he done for Jake and Tom Burden?" The old man nodded. "Braced them over in Dade. Killed them both before they could get off a shot."

Slocum turned, looking down at the old man. "I heard. You got any more good news for me, Pike?"

"No, sir, that's it, I reckon." Pike looked over at the wolf hunter. "Rider came through couple days back with the news. Was wondering what it was all about is all."

"I wouldn't know." Watt looked across the street.

"I'll tend to your horses then." Pike hesitated. "You know that young man is as hard as they come."

"Good, you do that." Watt ignored the last remark.

"Yes, sir."

Pushing through the front door of Dora's Boarding House and Café, Slocum studied the familiar room carefully before motioning Tolman to a seat in the rear. It was late afternoon so the place was empty of customers. Hearing the bell, attached to the door, Dora came bustling from the back kitchen.

Stopping cold, she stared in disbelief at the tall buckskin clad figure and the Indian sitting at the back table. "Watt!"

"It's me, Dora." The big man stood up. "How are you?"

"I'm fine." She moved closer, looking down at Tolman. "And who is this young gentleman?"

"His name is Tolman, and yes, he's Kiowa." Slocum frowned slightly. He had never mentioned Tolman to Dora, nor brought him to Amarillo.

"Kiowa?"

"That a problem, Dora?"

"No, I'll get y'all some coffee." The woman smiled. "Anyone who is a friend of yours is a friend of mine. You know that."

"Fine, fine."

Pouring some coffee, she smiled. "What are you two doing here?"

"You won't believe it, but Brother Wes sent for me." Watt picked up his cup. "I hardly believe it myself."

"I know, one of you Slocums was in here a few days back looking for you."

Slocum nodded. "Yeah, I heard a young fellow was looking for me."

"We heard he found the Burden brothers too."

"Good news seems to travel fast in these parts."

"Good news for some, but it puts a stamp on the boy." Dora frowned. "There sure isn't no one gonna miss them two no-account horse thieves."

"How's that put a stamp on the boy?"

"Already the name Reed Slocum has spread around these parts like wildfire." Dora shook her head. "They'll always be some fool wanting to find out exactly how fast he really is."

"I don't believe he's looking for trouble with a gun."

"Maybe not, but trouble has a way of finding a man." Dora looked across at the big man. "I'll get you two something to eat."

"Thank you, ma'am." Watt nodded. "We're getting mighty hungry."

"Ma'am? It used to be Dora." The woman smiled slightly.

"That was a while ago."

"Yes, I guess it was at that." The pretty woman smiled down at him. "You still got your Kiowa woman with you?"

"I do." Slocum nodded at Tolman. "This young man here is her son."

Looking hard at the youngster, Dora nodded. "Uh huh, and his father?"

"Tolman is my son." Watt stared sharply at the woman.

"Well, now you have two sons. Both of them are nice looking young men, Watt."

Placing fried potatoes and steak before him, she watched as the huge hands picked up the eating utensils.

"Thank you, Dora."

"You meet up with the boy?"

Nodding between bites, Slocum looked up at her. "Yep, I met him."

"He's a dead ringer for you, Watt." Dora looked over at Tolman. "Just like Tolman here, only lighter skinned."

"This is good steak."

Dora shook her head as he avoided the subject. "You tell him who you are?"

"I figure he knows."

"You know what I'm asking, Watt Slocum."

"No, we didn't have time to get sociable."

"Didn't have time?" Dora smiled. "Why are you here, Watt?"

"Well, it was either agree to help Wes, or fight the boy."

"He was going to fight you? I don't believe that." Dora shook her head.

"The lad's a Slocum, mighty set and hardheaded in his ways."

"And you think he would have actually tried to fight you?"

Watt quickly told the woman about Lee Hargrove's abduction by Keeler and his men, and his brother, Wes Slocum, sending for him. Then, he told her about making a deal with Reed to go after the Hargrove girl before riding on to Amarillo.

"Yes, I do believe if I hadn't agreed to help Wes, I would have had to fight him."

"I can't believe that, Watt." Dora shrugged. "He seemed like such a nice young man."

"Sure as I'm sitting here, I do, Dora." Slocum frowned. "He said he'd fight me, and I believed the look in his eyes."

"And you didn't want to fight your own son?"

"No." Slocum finished his coffee. "For a sprout, he's hard clear through. I believe he'd have used his fists or that big forty-four he wears."

"He used it on the Burdens for sure."

"He did for a fact." Watt nodded. "Bannock said they didn't get off a shot."

"I guess he came by it honestly." Dora shrugged. "You staying the night?"

"No, I'm riding on as soon as my horses rest up a bit and get good feed in them." Watt looked over at Tolman. "You get enough to eat?"

"So, you're actually going to go help your brother Wes?" Dora looked strangely at the tall man. "After all these years."

"Said I would, and gave the boy my hand on it."

"I'll put you up some sandwiches for the trail." Dora smiled at Tolman as she filled his coffee cup. "You'll stop on your way back through won't you?"

"Thank you, Dora." The big man nodded. "We'll see, when and if I get back."

"Why are you doing this, Watt?"

"Other than giving my word, I really don't know." Studying the coffee mug, Watt shrugged. "I don't know exactly what this is all about, but it must be mighty important for my dear brother to send the boy this far north to find me."

"Does Tolman speak English?"

"I speak English, ma'am, or Kiowa." Tolman looked at the woman. "I can even read and write."

"Excuse me, Tolman. I didn't mean to be disrespectful." Dora blushed.

"You weren't, Dora." Watt spoke up. "You were just being curious is all, like most women."

"Have you met your brother yet, Tolman?"

The dark head nodded. "I have seen him, but we have not spoken."

"I think you'll like him." Dora touched the young one's shoulder. "You two are a lot alike in ways."

Watt stood up. "We'll stop in on our way back through, providing we get back."

"I'll be waiting. You two take care of yourselves."

Tightening up his cinches, Watt swung up into the saddle and tossed the old hostler a silver dollar. "We'll be seeing you, old man."

"Where you riding, Mister Slocum?"

"Now, old man, you know I ain't about to tell you that."

"Figured so." Pike laughed. "Well, you ride light in your saddle and watch your backsides."

"Likewise, Mister Pike."

"You ain't gonna tell me?" Pike looked over at Tolman curiously.

Sitting his horse, Slocum looked down at the old hostler. "You're right, old man, I ain't."

"You know this boy will be about as welcome east of here as a case of smallpox." Pike looked up at Tolman. "Watch out, there's been Comanche trouble, raiding and killings all through south Texas. People are pretty hostile."

"Thanks, Pike. We'll be careful."

"Yep, old Buffalo Horn and Quanah have been making a pest of themselves down along the Peace River."

"Haven't heard about that yet."

Checking the loads in his pistol, Watt turned the bay horse to the east, away from Amarillo. Figuring they had two to three weeks to reach Doan's Crossing and rendezvous with the Bar S herd, he didn't push the horses hard. He knew no one would be looking for him heading east, so he rode easy. Out there, he wouldn't have to be on guard for an enemy. Still, he was well known and the name, Watt Slocum, was hated and loathed by many, respected by few. Wherever he rode in this country, he would be recognized. His size alone would give him away, and there were so many that knew him by sight. He had run roughshod over many a man since leaving the Bar S so long ago. For many years now, with every passing day and mile, he watched for the ghosts of his past to catch up to him.

The memory of his wife, Rebecca, who was killed, had made him as mean as a wounded bear for years. Now, with so much time passing, he still remembered her death, but the years calmed him taking most of his viciousness away. He knew his brother, Wes, had been right for banning him from the Bar S after he had killed Freckles Johnson. Still, the man had been responsible for getting Rebecca killed, and he deserved to die.

One freezing winter morning, while Watt was out helping with the herd, Johnson had put Rebecca on a half-broke bronc, then just stood by laughing as the horse bucked around the corral, finally throwing her into the snubbing post and breaking her back. Watt shook the sad memory from his mind. He had almost forgotten, but when the boy showed up, looking for him, all the memories came flooding back as strong as ever. The youngster was the spitting image of Watt, except he had his mother's eyes.

CHAPTER 6

Bannock and Lone Bear suddenly pulled their horses to a stop when two riders appeared out on the flats just ahead of them. The two sat their horses and stared across the space that separated the two parties. Reed reined in beside the two Kiowa and looked over at the riders.

"We got trouble?" Reed eyed the two men.

"Much trouble, young Slocum. These same bad men we follow." Bannock nodded. "Comanche, him called Hawk. Very bad Indian."

"There's only two men out there." Reed looked around at the surrounding grassland. "Where are the others?"

"It only take one bad man to kill."

"What do you mean?"

Bannock nodded. "I think they only come here to kill you. They not know you are a Slocum."

Lone Bear studied the two men as they waited across the space of fifty yards or more. "Hawk knows we ride for Tall Pine. They no want trouble with him."

The redhead dismounted and walked several paces out in front of the Comanche who held the horses.

"I think they come to kill you, young Slocum." Bannock repeated as he looked across at the redhead who moved even closer toward them. "Him name, Red Jack. Him bad man. I think Keeler send him to kill you so you not follow them farther."

"He looks like a bad man." Reed studied the redhead standing arrogantly in front of them. "He's ugly enough."

Lone Bear shrugged. "Somehow, Keeler knows you follow them to get girl back and they not want to give up squaw."

"What about you two?" Reed watched as the redhead moved a few steps closer, then stopped. "They aim to kill you too?"

"We Kiowa, they no worry about us." Bannock nodded. "We just Indians to them, no worry."

"So they're just after me?"

"They just come after you, young Slocum." Bannock nodded. "They not want you to follow them to Comanchero country."

"My name is Reed."

"You make fight with red-haired one." Bannock slipped from his horse. "We take care of Comanche if he comes to fight."

"I reckon that's what he wants alright." Reed looked at the redhead. "But, I ain't quite sure why."

Reed dismounted and walked a few paces toward the redhead. He had never seen such an evil face as the one standing, grinning at him, several feet in front of the Comanche. Stopping forty feet from the man, Reed flipped the tie-down thong from his forty-four.

Reed jabbed his thumb back at Bannock and Lone Bear. "They say you've got business with me?"

Red Jack smiled coldly, then looked back at Hawk. "They're wrong. We don't have business with you, we just want to kill you is all."

"Why?" Reed shrugged. "I don't even know you."

"Hawk here told Mister Keeler you've come after the blond-headed girl. He doesn't have any plans of turning her loose."

Reed didn't take his eyes from the gunman. "Releasing her is better than dying, Mister Red Jack."

"You know me then?"

"Red Jack, yep, I know you." Reed motioned at Lone Bear. "Bannock told me who you were, and how sorry you are."

"Now, that's not at all sociable, young fellow." Red Jack smiled showing his yellow teeth. "Who are you anyway?"

"Name's Reed Slocum."

"Slocum." The man's eyes narrowed. "You related to Watt Slocum, the wolfer?"

"My uncle."

"You're the one that killed the Burdens back in Dade." Red Jack swallowed hard. "We heard about you and the Burdens going at it when we passed through."

"I am the one that killed them." Reed smiled. "And I'm the one that's fixing to kill you, Red Jack, right here."

Reed hardly spoke his last word when both guns roared as the sound reverberated across the flats. Seeing Red Jack thrown backward from the heavy slug, Hawk slipped on the side of his horse and pounded away, back to the south. Firing their Henry rifles several times at the retreating Comanche, Bannock and Lone Bear walked over to where the dead body lay sprawled in the dust. Looking at Reed, they nodded their heads. They knew this one was a true warrior. His face was a mask as no emotion showed on the young man's face.

Rolling the dead man over, Bannock smiled as he pointed at the bullet that had hit plumb center in the man's chest. Reloading the empty chamber of the forty-four, Reed holstered the heavy pistol and turned to his horse.

"Red-haired one, I think him good dead white man now." Lone Bear laughed. "This crazy one kill many Indian and white."

"You never did answer me. Who is the Indian that rode away and why is he riding with white men?"

"That one called Hawk. Him one bad Comanche." Bannock pulled the saddle from the dead man's horse and turned him loose. "Hawk has no people since Quanah banned him from the Comanche Tribe. Now, he rides with whites."

Reed nodded. "Now, what do we do?"

"Now, Hawk go back and tell bad man you kill this one. It would have been better if our bullets had found the Comanche's body."

"You still want to go after girl?" Lone Bear pulled Red Jack's weapons from his body. "When Hawk tells them what happened, Keeler may come for us. We must watch trail ahead very close now."

"I'm going after her." Reed pulled himself into the saddle. "Are you two going with me?"

"Tall Pine told us to stay with you." Bannock nodded. "We stay with you."

"Tall Pine?"

"The one you call Watt Slocum." Bannock looked closely at Reed. "Him our blood brother. We do as he asks."

"Thank you." Reed was relieved. He needed their help tracking the outlaws that had taken Lee Hargrove or if he ran into anymore of the wild tribes roaming this far out on the Llano Estacado. "Let's ride."

Hawk rode into Keeler's camp, concealed on the bank of a small stream. Dismounting, he turned his sweating horse loose with the others. The animal was too tired to roam far. Walking to where Keeler and the others sat around a small fire, Hawk squatted down, helping himself to some coffee.

"What happened?" Keeler could see the sullen look on the warrior's face. "Where's Red Jack?"

"Red Jack, him dead."

"Dead?"

"White man with Bannock and Lone Bear kill redhead, bang bang." Hawk pointed his finger at the fire and made a shooting sound. "The young white that follows, him bad man with gun."

"Did Red Jack get a fair break?" Waco spoke up.

Hawk nodded, then smiled. "Redhead one, reach for his gun first."

"What's so funny, Hawk?" Waco watched the dark face. "What?"

The Comanche looked over at the young outlaw. "This one faster than you. This one, he kill all of you maybe."

"You sure of that?" Waco sneered. "You want to try me, Injun?"

"You ride back that way and make fight with white man that kill Red Jack." Hawk shrugged. "You no scare Hawk, white man."

"Stop it, both of you." Keeler stood up and paced nervously. "What do you think, Bodie?"

"I told you already." Bodie shrugged, ignoring the looks that Keeler was giving him. "Turn her loose."

"Okay, so you told me." Keeler looked to where Bodie sat beside the girl. "Maybe, I'll send you back to take care of this fighter."

Bodie laughed. "That's fine with me."

"Him say his name Reed Slocum." Hawk spoke the name, making Bodie jerk his head up. "I hear this one tell redhead one. He say you send squaw back, he go back, no kill you."

"What was Red Jack's answer?"

"He tell young one, him come to fight." Hawk shrugged. "Then bang bang, him one dead redhead."

Hawk was lying, he had never spoken to the white man, Reed, but now he had a bad feeling about this one following them. If he could get Keeler to turn the girl loose, they might be rid of the menace trailing behind them. The Comanche knew men, and the young white with the fast gun was a dangerous one to make an enemy of. Hawk could see the cold, deliberate way he had killed the redhead, then looked to where he was sitting. There was something about the young white hunter, and now he had become a killer in his own right. The Comanche knew as long as they kept the white girl captive, the ones behind them would follow. He also knew the Comanchero leader, Juan Valdez, allowed no white man to enter or be brought into Comancheria without his permission.

"Tell me, Hawk." Keeler looked over at the Indian. "Do you think I should send the girl back?"

"I think Keeler should do what he wishes with squaw." Hawk swallowed some coffee. "I cut squaw's throat if Keeler says so."

"Good answer, Injun." Waco laughed. "I say we all go back and kill him."

"Me, no go back." Hawk pointed over at the girl. "This white man is bad medicine. I think spirit people help him. She just squaw, not worth getting killed for."

"This Slocum sure has you buffaloed, Hawk." Waco sneered. "I believe you've turned yellow."

"One does not tempt the spirit people." Hawk nodded solemnly. "I say this one more time, turn the woman loose or we all die."

"Do you really believe this spirit stuff, Comanche?" Waco laughed again. "Or are you just scared to face this white man?"

"I watched this one kill the redhead." Hawk looked over at Bodie. "I say he will kill all of us if we go back."

Keeler was shaking his head as he listened to Hawk. "Hawk, you don't really believe what you're saying?"

"He has Kiowas, Bannock and Lone Bear, with him." Hawk nodded. "You not be able to ambush white man as long as they lead him."

"So, they're just two Kiowa." Waco sneered. "Just Indians."

"If we cannot ambush this one, then we have to stand in front of him to kill him." Hawk shook his head. "Bannock and Lone Bear great warriors. They very hard to kill."

"There's four of us, against one kid." Waco sneered.

"Three, I tell you. I will not ride back and fight this one."

"Two." Bodie spoke up. "I'm not going back either."

"Cowards." Waco screamed. "You're both yellow, scared of one green kid."

Hawk shook his head. "Not cowards. I tell you again this one, maybe spirit person. I never see him pull gun, it just appeared in his hand."

"Like magic." Keeler scoffed. "For Pete's sake, Hawk."

"You laugh. I stay here watch squaw. You and Waco go back this time." Hawk raised his rifle slightly expecting Keeler or Waco to draw. "I not go."

"You'd like us to leave the woman with you, wouldn't you, Hawk?" Waco grinned. "Yeah, you'd like that very much."

Cussing, Keeler whirled toward the horses. "We're riding south, right now. We'll let the Comancheros take care of this one."

Hawk looked over at Bodie and nodded. "These two bad men when they fight weaker ones. Now, they not so brave."

"Tell me, Hawk." Bodie looked at the Comanche. "Is he really all that fast?"

"This young one is a killer. His hand faster than eye can follow." Hawk spread his hands. "Hawk say no more, but they better release white woman or they all be dead men. This one's eyes are dead when they look at you. I tell you, white man, he is spirit person. I feel this thing."

Lone Bear rode far ahead of Bannock and Reed as he followed the track of the Comanche that led back to the south. As they continued south, across the lower plains, the air became hotter and heavier than the thinner, cooler mountain air. However, the air was still fresh and clean as Reed took in a deep breath. He was accustomed to the plains more so than the mountains but he had heard it took a while to get used to the thinner air higher up.

The ones ahead continued south, moving deep into Texas and the Staked Plains. Bannock said they would take the girl to trade with the

Comancheros who had hidden camps far out in the flat grasslands. He also said the ones ahead had picked up their pace so they had to travel faster.

As they leveled out on the plains, the grass was so high it brushed against their horses' bellies. The deep grass allowed them to easily follow the broad, beaten-down path the ones ahead had made. Reed looked behind him at the high slopes they had just ridden down from, then turned to look out across the vast expanse of grasslands that covered everything in sight. Not a tree or shrub showed anywhere before them, and no landmarks to point their way.

"How does the Comanche find their way around out here without getting lost?" Reed looked over at the Kiowa. "The grass flats all look the same to me."

Bannock shrugged and tapped his head. "They follow sun and stars. They have something up here that guide them."

"You mean like a white man's compass?"

"I see watch that tells which way a white man should ride." Bannock nodded. "Indian no need this watch."

Reed looked over at the Kiowa. "Tell me, Bannock, why would they take one lone girl so far into these lands to trade?"

"Girl very pretty, yellow hair, and she young. Yellow hair highly prized here. Valdez will give much gold for her." The warrior's face hardened. "Maybe these bad ones have stolen guns or horses to trade also."

"What will Valdez do with her?"

"Sell her, trade her, or maybe send her to Mexico." Bannock shrugged. "She go where he get most money or guns for her."

"Can we catch them before they reach Valdez?"

"If red-haired one hadn't come after you, we would already have caught up with them."

"You're telling me the Comanche went back and warned them?"

"Yes, Hawk warn them. Now, they watch for us." Bannock pointed down at the tracks. "And they travel much faster."

"Would they kill the girl if we get close?"

"They kill, but they no give woman back."

Reed looked about the land. "This is dangerous country."

"Very dangerous land, young one." Bannock laughed lightly. "We better catch them quick, or we lose our hair maybe."

"I've fought Comancheros and Comanches before, down on the Brazos."

"You fight Kiowa?"

"Yes."

Bannock nodded and kicked his horse. "We catch Lone Bear and make camp for night."

"I'm not tired."

"Maybe you no tired. Maybe horse tired."

"Maybe." Reed felt embarrassed. He had been thinking only of himself.

The small fire flickered, sending a hazy light against the rock wall where they had made camp. The hobbled horses grazed behind them in a small area surrounding a seep hole of water. A shallow stream was a bare trickle coming up from an underground spring irrigating the sparse grass the horses ate. Reed tasted the water and filled up his canteen. The water tasted as if it was touched with iron or some other compound, but it was better than going thirsty.

Lone Bear rode in and turned his horse loose with the others. "Bad men one day ahead. I find nothing but their tracks."

"Hawk rode hard to get back to tell bad man of redhead." Bannock leaned back against his sleeping robe. "I would like to hear what Comanche said."

Reed watched as Lone Bear poured himself some coffee. "Can we catch them?"

"We see. Maybe one day, maybe more."

"Why do you ride after this girl, young Slocum?" Bannock asked. "You hardly know her."

"I made a deal with the one you call Tall Pine." Reed nodded. "I would get the girl if he would go help his brother."

"Tall Pine, him no like his brother?"

"It's a long story, Bannock. He likes his brother alright, but there's been trouble between them." Reed tried to explain. "Now, his brother is hurt bad and needs him."

"You would have killed Tall Pine if he not help his brother?" Bannock asked Reed.

"I gave my word to bring Watt Slocum home, but I don't know if I would have drawn my pistol." Reed shrugged.

"You would have killed?" Bannock asked again.

Reed looked into the fire and shook his head. "I don't know, Bannock."

"We never see Tall Pine give in so easy. We think him no want to fight you."

"Wonder why?" Reed had thought this too. "I know he wasn't scared, and he sure doesn't mind fighting others."

"Others he fight, but he not fight his own son."

"What?" Reed looked over at Bannock. "I'm not his son."

"You son of Tall Pine, young one." Lone Bear nodded. "Look in water and see yourself."

Bannock looked at Reed curiously. "How you not see this?"

Reed shook his head slowly. So that's what happened. He thought Watt Slocum, the scourge of the Colorado, had given in way to easy. Why hadn't Uncle Wes told him about his father over the years? Now, he knew what his uncle had meant when he said Reed was the only one he could send after Watt that the man wouldn't kill.

"Nobody ever told me." Reed shook his head bewildered. "I never even knew he existed until a couple weeks ago."

"You same as Tall Pine." Lone Bear poured himself more coffee. "And Tolman is your brother."

"How's that?"

"You fight, you kill. You have no sympathy for ones you shoot."

"You saying I'm cruel?"

"No cruel, just have hard heart." Bannock nodded. "You fighter, same as Tall Pine."

Lone Bear laughed lightly. "Maybe more killer."

Nodding, Reed poured himself some more coffee and thought about Watt Slocum. He knew now what Dora had been trying to tell him back in Amarillo. Never would he have guessed he was the son of the one he thought was his uncle. He wondered why Uncle Wes hadn't told him. He knew his uncle was ashamed of his brother for killing Freckles

Johnson, and had made him leave the Bar S. Surely that wasn't enough, there had to be more reasons for keeping such a secret.

"He ever say anything about my mother?"

Lone Bear shook his head. "Him no speak of her, never."

"Her name, Rebecca, is all we know." Bannock added. "I once see picture Tall Pine has. She very beautiful woman."

Bodie Paul shook his head as he listened to the talk between Keeler and the others. If Keeler would only release the girl, they could ride on without the threat of Reed following them. He knew to argue anymore about releasing the girl was futile and could be dangerous. Keeler had his mind made up and wasn't going to let the girl go, no matter the consequences. All day, they had ridden south, speaking hardly a word between them. Bodie knew Keeler was worried. Instead of sending Hawk to ride point, watching for enemies, he now had the Comanche following behind, watching their back trail. Near sundown, they reined in at a small water hole, dismounted, and hobbled their horses on the tall grass.

"Get you something to eat and rest. Come daylight, we're riding hard." Keeler looked around the small group. "Any arguments?"

"We headed for Comancheria or do we go after Reed Slocum?" Waco looked at the girl.

Hawk shook his head and repeated himself. "Bannock and Lone Bear lead young Slocum. You never get close enough to kill him by ambush."

Keeler shook his head. "We're headed for Valdez. Anybody got any different ideas can say so now."

"We're gonna let Valdez kill Slocum for us, Keeler?" Waco grinned. "Kinda makes us look like cowards, don't it?"

"Maybe Valdez will let you and this young Slocum go at it, providing he catches them."

"Alright by me." Waco smiled. "I don't figure Hawk knew what he seen back there."

Hawk could only shake his head. "Maybe you not be alright when you face this one."

"You sure, Comanche?" Waco laughed out loud. "Why?"

"This one maybe meaner than Tall Pine Slocum." Hawk looked disgustedly at Waco. "Big Slocum may just fight with you. This young one, he kill you, then walk away like nothing happen. With Bannock and Lone Bear's help, this one fast becoming a hunter and killer of enemies."

As the sun broke out in the eastern sky, Keeler had the men mounted and riding. He sensed the Comanche's worry and now it settled on him. He had never known Hawk to be afraid of anything or anybody, but this young Slocum had the warrior's nerves stretched tight. Over the years, riding with the Comancheros and being around the Comanche, he had learned to respect their belief in the spirit people. He had seen many times when the medicine men in the villages predicted something that happened the way they said it would. No, he didn't take Hawk's worries lightly. He knew the man was no coward. Quanah Parker himself had banished Hawk from his people, the Quahadi Comanche, for being too cruel against his own people. Being too blood crazed in battle, the warrior definitely was no coward. Ahead, he would find safety in Valdez's camp from whoever followed. Keeler wasn't a coward himself, but Hawk had him spooked with all his spirit talk about the young gunman following them.

Waco rode his horse alongside Bodie and grinned. "I think Hawk has old Keeler really spooked, don't you, Bodie?"

"I'm a little spooked myself." The small man nodded. "I've heard about the Comancheros and what they're capable of doing to a man."

"I take it, you've never been around Comancheros before?"

"No, I'm still alive." Bodie shook his head. "And I sure don't relish being around them this time."

"You see that feathered lance sticking out from Keeler's rifle scabbard?" Waco pointed. "The one with all the feathers?"

"I see it."

Waco grinned. "That's our pass. The lance will get us safely through these lands. At least until Valdez sees what we've brought to trade."

"You mean the girl?"

"That's it." Waco laughed. "When that Mexican sees that blond hair, we'll have a free hand in that Comanchero camp."

"Then what?"

"Well, hopefully, if he takes a real shine to the girl, we'll all make a small fortune in gold. Then, we'll ride back out and steal some more horses or something."

"I take it you've been here before, and if he doesn't want the girl?" Bodie questioned.

Looking at Lee, the gunman smiled. "Oh, he'll want her alright."

"But, what if he doesn't?"

"Then, my friend, we could be hung upside down to dry out." Waco smiled coldly. "Yeah, I've been here twice. I had the creeps both times."

"You, Waco, admit having the creeps?"

"I admit it." The young gunman shook his head. "Wait till you see the cutthroats we're fixing to meet. Those old boys give me the wobbles. They make the Comanche seem like children."

"Tell me about Juan Valdez."

"All I know about him is he ramrods this outfit." Waco shrugged. "His name is Juan Alonzo Valdez. His folks used to own most of this land before Sam Houston whipped old Santa Anna and drove them out."

"So now he's out to get it back?"

"No, Bodie. Even Valdez knows he'll never get his land back." Waco smiled. "But, he's sure gonna make enough money out here to buy him some more down in Mexico."

"What kind of man is he?"

"Only two words fits him, mister, that's cruel and crueler."

"A bad one is he?" Bodie looked over at the girl. "What about her?"

"I sure wouldn't want to be in her shoes." Waco shrugged. "No, sir, not for all the money in Texas."

"That bad?" Bodie looked over at the exhausted and disheveled girl. "Is he that bad?"

"Whatever is in her future, I'll guarantee you, it won't be good."

For five days, Keeler led the small party deep into the Llano Estacado, knowing any minute, the wild Comanche or the white men that rode behind them would appear out of the grasslands. Two days ago, he unwrapped the feathered lance, Valdez had given him, for safe passage through these lands. Keeler knew it would keep them safe at least until they reached the Comanchero's headquarters.

So far, they had met only a few wandering hunters, not the murderous wild men of the Comancheros. Several times, Keeler had sent Hawk to watch their back trail for any signs of the ones following them.

He knew if Valdez hadn't moved his camp from the large valley, they were only a day's ride away. Letting the horses drink from a large wash, Keeler studied the trail behind him. He couldn't figure why the Kiowa and the white man hadn't caught up with them yet.

Raising their heads as water dripped from their muzzles, the horses pricked their ears as several riders surrounded Keeler and his men. Quickly, Keeler raised the feathered lance high for all to see. At least thirty Comanche and several Mexicans sat looking down at them.

"Well, boys, we found them, I reckon." Waco looked around at the riders. "Kinda makes your spine tingle, don't it?"

"No, sir. I'd say they found us." Bodie studied the wild mean-looking riders. "And my spine is too scared to move or tingle."

Kicking his horse, Hawk rode out of the wash and started talking to what appeared to be the leader. Nodding, the Mexican looked the girl over closely, then motioned for them to follow him as he reined back to the south.

"What now?"

"Well, Mister Bodie Paul, I reckon you'll get to meet Valdez." Waco grinned.

"You think they know about the ones following us?"

"Not yet, but Keeler will tell Valdez. He has to tell him in order to save our necks." Waco shrugged. "That Mexican takes a mighty dim view of anybody coming into his land without his permission."

Leaving Lone Bear and Reed behind, Bannock slipped closer to watch the proceedings. They had ridden their horses almost into the ground and just about caught up to Keeler and his riders when suddenly the Comancheros surrounded the gang as they watered their horses. Bannock had almost given the signal to attack, but remained hidden when the riders appeared out of the tall grassy plain. Bannock watched as Hawk talked with the leader of the Comancheros, and when they finished talking, they rode on to the south. Bannock had hoped to catch up with Keeler before they met up with the Comancheros, but now it was too late. Disappointed, he ran back to where Reed and Lone Bear were waiting.

"We too late. Now, Comancheros take them to Valdez." Bannock shrugged as he looked at Reed. "We go home now."

"No!" Reed spoke up. "We go after the girl."

"Girl good as dead now. We no can get back." Lone Bear shook his head. "We leave this place."

"How much farther is their main camp?"

"Short ride, maybe be there by sundown."

"Then, I'm going on."

"This place, they take her, has many Comancheros. Bad people, armed camp of warriors." Bannock placed his hand on Reed's arm. "You do this, then you dead man."

"I've got to give it a try." Reed shrugged. "I gave Tall Pine my promise to do my best to get her back."

Bannock moved beside Lone Bear and spoke for several minutes in Kiowa. "If young one is gonna be so foolish, then we be foolish too."

"I'm not asking you to." Reed protested. "You don't have to risk your necks to help me."

"You not know camp, we do." Bannock shook his head. "Without us, you get yourself dead."

"And Tall Pine wouldn't like that."

"We wait here until sun goes down, then move when dark times come."

Reed thanked the two warriors. "You know where they'll keep her?"

"One with her beauty, Valdez not let out of sight." Bannock smiled. "We find her in his hacienda."

"If we don't get her back, I will kill the one Keeler before we ride away from this place." Lone Bear touched his knife.

"We'll get her back or die trying." Reed nodded grimly.

Valdez looked up as Keeler and Lee Hargrove were ushered into his headquarter's building. His eyes quickly turned to where the girl stood trembling beside the big white man. The dark eyes of the Comanchero leader were fixed on the girl, blatantly admiring her beauty. Even unkempt as she had become after the long ride, she was still beautiful. The tall Mexican smiled and bowed. He was stricken with the woman. Juan Valdez was light complected, straight as an arrow product of the aristocracy that once ruled Mexico and all of Texas. Sporting a small mustache, the handsome leader of the Comancheros was well-mannered and polite as Keeler introduced Lee.

Walking around the girl, he smiled. "How old are you, señorita?"

"Seventeen."

"You must be very tired and in need of freshening up." Valdez clapped his hands, summoning a housemaid. "See that she has a bath and a new wardrobe before dinner."

"Sí, Patrón."

"Let her rest a little while."

"Sí, Patrón."

Watching as the girl was led from his parlor, the tall Mexican smiled and looked over at Keeler. "Well, now, Señor Keeler, you have come a long way, but I believe it will be worth your trouble. Shall we have a drink to let's say, wash away the dust of the trail?"

Keeler nodded. Valdez seemed like a well-mannered, polite host, but he knew the Mexican's reputation. He could become as deadly and vicious as any of his men outside. He couldn't blame the man, as he thought he had been robbed and cheated out of his inheritance and titles by the land-grabbing gringos coming into Texas. The proud aristocracy that once owned all of Texas was now dispossessed and driven back into Mexico, exiled from their hereditary estates. Juan Valdez's father, a proud man with a land grant from the King of Spain had been slain in his own doorway by revolutionaries riding with Houston. He would not concede to their wishes and leave his hacienda, so they shot him down in front of his young son. Hatred and blood revenge against the Yankee invaders, then became Juan Valdez' only reason for living. He had put up with Keeler only because of the guns and women the man brought with him on each visit.

"Thank you, Jefe." Keeler bowed slightly as he took the glass of Sherry. "Señor, before we speak of the price, I must tell you, there may be men following us to get her back."

"Señor Keeler, you know my rules about interlopers in my country." Valdez stared hard at Keeler. "I allow no one to enter my lands without permission. You know that law very well."

"I do, Jefe." Keeler nodded. "It was an unfortunate mistake. I assure you, señor, it will not happen again."

"Why did you let them come this far?" Valdez swirled the Sherry in his glass, clearly irritated. "Are they Texas Rangers?"

"No, señor, worse I fear." Keeler's hand shook slightly as he held his glass. "Two Kiowa and a young white man."

"And you fear these?" Valdez was curious as he knew Keeler was mean and cruel himself. "Why, señor?"

"The young white killed one of my best men." Keeler turned his eyes. "Hawk says the spirit people would have let him kill us all."

Valdez laughed. "So now you believe Comanche superstition?"

"I believed his words." Keeler blushed. "I would have sent the woman back, but with her beauty, I knew you would admire one such as her."

Nodding, the Mexican smiled at Keeler. "Go upstairs, my friend. Clean yourself up for dinner, then we will discuss the price of shall I say, so comely a beauty."

"Gracias, Jefe."

Lone Bear followed closely behind the Comancheros as they led Keeler and his men south. Both of the Kiowa warriors had ridden to this canyon, the Comancheros' camp, many times before to trade horses and guns they had stolen. Since becoming blood brother to Watt Slocum, they had never returned to the canyon or the Comancheros again. Tall Pine paid them well for hunting, but he forbid any killing or stealing. Now, they were sitting their horses less than a mile from the entrance of the deep canyon.

Bannock nodded at Reed and Lone Bear. "We go. I know Valdez. Tonight he drink wine and eat much to celebrate Keeler bringing him girl. We must go now in the dark and get her out before the rising of the sun. Listen close, this time is our only chance to take girl from stronghold."

"Why is that, Bannock?" Reed shrugged. "Why is this our only chance?"

"By now, Keeler told him of us. Tomorrow, he send riders to search for us." The warrior explained. "We must take girl and be far away before this place awakens with the new sun."

"They will come after us like crazed wolves, and he has the best of trackers." Lone Bear added.

"Tonight, if you must kill, use knife, no guns." Bannock looked at the men. "We go."

CHAPTER 7

At dusk, after Reed and the two Kiowa had ridden hard, they sat on a slight knoll observing the large Comanchero stronghold. The camp lay in a large box canyon guarded by high canyon walls. Only one trail exited on each end of the deep gorge. They could see many Mexican, White, and Comanche men walking around the huge campfires that lit up the grounds and buildings around the compound. Reed guessed at least one hundred Mexicans and whites were in the canyon, not counting the Comanche warriors. A lone guitar strummed a lively song as women danced around fires to the cheers of the drinking men.

"They have good time down there." Bannock nodded quietly. "Pretty soon, maybe they all sleep."

"They always drink too much." Lone Bear shook his head. "Much whiskey and plenty of women is how Valdez keeps their loyalty."

"Where will they keep the girl?" Reed searched the buildings with light coming from the windows.

"There, in big house at far end, is where Valdez has her." Lone Bear pointed with his chin. "That is his lodge."

"Valdez is a fool." Bannock nodded. "He thinks no enemy can get through camp to his lodge without being seen."

"Valdez is a smart leader, but in this belief, I agree, he is a fool." Lone Bear grinned.

"When will we move?"

"Soon." Bannock nodded. "Lone Bear go to corrals and get us fresh horses. Pick out only best. We may be in for long run."

"Where will we meet?"

"There, in shadow by post." Bannock pointed at a far lamp post.

"What about the night guards that watch the camp?" Reed had seen the men standing along the ridge that led into the camp. "If anything happens, they will be hard to get by if we have to run for it."

"Soon, they change guards for evening meal, then we strike." Bannock touched his knife. "I take this side of ridge, you take other side. Make no sound, let none of them live. Lone Bear bring horses."

"He may be seen."

"In dark of night, they think he is one of them." Bannock looked over at the dim face. "If you want girl, young one, you must kill them. Do not miss."

"I want the girl. I won't miss."

"You see lamppost at edge of village, study it, do not forget it." Bannock nodded.

"I see it."

"We meet there when guards are dead." Bannock looked at the other Kiowa. "Lone Bear wait at farther post with horses."

Reed removed his boots and tied them around his neck. Wrapping his feet in soft strips from his blanket, that he cut up, he secured the strips tightly with leather thongs. Bannock warned him not to make a sound. Crossing the deep gorge, Reed could feel the hard stones beneath his feet as he moved cautiously to the first guard. Slipping soundlessly across the rocky trail and almost up to the guard, Reed crouched and watched the man light a cigarette. The man's full attention was focused on the activities below. His eyes were fixed on the dancing women as the music drifted upward. Looking down at the skinning knife, Reed shrugged and moved forward. The sharp-pointed blade did its job as Reed's powerful arm encircled the guard's throat, cutting off any cry as the knife sunk deep into the man's back. Wiping his blade as he slowly lowered the guard, Reed searched out his next victim. The guards were easy victims. No threats from the outside made the guards careless and not as alert as they should be plus Reed smelled the strong odor of whiskey on their bodies.

Bannock appeared out of the shadows as Reed trotted quietly toward the lamp post. "How many you kill, young one?"

"Three." Reed was almost sick to his stomach for killing so coldly, but he wasn't about to let Bannock know.

Handing Reed a serape and a Mexican sombrero, Bannock nodded. "Good. Wear this, young one."

The hat was far too small for Reed's large head. Quickly cutting the hat, he pulled it down hard the best he could. Following Bannock's lead, pretending they were just a drunk Indian and Mexican, Reed staggered behind the warrior toward the big house.

"There are guards around hacienda." Bannock whispered quietly. "We walk by house and see how many."

Bannock was right as two guards stood watch outside the doors, and their big sombreros revealed they were Mexican, not white. Bannock waved drunkenly at the guards as they weaved past the doorway. Slipping alongside the adobe building to an open window, the two men looked inside where Valdez was having supper. Only Keeler, the girl, and one Comanche sat at the table with Valdez.

"That is Lobo Cayuse, chief of Comanche that ride with Valdez." Bannock whispered as he studied the inside of the room. "Him one mean Comanche."

"What are we gonna do?" Reed whispered back.

"Keeler him drunk. Lobo Cayuse him drunk." Bannock smiled. "Soon, they all go to sleep maybe."

"And Valdez?"

"If we can get girl away, good, if not, we kill Valdez and take."

"That'll stir up a hornet's nest."

"Without head, snake die quickly, me betcha." Bannock shrugged. "Valdez, him big chief here, no others."

Valdez watched as Lobo Cayuse started to close his eyes and slip forward to the table, passing out from the strong spirits he had taken in. Smiling at the girl, he tossed Keeler a leather pouch full of gold coins.

"I believe that, Señor Keeler, will settle our account."

Keeler nodded drunkenly. "What about the ones following me, Jefe?"

"I will send men in the morning to capture these fools." Valdez grinned over at Lee. "Then you and your men will watch as they die for daring to enter my lands."

"Your land, Señor Valdez?" Lee laughed sarcastically. "This is Texas, not Mexico."

"The young lady has a smart mouth, Señor Keeler, but I will soon teach her to respect her elders." Valdez smiled across the table as he toyed with a goblet of whiskey. "She will learn."

"First time I've heard her say anything." Keeler looked across at the girl. "Well, morning comes early, señor. Thank you for your generosity and your fine brandy."

"Of course, señor. You and your men will be my guests until we capture these interlopers." Valdez tapped the side of his glass. "Do you understand?"

"Yes, señor, completely." Keeler knew Valdez had just given him a warning. If the three that followed him and his men here weren't captured, then it could go bad for them.

Bannock and Reed watched as Keeler stood unsteadily and exited the room, leaving only Lee, Valdez, and one servant. Nodding for Reed to follow him, Bannock staggered back down the ally and up onto the porch where the guards reached out to turn them around. Again, the sharp knives cut deep, silently doing their bloody jobs.

Slipping quietly inside the house, Bannock peered into the long room where the girl and Valdez were looking across the table at each other. Valdez wasn't drunk, but he had consumed enough alcohol to dim his usual vigilant watch.

"Tell me, shall I keep you or send you to Mexico?" Valdez smiled broadly at the girl.

Only silence came from Lee as she looked disdainfully at the tall Mexican. Reed watched as Valdez motioned for the serving man to leave the room. Seeing his chance, Bannock moved silently across the room and placed his knife at Valdez's throat. Lee leapt from her chair, throwing herself into Reed's outstretched arms. Complete silence inhabited the room as Bannock ushered Valdez toward the door.

"Señor, you don't think you will escape from here?" Valdez quieted as the knife bit into his skin. "You are very foolish."

"We will, or you won't." Bannock heard a sound from behind the room's curtain and motioned at Reed.

Only the sound of a moan came from the backroom as Reed disappeared behind the curtain separating the rooms. Bannock quickly gagged Valdez and tied his hands behind him. Lee pulled away from Reed as he ushered her outside, following Bannock.

"You killed that man."

"He would have given out an alarm and we might have been caught." Reed tried to reason with her. "I had to."

"It was cold-blooded murder."

"Yes, it was, Lee, just like they killed your pa."

"Not that poor man back there." Lee shook her head. "He had nothing to do with it."

"Be still, woman, before you get us all killed." Bannock grabbed the girl's arm roughly. "He had to be silenced quickly."

"As you will be, mister, if you make one false move." Reed pushed his knife under Valdez's nose. "You, comprende?"

Wrapping a serape around Valdez and keeping to the dark shadows, they slowly made their way back to where Lone Bear waited with the horses. Very few people still sat around the low burning fires and most of them were drunk. Reed couldn't understand why a leader like Valdez would let his men drink so much. Even the guards had been consuming whiskey and tequila, making them careless and easy to overpower.

The form of Lone Bear and the stolen horses revealed themselves out of the dimness of the night. Suddenly, as the Kiowa greeted Bannock and looked curiously at Valdez, sounds of gunfire at the end of the village awakened the drunken compound.

"Someone has found the dead ones we left." Reed looked toward Valdez' house that had become a beehive as Comanche warriors carrying torches streamed from their lodges.

"We go quickly." Bannock lifted the girl on a saddled horse. "You hang on, woman. No fall off."

"Hang on, Mexican. We don't want to lose you now." Reed helped the bound man into the saddle. "That would be a shame."

Reining the excited horses back through the gorge that led them into the compound earlier, Bannock led Lee's horse in a dead run. From above on the ridge, gunfire rang out as one gunman fired at the retreating riders. Lone Bear slumped sideways on his horse as Reed tried to grab him. Reining in as they cleared the canyon entrance, Reed dismounted and hurried to the grimacing warrior's side.

"Where did they get you?" In the dim moonlight, Reed could barely see the wounded man.

"Back." Only a grimace came from the warrior.

Examining the bloody gash in the warrior's back, Reed found a jagged tear where the bullet had plowed along Lone Bear's back. Luckily the wound wasn't deep, but Reed knew it was painful. Quickly packing and wrapping the wound, Reed looked over at Bannock.

"His wound will be painful, but not deadly."

"We must go." Bannock looked at Lone bear. "I will lead your horse."

"No, I am not a child." Lone Bear refused to give Bannock his reins. "You take care of the woman."

Reed looked at the entrance of the high gorge leading down into the stronghold. "Bannock, is this the only entrance to the camp?"

"No, but it long ride around from other side."

"How long?"

"Canyon prevent riding straight here." Bannock shrugged. "Maybe three, four hours."

"Lone Bear is hurt, and you've got to get Lee back safely." Reed looked over at Valdez. "I will wait here with Valdez and try to slow them down."

"They will kill you, young one." Lone Bear shook his head. "Do not do this."

"Go, before they get organized and come here."

"We go." Bannock turned his horse. "Stay safe, young one."

"You keep her safe."

"No, we can't leave you all alone." Lee tried to protest as Bannock led her and Lone Bear away in a hard lope. "No, Reed."

Reed watched as the three riders disappeared into the dark, listening until the sound of their horses could no longer be heard. Turning to where Valdez sat his horse, Reed jerked him bodily from the saddle. Removing the gag from the Mexican's mouth, Reed pulled his skinning knife.

"You know, Señor Valdez, I will use this." Reed waved the knife threateningly.

"You have proven your cruelty many times this night." Valdez spit, clearing his mouth. "I believe you."

"Remember that, and don't give me any problem."

"Señor, you are outnumbered by hundreds." Valdez laughed nervously. "Even you cannot fight so many."

The pass where they stood was narrow, allowing only three or four riders to pass at the same time. Checking his Henry Repeater, Reed nodded.

"You reckon the ones coming out of that pass will shoot with you standing out in front of me?"

Valdez shook his head. "You are a very smart, young man, but they will come around behind you, and soon I think."

"When they do, both of us may breathe our last." Reed stuck the blade closer to the man's face. "You ever been cut with a knife, Señor Valdez?"

"Sí, señor. In my profession, sometimes my enemies try to kill me."

Reed could clearly hear the sound of approaching horses. Daylight was just beginning to lighten the pass enough for him to see the riders as they emerged from the mouth of the canyon. Two riders appeared first and then others could be seen behind them.

"Well, let's hope your men don't act foolishly." Reed warned. "You stand real still now, you hear?"

Resting the barrel of the Henry over Valdez' shoulder, Reed fired off three quick rounds, dropping two of the approaching men from their saddles. Yelling in defiance, the next three men in the pass started to charge forward until they recognized Valdez standing in front of the white man. Again, the rifle barked dropping two more men onto the hard ground. Retreating out of sight of the dangerous rifle, Reed watched as they dismounted. Aiming the rifle again so the bullets would ricochet after hitting the other wall, Reed watched as a horse screamed and went down in the pass. Quickly reloading the rifle, Reed removed the weapon from Valdez' shoulder.

"Your men are kinda dim-witted."

Valdez looked where one of the downed men was struggling to crawl. "You are a cruel killer, white man."

"You ain't seen nothing yet, Comanchero." Reed raised the rifle and killed the crawling man. "Men that steal and buy young women, I consider dogs, mister, and I shoot rabid dogs."

"You, señor, are cold blooded."

"You're right, and you could be next." Reed tapped the man's back with the rifle. "You best yell over there and tell your people to stay back or you are next."

"You cannot hold them back for long."

"Long enough." Reed hoped Bannock was making good time in his retreat to the north. "You best get to yelling, Señor Valdez."

"You wouldn't dare kill me." Valdez laughed. "Then you would be dead yourself."

"I doubt I place as much value on my life as you do on yours. Now, start yelling." Reed grinned and pushed the hot barrel against the Mexican's neck. "Hot ain't it, Valdez?"

Valdez could hear the coldness in the young white's voice. He wasn't bluffing. He would kill him as quick as he had killed the wounded one. Calling out for his men to stay back out of harm's way, Valdez turned red with rage.

"I care for my people."

"Yeah, I'm sure you do." Reed spat. "But, I bet you care a lot more for your own hide and your silly pride. You didn't care much about that poor girl."

"You do not have pride?" Valdez shrugged "The woman was not harmed."

"Well, Valdez, I was always told pride goes before the fall." Reed tapped his shoulder with the rifle.

Turning his attention back to the small pass, Reed watched as several Comanche warriors raced through the gorge despite the Mexicans trying to stop them. He had to admit the warriors were magnificent as they rode straight into his rifle, yelling like demons.

"They sure don't learn, do they?" The Henry spoke again dropping the first three riders to clear the pass. Again and again, the rifle roared knocking warriors from their racing horses. As two warriors cleared the deadly rifle and came closer, Valdez blinked as the forty-four spoke, killing the last two warriors.

The reverberations along the high gorge quieted as the rifle smoke cleared. At least ten bodies lay dead or dying along the gorge. Reloading his weapons, Reed looked for any other threats as he waited beside Valdez.

"You are a very efficient killer, señor." Valdez shook his head. "Cold hearted for one so young."

"I'd call it self-defense. I believe they were trying to kill me." Reed frowned over at Valdez. "Remember, mister, you and Keeler started this dance."

"And you aim to finish it. Is that right?"

"To your last man if they don't keep back." Reed studied the gorge. "Mister Valdez, you can count on it."

Two hours passed. Reed knew his time for retreating away from the gorge before the others had time to come around the canyon to his rear was growing near. No other fighters ventured forth from the mouth of the canyon to ride into his deadly fire.

"I will make you a deal, Valdez."

The Mexican looked over at the tall man. "And what is that, señor?"

"Yell out and tell them to stay where they are for three hours and I will let you live." Reed nudged Valdez with his rifle.

"And if I don't?" Valdez sneered.

Reed pulled the skinning knife. "I'll gut you, right here and now, without blinking an eye."

"Keeler said you were related to the one called Tall Pine." Valdez looked across at the pass. "I believe you are meaner and colder blooded than the big one we have heard of."

"You and Keeler have made me what I am."

"No, señor, killing has always been in your blood." Valdez shook his head. "The girl just made it awake and come out."

"You choose, mister. Live or die, start telling them."

"I will give the order." Valdez nodded. "But, will you keep your word."

"I should kill you, mister, but I'll keep my word." Reed nodded. "I'm not in the habit of lying."

"I will walk a little closer so they can hear my words."

"You try anything and I'll drop you." Reed raised the rifle.

"I do not doubt your word, señor." Valdez started forward slowly.

Reed looked up at the sun, then back down the trail toward the gorge. By the sun, he guessed his three hours were up. Valdez's men would be coming around, behind him. Dismounting, Reed pulled Valdez around and untied his hands.

"Walk, Valdez, and hope that we don't cross trails again."

"My horse?"

"You won't need your horse, but I might." Reed mounted and turned the horses. "Don't send your men after me or there will be a lot more dying."

Valdez rubbed his wrists as he looked up at the young man. "Adiós, señor. Perhaps, we will meet again."

"Be smart, Señor Valdez. Go back to your camp. You have lost nothing so far but a little pride."

"But, Señor Slocum, to a Valdez, pride is everything."

"Maybe, but I'd say losing a little pride beats dying, wouldn't you?"

Valdez watched as Reed rode away and was hidden by the tall grass, disappearing into the western grasslands out of his view. Hate dripped from his lips as he cussed the gringo for entering his lands and making a fool of him. Not to mention the twenty or so dead ones strung out through the gorge and all the way to his hacienda. Too proud to walk, he found a comfortable rock outcropping and sat down. He knew his men would be riding up before long. They were loyal men, but he always wondered how long that loyalty would last if he didn't make them money, feed and furnish them with a place to hide out.

He knew if he was killed, the Comanche would just fade back into the Llano Estacado, and the Mexican riders would return to Mexico. But, the gringos who rode with him were all wanted men, hunted by the military and the man hunting Texas Rangers. These whites had to stay loyal to him since they had nowhere else to turn for safety. Most had reward posters on their heads. Riding into Mexico could easily get them killed for the bounty.

Catching sight of the oncoming riders, he watched as they rode warily along the trail toward him. They all had a good taste of the youngster's accuracy with the Henry Rifle, and none wanted to be his next victim.

Pedro Garcia, his number one pistolero, and Segundo were the first to reach him and dismount. "Jefe, thankfully you are safe."

"Sí, Pedro." Valdez took the canteen of water offered him. "Gracias, amigo."

"You are not hurt?" Keeler stepped down from his horse. "Slocum did not harm you?"

"No, I am not hurt." Valdez shook his head. "The young gringo kept his word and let me go."

"What is your wish, Jefe?" Garcia asked Valdez. He had been a longtime follower of Valdez, loyal to a fault. "The gringo, he retreats behind the rocks and picks us off one by one."

Valdez looked to where he had last seen Reed. He had ridden due west, while the two Kiowa with the girl had headed north. He knew the youth had less than a two-hour head start on them while the Kiowa had maybe a five-hour lead.

"Pedro, you will take trackers and follow the trail of the woman." Valdez slapped his leg with a rawhide riding crop Garcia had handed him. "I will ride with Keeler and his men after the young one."

Garcia pulled Valdez off to one side, out of earshot. "Jefe, I do not trust these gringos."

"Do not worry, Pedro." Valdez shook his head. "I will take many men with me."

"I trust no one, not even our Mexicans." Garcia grumbled. "I do not wish to leave you alone."

"I want the blond-headed señorita back, amigo." Valdez nodded. "Do you understand?"

"I understand, señor, but I fear for your life." Garcia explained.

"I will be okay, compadre." Valdez nodded. "Go after the woman for me."

"I promise I will bring her back, Jefe." Garcia smiled. "This one, she has much beauty."

"More than any woman I have ever known."

Reed rode the horse in a high lope as he led Valdez's horse. He could see the trail he was leaving as he passed through the high grass. Turning north to the high plains, he kept the horses moving at a fast clip. He knew the Comancheros would be coming soon. If his figuring was right, he was at least two hours in the lead. If he could reach the beginning of the mountains, his trail would be much harder to follow. Reed knew the deep pride the Mexican carried, and that pride would have the bandit leader following him as fast as his trackers could pick up his trail.

Keeping a close look out on his back trail as well as in front of him, Reed pushed the horses hard. He had to get out of the grassy plains, where the advantage would be equal to both hunted and hunters. His passing in the tall grass left a trail any blind man could follow. Finally, the horse he rode could run no further. He quickly transferred his bags and weapons to Valdez's horse, then turned the tired horse loose and moved on. He wondered how Bannock and Lone Bear were faring. He figured Valdez would probably send other riders and trackers after them.

Topping out on a high ridge, Reed studied the valley he had just crossed. Far out on the grasslands, tiny dots showed up following the trail he had just ridden. Reed figured the riders at best were at least two hours behind him. He wondered if Bannock could stay ahead of his pursuers, burdened with the girl and the wounded Lone Bear. Studying the oncoming riders carefully, he turned his horse to the north. He would cut back to the northeast and try to pick up Bannock's trail. He knew Bannock would ride straight for the wolf camp and then on to Dade, but were there enough able bodied men in that small town that would dare fight the Comancheros following them?

The horse he rode was tired, but he hadn't carried the weight near as far as the other horse had. Leaving the grasslands, the terrain rapidly changed from tall grass to hilly ridges, barren of hardly anything except sagebrush, small pinyons, and rock passes. Reed knew he would be easily spotted by his pursuers out here in the open. Kicking the horse into a slow lope, he headed for a ridge that would obscure him from their sight. Topping out on the ridge, Reed dismounted and loosened the cinches of the tired animal. The men behind him weren't in sight yet so he let the horse rest a spell. Pulling extra shells from his saddlebags, Reed replenished the ammo belt Lone Bear had given him.

The sweaty bay gelding had quit blowing and was scavenging around the sparse grass that was to be found. Taking one last look across the broad expanse of grass below, Reed led the horse to the northeast.

Hitting a dog trot, he led the horse for several miles through the semi desert land until he again started to climb. Topping out another small hill, he was happy to find a small mountain stream flowing downward through the passes. Watering the horse and refilling his canteen, Reed tightened his cinches and moved on across the trail. Now, the trail behind him was sheltered by the higher hills so he would not be able to see the ones that were following.

For a full day and into the night, Reed moved forward, occasionally walking to let the tired gelding rest. The horse he rode was weary, but he was a good solid animal with the heart to carry his rider on. Reed figured the horses that carried his pursuers were as tired as his animal was, but still, he worried. He had heard tales of how the Comanche could ride a horse twice as far as a white man could before it died. Turning east, onto a heavily traveled trail, Reed found the tracks of Bannock and his pursuers. Even in the poor light of the coming darkness, he could make out the tracks of many horses heading to the north.

It had to be Bannock's tracks he was looking at. Walking and leading the horse, Reed followed the tracks slowly through the late evening. He remembered this part of the trail, but with darkness moving in, he was forced to stop at another hole of water. Unsaddling the animal, he hobbled him and turned him loose on a small patch of grass. Ahead were the ones that pursued Bannock and behind him were the ones that were following his trail. Now, he was caught in the middle between two parties of Comancheros. Reed wondered if Keeler and his men were in one of these groups, or maybe Valdez had them killed.

Reed couldn't read sign like Bannock or Lone Bear, so he had no way of knowing how long ago the ones he followed had passed heading north. Nevertheless, he had no doubt somewhere ahead, between him and Bannock, were the Comancheros and maybe Valdez himself riding to overtake the woman. Unable to sleep, Reed saddled the horse and started up the hilly trail. He had to take the chance of losing the tracks in the darkness, but he needed to travel in the cool of the night and overtake the ones ahead. Bannock would know he was being pursued, but with the girl and Lone Bear hindering him, could he outdistance the Mexicans and Comanche? The Comanche were born horsemen, riding for days without tiring, and the Comancheros would stay with the

Comanche. To help keep Lee safe, Reed had to keep going until he caught up with the ones ahead. He couldn't let the girl fall back into the hands of Valdez again.

Reed no longer worried about the ones following him since they would eventually show up and then would be the time to worry. With the break of day, he breathed a sigh of relief. Before him on the sandy trail lay the tracks of many riders, maybe fifteen horses had passed recently. Kicking the tired gelding, Reed moved on at a slow trot. Nearing dark, after another long day in the saddle, Reed led the horse and moved ahead on foot. Staring over a small ridge, he quickly ducked back as he almost walked into plain view of the ones ahead. Dropping the reins, he crawled back up the ridge and peered down the trail at a small stream. Ten horses stood hobbled and grazing alongside a stream. Looking down on the riders, lounging around the fire, Reed counted three Comanche and the rest were Mexican.

He knew the Comanche were probably the trackers and the Mexicans were probably Valdez's hired killers, the best he had. Valdez was not in this group. Reed figured with his pride, he was with the ones following him. He knew the Mexican leader would want to be in on his death, perhaps killing Reed himself. Reed watched for an hour as darkness surrounded the Mexican's camp. No guards were posted and all the riders were rolled up in their bedrolls against the chill of the higher elevation. Whoever was leading this group of killers was mighty sure of himself or downright stupid for not posting a guard.

Reed surveyed the terrain of the small dipped out hollow where the riders had made their camp. He knew it could be dangerous, but if he was lucky, he could surpass the camp on the west side, downwind of the camp. Hopefully, he could slip by the camp without catching the other horses' attention and the east wind would not change when he crossed the small canyon. Carefully checking over the land, he had found no crevices he or the horse could stumble into in the darkness.

Holding the horse up close, in case he tried to call out to the other horses, Reed started to skirt the camp. Even with the chill of the night, sweat covered his shirt from the strain and tension. Slowly, foot by foot, Reed passed the sleeping camp, then finally continued on to the trail ahead. Mounting the gelding, he moved forward, looking for a good place to make another stand. He needed a small pass, one that couldn't be skirted by men on foot, where he could slow down the pursuers. He had to give Bannock time to open up his lead on the ones pursuing them.

Reed remembered this part of the trail when Bannock had led them south into the grasslands. Boulders and rock skirted the rocky passes as he followed the tracks of the Kiowa and girl. Sweat stains covered the dark neck and flanks of the horse as the animal topped over the lower pass. Ahead, lay a long flat, then another mountain trail that wound slowly up to the next pass. Reining in the tired gelding, Reed dismounted and pulled the Henry from its saddle scabbard. He gauged it was at least two hundred yards to where the riders would be coming into view. They would have to cross a lot of open ground before they could reach him. Studying the landscape, Reed could see no way the Comancheros could skirt around him without costing them a lot of time. Hobbling the horse out of sight, Reed laid out his bandoleer of shells, then found himself a good rest for the rifle.

Looking up at the sky, he figured it was almost noon when the riders finally appeared far down the trail. Three Comanches were in the lead, followed by a huge Mexican in a black sombrero. They were too far to make out their faces, but he could see all carried rifles across their pommels. Reed had no qualms about killing them from ambush, as they would pay him the same compliment if the hands were reversed.

Reed figured they were a little over a hundred fifty yards from him when he dropped the first Comanche from his horse. The carrying of the sound from the rifle took time giving him another easy shot before the riders panicked and rode in different directions, trying to find a safe haven to hide behind. Two Comanches were down as Reed tried for the third. The warrior rolled to the side of the running horse hiding himself from sight. Turning the sights on the racing horse, Reed dropped the animal, then killed his rider as he tried to dodge behind a large rock.

Garcia watched as the three Comanches died in less than a minute. "Mío, mío." The dark face scowled as he looked to where the sound of the rifle came from. "This one is the devil himself come after us."

"He has killed all our trackers!" Another rider exclaimed as he looked at the dead Comanches.

Retreating out of range as Reed knocked one last Mexican from his horse, Garcia yelled out in rage and shook his fist. He had lost four men and there was no way to get across the flats to the shooter without losing several more.

"What will we do, Juan?" A very young Mexican with two bandoleers of shells belted across his chest asked. "We can ride around, but it will take several hours."

"If we charge the gringo, we will lose many men. We must wait until dark to cross." Garcia shook his head. "This one has chosen a good place to fight. We cannot go around him. You are right, it would take too long."

"If we wait, he could be far away by dark." The young one whipped his horse hard. "I will kill this one."

"No, Carlos, no!" Garcia watched as the bay horse of the youngster charged across the flats into certain death. The young Mexican was halfway across the flats, racing his horse hard, when the smoke and blast from the rifle sounded. The small body of the Mexican was thrown back from the impact of the heavy bullet.

Crossing himself, a scar-faced Mexican looked over at Garcia. "Valdez will be mad at us for letting his nephew get killed like this."

"Carlos was stupid. It was not our fault, Raoul." Garcia stared at the fallen body. "But, the young one, he was very brave."

"Brave, maybe, but also very foolish." The Mexican nodded. "I'm afraid the same fate awaits for all of us if we try to cross now."

Garcia sat staring out across the flats. The youngster was no coward, but to charge into this one's rifle had been suicide. "If we charge across now, Raoul, most of us will never see tomorrow."

"Who is out there, Juan?" Another small Mexican peered across the flats. "I do not think the Kiowa we follow can shoot that good."

"I think it is the young gringo." The dark head shook. "Somehow, he must have gotten around us while we slept like babies. It must be him. Who else could it be?"

"Perhaps they are Texas Rangers?" The little man shrugged.

"No, the rangers would not kill from ambush as this one has done." Garcia frowned. "It is the same white hunter that followed Keeler and his men to our country."

"The next time I see this gringo Keeler, I will cut out his heart and roast it." Another Mexican swore. "He has brought death to so many of our compadres."

"And I will help you, amigo." Raoul nodded.

From higher in the mountains, Bannock and Lone Bear listened to the far off rumble of gunfire. Turning in their saddles, the men waited for the sound to come again. The sounds of a rifle's blast could be heard faintly but then only silence came from the grasslands.

"What do you hear, Bannock?" The disheveled girl watched the faces of the two Kiowa.

"Gunfire, but it is a long way off." The warrior nodded. "No sound comes now."

"Here in the high mountains sound carries far." Lone Bear strained to hear more gunfire. "It must be the young one."

"Can't we go back and help him?"

"No, woman." Bannock shook his head. "He has given his life to save ours, we cannot go back."

"But, he is alone against so many, he will be killed."

"Then we remember him as a brave warrior." Lone Bear kicked his horse. "He's given us time, maybe our lives. We must ride."

Reed looked across the flats where the small body of the one he had just shot lay. He shook his head wondering why this one had been so foolish to throw his young life away. Peering down the sights of the Henry, he held it high on the gathered horsemen who screamed in rage and waved their rifles. He knew it was a long shot for the rifle and he would probably miss, but he wanted the ones over there to know he still was covering the flats. Maybe a close shot would discourage them from charging in force toward him. The recoil slammed against his shoulder as the sound of the rifle blasted. Across the flats, one of the Mexicans was flung back from his horse. Reed nodded as the others retreated behind rocks out of harm's way. Mounting the tired gelding, he turned back to the north. He didn't figure anyone would dare try to cross the clearing until dark.

Chapter 8

Watt Slocum looked back as the smoke and noise from Amarillo faded from his view. Trying to remember the last time he had been across the Red at Doan's, he tried to calculate how much time he had to reach the crossing. Reed had said, maybe three weeks before the herd hit the trail, so he figured by riding steady, he had plenty of time. If he needed fresh horses, Watt knew there were plenty of people in north Texas that could supply him with them. He had friends in the panhandle, but he also had many enemies. The Kiowa and Comanche were his brothers and many of the outlaws that rode this flat country were well known to him. He left them alone and they treated him likewise. Sitting his horse in the middle of the east-west trail, he motioned for Tolman to follow, then turned the big horse to the south. He was curious, so before joining with the herd, he decided to ride to the Bar S to check on his brother and tell him about Reed. No faster than a trail herd moved, ten to fifteen miles a day, on a fresh horse he could catch up to them well before they reached the Red River Crossing.

Rotating between walking, trotting, and a slow lope, Slocum was covering the long miles back to the Brazos River. Many years had passed since he crossed this part of Texas, and the land brought back many old memories. Rebecca's smiling face as she held their newborn son, flashed before his eyes, and for him, the happiest of days before Freckles Johnson had recklessly caused her death. Shaking his head, he looked down at the crossing on the Bosque River. Not as large as the Brazos, but still a good-sized river that never went dry during the hot months.

The main house of the Bar S was only a few miles further to the south. Kicking his horses into a slow ground-eating lope, he covered the last miles quickly. Riding through the gates into the ranch yard, Watt dismounted at the tie rail. Looking around the quiet ranch yard, he knew either the men were out on round-up or they had already trailed the herd north. Nodding for Tolman to follow, Watt tapped on the door and was surprised when a young woman answered his knock. Nodding at the woman, the tall man stepped back as she opened the screen door.

"Yes, sir?"

"I'm Watt Slocum, come to see my brother if he's still above ground."

"I know who you are." The woman looked over at Tolman. "This one I don't know."

"This is Tolman, my son."

The woman nodded coldly, then ushered him inside. "He's still alive, if that's what you mean."

"It is."

"I thought you were supposed to meet the herd at Doan's Crossing."

"Have they already pulled out?" Watt looked around the large room and it hadn't changed the least in the years he had been away. "We didn't see any hands as we rode in."

"The herd left out two days ago."

"Good, then I won't have any trouble catching up to them, will I, ma'am."

"I doubt you will." The young woman turned and led the way to the bedroom. "Your brother is through here." Stopping at the doorway, she looked up at Watt in disgust.

"Apparently you don't like me much, ma'am."

"You could say that again, Watt Slocum." The dark eyes glared up at him. "I despise you."

Smiling, Watt spoke to her back as he pushed into the room where Wes Slocum lay in bed. "Well, lady, I don't remember you, but at least you're honest."

"I tend to say what is on my mind."

Entering the bedroom, Watt looked down at the hurt man. It was plain to see the pain in his brother's face. "From what Reed said, I didn't know whether I'd find you alive or dead."

"I'm mostly alive, Brother, but just barely." Wes looked up at the unkempt man. "It's good to see you. I figured you'd be headed for the Red."

"There's plenty of time to catch the herd." Watt pulled up a chair by the bed. "This is my son, Tolman."

Wes took in the long black hair and the buckskin hunting shirt and nodded. "A person could mistake you for an Indian."

"Kiowa." Tolman looked down at the hurt man. "At least half."

"What are you doing here, Watt?" The hurt man looked over at the unkempt figure sitting beside the bed. "Figured you'd be on your way to the crossing, providing Reed found you."

"Came to check on you and get the lowdown on what I'm up against out there."

"You mean you didn't want to see if I had gone under and you inherited the ranch?" Wes nodded slowly. "Well, as you can plainly see, I'm still breathing."

Watt stood up and stepped back. "Get this straight, dear brother, I don't give a hang about your precious ranch. I can ride back north right now."

"Just like that, Watt?" Wes moved slightly. "You ain't changed a bit."

"I'm only here because I didn't want to have to kill the boy." Watt looked down at the injured man. "I don't give a rip about you or this ranch."

"He threaten you, did he?" Wes laughed lightly. "Sit down, Brother. Sit down and calm yourself."

"He's got sand in his veins for sure." Watt nodded. "You put the boy in a dangerous situation by sending him out there."

Ringing the bell by his bed, Wes looked over as the doorway darkened. "Fix my brother and nephew some vittles, will you, Jeanne?"

Looking hard at Watt and Tolman, she nodded without answering and turned from the room.

"She's got a real hate against me, liable to poison me."

"Her brother was Andrew Long. The man you almost beat to death one time down at the Brazos Crossing, remember?"

"Yeah, I remember. You know, he started that ruckus." Watt shook his head. "Whatever became of that loudmouth?"

Wes nodded. "Longley killed him at the crossing. I reckon they were fighting over the same woman."

"Longley?" Watt smiled. "Andy Long braced that killer?"

"Wasn't much of a fight, so I hear." Wes grimaced. "More like murder in my books."

"I reckon it was." Watt nodded. "Longley was a bad actor with a mighty fast gun."

"Where is Reed? Why isn't he with you?"

"Well, brace yourself, Brother." Watt quickly told Wes where Reed was and what he was doing.

"You let him go alone?" Wes swore. "What were you thinking?"

"The same thing you were when you sent him after me." Watt frowned. "Your herd of cows."

"But alone, he's just a youngster."

"Not alone, Brother. He's got my best two men riding with him." Watt swore. "Besides, if anything happens to him it's your fault."

"My fault?" Wes shifted in his bed. "How do you figure that?"

"You think more of this ranch than you do of your own nephew." Watt frowned. "You sent him on a man's job."

"I had no choice. Without your help, we'd all lose this place."

"Well, as you say, I had no choice either." Watt seemed to smile. "If I hadn't agreed to his terms, he might have shot me."

"You don't believe that."

"I'm here ain't I? That lad's a hard shell for sure." Watt shook his head. "Yes, I do believe he would have shot me."

Handing Watt and Tolman a tray of biscuits, ham, and eggs, Jeanne looked at Tolman and shook her head. "You want anything, Mister Slocum?"

"No, thank you."

"Thank you, ma'am." Watt sipped the hot coffee. "We're famished."

"Choke on it for all I care."

"Thank you again, ma'am." Watt smiled at the woman as she left the room. "Where did you find that spitfire?"

"I didn't, that no-account Doctor Samuel S Boudean set her on me when I got laid up." Wes smiled. "Wasn't much I could do about it at the time. Now, I find I couldn't do without her."

"Sounds like a good idea to me." Watt nodded. "You look like you need some seeing to."

"Well, I reckon I do at that." Wes looked up at the big man. "When you pulling out?"

"I'll switch horses with you, then we'll ride into town and get us a bath, haircut, and some new duds. Then, we'll catch up with the herd." Watt finished his food. "You need anything, Brother?"

"You better get the boy some new duds, and you might cut his hair." Wes nodded at Tolman. "Kiowa ain't thought of too highly around here."

"Is that what you think of me, Uncle?" Tolman set his plate down and stood up. "And, no man is cutting my hair."

"No, boy, not me personally, but that's what others around these parts think."

"Tolman wait outside for me." Watt looked over at Wes. "Now, what have you got me into?"

"You'll be up against Rail Johnson and his hired guns, after you cross the Red."

"Rail Johnson… thought you and him were friends?"

"Not anymore." Wes replied. "Tell me, will you be coming back to the ranch after the drive?"

"No, don't reckon I will." Watt explained. "It doesn't look like my son would be welcome here."

"You know the feelings around here, Watt, against the Kiowa and Comanche." Wes sighed.

"Tolman is my son." Watt frowned. "Where I go, he goes."

"When folks look at him all they see is a full-blooded Kiowa." The rancher shook his head. "What about Reed, your other son?"

"Bannock and Lone Bear will keep him safe." Watt assured him. "He'll be back here before we finish the drive. I'll check on him before I head back north."

"I guess this Bannock and Lone Bear are the men you said were good, and they're Kiowa too?" Wes questioned.

"None better." Watt stood up and looked down at his brother. "Adios, Wes. I'll get your herd through just fine."

"You take care of yourself, Watt. Watch out for Rail Johnson and his bunch." Wes nodded. "Don't expect any trouble from him until you cross the Red."

"I'll do that."

"Tell old Henry down at the barn to saddle up the chestnut and the long-legged bay for you."

"I'll do this for you, Wes, but don't expect to see me again."

"I don't have anything against your son, and I want you back here on the ranch with the rest of the family." Wes stated.

"And my wife, Nakima, will she be family too?"

"That's not fair, but yes, if you want her here, so be it." Wes frowned.

Nodding, Watt passed from the bedroom and started for the kitchen door. "I'm sorry I was rude, Mister Slocum."

"Don't be, ma'am. I should have killed your brother that night on the Brazos."

Walking to the bedroom door as Watt left the house, Jeanne looked in on Wes. "He's a hard man and he stinks."

"Yes, he is, Jeanne. The stink will wash off, but the hard will never leave that one."

"His son seems hard too, but he's a nice looking youngster." Jeanne smiled.

Watt Slocum, with Tolman following, rode the big chestnut horse down the street of the town of Brazos Flats, looking at the slab-sided buildings as he passed. Reining in at the red-poled barbershop, he dismounted, then entered the shop. Seeing the bloody hunting shirt and the uncouth look of the man, the barber smiled weakly and watched as two other customers left hurriedly.

"Can I help you, sir?"

"I need the works, barber. Bath, shave, and haircut." Watt nodded at Tolman. "And he needs a bath."

Looking at Tolman, the barber shook his head. "But, sir… I can't."

"Show him the bath, mister." The words were hard and cold as Watt tapped the blade of his knife.

"Yes, sir. Be seated while I get some hot water boiling."

"I'll walk across the street and get us some suitable clothes before I take my bath."

"Yes, sir… yes, sir." The small barber mumbled and disappeared behind the curtains where the tubs waited. "You sure need some."

The inside of the large mercantile store smelled and looked like hundreds of others that dotted the land across Texas. Out of necessity, the mercantile carried everything needed to feed, clothe, and keep a family taken care of year round. Watt eyed the tall figure standing behind the counter as he crossed the room to where the stacks of clothes lay. Busy picking out two sets of clothing for himself and Tolman, he sensed the clerk approach.

"Hello, Watt Slocum."

"Mister Davis."

"It's been a while, Watt. How have you been?" The storekeeper looked curiously at Tolman.

"I'll take these shirts and pants." Watt handed the clothes to the clerk.

Davis looked down at the moccasins covering the huge feet. "Boots?"

"These will do just fine." Watt looked down at his feet.

"How is Wes doing?"

"Fine, his nurse is taking good care of him."

"Yes, Jeanne Long is a fine woman." Davis took the money Watt laid out on the counter. "I reckon you remember her?"

"I do now." Watt nodded and walked out.

The storekeeper watched as the big man crossed the street, stepping nimbly on the walkway. "You ain't changed a bit, Watt Slocum. Still hard as nails and twice as cold."

An hour later, stepping down from the steps of the barbershop, Watt looked and smelled like a new man. A bath, close shave, haircut, and new clothes made him look younger and smell better. No one would have recognized him for the man that went into the shop earlier. Tolman felt the smooth dark blue calico shirt that covered his upper body and smiled. Stepping upon their horses, the two men kicked the horses into a short lope back to the ranch.

"You should have let the barber cut your hair, Tolman." Watt smiled at the young man's free-flowing, long, black hair. "Somebody out here might take a hankering for it."

"I may be scalped, but I will never cut my hair."

Laughing, Watt kicked the horse back toward the Bar S.

"Well, now, you look like a lot different, Brother." Wes looked up as Watt walked into the room. "And so does Tolman."

"We'll be headed out now, Wes." Watt looked at the injured man. "I hope you heal up real quick like."

Rising slightly from his bed, Wes warned. "You watch yourself when the herd crosses the Red into the nations."

"I'll need some pocket money if you have any?" Watt looked about the room. "For supplies and such if we run short."

"Look in the top desk drawer and take what you need." Wes offered.

"I should pick up the drag in a couple days, maybe three. I'll keep my eyes peeled for Rail Johnson." Watt assured him and turned for the door. Passing the woman as he left the bedroom, he nodded slightly. "Take care of him, Miss Long."

"You take care of yourself, Watt Slocum." The woman smiled. "And your son, Tolman."

"Well, thank you, ma'am." Watt was surprised. "You've changed."

"I was wrong before." Jeanne dropped her eyes. "I knew what my brother was. Well, let's just say he was not a good man."

"Thank you, ma'am."

Stepping down from the porch, Slocum watched as the high-stepping, buggy horse of Sam Boudean came trotting into the yard. Untying his horse, Watt turned as the buggy stopped beside him.

"Watt Slocum in the flesh." Boudean smiled. "I wouldn't have believed it if I hadn't seen you for myself."

"Howdy, Doctor Sam." Watt nodded. "It's been a spell for sure."

Looking at the doorway, Boudean removed his black bag from the buggy. "How's your brother today?"

"You're the doctor, Sam." Watt's words were crisp. "He's your patient."

"You've seen him since I have."

Watt nodded. "He was talking pretty clear when I left him just now."

"Well, I better get inside." Boudean nodded at the tall man. "You ain't changed a bit, Watt Slocum."

"Well, neither have you, Doc."

Kicking the chestnut into a lope, Watt headed east, away from the ranch. With any luck at all, they should pick up the herd in no more than three days. As slow as the herd was moving, he would have plenty of time to catch up with the drag of the drive. He didn't know how the herd was split up between steers and cows, but there should be no calves. The herd would be fresh and making good time the first few days on the trail. Still, there was no need to kill the horse or himself in a wild race to catch up. He and Tolman would ride easy, taking care of their horses in case they were needed. The herd would be safe until they reached the river. Even Rail Johnson wouldn't buck the Texas Rangers, so they were in no hurry.

Valdez rode into the rock outcropping where Juan Garcia and his men waited, hidden from the long-shooting rifle that had killed so many of them. Dismounting, as the Mexicans rose from their hiding places, Valdez looked around the group in rage.

"What are you doing here?" The tall Mexican looked out across the flats at the dead bodies. "What has happened?"

"I am glad you are here, Jefe." Garcia couldn't look the man in the eyes. "There is one over there that has the eyes of an eagle."

"Whoever this one is, his rifle doesn't miss when he fires." Raoul added.

"Where is he?" Valdez studied the far rock outcropping with his eyes ablaze. "Where?"

"Over there, behind that flat rock."

"It is the young one, Slocum." Valdez mounted his horse. "We followed his trail back to this place. Let's ride."

"It is dangerous, señor." Garcia grabbed the reins of the horse. "The one over there is a very good shot. He doesn't miss."

"We ride. I am dangerous too!"

"Wait, Jefe. There is more." Garcia nodded far out on the flats. "That is Carlos lying there."

"Carlos, what is he doing here?" Valdez shook his head in dismay. "My nephew is dead?"

"Sí, señor." Garcia dropped his head not knowing what to expect from Valdez. "He followed us… said you sent him to help."

Valdez lowered his head for several seconds. "I told the boy to stay at the hacienda where he would be safe."

"He charged the one over there alone, before we could stop him." Garcia shrugged. "He would not listen, Jefe. I am sorry."

"He was strong headed for one so young." Valdez studied the still body. "Now, he is dead."

"Everyone liked Carlos. We are all sorry."

"What will we do, Jefe?" Raoul spoke up. "To ride out there means certain death."

"Go back and tell Keeler and his men to come up here."

Minutes passed, then Keeler rode up beside Valdez and looked out across the flats. Five men lay dead out in the sun and one lay covered with a serape behind him. Looking at the dark face of the tall Mexican leader, he kept quiet.

"You and your men, señor, will lead us across the flats." Valdez's voice came out cold and hard. "You brought this killer here. Now, you will face his rifle first."

Keeler knew better than to argue. Valdez had at least twenty-five men left backing him. "Sí, Patrón."

Motioning for Waco, Bodie, and Hawk to follow him, he kicked his horse into a trot toward the far rocks. He looked at the bloody bodies as he passed each dead man and shook his head. Keeler knew if young Slocum was still watching them from the rocks ahead, they could all wind up dead men. Looking behind him, he watched as Valdez and his men left the safety of the rocks and followed them at a distance.

"This is pure suicide, Keeler." Bodie spoke up from his right side. "We're sitting ducks out here."

"You have a better idea." Keeler frowned. "That's Valdez's nephew laying in front of us. It'd be suicide to refuse to go farther, Mister Paul."

"Then, we may all be dead men already."

"He figures we brought this trouble down on him." Keeler looked over at Bodie. "And I reckon we did at that."

"What are we gonna do?"

"Let's charge them rocks. Maybe, he won't be able to get us all." Waco spurred his horse hard, yelling as he fired his pistol.

Racing into the rocks, Waco whirled his horse, finding Reed had already vacated his place behind the boulder. After killing so many, several empty casings from the Henry lay on the ground where Reed had fired and then ejected them from the rifle.

"He's gone." Waco looked up the trail. "He's like a ghost."

Hawk studied the tracks that rode away from the flat rocks. Kneeling, he traced the hoof prints with his finger. Looking up at Keeler, the Comanche pointed north. "Him gone maybe one hour, maybe more. For once, Waco, you are right."

"What do you mean, Injun?" Waco didn't like Hawk.

"I told you before, this one we follow is a spirit person." Hawk nodded solemnly.

Keeler looked to where Valdez stood over the young Mexican's body. "You boys, spread out a little and be ready in case we have to fight our way out of this mess."

"You think he'll try to kill us, Keeler?" Bodie watched as the small body was being placed across a horse.

"Wouldn't you if that were your kin?"

Bodie nodded. "Reckon I would at that."

Valdez reined in and looked at Keeler. "The gringo killed Carlos."

"I am sorry for your loss." Keeler nodded. "We all liked the boy."

"I do not want your sorrow, señor. I want you to kill the one that has done this thing." Valdez crossed himself. "Now, ride!"

"You have my word, he's a dead man when we catch up to him." Keeler looked over at the Mexican.

"And you have my word, señor." Valdez nodded. "If you don't kill him, we will kill you."

Keeler knew the closer they rode toward Colorado Territory the better their chances of surviving this debacle would be. Valdez and his riders were all Comancheros, and in that land, every hand was against them. If discovered, they would be a long way from their camp and safety. He also knew Valdez would eventually try to kill them once their usefulness in finding Slocum was finished. For now, the girl was no longer on the Mexican's mind. Now, he grieved for one he thought of as a son. All he wanted was revenge against the one who had killed the young Mexican, Carlos.

"We will find the young white who has done this thing."

Valdez fastened his black eyes on Keeler. "You better, señor. You're dead if you don't."

Motioning at Hawk to lead out, Keeler looked over at Bodie and shrugged. "At least we're still breathing."

Hawk was an experienced warrior and many times he had been on raids across the endless Llano Estacado. All Comanche warriors were great horsemen, so he knew the horses they rode were jaded from the many miles they had traveled following the white. The white was better mounted as his horse still stepped out strong, not dragging the toes of his hooves. Hawk read the tracks on the trail plainly and knew fresh horses would be needed if they were to overtake the young white. Trouble was, in the vast emptiness of the plains, horses were scarce. They had to ride to one of the big ranches further east to steal the horses needed. However, to leave the trail they followed could cause them to lose Slocum in the vastness of the grasslands. A windstorm or a thunderstorm could erase the tracks before they could get back.

Reining in, he waited for Keeler to catch up. "The young one ahead is riding a stronger horse. Ours are finished."

Valdez reined in beside where Hawk and Keeler were talking. "What is wrong?"

"The white man rides a stronger horse. If we are to catch him, we need fresh horses."

Valdez was a horseman and he knew the Comanche spoke the truth. The horses were exhausted. "Stay on the trail. I will speak with Garcia."

"The nearest ranch from here is due east about thirty or so miles." Keeler nodded. "But, the Slash H has many men riding for them."

"I will speak with Garcia. We have a few Comanches still alive. He can take them." Valdez rode back to where the main body of Comancheros waited.

Hawk watched as seven riders split off from the main body and rode due east. Five Comanche riders and two Mexicans were in the group. Kicking his tired horse, Hawk kept following the fresh tracks.

Raoul rode up beside the Comanche and Keeler to deliver a message from Valdez. The Mexican looked hard at Keeler and Hawk. "He says we are to follow this one. He says he will cut across and catch up with us."

Keeler kicked his horse. "We'll follow as fast as our horses will allow."

Reed was watching from behind another outcropping of rock as the three men pointed at the tracks and carried on a conversation. He recognized one was a Mexican, a Comanche, and a white man he had never seen before. He kept his eyes riveted on the Comanche, their tracker, as the Mexican rode back to the main body. Lining up the Henry's sights on the one he thought to be the most dangerous to him, Reed squeezed the trigger slowly. Shocked, he looked over his sights as a Mexican interceded himself in front of the Comanche just as he squeezed the trigger. Reed watched as the rider was knocked from his saddle.

Again, the rifle roared missing the Comanche who had slipped beneath his running horse and retreated safely out of range of the deadly weapon. Reed dropped one other Mexican from his saddle, who hadn't reacted quick enough to reach safety. Valdez looked down at the fallen men, then his blazing dark eyes focused on Keeler.

"Now, señor, it seems you have lost me more men." Valdez touched the butt of his pistol. "I want that man out there dead. Do you understand?"

Keeler nodded slowly, he could see death in the Mexican's eyes. Motioning to his men, he rode back out on the flat racing toward the place the firing had come from. They all knew there was no choice for them, to refuse would get them shot down where they were. Spread out so the shooter couldn't get all of them, they ran their worn out horses toward the rocky outcropping. Again, like the previous time, reining in behind the rock wall, they found whoever was doing the shooting had vanished. Slipping from his winded horse, Hawk picked up two empty casings.

"It's got to be Slocum." Waco looked at the casings Hawk held. "It has to be him. No Kiowa can shoot like that."

Bodie looked out across the flat trail where the dead man lay. "Good shot for a Henry. Must be a hundred fifty yards to where he hit that Mexican on the run."

"He's a dangerous man." Keeler watched as Valdez advanced. "So is the Mexican coming."

"You hesitate to ride, señor?" Valdez questioned. "Why?"

"Just letting our horses blow a minute or two when we found these." Keeler held out the spent shells.

"From now on, one of your men will ride point." Valdez pointed at Bodie. "He will be our next dead one. I will lose no more of my men."

Keeler nodded. "I will ride with him."

"No, señor, you will ride with me." Valdez nodded. "I wouldn't want to lose you. Your death will not be so fast or so easy."

Mounting, Bodie kicked the tired animal following the trail headed north. Hawk and Waco kept close behind him. "Which one of us do you think old Slocum is gonna kill next, Injun?"

Hawk looked over at the young killer shaking his head. "I do not know this thing, but he will kill again unless we leave this place soon."

"Tell me, Hawk." Waco asked. "Just how are we gonna get ourselves out of this mess?"

Shrugging, the Comanche looked back at the main party of riders. "Our horses too tired to escape now. We cannot outrun Comancheros, and if we run, we could run into young white man who will be waiting."

Waco laughed. "Seems Mister Keeler has gone and got us between a rock and a hard place, Hawk."

"Rock and hard place?" Hawk looked at Waco.

"It's a white saying, Hawk." Bodie shook his head. "It just means we're in plenty of trouble."

The Comanche nodded slowly. "For once, white man is right. We in much trouble. The one ahead is a spirit person."

From his vantage point further along the mountain, Reed watched the advancing horsemen. For two days, he had kept in front of the ones following. Only the powerful horse under him kept him safe and out in front of the Comancheros. The Henry lay across a flat rock with several shells lying beside it. Raising the rifle, Reed sighted down the barrel at the nearest rider. The finger tightened slowly, then Reed lowered the rifle and studied the man. Something about the way the rider sat his horse was familiar, so Reed held his fire.

Bodie Paul, the name rolled off Reed's tongue in shock as the rider's face came closer. Pulling the rifle back, Reed mounted and retreated up the dusty trail. Bodie's face flashed before him, the face of a friend. The man that had taught him all he knew about a pistol. He had grown to think of Bodie as family, and he couldn't pull the trigger. Bodie had now become his enemy, riding with Valdez and his cutthroats. Reed cussed as he should have fired. Back there he had his chance of narrowing the odds against him but he couldn't kill Bodie Paul in cold blood. For now, he would just stay ahead of Valdez until he could ride closer to Dade. This far north, deep into dangerous country for the Comanchero, maybe Valdez would give up and turn back to the Llano and safety.

Hawk studied the tracks where Reed had stood, then turned to where Bodie sat his horse. "Young Slocum let you live and rode off, why?"

"How do you know he let me live?" Bodie turned his head.

"There where he wait. There where he laid rifle. Look, white man, see scratch mark on rock?"

Bodie looked down at the tracks and frowned. The Comanche had sharp eyes and missed nothing, so there was no use lying. "We used to be saddle pards."

"Maybe, old Bodie saved all our lives." Waco laughed.

Bodie looked north muttering to himself. "And maybe, just cost him his own life. Ride fast Reed Slocum and never look back."

"You knew all along who has been following us?" Hawk looked over at Bodie.

"I guessed."

"You should have told Keeler."

"Would it have made any difference?" Bodie shrugged. "I told him to turn the woman loose. If he had listened, we wouldn't be in this mess."

Waco grinned. "Why you're just full of surprises, Bodie. Tell me, is young Slocum as fast with his pistol as old Hawk here says?"

"You'll just have to try him to find out, I reckon." Bodie grinned. "Sure way to commit suicide I'd say."

"For who, Bodie?"

"Try him."

"I aim to, just as soon as we catch up."

The morning of the second day as Keeler rolled from his blankets, a lone Comanche came riding into camp, leading a second horse. Looking down as Valdez raised to his feet, the Comanche's hands started speaking. Nodding, Valdez turned to where Keeler stood.

"This one says fresh horses are coming, señor." Valdez looked up at the warrior and pointed. "He says they will be waiting when we reach the mountains."

"Will they be ahead of Slocum?"

"No, but they will be closer to him and we will have fresher horses than he is riding." The tall Mexican smiled coldly. "Now, we will run him down quickly."

"Maybe we can catch him out in the open for once."

"Perhaps." Valdez smiled coldly. "If you and your men are lucky, señor."

"Let's ride, Jefe." Keeler turned to wake up the rest. "I want this one bad."

"Not as bad as I want him, señor." The dark eyes stared holes in Keeler's back.

"We need to catch him before he reaches Dade."

"I have heard this is just a small place." Valdez frowned. "If I have to, I will kill everyone there to find him."

"And if he makes another stand?"

Valdez nodded grimly. "Then, Señor Keeler, we will all charge him in mass. Some of us will perhaps die, but it will be finished."

"You know you will be his first target when he sees you."

"I don't think so, señor." Valdez laughed cruelly. "You and your men will be the first ones that come into his sights."

Keeler shook his head slowly. "So be it. I will personally lead the men."

"Yes, you will."

Reed saw the riders in the lower lands coming in from the east. He could see six riders, and each man was leading several horses. For several days, he had managed to stay ahead of the men following him, but now with fresher horses coming, he knew they would run him down quickly. Turning the horse, he started north at a slow trot, looking for another good place to make a stand. If Valdez and his men caught up, Reed was determined they would pay dearly before he fell.

Climbing steadily for a whole day, the horse finally played out and Reed had to lead him. Studying the uphill climb as he followed the trail, Reed continued to search for a good place to make another stand. Watering the thirsty horse and refilling his canteen with fresh water at another small water hole, Reed looked back down the mountain. No riders were in sight, but surely they had gotten the fresh mounts by now and would be on their way.

Bannock led Lone Bear and Lee Hargrove into the wolf camp of Watt Slocum where they were met by Nakima and several Kiowa warriors. As they slid from their tired horses, completely exhausted, Lee could hardly walk and had to be helped to a place by a small fire. Tired, dirty, and unkempt, she grabbed Bannock by the arm as he turned back to where Lone Bear was talking with the other warriors.

"I am safe now, Bannock." She looked up into his eyes pleading. "Return and help him if it's not too late. Please, my friend."

"I will talk with the others." Bannock smiled. "It is up to them whether they go or not."

"Hurry, Bannock." The girl held his arm. "I fear for him."

Bannock nodded. "You like the young one?"

Blushing, she nodded. "I just don't want him killed is all."

"I will speak with the others." The warrior smiled and walked away.

Nakima walked beside Bannock as he returned to where Lone Bear and the other Kiowa men stood. "You must go help my husband's son, if you can, Brother."

"We could lose many of our people." Bannock looked back down the trail. "There are many Comancheros coming, Sister."

"What is to be will be. You gave Tall Pine your word to help and protect the young one." Nakima shook her head. "I do not know this young one yet, but he is as Tolman, a son to me."

"I said I will speak with the others."

"You said he stood between you and the Comancheros and held them back while you escaped." Nakima argued. "You owe him your life. Now, save his if it is written."

"We heard gunfire across the mountain, but it was far off. We know nothing more."

"Go, Brother. Ride swiftly and try to save Reed Slocum."

"You go back to fire with the woman." Bannock ordered Nakima, then walked to where Lone Bear sat with several warriors. One of the women brought him a plate of food, then quickly left the men.

"What will Bannock do?" Lone Bear looked to where the warrior sat.

"Nakima says we should go help the young one." Bannock looked around the fire at the gathered warriors as he ate. "I will go. Who rides with me?"

"There are not many of us." An older warrior spoke up. "Who will guard our women?"

"I will only take five warriors with me." Bannock shrugged. "The rest will stay for the women."

"Why do we help this white man?" The same warrior spoke up again. "He is not our blood or our problem."

"I will ride as soon as I catch a fresh horse." Bannock tossed the plate at the warrior's feet. "I gave my word to Tall Pine, and yes, he is my problem."

Three warriors stepped beside Lone Bear as Bannock glared at the warrior. Bannock looked at the others and nodded. With only five fighters against the many Comancheros with Valdez, they would be badly outnumbered, but he knew Valdez wanted the girl. If they did nothing to stop the Mexican, then the Comancheros could possibly continue to ride north and attack their camp.

Lone Bear stood beside Bannock. "Bring fresh horses and extra shells for our rifles quickly. We ride."

Pulling the older warrior aside, Bannock looked hard at the warrior. "You keep guards out, Latoona, until we return. If anything happens to Nakima or girl, you will answer to me and Tall Pine."

"We will watch like the night owl."

Bannock nodded. "See that you do."

"How far away is the white one?"

"I do not know, maybe a day." Bannock took the offered food and shells. "If he still lives."

CHAPTER 9

Watt Slocum sat his horse on the bank of the Red River as he looked out across Doan's Crossing. He had never been to this crossing, but he understood two brothers ran a trading post and had corrals set up about a mile or so across the Red. Besides drovers pushing several herds north in the spring, many Kiowa and Comanche people inhabited the post. Riding at a steady gait, Watt and Tolman had taken three days to catch up to the Bar S herd. The words of Wes Slocum came back to him as he watched the slow moving river. He remembered his brother's last words were to watch out for Rail Johnson and his henchmen after the herd crossed the river. The big man nodded slightly. Tomorrow, he would push the herd across the Red, then deal with Johnson if he had too. Riding back to where the Bar S riders were bedding the herd down after they had been watered, Slocum dismounted beside the chuck wagon.

"How's the river look?" The grey-haired cook tossed Watt a hot biscuit. "Can we cross?"

The big man bit into the biscuit and shook his head. "Your cooking is getting better every year, Louie."

"Well, thankee, Mister Slocum… and the river?"

"We'll start them across come sunup." Watt watched as Emmet Tabor came riding in. "Have the chuck ready before daylight."

"Yes, sir… boss." Louie Bates was getting up in years, working for the Bar S for almost forty years. He had practically raised the wild Slocum brothers since they were born. First as a bronc buster, then as a cowhand, and now, after slowing down from carrying many broken bones, he was the cook. Over the many years, he had never missed one trail drive. Now, he was delegated to drive the chuck wagon and do the cooking, and doctoring when needed. Still, the chuck wagon was his sole domain, and anybody wanting to eat dared not cross or sass the old man if they were hungry. Louie Bates and his brother, Henry, back at the ranch were kinda like hierarchy now. They both started riding for the Bar S when Wes and Watt's daddy had founded the brand. Wes had offered Louie a full retirement, but the old bronc buster had scowled, saying he wasn't ready for the rocking chair yet. Being demoted from a top hand to a cook would have insulted many a cowboy, but not Louie Bates. He was a practical man that knew his time in the saddle was over. Now, he was thankful that Wes Slocum still let him work as a man should.

Tabor reined in hard and looked over at Watt. "We may have bad trouble, boss."

"Is there any other kind? Spit it out, Emmet."

"Couple of the men thought they seen riders dogging our heels this afternoon." Tabor shifted in his saddle. "You know, if Johnson stampeded our cows on this side of the river, it would take days to round them all up."

"That what you figure they're up to?" Watt twisted in the saddle to study the herd.

"If some of them old mossy horns get to running, shucks, they may run clear back to the Bar S before we could stop them." Tabor swore. "Well, sir, maybe not quite that far, but they would scatter to the four winds for sure."

"You could be right." Watt agreed. "We'd probably not get them all gathered again before late summer."

"What do you want me to do?"

"Just send out the nighthawks like normal for now. After dark, we'll ride out." Watt looked down at the cook, then at the biscuit. "By golly, I might give you a raise, Louie."

"Humph." The old man growled before turning back to his cooking. "That'll be the day."

Tabor looked over at Watt. "I don't mean to pry, boss, but what about Reed?"

"I don't know, Emmet. I left him up north to take care of a little problem." Watt shook his head. "I'm a little worried myself."

"Did you get to talk with him?"

"I did."

Tabor smiled. "He's quite a young man, ain't he?"

"I'd say that was putting it mildly." The big man half smiled. "He's a handful alright."

"Well, I wouldn't worry too much about him. Anybody that crosses him will probably have their hands full." Tabor winked. "He's a chip off the old block. He'll be okay."

"I hope so." Watt looked to the north and west. "I hope so."

Supper was finished as Watt passed through the relaxing riders and nodded at the ones he needed. Collecting the riders away from the fire, he kept them cloaked in darkness. Six of the older hands stood waiting by the picket line as he stood before them.

"Alright, boys… tonight, you may get a chance to earn your pay." The big man looked at the small group. "You boys up to a fight."

"Shucks, Watt, we thought we had already earned it." Joe Casper laughed. "You sure have been pushing us hard ever since you caught up."

"Well, tonight might just be a bonus for you, Joe." Watt nodded. "You seem to be spreading a little around your belt."

"What's going on, boss?" Howe spoke up. "Who we chasing tonight?"

"Emmet says we've had company shadowing us all day." Watt answered the bowlegged rider. "I've sent Tolman to find them."

"You think that one Kiowa can find somebody out there?"

"If they're out there, he'll find them." Watt frowned slightly. "I'll guarantee it."

"You trust a Kiowa, Mister Slocum?"

"This one I do, Cates." Watt turned on the tall drover. "I wouldn't say another word, were I you."

"Yes, sir."

"Fork 'em, boys. We'll meet him on the south side of the herd."

The Bar S riders didn't know Tolman was the half-breed son of Watt Slocum. He was two years younger than Reed, but at seventeen, he had already become a man. Not quite as tall as Reed but he was straight as an arrow and muscular for his age. He had the dark complexion of his mother that marked him as an Indian. Like his mother, he seldom spoke, letting others do most of the talking when he was around whites.

Slocum was proud of Tolman. He never bragged on the young man, but there was pride in his eyes when he looked at him. Straight across the shoulders, for his young age, he carried himself with pride and dignity for all to see. From when he first walked, Bannock, brother of Nakima, had taught him the way of the Kiowa, and no other interfered. As his uncle, it was Bannock's duty to teach the youngster the art of war, tracking, and killing. Tolman had learned his lessons well in his short life. He had the Kiowa coloring, but the rest of him was pure Slocum.

None of the riders heard or noticed Tolman as he suddenly appeared beside them from the dark. He seemed to materialize before their eyes. Pushing his horse close to Watt, he whispered quietly.

"Twelve whites are waiting there." The dark head motioned to the east.

"Are there anymore on the other side of the herd?"

"No more, just these." Tolman replied. "These bad men. They plan to stampede the herd right through night camp, maybe kill some riders."

Nodding, Watt looked about at the gathered faces. "You boys heard him didn't you?

"We heard him, Watt." Tabor nodded. "What's your orders, boss?"

"Stay single file and keep quiet." Watt motioned at Tolman. "Lead us to where they're waiting."

An hour later, Tolman reined in at a small stand of blackjack trees and pointed to the west. A small fire blazed brightly across the flats, almost two miles away from where the herd was bedded down.

"They are stupid fools showing a fire like that." Watt could only shake his head. "Alright boys, we'll circle them quietly."

"We gonna kill them, boss?"

"No shooting. We sure don't want to stampede our own herd." The big man warned. "Let's go, spread out and we'll catch them in a circle."

With his riders completely encircled around the men sitting about the fire, Slocum rode into the camp. Twelve men leapt to their feet as they looked up at the huge man sitting on a chestnut horse.

"If you boys reach for your guns, you're dead men, I guarantee it." Watt looked around the fire.

"Shuck them pistols into a pile quick." Tabor spoke from out of the dark.

A rider in a black vest grabbed for his holstered gun and was flung backward as Tolman's arrow ripped into him. The reflection of the fire showed the feathered shaft stuck clean through the man's chest.

"Shuck 'em." Tabor repeated. "Make it quick. Ain't gonna tell you boys again."

Seeing the rifles leveled at them as the Bar S men appeared in the light, every hand relaxed, moving quickly away from their pistols.

"What you men want? We ain't done nothing. We're just riding by."

"Well, if it ain't Dan Hickman." Watt dismounted and walked to where the tall, rangy speaker stood. "You still riding for Rail Johnson, I suppose."

"Well, what of it?"

Only the hard slap of Watt's huge hand sounded as Hickman was knocked, rolling through the fire. Looking around at the other nervous faces, the big man nodded coldly. "Any you other boys want to say anything smart?"

"About what?" Another rider spoke up. "Like Dan said, we were just passing through these parts."

Watt shook his head. "You boys sure are tight mouthed. Who you're riding for is what I want to know and what I aim to find out, pretty quick."

Not a word came from the men as Hickman managed to stand to his feet. Only sour and grim looks came from them, but not one Johnson rider spoke a word. Walking to where a saddle lay on the ground, Slocum untied the rope.

"What you aiming to do with that, mister?" A younger rider studied Watt nervously. "Ain't no call for a rope."

"Well, young feller, I'll tell you." Watt looked up at a tree limb. "I aim to hang you boys for rustling."

"We ain't stole nothing." Hickman spoke up. "That would be murder."

"Whatever it'll be, Dan, you'll be dead and I doubt it'll matter much."

"Yes, sir. We ride for Rail Johnson." The young rider blurted out. "Don't hang me, please."

"Shut your trap, Evers, you sniveling coward." Hickman back-handed the young rider.

The singing of the lariat as it settled around Hickman's neck could be heard as Watt tossed the rope over a low limb. Keeping the rope tight as he stepped up on his horse, Watt dallied the horn and backed the chestnut away from the tree. The hemp smoked a little as it burned into the limb from the weight as Hickman's feet left the ground kicking. Grabbing at the choking rope with both hands, Hickman kicked several times, then strangled as the hemp burned into his neck. The young rider, Evers, passed out, falling in a heap as Hickman choked and finally hung limp.

Dismounting, Slocum left the horse standing with the body swinging, then walked to where the men were quaking in their boots. The big man retrieved another rope and looked coldly at the riders. "Who's next? I'm gonna ask you just one more time. Why are you here dogging this herd?"

Dropping their heads, Boone Hames spoke up. "Well, it don't matter now, you're gonna hang us anyway. We were paid to stampede your herd and wreck your camp."

"You could have killed some of my men." Watt frowned. "Running cattle have a way of stomping on men pretty good."

"Yes, sir." The rider nodded slowly. "That was the plan."

"Who are you working for?" Slocum shook out the rope. "Say it out plain for everyone here to hear."

"Rail Johnson."

"Each of you say the name."

Every rider spoke the name Rail Johnson. Looking at the big man with the rope, they all knew they were fixing to meet their maker. The name, Rail Johnson, was repeated until every man had spoken it. Mounting the chestnut, Watt stepped the animal forward, lowering Hickman's body to the ground.

"What we gonna do with them, boss?" Tabor looked at the scared men.

The big man looked down the line of cowed men. "I ain't gonna hang you this time. We're just gonna put you across the Red tonight.

You boys ride anywhere you want, but don't let me catch one of you back in Texas or I'll finish what I started here. You understand me?"

Every head nodded with relief as they looked up at the man who sat glaring down at them. Nodding over to where Tabor stood, Watt waited.

Tabor rode his horse forward. "You boys get saddled up quick, then we'll take us a ride down to the crossing." Tabor nodded down at Hickman and the other dead man. "What about the bodies, Watt? You want us to bury them?"

"What bodies, Emmet?" The chestnut horse turned. "Give these boys a little taste of your hemp ropes, then send them across the river."

"Yes, sir." Tabor nodded as the big man and Tolman rode off.

"Man, Emmet, I've heard what a hard case he is, and now, I've seen it for myself." Howe wiped his face. "You know these men hadn't done anything yet. You could call what he just done murder."

"It wouldn't be healthy if someone did, Howe." Tabor smiled. "I didn't see anything myself. Did any of you other boys see anything?"

Not a word was spoken as the men sat their saddles.

"I reckon I didn't see anything either." Howe spoke up.

"Why, Mister Hank Howe, you've just added maybe forty years to your life." Tabor laughed as he started the men for the crossing at Doan's. "Forty years."

"Yeah." Howe agreed as Watt disappeared in the dark. "I believe you, Emmet."

"You boys see anything like the way that Injun kid killed that gun sharp?" Another rider spoke up. "Didn't blink an eye, no sir, not one blink, and he's just a young one."

"Just so you know, Rudy, that youngster you keep calling a Kiowa is Watt's kid."

"You're kidding." The one called Rudy swallowed hard. "Why didn't you warn me?"

"No, I ain't kidding, cowboy. He'll have you for breakfast if he hears you say any more about the boy." Tabor kicked his horse. "Now, stop your jawing and let's get these boys across the river."

Reed's horse was finished, leaving him afoot. He knew he couldn't evade being tracked down by the Comanches with Valdez for long.

Now, all he could do was seek out the best place to make a stand. Unsaddling the horse, he packed his saddle, canteen, and blankets into a small enclave that protected him from three sides and gave him a good field of fire. He knew if Valdez charged en masse, he could get a few but not all before they surrounded him. Twice, the Comancheros had only sent a few riders across to attack him. This time, he knew they would change their tactics and would all charge him at once. Laying out his rifle and shells, Reed took a long pull on his canteen, then settled down to wait for the Mexican's arrival. After the long chase, Reed was well aware he had been lucky to stay alive this far.

Reining in his fresh horses, Valdez stopped beside the few remaining Comanche trackers he had left. One of the warriors pointed out across a flat field at the tall outcropping of rocks.

"Him wait there."

Valdez studied the rocks, but couldn't see anything. "You sure he's there, Wild Horse?"

"Wild Horse sure." The warrior nodded. "You no believe me, you ride out there and find out for yourself."

"I'll take your word on it."

The Mexican looked at the warrior. He didn't like Wild Horse's disrespectful mouth and never had. Nevertheless, the Comanche was a great tracker and fighter, plus he was the youngest brother of Lobo Cayuse. Valdez needed the warrior, so he had to disregard the man's arrogance and demeanor. Wild Horse demanded respect since his bravery in battle had been proven many times against the Rangers of Texas. Also, he couldn't afford to insult Lobo Cayuse and lose the Comanches he led.

"What would you do, Wild Horse?" Valdez looked across the field.

"I would tell you to turn back and leave this one." The warrior shrugged. "I think he is bad medicine."

"He is that. He has killed many of our people already." Valdez nodded. "Hawk says the spirit people protect him."

"And he will kill many more if you charge across there." Wild Horse shook his head. "I know you will not turn back, so tell me, what will you do?"

"Will you ride with me if I lead my men across?" Valdez studied the dark face.

"I am no coward." The warrior frowned slightly, knowing many were fixing to die. "I do not like it, but I will ride with you."

Keeler rode up to where Valdez and Wild Horse were studying the far rocks. "Are we going across, señor?"

"Bring your men up here."

"I reckon we're leading the charge?" Keeler nodded across at the huge boulders.

"You and your men are." Valdez sneered. "You said you wanted young Slocum. There he is, señor. Go get him."

Sitting behind Keeler, Waco spoke up. "With your permission, I'll ride over there and kill Slocum."

"You, señor?" Valdez scoffed. "He will kill you before you get across the field."

Waco shook his head. "If he does so be it, but I don't think he will shoot if I go alone."

"You are a very brave man or a fool, señor." Valdez laughed. "Which is it?"

"Maybe a little bit of both, Señor Valdez." Waco grinned. "But, if it works, it'll beat getting more of your men killed."

"I'll cross with him." Bodie spoke up.

"No, I'll kill him alone." Waco shook his head. "I don't need you."

"You need me. I'm going."

"Enough." Valdez held up his hand. "Go, both of you."

Wild Horse looked over at Hawk and spoke to him in Comanche. "Why do you ride with these pigs?"

"For the same reason you ride with Valdez." Hawk smiled. "We both know the Comanche are a beaten people. I myself will not live on a reservation and take the white man's handouts."

"Quanah Parker and Buffalo Hump still ride the Llano Estacado." Wild Horse shrugged. "They have not been defeated."

"The whites are many." Hawk shook his head. "The day of the Comanche is numbered, and soon, we will be gone from this land."

Waco tied a white rag to his rifle's barrel, then with Bodie following started across the wide expanse straight into Reed's guns. When the two riders were halfway across the flats, the roar of the rifle sounded and dust kicked up a few feet in front of their horses. Waco raised the flag higher and continued forward as another shot was heard from behind the rocks.

"The white hunter will kill both of them fools soon." Wild Horse remarked.

"Be ready, señor. When they fall, you and the Comanche will lead the charge." Valdez looked over at Keeler.

Keeler looked at the Mexican without blinking. "As I believe I am fixing to die here and now, tell me something, Señor Valdez."

"What do you wish to know, Señor Keeler?" Valdez smiled coldly. "Every man should have a last request, don't you think?"

"Why are you so set on killing this one gringo, or is it the woman you want?" Keeler questioned.

The cold, smoldering eyes fixed on Keeler, emitting hate. "It is not the woman. Now, I must kill this one first, then I will go after the woman."

"But why, señor? You have lost so many men."

Valdez nodded. "That is exactly why this one must die. I have lost many men and the ones that live have no respect for me as a leader anymore."

"That is not so, Jefe." Garcia spoke up. "The men respect you as they would no other."

"If the gringo defeats us and lives, I will lose face with them." Valdez glared over at Keeler. "Do you know what it is like to lose your pride, to have your insides laid bare?"

"And if we kill young Slocum?"

"I will have my pride and respect back, and then I will go after her."

As the two riders under the flag of truce rode closer, Reed recognized Bodie Paul but the other man he didn't know. Sighting down the barrel, he held the sights dead center on the younger man's chest. He couldn't believe Bodie was riding with these killers. The Bodie Paul he knew would never have done such a thing.

"That's far enough. You take another step and I'll drop you right there."

"Why don't you come out in the open. Just me and you will go at it with our pistols." Waco lowered the flag. "Just you and me, Mister Slocum."

"Reed, it's me, Bodie Paul." The smaller rider called out. "You remember me, lad?"

"I remember you, Bodie. What are you doing riding with this scum?"

"The usual story for a saddle bum, I reckon. Broke and hungry will cause you to have strange bedfellows."

"This is gonna get you killed, Bodie." Reed studied the small man. "You know that, don't you?"

Bodie ignored the question. "Waco here wants to prove how big a man he is to Valdez by killing you in a fair stand-up fight."

"Tell me, Bodie, why should I let him prove anything out here in the middle of nowhere?" Reed scanned the flats for a trick of some kind. Seeing no movement from the rocks, he turned his attention back on the two riders in front of him.

"Waco here figures it's his only chance to get out of this mess alive." Bodie looked over at the gunman. "If he kills you, it could be Valdez and his men won't kill him."

"I doubt that Mexican will let him live, whatever happens." Reed scoffed. "I've killed too many of his men and made a fool of him."

"You kill me, boy, and just maybe the ones behind us will ride off and let you live another day." Waco looked back over his shoulder. "They all think you are a spirit of some kind, but then again, maybe not."

"And you, Bodie, what part you got in this?" Reed studied the two men.

"I'm neutral, Reed." Bodie raised his hand. "This is between you and Waco here."

"I'd rather just kill both of you where you sit." Reed raised the rifle.

"You do that, Slocum, and it'll just prove what a coward you are." Waco spit and taunted Reed. "You know you ain't man enough to face me."

"Coward? Outnumbered twenty to one and you're calling me a coward?" Reed laughed. "You're the coward, mister, taking an innocent girl like you did."

Waco sneered. "Step out and let's just find out who's the coward. Providing that is, if you've got the guts, Mister Slocum."

Sitting a few feet behind Waco, the smaller man waved his hand slightly, trying to convince Reed he was on his side. Reed nodded, acknowledging he understood what Bodie conveyed to him.

"Alright, gunfighter." Reed laid his rifle down, but he wasn't sure what Bodie had in mind. He only knew if he killed Waco, there would be one less to fight. "We'll do it your way. I'm coming out."

Grinning, Waco dropped from his horse and checked his pistols as Reed walked out into plain sight. The low-slung guns and swaggering body motions of the slender man told Reed the man was cocksure of himself and dangerous. Reed watched as Bodie led the gunman's horse out of danger of flying lead. Then, as the gunman approached to within thirty feet of where he waited, Reed readied himself.

"What is the small one doing?" Valdez watched as Bodie moved aside. "He does not help fight the white."

Keeler shrugged as he watched the two men face off in front of each other. "I figure if Waco goes down, Bodie will kill Slocum."

"He should fire with the other one." Valdez watched the scene unfolding in front of him.

"My men have their pride too, señor." Keeler watched as the Mexican smiled coldly.

"Well, boy, get ready to meet your maker." Waco crouched slightly.

Reed smiled as he dropped his hand beside his pistol. "I'm ready, bigmouth."

Faster than an eye blink, both pistols roared, echoing along the rock walls. Another shot sounded as Waco's dying reflexes squeezed off another round into the ground. Staggering several steps forward, his face a mask of surprise, the gunman slowly collapsed pitching forward. Turning his gun to where Bodie sat his horse, Reed watched the man.

"We've only got a few seconds, Reed, before they'll be on top of us." Bodie dismounted.

"What's holding them?"

Bodie looked over to where Valdez and his men were sitting their horses. "They're waiting to see if I can take you, I reckon."

"That what you're figuring on trying?"

"Nope." Bodie smiled. "When I nod, get your rifle and let's get out of here quick."

"My horse's give out. He can't run any farther."

Bodie shook his head. "These two are fresh. Comanches just brought them to Valdez this morning."

Reed knew he had to trust the man. There was no way he could hold off the Comancheros alone. With a nod, Bodie led the horses toward the rocks as Reed bolted back to retrieve his rifle and canteen. Yells of rage and screams from the Comanches could be heard as they charged forward, past Keeler and Valdez across the flats, firing their rifles wildly.

Swinging upon the horses, Reed and Bodie raced to the north. Less than two hundred yards separated the two parties. Reed could hear the shots being fired behind them. Turning in his saddle, he could see the smoke belching as the rifles were fired. The mountain trail they were following was a maze covered in boulders and small rocks. Reed whipped the racing horse with the barrel of his rifle as he pushed the horse into a hard run, trying to widen the gap between the two parties. It was too late when he realized the Comanches following had kept the fleetest horses as they were gaining on them.

Yelling over at Bodie, as the Comanches far out in front of Valdez came ever closer, Reed pointed at a near boulder. "Rein in when we get to those big rocks and we'll try to slow some of them down a bit."

Reining in their horses behind the nearest boulder, big enough to shield the animals from being hit by ricocheting bullets, Reed and Bodie slid to the ground. Laying their rifles across the boulder, both men started firing at the oncoming warriors. Horses and men dropped as the Henry Repeaters did their bloody work. Quickly mounting as the last Comanche reeled from the screaming bullets, Reed and Bodie raced away. Valdez screamed in rage as he reined in and watched as the Comanches were being knocked from their horses.

Slowing their horses as they watched the riders following them stop where the bodies lay, both men grinned.

"Maybe that will slow them down some, Bodie."

Suddenly, the small man stiffened and slid from his saddle. Reed looked to where a rifle, belching smoke and lead, had sounded. A lone warrior sat his horse, raising the rifle in triumph. Slipping from his horse, Reed turned the small man over to find his chest covered in blood. The grey eyes of Bodie stared blankly at him. Swinging upon his nervous horse, Reed took one look to where Hawk was racing toward him. Again, Hawk's rifle spoke, kicking up dirt under his skittish horse. Grabbing the reins from Bodie's horse, Reed slapped his animal hard and raced toward another pile of boulders.

Valdez had only fifteen able-bodied men left. Wild Horse and his Comanches had all been killed in the last charge. Running his horse hard, Valdez watched as Hawk fired round after round at the fleeing white. Perhaps this one was protected by the spirit people as the bullets had passed all around the fleeing man without touching him. Watching, as Reed disappeared behind another pile of boulders, Valdez pulled his blowing horse back to a walk.

He would let Hawk ride forward to see if the white was again waiting to ambush his men. This white was a crack shot and almost every time he pulled the trigger, Valdez lost a man. Using the boulders for protection as he was doing, Valdez knew he could lose all his men. The Mexican was crazed with hate. If the white barricaded himself behind the rocks again, this time he would spread his men out across the trail and charge all at once. He watched as the Comanche slowly made his way into the rocks and disappeared. As Valdez waved his men forward, a rider reined his horse in front of him.

"It is no good, Jefe." Garcia held out his hand. "The gringo will kill all of us if we continue this madness."

"Do you want me to run?" Valdez shook his head. "Is this what you would have me do, hombre?"

"I want you to live, Patrón. The next bullet could find your body."

"Or yours."

"My life does not matter." Garcia shook his head. "Let us return home and fight this one, another day."

Valdez looked over at Garcia. "What do you mean?"

"We will go home and let this one think we have given up." Garcia smiled. "Then we will rest our men and attack the rancho where he lives, when he doesn't expect us."

"We do not know where his rancho is."

"This one does." Garcia pointed his rifle at Keeler. "He told me he did."

"Do you know where this one lives, señor?"

Keeler nodded, looking down at the dead body of Bodie. "The small one there used to work on his uncle's ranch."

"And this one and the woman will be there?"

"I think they will, but it's far to the east." Keeler had no way of knowing for sure, but any lie to get them away from this craziness would do.

Hawk rode from behind the boulders and motioned with his arm for Valdez to ride forward. The Comanche shook his head as he counted how few they were now. When they had started from the stronghold of the Comancheros they numbered at least forty, and now there was less than fifteen. He had to respect the young one ahead. He was a brave man with the eyes of an eagle and the heart of a bear.

"Soon, we will be clear of these rocks and into the woodlands of the mountains, but his rifle could still kill many before we reach the trees." Hawk nodded as Valdez and his remaining men rode up.

Valdez looked at the warrior, then back up the trail. He knew no matter whether he continued the chase or turned back, he had lost face with his men and the Comanches. One young white all alone had beaten him and his men. His pride told him to continue with the pursuit, but he knew to do so could cost him more men.

"Can we catch him?" Valdez looked over at Hawk. "Can we kill him?"

"Maybe we can do this but how many more men do you wish to lose?"

"We will follow him until dark, then we will decide."

Bannock, Lone Bear, and the other four Kiowa warriors had heard the gunfire further down the mountain trail. Scattered patches of boulders lay protruding from the ground like mushrooms along the trail. Watching as a lone rider came into view, they hid their horses behind a boulder and waited. Several times, the rider had reined in studying his back trail as he came closer to their hiding place.

"It is the young Slocum." Bannock smiled. "He still lives."

Lone Bear nodded. "We better let him know we are here."

Whistling loudly, Bannock waved his arm, then ducked back behind the boulder as Reed raised his rifle. Seeing the weapon lower, the Kiowas rode out from behind the large rock. Recognizing the warriors, Reed kicked his horses into a slow lope and rode to where they sat their horses. Smiling, both Bannock and Lone Bear nodded across at the young white.

"We hear much shooting. We come to this place to see if you still live." Bannock smiled. "We bring these warriors with us."

"For a spell it was mighty close back there, but I'm still alive." Reed looked behind him. "It's good to see all of you."

"And it is good to see you, young one."

"The girl?"

"She waits with Nakima. She is safe." Bannock assured him.

"Good, I'm glad she is safe." Reed felt relieved.

"Does Señor Valdez still follow?"

"I don't know. He was still following a little while back."

"You wish to ride to the girl?"

"No." Reed shook his head. "We will wait here to see if the Mexican comes. If they still follow, we will kill them."

"How many are left?" Lone Bear looked over at Reed.

"I don't know, maybe fifteen."

"You have killed many." Lone Bear nodded at the others. "Yet, you are not even scratched."

"Many." Reed looked around at the boulders. "They couldn't get at me for these rocks."

"The Comanche?"

"They were brave warriors. They charged straight at me, but now, all are dead men."

"You have killed all the Comanches that rode with Valdez?"

"All that I could see."

Bannock shook his head in dismay. "All of them?"

"All but the one that helped take the girl."

"Hawk." Lone Bear shook his head. "Are you sure he is the one that lives?"

"I'm sure. I remember his scarred face." Reed nodded. "He was with the red-headed one I killed."

"Yes, he was with the red-haired one. Hawk is a mighty warrior and dangerous enemy." Lone Bear shook his head.

"He killed the small one that rode with Keeler." Reed added.

"Why would he kill this one?" Bannock was curious. "One that rode with him?"

"His name was Bodie, and he tried to help me." Reed explained. "He was my friend. We rode together many moons ago."

"Wild Horse, the brother of Lobo Cayuse." Bannock looked at Reed. "Did you kill him?"

"If he was with the Comanche, I did."

"He was a great warrior." Lone Bear shrugged. "Lobo Cayuse will not like this. He will be saddened."

"Well, he's a mighty dead warrior now."

Bannock nodded. "Wild Horse always rode the war trail with the Comanchero."

"Well, looks to me like he rode one too many this time." Reed studied his back trail.

Valdez raised his hand and stared across the last flat before the trail started upward into the higher mountains. He could see seven riders sitting their horses far up on the trail. The distance was still too great to see them plainly, but he knew the young white was one of the seven. He could tell the others were Indians, probably the same ones that had helped steal the girl away from his camp. He studied the riders wondering if the woman was still with them. Anger filled his head, causing his face to turn red with rage. Here were seven men scoffing at his Comancheros, the most feared killers on the Llano Estacado. To let them ride away unchallenged would cause him to lose face even more.

"Ride away from this, Jefe." Garcia pleaded, staring across the flats. "He tries to make you mad enough to charge."

"It could be a trap, señor." Keeler spoke up. "He could have all of Slocum's Kiowa with him now."

"We have lost enough, Patrón." Garcia shook his head. "Por favor, leave this place now."

The tall Mexican dropped his head. He knew the two men spoke the truth, but his pride said to charge across the flats even if it meant his own death. Back at the stronghold, he would never be able to look his followers in the face after they found out how many men he had lost to one lone white. The Valdez name had always been unblemished without shame, but now?

Hawk reined in his horse and studied the face of the Mexican. "The white and six Kiowa wait for you to charge."

"These men say it will get us all killed." Valdez looked at the dark eyes of the warrior. "What do you think?"

The Comanche looked around at the beaten Mexicans that rode with Valdez. "You already got Wild Horse and all his men killed. Why do you not attack and get the rest who ride with you killed?"

"Yes, you are right. I have lost many men." Valdez's words were like ice as his finger touched the butt of his pistol. "Be careful what you say."

"You will kill me for speaking truth?" Hawk scoffed and jabbed his finger. "If you want to kill someone, go kill the white that waits there."

"Ride away, Patrón." Garcia begged. "Do not listen to Hawk. Do not let him get you and the men killed this way."

"Do they have any more men with them, Hawk?" Keeler questioned the Comanche.

Hawk laughed lightly. "Six will be more than enough to kill these."

"Enough!" Valdez seemed to scream in desperation. "Say no more, warrior."

"I say this… these men are beaten before they charge." Hawk pointed at the Mexicans. "Look at their faces."

Valdez watched as Bannock and Lone Bear circled their horses and raised their rifles provoking him to charge. Looking around at his men, the Mexican knew Hawk was right. His men had lost heart for another confrontation with the sharpshooting white. He knew they would follow him if he ordered them forward, but they already felt they were dead men. None of the riders would look him in the face.

"Leave this place, Patrón." Garcia pleaded again. "If we go forward, none will see the new day."

Nodding, Valdez turned his horse and started back south toward the vast grasslands of the Llano Estacado. Shame turned his face beet red as he turned away from only seven men. He wondered, would his men think him a coward now and maybe desert him.

Looking over to where Keeler and Hawk sat their horses, Valdez motioned at them. "You will ride with us."

Keeler only nodded as he fell in behind the Mexican's horse. Looking over at Hawk, he smiled slightly. He had no choice but to follow the Mexican, if he refused, he knew Valdez would order them killed. If he tried to escape toward Reed Slocum, he knew the white would probably kill him. The trail back to the Comanchero stronghold was long. Hopefully, somewhere along the way they could find a chance to slip away from of the Mexicans.

Valdez reined in and looked at the Comanche. "I will pay Hawk many horses and much money if he will bring the yellow-haired one back to me."

"You would pay so much for a squaw?" Hawk shook his head. "How many horses will you pay?"

"Twenty horses for the blond-headed squaw." Valdez nodded. "If you do this, I will free your patrón here and let him have his life back."

Hawk looked to where Keeler sat his horse. He could care less whether Valdez killed the white man or not, but the horses. "Tell me, how many horses will you pay for the killer of your men?"

"Twenty horses and gold for the woman." Valdez held up his hand. "And if you bring the scalp of the one that has killed my men, I will give you twenty more."

"Follow them, Hawk." Keeler spat. "Kill Slocum when you can."

Nodding, Hawk looked at the Mexican. He was thinking only a fool would pay so much for a squaw, any squaw. "I will bring her and the scalp back to you."

Reed watched as Valdez and his men turned to the south and disappeared. Lone Bear looked over at Bannock and nodded. Valdez had lost many men in this wild chase after Reed Slocum, still he couldn't believe the Mexican was giving up and returning to his own lands. Lone Bear knew Valdez since he had ridden with him in his youth. He couldn't believe the proud Comanchero leader was giving up in defeat. Still, the man had lost most of his men. Now, he faced more than just one white man so he would be foolish to continue the fight.

"I will follow them to make sure it is not a trick." Lone Bear nodded at Bannock. "I will see for myself that they do not turn around."

"Be careful, my friend." Bannock looked over at the warrior. "Remember, Hawk is still alive."

"Hawk, hah." The Kiowa laughed. "He is just one Comanche."

Bannock whispered to the warrior's back as he loped his horse to the south. "Yes, my friend, but one very dangerous Comanche."

Reed watched as the warrior disappeared, then turned back to the north. "How far is it back to your camp?"

"Not far. We go quick." Bannock took one final look to the south, then motioned Reed to follow.

Chapter 10

Boone Hames rode his worn out horse into Rail Johnson's headquarters at the Rafter J Ranch and dismounted. Handing the reins to a barn hand, Hames rapped on the large oak door. A tall, square-jawed man opened the door and stared hard at the dusty rider before motioning him into the room.

"By you being here, Boone, something must have gone wrong." The tall rancher led the tired man into his study. "Let's have it."

"Yes, sir. Everything went to blazes." Hames cleared his throat. "I could use a drink, my throat is parched."

Pouring a full goblet of rye whiskey, Johnson handed it to the man. "Sit down and take your time, Boone."

Downing half of the glass, Hames coughed slightly, then looked sheepishly over at the rancher. "Dan is dead. They hung him, and Bob Gage was shot when he tried to pull iron on the Bar S trail boss."

"Dan dead?" Johnson shook his head. "They hung him?"

"Gage went for his gun first, but old Bob was dead before he cleared his holster." Hames nodded. "Yes, sir… Mister Johnson, then their trail boss hung Dan."

"Gage is dead too?"

"Yes, sir."

"He was a fast man with a gun." Johnson shook his head in disbelief. "Dead?"

"Not near fast enough. An Injun riding with the herd killed him with a bow and arrow."

"An Indian?" Johnson wiped his face. "Killed by an arrow you say?"

"Yes, sir. A youngster at that." Hames added. "Sent that arrow into old Bob without blinking an eye."

"What happened to the other men who rode with Dan?"

"After Gage went down, they tucked their tails like whipped pups." Hames took another drink of whiskey. "They were scared, I tell you."

"Then what happened?"

"Watt Slocum made every man say who they rode for."

"Watt Slocum?"

"Yes, sir… Mister Johnson, big man rough as a cob, I tell you."

"Then?"

"They whipped all of us pretty good with lariats and sent us across the river." Hames finished his drink. "Warned us not to ever come back."

"But, you did."

"Yes, sir. I owe you plenty." Hames replied. "I had to get the news to you."

"So Watt Slocum is the trail boss now?" Johnson poured more rye. "It figures, I understand Wes Slocum is laid up for quite a spell. Last week Watt was seen in town with an Indian boy."

"It was him alright. Watt Slocum is the one that did the hanging."

"Watt Slocum!" The words seemed strangled as they came out. "Watt Slocum, the killer of my brother is ramrodding the Bar S herd?"

"For a fact, boss." Hames finished his drink as Johnson flung his glass into the fireplace. "He's a hard one… coldest human I ever saw."

"Very well, I know." The lantern jaw seemed to harden. "Like I said, he's the one that killed my brother."

"I'm sorry, boss, but they were on us before we had a chance."

"Watt Slocum is half Indian." Johnson nodded. "I can understand you got caught, but at least you had the nerve to come back to tell me."

"The others are still running north, I figure." Hames shook his head. "That cold-blooded hanging, then the whipping by Slocum's men put a good scare into the boys alright."

"They probably are at that." The large head nodded. "Get some rest. Come daylight, we'll be riding out."

"Slocum has maybe twenty five riders with him." Hames poured himself another drink. "And that Indian that killed Gage."

"Go to the bunkhouse and get some rest, Boone." Johnson looked out through the window. "Send old Shorty in."

"With that Indian riding with the Bar S, they're sure gonna be hard to sneak in on."

"Then, we'll just have to kill the Indian, won't we." Johnson looked at the rider.

Shorty Winthrop limped slowly into the elaborate room and waited until Johnson looked up from his paperwork. Like most old ranch hands, the old hostler had been a real cowpuncher in his day. Now, he had grown old and had several broken bones to show for it. Johnson had relegated the old puncher to taking care of the saddle horses kept in the ranch's remuda.

"Get word to Lace Bradley. Have him come in quick."

Shorty nodded. "Yes, sir. He's out on the east pasture today."

"Bring him." Johnson demanded. "Fast."

"I'll send Junior to fetch him."

Bradley raced his leggy bay horse into the ranch yard and dismounted in a cloud of dust to find Rail Johnson already on the porch waiting for him. He had run the bay hard. The youngster, Shorty had sent, said it was urgent and he was needed back at the ranch quick. He knew Johnson would not have sent for him, saying hurry, unless it was something bad.

"You made good time, Lace." Johnson paced the porch.

"I got here as fast as I could, Mister Johnson."

"You did good." Johnson looked at the blowing horse. "Now, grab a fresh horse and get into town. Round up about twenty toughs and make sure Whitaker Jones is one of them."

"You need that gunman?" Bradley looked across the room. "He's a mean one, boss."

"I do, and he better be faster than Bob Gage." Johnson growled. "A lot faster."

"What's happened?"

"Watt Slocum's ramrodding the Bar S Herd." Johnson cussed. "One of his men killed Gage and hung Dan Hickman, then sent our other men north like a bunch of scalded dogs."

"That sounds like Watt Slocum. He's a bad one to fool with, I know." Bradley stated.

"I reckon you remember him as well as I do."

"I remember him alright. What's it been, about fifteen years now?" Bradley asked.

"Fifteen years and six months to the day that he killed Freckles."

"Watt Slocum bossing a trail crew for the Bar S. How did his brother Wes get him to ramrod the herd north?" Bradley shook his head. "I was there when he tossed old Watt off the ranch."

"Easy, Watt and that kid of his stand to lose the ranch if he doesn't get the Bar S herd to market." Johnson smiled evilly. "You know, I hold the note on everything Wes Slocum owns."

"I know, you told me last time we had a card game."

Johnson nodded. "S'pect, I was down in my cups that night."

Bradley shook his head. "So this is your chance to get Watt Slocum and the Bar S Ranch, all in the same day?"

"And that'll finish Wes Slocum too." Johnson smiled coldly. "Get moving."

"How much do I offer them for the job?"

"Bring 'em. I'll make it worth their time."

"You sure you want that killer Jones?"

"I do, unless you think you can take Watt Slocum alone?"

"I'll bring him." Bradley dropped his eyes. "I know I ain't near a match for that maverick. Last time we locked horns, he dang near killed me."

One day after leaving Lone Bear around dusk, Reed, Bannock, and four warriors rode into the wolf camp. Dismounting, as Nakima rose from her cook fire, Reed looked to where Lee Hargrove sat against the side of the cook wagon. If it hadn't been for the blond hair, he wouldn't have recognized her. Lee was dressed in a long, deer-hide dress that clung to her with moccasins covering her feet. Two days of rest and good food had done wonders for her.

Nakima looked down the trail behind them, then back at Bannock. "Where is Lone Bear?"

"He'll be along soon." Bannock smiled at his sister. "He watches to see if the Comancheros return to their own lands."

"The young one is not hurt?"

Bannock shook his head. "The young one is a great warrior. Maybe greater than Tall Pine."

"Never." Nakima looked at Reed. "He is so young."

"He is young, but he killed many Comanche and Comancheros before we got to him." Bannock shook his head. "He has become a hunter of men. A killer maybe."

"Tall Pine may not like this." Nakima looked to where Reed was unsaddling his horses.

"Tell me, Sister, would he rather have the young one kill or be killed?" Bannock smiled. "He is much warrior, it could not be helped."

Reed walked to where Lee was standing. "How are you, ma'am?"

"Thanks to you and Bannock, I'm fine." Lee smiled up at him. "You saved me from a fate worse than death at the hands of that monster Valdez."

"Are you rested?" Reed studied the girl. "Come morning, we must ride away from here."

"Back to Dade?" The girl shivered. "I don't ever want to go back there."

"What about your store?"

"My father was killed in that store. I could never go back in there." Lee argued.

"Is there anyone in Dade that might buy it?"

"I don't know, and I don't care." The girl shook her head.

"I've got to ride to the Bar S and check on my uncle. I think it best if you came with me." Reed suggested.

"I don't know, Mister Slocum." Lee looked around. "I feel safe here."

"You can't stay here, Lee." Reed smiled at the girl. "Valdez could ride back here with more men and kill these people. You know he wants you back."

"He made my skin crawl when he looked at me." The girl shuddered at the thought. "If he ever touches me, I'd kill myself."

"Then we must ride out as soon as Lone Bear returns." Reed looked to where Bannock and Nakima were watching them. "If you stay here, Lee, it could put them all in danger."

"You're saying Valdez wouldn't harm them if we're not here?"

"He's lost enough face. He cannot harm these Kiowa without enraging all the Kiowa and Comanche on the Llano." Reed explained. "If we leave, he will have no excuse to fight these people."

"I do not want them hurt because of me." Lee looked over at Nakima. "I will go with you, at least as far as Amarillo."

"I wish you would come back to the Bar S with me. There we can protect you. You will be safe at the ranch." Reed assured her.

The girl looked up at the tall youngster. "Let me take one day at a time, Mister Slocum."

Nodding, Reed turned back to where Bannock waited with the horses. The girl had changed. She was no longer the innocent sweet woman he had first encountered when he rode into Dade. The trauma she had been through the last few days had put a mark on her. Now, she was less trusting, and probably needed more time to forget and recover.

"What will young Slocum do now?" Bannock handed Reed the reins to his horse.

"When Lone Bear gets back, I will take the girl with me and leave this place."

"Where will you go?"

"Back to my uncle's ranch, the Bar S, down on the Bosque River."

"No, you must not take her there." Bannock shook his head. "This place is too close to the Llano. Keeler and the Mexican will know of this place."

"You think the Comanchero might come after the girl there?" Reed was shocked. "He'd ride that far?"

The dark head nodded. "I watch the way Valdez look at girl. One day he will follow you there. I know this. He wants girl back."

"You may be right."

"Take girl to Tall Pine where he takes cows."

"On a trail drive?"

"There she would be far away, safe from Valdez."

"I will think on your words, then decide after Lone Bear returns."

"Why do you wait on Lone Bear?" Bannock asked. "He will return here by and by."

Reed looked over at the Kiowa. "He came to help me, Bannock. I owe him."

Lone Bear rode in at daybreak as Nakima and Lee were cooking breakfast. Slipping from his worn out horse, the warrior walked to where Bannock and Reed stood. Blood covered his left arm.

"You have been wounded. Who shot you?" Reed looked at the bloody sleeve.

"Valdez and Comancheros go back south to their village." Lone Bear shrugged as Nakima examined his arm. "The wound is nothing, Nakima."

"Who shot you, Lone Bear?" Reed asked again.

"Did all of them go back?" Bannock looked across at the warrior.

"No, the Comanche Hawk was not with them." Lone Bear sat down as Nakima worked over his arm. "I was careless. Hawk and me shoot at each other."

Bannock questioned the warrior. "You not see him?"

"No, Hawk is great warrior." Lone Bear shrugged. "He came from behind rocks and shoot first."

"Did you hit him?"

"I do not know this." Lone Bear shook his head. "Maybe I shoot him, but he hide behind rock. If I follow to see if he still lives, I may be dead Kiowa."

"Why would he follow us alone?" Reed asked.

"Hawk follow to see where you take girl so he can tell Valdez." The warrior thanked Nakima as she finished wrapping his arm. "Valdez want yellow-haired woman. Me think him offer many horses to Hawk for her return."

"He would dare to follow her north all alone?"

"You will learn to respect this Comanche." Lone Bear nodded. "I tell you again, young one, Hawk is great warrior."

"Greater than you and Bannock?"

Bannock tapped his chest. "We are Kiowa. Hawk just a Comanche."

"Hawk may be greater warrior." Lone Bear only shrugged as Bannock glared at him. "Maybe."

Bannock held up his hands. "You and girl eat quick, then ride to white man village."

"What will Bannock do?"

"We ride out, try to find trail of Hawk. If he still lives, maybe we kill him." Bannock laughed.

"How will I know if you killed him?"

"You will not be able to know this thing." Bannock shrugged. "Lone Bear speaks truth, Hawk is great warrior of Comanche. We try to kill this one, but stay alert, young one, even after you reach cowherd."

"What do I tell Tall Pine?"

"Tell him, we wait here for him to return."

Bannock and Lone Bear watched as Reed and Lee Hargrove disappeared north along the path leading to the small town of Dade. Both men knew the young white was brave, but not sure if he was a match for Hawk if the Comanche still lived and managed to get past them.

"You take Apotte and Horse Killer. Go after Hawk." Bannock studied the trail.

"And what will Bannock do?"

"I will follow young ones to make sure they are not harmed."

"It is a dangerous trail you follow, my brother." Lone Bear flattened his hands.

"No more dangerous than when you followed Valdez south."

"Go then, we try to find Hawk and kill him."

Before riding out of wolf camp, Bannock warned Reed to watch the skyline and keep a sharp eye out, all around. If Hawk wasn't hurt, he could be out there somewhere and he was a deadly enemy. Riding most of the night, the small sleepy town of Dade came into view early the next morning. Reining in at the store, Reed tied the horses, then took Lee to what sufficed as a boardinghouse across the street. Many of the locals had already spotted them and closed in around the girl.

Helping Lee inside, Reed got her seated at a table when Sue Watson grabbed the girl in a big hug. "Thank heaven, you're safe, my dear."

"Yes, Mrs. Watson, thanks to Mister Slocum, Bannock, and Lone Bear."

"We're all so sorry about your dad." The woman tried to console her. "He was such a fine gentleman."

"Thank you, Mrs. Watson." Lee nodded tiredly at the woman.

"The town gave Mister Hargrove a nice funeral and burying." The woman assured her.

"Ma'am, would you fix Lee a bath, then go to the store and get her some clean clothes?" Reed asked the woman.

"I will as soon as she eats something." The woman smiled. "My dear, I have the keys to the store, would you like to go get the clothes you want?"

Shaking her head, Lee withdrew. "No, I never want to go in there again."

"I see. Well let me fix you some breakfast." The woman moved toward the kitchen. "Then we'll get you a bath."

"Mister Slocum hasn't eaten yet either." Lee added.

"Yes, of course, I will fix you both something."

Sipping on coffee, Reed looked across the table. "I know you're tired, Lee, but as soon as you bathe and change clothes, we need to ride on to Amarillo."

"I will be ready, Mister Slocum." Lee nodded. "I know we must stay ahead of Hawk, if he's following us."

"Hawk?" Reed didn't know the girl knew anything about the Comanche.

"Yes, Mister Slocum, I heard you and Bannock talking back at the camp."

After eating, while the girl bathed, Reed walked to the corrals where his saddle and pack horses were standing. Matt Foster, the owner of the stable, met him at the gate as he placed one foot on the lower rail. The horses were rested and looked good.

"Mister, you done a fine thing rescuing the girl." Foster reached out his hand. "We all thank you."

"You know anyone that might want to buy her store; lock, stock, and barrel?" Reed asked the man.

"Yep, Granger Ball might just buy it." Foster replied. "He's tried to buy it before. I'll get word to him."

"We're riding out shortly. Go get him now."

The man nodded. "You'll be wanting your animals, I reckon?"

"I will. How much I owe you for their feed and keep?"

"For what you've done, not a dime."

"I'm thanking you." Reed studied the corrals. "I'll need a fresh horse for the girl."

"That sorrel filly is a fine traveling horse and she's got a new set of shoes on." The hostler pointed at a deep sorrel mare.

"I'll swap you the two standing there for her." Reed pointed at the two horses tied in front of the store. "Providing you help me shoe my two."

"You figuring on a long ride maybe?"

"A real long ride."

"What brands are they carrying?" The hostler looked at the horses.

"Wouldn't know the brands. I took them from the Comancheros far to the south." Reed shook his head. "But, I'll write you a bill of sale in case someone claims them."

"Good enough." The tall man nodded. "I'll go find Mister Ball."

"You tell the people here that a Comanche warrior called Hawk could be following us." Reed handed the hostler a bill of sale for the two Comanchero horses. "Be careful, he's very dangerous and a killer."

"I know him. I seen him with Keeler and his cutthroats." The man shook his head. "Why is he following you?"

"The girl. He wants to take her back to Valdez."

"Valdez, the Comanchero?" The man's face lost color.

"That's him."

"We'll kill him if he shows himself around here."

Reed smiled. "Thanks friend, but I doubt you'll ever see him."

Reed finished shoeing his horses and resupplied his packsaddle with the food and supplies they would need as they traveled. Refilling his bandoleers with shells for his Henry and the forty-four pistol, he stepped out onto the store's porch. Lee had settled her business, selling the store to Granger Ball. Helping her onto the sorrel mare, Reed turned the horses down the dusty road to Amarillo. Without looking back, the two rode out of Dade leading the packhorse. Several of the townspeople stood in the street waving good-bye as they passed from sight.

Amarillo was only a day's ride from Dade, but Reed was taking his time, studying every mile of the trail before riding forward. He knew he would have no way of knowing if Bannock intercepted Hawk or if the Comanche was still following them. He believed Lone Bear when the Kiowa said Hawk was a dangerous adversary and could be on their trail now. Reed had killed the redhead and Waco, then Hawk had killed Bodie which only left two of the original killers that had taken the girl. The last he had seen of the leader, Keeler, was riding with Valdez and still very much alive. He had no idea if Hawk was following their trail or how far he would follow them.

Almost at sundown, Reed dismounted beside a small spring fed pool of clear water and pulled the saddles from the horses. To his surprise, the girl pitched in and gathered small dead limbs for a fire. Leaning back after finishing a meal of biscuits and dried beef that Nakima had given them, Reed looked over at the pretty girl.

"This would be fun if you weren't so worried." Lee sipped on her coffee. "What is wrong? You're scaring me."

"Nothing, just being careful is all."

"You think Hawk could be out there?"

Reed was surprised, not knowing she could detect the worry in his face. "You're safe, Lee. I'm not worried. It's just Bannock and Lone Bear told me to be watchful."

"We'll be riding together for some time." She frowned. "Be honest with me, please."

"Alright, Lee." Reed smiled. "You're right I'm worried the Comanche, Hawk, could be following us. He could be on our trail now."

The girl shuddered as she remembered the scar-faced Comanche. "If he is following us, we should be worried. He is a cruel man."

"I know, he's a killer. He killed a good friend of mine." Reed nodded. "Get some sleep, now. We'll ride out before daylight."

Seeing the girl had fallen into a fit full sleep, Reed picked up his rifle and slipped out into the dark. During the long night, animals scurried by where he sat watching over the camp and the girl. Several times, he drifted off into a light sleep, then jolted himself awake to stare down where Lee slept in her blankets. He cussed himself for falling asleep, knowing he could be killed and the girl retaken if the Comanche slipped undetected into their camp. Many times, he had ridden night herd on the Bar S Cattle Ranch, sometimes falling asleep in his saddle but this was different. If he fell asleep, he could die.

Reed studied the camp where Lee still slept as the first rays of morning sunshine burst over the horizon from the east. Nothing was amiss as the horses grazed peacefully on the sparse mountain grass. A lone coyote slipped stealthily away when he detected Reed's presence which was a good sign. Reed knew the coyote would have shied away and disappeared if any other human was near. Stretching, Reed walked back to camp and started saddling the horses. A good hot cup of coffee sounded good, but Amarillo was near. They should continue on and eat breakfast while the horses were grained and rested.

"You awake, Miss Lee?" Reed stood over the slight form as she jerked awake. "It's okay. It's just me, Reed."

"Oh." The small hands went to her disheveled hair as she stood up. "I must have died when I went to sleep."

"You were exhausted."

"Did you sleep?"

"I slept." He lied.

Reining in at the tie rail in front of Dora's Eatery, Reed dismounted and helped the girl from her horse. Walking onto the porch, they were met by the shocked restaurant owner.

"Lee Hargrove, you're back and safe." Dora herded the young woman into the restaurant. "Both of you sit down."

Reed watched as the girl took a chair, then turned back to the door. "I'll see to my horses before I eat, ma'am."

"You get yourself back here quick." Dora placed coffee in front of the girl. "I'll have your breakfast ready in a jiffy."

"Yes, ma'am."

The old hostler, Pike, came from the livery as Reed led the horses into the corral. "Seen you and the Hargrove girl ride up, Mister Slocum."

"Still having trouble sleeping huh, old timer?"

"Nah, I was feeding the horses." Pike looked over at the restaurant. "We heard about her pa getting killed. Figured with Keeler taking her, she was a goner for sure."

"She's fine, just a little hungry and tired."

"How'd you get her back in one piece?" Pike was being his usual nosey self.

"'Tweren't easy."

"Your uncle passed through here a few days back on his way somewhere east."

Reed nodded. "Wouldn't tell you where he was headed?"

"Nope, nary a word." Pike shrugged. "You should know Watt Slocum and his tight mouth."

"Nope, I don't know him at all."

Pike laughed. "No, I reckon you don't at that."

"Feed my horses and toss them some hay." Reed looked about the town.

"Sure enough will." The old man scratched his head. "You gonna want them today?"

"Yes, sir. I'll be riding on in two hours." Reed looked over at the eatery. "Put me some oats in a tow sack."

"I'll do it."

"You taking the girl with you?"

Reed shrugged. "Don't know yet, reckon that's up to her."

"If she's smart, she'll get away from this place." Pike rubbed his whiskered chin. "Go back east to civilization."

"Maybe she will."

"We heard about you killing Tom and Jake." Pike laughed. "Sure been kinda quiet and peaceful around these parts since their demise."

"Yeah, I imagine it has been."

The restaurant smelled of fresh baked bread and hot coffee as Reed entered and took a seat across from Lee. Eggs and ham on a huge platter were waiting on him. The girl had already finished her meal and sat back watching him eat. Looking up, as Dora walked to the table, she smiled.

"Hope it didn't get cold." Dora smiled down at him. "I had to get my bread in the oven for dinner."

"It's fine, ma'am." Reed buttered his biscuits and spread molasses on them. "Did Watt Slocum stop by here on his way through Amarillo?"

"Yes, your pa stopped here, Reed."

"How long?"

"Just long enough to eat and feed his horses."

Reed nodded. "Did he tell you where he was headed?"

"To the Bar S, I figure."

"He's supposed to meet up with the herd at a crossing on the Red River."

"If I know Watt Slocum, he'll check in with his brother before he does anything." Dora smiled. "He's the cautious kind. Call it a woman's intuition."

Pushing back his plate, Reed looked at the girl. "I'm headed east. Are you riding with me, Lee?"

Looking at Dora, the girl shrugged slightly. "I don't know what to do."

"You're welcome here, little lady." Dora smiled.

Reed nodded his head slowly. "Miss Dora, we've got more problems than where she should stay."

"What's wrong?"

"She needs to come with me." Reed stood up. "If I'm right, that fishing marshal of yours can't protect her."

"Tell me, Reed, is she in danger?" Dora looked down at Lee.

"She sure could be." Reed nodded. "I just don't know yet."

"We'll protect her here if she wants to stay."

"I guess you're counting on your marshal?" Reed shook his head. "Well, he can't protect her from what may be coming this way."

"I'm counting on the people of Amarillo to help."

"Going or staying is up to her, but I have to go. I'm riding on." Reed turned for the door.

"Is she in danger?" Dora asked again.

"I done told you. Now, ask her."

Watching, as Reed passed through the door, Dora smiled over at Lee. "You want to tell me about it?"

Lee stood up and looked down at the woman. "No, Miss Dora. One day I will, but for now, I best just go with Mister Slocum."

"If that is your wish, Lee?"

"If I stay here, I could put you in danger." Lee warned. "Maybe the whole town of Amarillo."

"What?" Dora looked up in shock. "How? From who, girl?"

"Good-bye, Miss Dora."

Pike and Dora watched from the porch of the café as Reed and Lee disappeared from their sight, following the east road. Dora looked around the dusty town wondering what the girl had meant by her final words before leaving the café. How could she, a mere girl, put a whole town in danger?

"Well, you're here. I reckon you decided not to stay in Amarillo." Reed looked at the girl riding beside him.

"No, if Hawk followed us to Amarillo, I could be placing Dora in danger along with many others." She shook her head. "It's best I go with you."

Reed looked at the pretty sorrel mare, she rode. The liveryman in Dade had been right, she was a saddle horse. Her fast running walk could carry a rider many a mile in a day, and not shake the person's insides to pieces.

"She is a beauty, isn't she?"

"Yes, she is. Thank you for her." Lee patted the slick neck. "Are we heading for your ranch now, Reed?"

"No, I don't think so." Reed remembered Bannock's words of warning. "I believe we're going to join up with the trail herd headed for Sedalia."

"Is that a far ride?" Lee looked back at Amarillo. "Sedalia?"

"Never been to Missouri before. I don't know for sure, but you'll be safer with the herd and Watt Slocum than you would be alone at the ranch." Reed explained.

Lee looked around the flat prairie land. "How are you going to find the herd out here?"

Reed smiled. "Why, my lady, we'll ride northeast and look for a large dust cloud."

"You're funny, Reed Slocum. I just hope you brought plenty of food."

"Why a little woman your size shouldn't eat much, Miss Hargrove."

"Will we make it, Reed?" The blue eyes looked to him for assurance.

"We'll make it." Reed smiled at her. "There's no one ahead of us, so all we have to do is keep moving."

"And stay ahead of Hawk?"

"If he's even following us." Reed turned and looked back at Amarillo.

CHAPTER 11

Valdez offered Hawk money and several horses if he would follow the white and Kiowa's trail north and return the woman. The Comanche couldn't believe such a price was being offered for a mere squaw, so he nodded at the Mexican and turned north.

Late in the afternoon, and only an hour's ride north, Hawk spotted a rider coming at a lope down the trail. Slipping his horse behind a large boulder, the Comanche hid and waited as the rider neared his place of concealment. The horse and man were still too far away to identify, but Hawk could tell the approaching rider was Indian by the way he sat his horse. Suddenly, he recognized the rider as Lone Bear of the Kiowa tribe, one of the three men he had been following. He was curious as to why the Kiowa was returning to the south alone unless he was looking for signs of the Comancheros. He smiled cruelly as he thought about killing Lone Bear as easily as swatting a mosquito. Squinting, the sharp black eyes of the Comanche narrowed as the rider came closer, riding right into his rifle.

Hawk had been promised money and horses, but he also knew if he failed to bring the woman back to the Mexican, Keeler would be killed. The Comanche had ridden with Keeler for many years, and the outlaw leader had always treated him fairly. Still, the white man's life meant nothing to him. He only wanted the bounty. He was no longer a young man, and with the promised money and horses, he could return south and live out his days happily. Bringing the scalp of this Kiowa to Valdez could earn him even more horses.

His eyes already found the track of the white's horse, and now, he would follow those tracks back to wherever Slocum had taken the yellow-haired woman. First, he had to kill the Kiowa who rode toward him. He could not let him discover the tracks he had left so plainly on the dusty trail behind him. If the warrior wasn't killed now, he could turn back to the north and follow him as soon as he discovered the tracks.

As a Comanche warrior, Hawk had pride and was no coward. The Kiowa were brothers to the Comanche so he would not kill the Kiowa from ambush. Sitting his horse, he waited until the horse's ears pricked, then rode forward onto the trail to intercept the Kiowa. As the Comanche suddenly appeared from behind the boulder, both warriors fired their rifles at the same time. Hawk felt the hot bullet graze his side when the Kiowa fired. He watched the Kiowa fall, but had no way of knowing how hard he had hit the warrior. He wouldn't dare ride forward to see if the Kiowa was dead, as it could be a trick to lure him in. Kicking his horse hard, Hawk raced to the east away from the Kiowa's rifle. He would ride east, hoping Lone Bear would think he was badly hurt and had to quit the chase. If the Kiowa was dead and he wasn't followed, he would change direction and continue to the north, intersecting the trail of the young white. He wanted the money and horses Valdez had offered for the girl, but he wanted to kill young Slocum as well. Too many Comanches had died by this young killer's hand. Slipping from his horse, he caked mud against his side to stop the flow of blood.

After a hard day's ride, Hawk circled back to the north intersecting the trail, picking up the tracks of the riders heading toward the small village of Dade. Dismounting and slowly sorting out the tracks, Hawk tried to figure out the many tracks covering the ground. He did not know the sign Lone Bear's animal made so he couldn't tell if the horse's tracks were among the ones on the trail. He still didn't know if the warrior had lived or died. Easing up on his horse, Hawk looked down at his bloody side and smiled. The spirit people had been looking over him. If the bullet had been another inch over, he would be mighty sick. He knew he had been foolish and should have killed the Kiowa without warning. Nevertheless, Hawk carried the pride of all Comanches and would not kill another, even a Kiowa, from ambush.

Hawk recalled, all his life since his youth, he had been a warrior riding with the Quahadi Comanche. He had learned the ways of the Comanche warriors and became a deadly tracker and killer. All the Comanche and Kiowa Nations feared him as he had become a ruthless warrior with a fiery temper. Finally, after killing a tribal chief over a squaw, Quanah Parker himself had banished Hawk from his own people. Quanah was the one warrior Hawk respected. He had said nothing when the Comanche Chief had told him to leave his people forever and never to return. To kill the tribal chief over a woman had been wrong and now he rode alone without a people. Five years had passed since he had left the Comancheros and joined with Keeler and his band of killers. Killing a white man was nothing to Hawk. He believed the whites were interlopers; something to be despised and killed.

Reining in, he looked up the narrow trail he knew would lead to Tall Pine's camp. The big hunter had been camped there in the high mountains for two years. Hawk studied the trail, then kicked his horse forward, following the fresh tracks of two horses he found on the trail. There was no need to stop, he would bypass the Kiowa camp of Slocum and ride straight to the village of the whites. He figured the woman would want to return to the white village as fast as she could. Hawk laughed that the yellow-headed one thought she would be safer in the small white village, than with the Kiowa.

Darkness fell across the small town as Hawk dismounted and tied his horse to the corral. Moving forward slowly, he looked through the dirty window pane to where a lone white sat before an open fire. Slipping into the corral, he passed quietly through the horses until he found what he was looking for. Two bay horses stood in the lot, still salty from sweat. They were the horses the young white had taken from the dead Comanche warriors back at the last meadow fight. He knew the woman and his quarry were here in one of these lodges, but which one?

Moving through the shadows of the small town, Hawk looked into each lit room. Finally, frustrated after searching the last building, he returned to the stable and silently entered the building like a ghost. Pulling his sharp skinning knife, he moved without making a sound behind the unsuspecting sleeping hostler. The knife touched the throat of the dozing man, bringing him awake with a start.

"You are dead, white man, unless you tell me where yellow-haired woman is."

The stable man froze with terror as he awoke feeling the blade cutting into his throat. Nodding slowly, he swallowed hard in fear as the pressure of the knife relaxed. "They're gone."

Hawk moved in front of the shaking man and looked down. "Tell me, where have they gone?"

"You're Hawk, the Comanche that was with Keeler."

"I Hawk." The warrior nodded. "Speak and you live this night."

The voice trembled. "If I speak, I will be a dead man."

"Tell me where squaw has gone and you will live. I have no use for old white man's life." Hawk threatened him.

"They rode east to Amarillo."

"When they leave this place?"

"Yesterday, sometime in the afternoon."

"Do you speak truth, old one?"

"I told you the truth, to my disgrace." The hostler shook his head. "I'm a coward."

"In the face of death, old man, maybe we all are." The sharp blade cut deep. "Now, you not worry about it any longer."

Cattle bawled as riders slapped their lariats against their leather chaps. They whistled and yelled as the longhorn cattle waded into the muddy river. The river was down with only a few yards of swimming water to cross. Watt Slocum and Emmet Tabor sat their horses on a sandy bank, watching as the long train of cattle stepped into the river and waded to the far bank.

"Pretty sight ain't they, boss?"

"I reckon, but not as pretty as a herd of buffalo grazing on the open grasslands." Watt nodded. "Not near as pretty."

"Most of them old buffs are long gone now." Tabor watched a rider turn back several stragglers.

"There's still some herds to the north." The big man shrugged. "Nothing like when I first rode that way though."

"We gonna stop over at Doan's tonight?"

"No, I want to get as far from the river as we can before nightfall." Watt flicked his reins absently. "You send Louie across to get supplies."

"Okay, boss. You figuring on trouble?"

"Trouble, Emmet? There's always trouble of some kind lurking around the next bend." Handing Tabor a few gold coins and some paper money, Watt smiled. "You never know. I've been away too long from this business."

"You're thinking of Rail Johnson ain't you?"

"Rail used to be a top hand." Watt nodded. "He was a real tough one in his time."

"He still is." Tabor agreed. "Tough as nails and he's turned mean to boot."

"Well then, I reckon we better be looking for trouble." Watt turned his horse away from the crossing.

"Where's Tolman?"

"Watching our back trail about three miles back, I reckon." Watt replied.

"He's a good one to have on your side."

"The best."

Crossing the Red had taken longer than Watt expected. The herd was less than five miles from the trading post when he ordered them to bed down for the night. Watt sat in the early night hours listening to the riders as they moved around the cattle, singing and soothing them as they quieted for the night.

Watt nodded as Tolman slipped silently up beside him. "Where's your horse?"

"I left him back a ways." Tolman smiled. "In the dark, I did not want your men to shoot me for an Indian snooping around."

"See anything?"

"Only a few Kiowa waiting to peel off a cow or two."

"You talk to them?"

"I told them we would leave them a few steers along the trail, if they tell us of anyone following the herd." Tolman nodded. "They agreed."

"Good, go get your horse. Louie should have some supper fixed up by now." Watt watched the straight-shouldered youngster move like a cat toward his horse. He doted on the young man. He hadn't been around to see Reed grow, but he had never let Tolman out of his sight since he was big enough to sit a horse. Along with Bannock, he had taught Tolman everything he knew about hunting, tracking, and killing, if need be. The youth was solemn like most Kiowas and didn't speak much, but a man could ask for no better son. Reflecting on the courage he had felt in Reed, he knew he had two good sons any man could be proud of. Tolman was Kiowa and Bannock had instilled in him the pride of a Kiowa warrior. Watt could sense Reed was different, even young as he was, the youngster was already hard as nails. Bannock had told how Reed hadn't blinked an eye when he killed the two Burden brothers. Hopefully, someday he would get to know his son, Reed Slocum, better.

For days, Watt had pushed the herd hard to reach the banks of the Washita River so they could spread out along the sandy banks to graze. He wanted to reach Sedalia ahead of the other herds, but he wanted the cattle in good flesh when he arrived there. Tolman had ridden back toward the Red for two days and hadn't seen any signs of another herd or Johnson's riders.

Louie was ladling food onto the hungry drover's plates when Watt saw Tolman ride in and unsaddle his horse. Walking over to the remuda, the youngster saddled a fresh animal.

"You headed out again?" Watt asked.

Looking at the eagle feather Tolman held in his outstretched hand, he nodded. "People of the Kiowa wait for me to counsel with them."

"You want company?"

"No, I will go alone." The dark head nodded.

"You reckon they seen something?"

"Maybe, I will take a bottle with me." Tolman grinned. "That will help loosen their tongues."

"Boy, you be careful out there." Watt looked at the handsome youngster. "You're Kiowa, you look Kiowa and talk Kiowa, but you be careful anyway."

"I will return when I find out what they wish to speak of." Tolman swung up on the horse. "Tall Pine should not worry. They are my people."

Watt watched as Tolman rode to the grub wagon and took some biscuits from Louie, then turned back to the south. He hated the boy going by himself, but he knew the Kiowa would disappear if anyone rode with Tolman. In the Nations, everybody was an enemy, especially the white man. It was a wild, thinly populated land with many predators roaming the country, both man and animal.

Dora stood on her café porch watching curiously as men milled around over at Pike's stables. Leaving her porch, she made her way to the crowd and pushed her way through the men to the livery entrance. She almost fainted in revulsion as she looked down at the bloody body of the old hostler Pike. Stepping back from the bloody scene, she looked around at the men.

"Who would have done such a thing?" One of the locals asked as he retreated away from the body. "Carve up old Pike like that."

"That's Injun work." An older man spoke up. "I've seen the Comanche cut up a man like that before."

"But why?" Another townsman spoke up. "Pike never did no harm to anyone."

"Pure meanness that's why." The first man spoke again. "Injuns don't need a reason to kill a man."

Dora remembered Lee's words about putting them all in danger if she remained in Amarillo. Whoever was after them must have tracked their horses to Pike's livery and killed the old man. Now, whoever had killed him could be following Reed and Lee to the east. Turning, as Dall Logan pushed through the crowd, she watched as the marshal peered down at the body.

A young boy ran up and pointed to the rear of the stables. "There's another dead man back there, Marshal Logan."

Walking to the rear of the stable the marshal found another body, but this one wasn't as mutilated as Pike. Rolling the body over as several men pushed in behind him, the skinny marshal shook his head.

"It's Sly Willoughby." Logan looked down at the bloody corpse. "Been scalped too."

"Why would anybody kill Willoughby, the town drunk?"

"I done told you, Injuns don't need a reason to kill." The old man spoke up again.

Logan raised his hand for silence. "Now, we don't know this was Injun work."

"You blind, Dall." The old man looked around the dirt floor. "A buffalo sure didn't put those moccasin tracks around his body."

Shaking his head, the skinny marshal spoke up. "I didn't see them at first, but you're right, Miller."

Dora watched as the men came back to where Pike's body laid beside his wooden chair. Why had the Comanche killed a helpless old man? Maybe he had cut on Pike until he told where Lee and Reed had ridden off to and then finished the poor old man. But, why had he killed the old drunk Sly Willoughby? Maybe Sly had seen the killer and gotten himself killed so he couldn't spread an alarm.

"What are you gonna do, Logan?" An older man asked.

Marshal Logan shook his head. "I don't know. We haven't had any Indian trouble around here in years."

"Well, seems like you've got it now, Marshal."

"We need a tracker." Logan rubbed his chin. "I'll send for Watt Slocum."

"He ain't here." Dora spoke up. "He rode east several days ago."

"What about Wilbur McKay?" The old man looked at the marshal. "He used to be good."

Logan shook his head. "That was ten years ago. He's about blind now."

"We need him, half blind or not." Abe Miller explained. "Ain't no one here got enough grit or know how to track an Injun."

"I'll ride out and ask him." Logan looked about the crowd. "Two of you men stay here and make sure no more tracks are messed up while I'm gone."

"I ain't risking my neck out here all alone." A townsman backed away. "No, siree."

"I'll stay, Marshal." Old Miller shook his head at the retreating men. "Whoever done this is long gone now."

Wilbur McKay was an old mountain man who had done some scouting for the army out on the Llano. Retiring to his small ranch outside town, he rarely made an appearance in Amarillo. Well thought of as a fighting man, he occasionally helped track down horse or cattle rustlers. The harsh winters and hot shimmering summers had beaten his skin to a leathery dark brown. Logan knew the old scout didn't have the keen eyesight, he had possessed just a few years back. However, if he could track the killer just to see where he was heading, that would be a big relief to the residents of Amarillo. Whoever had cut up the two men at the livery was much too dangerous a man to leave lurking about in the community to kill again.

Two hours later, the slender buckskin clad scout studied the tracks for several minutes before straightening and looking at Logan. The old mountain man had to be well into his sixties. The sun-beaten, wrinkled face holding the deep set grey eyes was creased from the constant wind that blew across the Llano. Even at his age, his step was still spry as he moved around the bodies.

"Comanche... and he was in a hurry." McKay pointed at a stall door where a hawk feather was hanging. "It was old Hawk, the renegade. That's his trademark hanging there."

"Hawk?" Logan looked over at the tracker. "We didn't see the feather. You know him?"

"Meanest Comanche on the Llano." The old scout pointed at the feather. "That's his calling card. I've tracked that buck for the army many a mile a few years back."

"Army never caught up with him?"

McKay laughed. "Caught him? Shucks, we never even seen him. He's slicker than a greased pig."

Logan shook his head. "Army give up did they?"

"They wore out many horses chasing Hawk, but they never caught him." The old scout replied.

"Where's he been and why is he here?"

"Quanah banned him from the tribe and I figure Hawk took up with the Comancheros." McKay stepped around Pike's stiff body. "I couldn't tell you why he done this, but one thing's certain, that Comanche means business."

"Can you track him, McKay?" Logan asked. "I mean with your eyes and all."

"Maybe, maybe not with my eyes, but if you're willing to take a posse out after him, I'll give it a try." McKay looked curiously at the marshal. "It's a waste of time, Logan, but it's your call."

"Why is it a waste of time?"

"Trying to track that buck out here would be like tracking a flea on a dog."

"That bad, huh?"

"The Llano is his backyard." McKay frowned. "He knows it like the back of his hand. He's a fighter, one of the best, and Mister Marshal, he loves to kill."

Listening to the conversation, Dora stepped closer. "I think I know where he's headed, Marshal."

"What would you know about it, Dora?"

"Lee Hargrove said somebody was after her and Reed Slocum."

"You mean the same Reed Slocum that gunned the Burden boys over in Dade?"

"The same." Dora frowned. "Remember, Marshal, they drew on him first."

"Why would one lone Comanche be after them?" McKay looked at the woman.

"For some reason, I figure he wants the girl. She's very beautiful you know." Dora shrugged. "Lee wouldn't tell me anything, just that we all might be in danger if she remained and tried to hide here."

"Apparently, she was right about that, Marshal." McKay looked down at the dead hostler. "He sure did a job on poor old Pike."

"Reed was headed for his uncle's ranch down on the Brazos when he left here." Dora studied the thin marshal. "The Bar S Ranch is where he was headed."

Logan looked over at the woman. He wanted a way out of this mess, but he knew he had to do something. He had to put on some kind of pretense of looking for the Comanche.

"Me and McKay will ride out on the south road and see if we can pick up any tracks."

"I'll trail with you, Logan, but he's long gone." McKay shook his head. "He's done his killing around here for now."

Dora watched as the two men rode out of town in a slow lope. She knew the marshal's heart wasn't in finding the Comanche. If he had been serious, he would have deputized several men to ride with him.

Then again, she knew there were very few men in Amarillo that were willing to endanger their own lives pursuing the Comanche. Especially when they found out it was Hawk they were after.

Two miles out of Amarillo, McKay held up his brown hand and pulled his horse to a stop. Dismounting, he knelt and studied the tracks along the dusty road. The old dim eyes blinked several times as he traced the many tracks leading east.

"If I'm guessing right, one horse took this road east just a few hours ago." McKay studied the tracks. "Probably after he done for old Pike and Sly."

"That's a pretty long lead."

McKay shrugged. Like Dora, he knew Logan was looking for a way out of following Hawk. "I figure the other tracks belong to young Slocum and the girl."

Logan straightened his thin frame and studied the dusty road leading east. "You figure you can follow his trail?"

"I can, providing he don't get smart to us and start covering his tracks."

"What do you figure our chances of catching up to him?"

"Of finding him, pretty slim." McKay added. "Of getting ourselves killed if we do run him down, pretty good."

"I think it's a waste of time." Those few words were enough and all Logan needed to hear. "What do you think, McKay?"

"I'm just a tracker, Marshal. I don't get paid to think." McKay smiled to himself as the marshal was sure doing his darnedest to wiggle his way out of this mess. "You want me to track old Hawk, just speak up and I'll give it a whirl."

"No, we'll let him go. This isn't my jurisdiction out here."

McKay stepped back on his horse, shaking his head. Logan was a coward. How the town ever pinned a marshal's badge on him was a curiosity. "You're the boss, Marshal. I'm heading home."

Logan and McKay had hardly ridden out of town when a lone rider whipped his sweating horse to a stop in front of the gathered towns-people. Sliding from his blowing gelding, the young rider looked around at the crowd by the corrals.

"Lonnie Marlow, what's your hurry son?" Old man Miller looked at the worn out horse. "You dang near ran your horse to death."

"I was sent to sound the alarm, Mister Miller." The young rider was trying to catch his wind. "Matt Foster was killed yesterday in his livery barn."

"Matt?" Dora shook her head in shock. "Matt Foster's dead?"

"Yes, ma'am, they found him yesterday morning at daybreak." Marlow seemed to shake. "I found him. His throat had been cut."

"You poor kid."

"They sent me here to warn you folks." The youngster nodded. "We think a Comanche who rides with Keeler and his bunch is following Lee Hargrove and young Reed Slocum. If it's Hawk, he is one dangerous Indian."

"You rode out here all alone?"

"I waited until daybreak. No one else would come. I figured you folks needed to know."

Stepping aside, Miller let the young man see the body of Pike. "Your Comanche has been here already, but we're thanking you for risking your life to bring us the word, Lonnie."

"It seems like this country is kinda running short of liverymen." The words came blurting out of the lad's mouth.

Rail Johnson sat his horse with several other riders and waited as Lacy Bradley and Boone Hames crossed the river toward them. Reining in their wet horses, both men looked across at the Rafter J owner.

"Storeman over at Doan's said the Bar S herd crossed two days ago." Bradley smiled. "Twenty riders, a big man ramrodding the outfit, and a Kiowa youngster."

"That's it, the trading post say anything else?"

"Just that their cook bought supplies for the drive is all." Hames nodded. "Slocum didn't show himself, just sent the cook in."

"How did you get a count on the Bar S riders?"

"One of Doan's hunters watched as they passed."

Johnson scowled. "I doubt any of the hunters at Doan's can even count."

"I reckon this one could, boss." Hames shrugged. "He knew exactly how many were on the Bar S crew."

Johnson looked across the river. "That should put the herd about two days north of the Red."

"Give or take a half day." Bradley agreed. "Same hunter told us the herd was stepping out pretty good."

"We'll give Mister Watt Slocum two more days. That'll get him far enough away from Doan's." Johnson smiled. "Out in the Nations, it's no man's land. I guess they could fall into bad trouble from the Kiowa, Comanche, or somebody."

"Wouldn't that be too bad?" Hames laughed. "Just awful."

Johnson looked about at the hard gun hands he had hired and shook his head. Every one of them were killers and most were on the dodge from the Rangers or some other law enforcement officer. He thought about his brother, Freckles. In two days, he would use these men to destroy the man responsible for his death. Wes Slocum had been his best friend at one time, but after his brother Watt killed Freckles, they had drifted apart, becoming mortal enemies. Wes had laid the blame for Rebecca Slocum's death at his brother Freckles' feet and Rail Johnson had never forgiven him for his accusations.

"Hames, you and Cole catch up to the herd, tail 'em and keep us posted on their whereabouts." Johnson looked over at Cole Sanders. "Now, you boys can earn your pay for a while."

"You're the boss, Mister Johnson."

Johnson watched as Hames and Sanders filled their saddlebags with cold biscuits and hardtack, then recrossed the river. On the north side of the Red was Indian Territory, no man's land to some. Luckily, the hard fighting rangers didn't have jurisdiction on the other side. They were forbidden to cross the Red for any reason. That left only the marshals out of Fort Smith, Arkansas along with Indian police to patrol what everyone called the Nations. Like the vast Llano Estacado, every type of saddle tramp and outlaw terrorized the territory, committing every crime in the books, even some that weren't.

Johnson was no fool. He knew Watt Slocum would be waiting somewhere ahead. The big man had a sixth sense when it came to spotting danger. But, the man didn't know how many riders would be riding against him. Twenty ordinary cowhands, even with Watt Slocum leading them, were no match for the killers he had hired. Johnson grinned evilly. He would hit the Bar S herd hard, kill the drovers and push the herd on north, then sell them in Sedalia. Wes Slocum would be finished, lose his precious Bar S Ranch, and Rail Johnson would have his revenge. It had been a long time coming, but now only days ahead, it would be finished and over with. Freckles Johnson would be avenged.

"We'll cross the river and make camp north of Doan's." Johnson kicked his horse.

"Can we pick up a couple bottles at Doan's?" One of the riders laughed. "I'm mighty parched."

"Fill your bellies with river water as we cross." Johnson frowned. "I don't want anyone from Doan's recognizing us."

"Shucks boss, there ain't no law over there, but a few marshals and some ragtag Indian police."

"No whiskey and that's final."

"You're the boss."

"I am, and if you men want to get paid, don't you forget it for a minute." Johnson looked at the riders. "Now, let's get across the river and make camp."

CHAPTER 12

Reed pushed the horses steadily to the east as they followed the wagon road away from Amarillo. Something nagged at him, causing him to twist around in his saddle several times to look back at the long flat road. There was no way of knowing for sure, but he felt someone was following them. Reed figured the Comanche Hawk was following maybe because he had evaded Bannock and Lone Bear. If it was Hawk, Reed couldn't understand why the Indian would risk his life to follow him and the girl so far to the east. The girl was beautiful, but there were many squaws in the Comanche villages. Shaking his head, he thought maybe his imagination was playing tricks on him.

"You feel something's wrong?" Lee was watching as Reed looked back several times. "Is someone following us?"

"No, I'm just trying to make sure we aren't being followed." Reed tried to reassure her. "Old habit, I watch my back trail a lot."

"Old habits, huh." Lee shook her head. "I didn't think you would be old enough to have old habits."

"Well, Miss Hargrove, I am and I do."

"You lie, Mister Slocum, you think Hawk is following us." Lee frowned. "Why do you say that?"

"It would be like Valdez to send Hawk after me." She shivered. "That Mexican wants me back as you well know."

"Yes, I lied. I was trying to keep you from worrying." Reed smiled. "But, I don't think the Comanche would dare ride this far east, even for one as beautiful as you."

"So, Mister Slocum, you think I'm pretty?"

"Yes, ma'am. I do for a fact."

"Well, you don't have to lie. I'm the one he's after."

"It's nothing, just a feeling I have." Reed smiled. "And you are very beautiful."

Lee smiled. She had never been told that before. She had seen the way men looked at her but she never considered herself pretty at all. "Well, thank you, sir."

The sun was setting as Reed reined in at a small water hole nestled deep in a growth of live oak trees. Dismounting, he quickly unsaddled and watered the horses. Hobbling the animals near the water, Reed turned to where Lee was gathering dry wood for a fire.

"No fire. We'll make a cold camp tonight." Reed looked down at the girl.

Shrugging her shoulders, Lee turned to the saddlebags. "I'll get us something new for our supper tonight."

Reed was curious. "Oh, what would that be?"

"Tonight, we're gonna have jerky and biscuits." The girl grinned.

"And that's different?"

"Yes, sir, it is." Lee laughed. "Last night we had biscuits and jerky, if you remember."

"Oh yes, you're right that is different… sounds wonderful."

Lee looked over at him. "I'm starved."

"Good, eat and get settled in for the night. I don't want you moving about in the dark." Reed checked the loads in both his rifle and pistol.

"You think he's out there, don't you?"

"He's out there." Reed nodded. "Somehow, I can almost smell him."

"How do you know?"

"I don't know positively, it's just this feeling I have."

"What should we do?" Lee looked around the darkening shadows. "I'm scared."

"We've got two good watchdogs standing there." Reed smiled, nodding at the horses. "They'll let us know if anyone comes near."

"I hope so." Lee shrugged. "If he gets close, he might kill you and drag me back to Valdez."

"I ain't dead yet." Reed understood her fear of the Comanche and being brought back to the Mexican would be worse than death itself. "You try to sleep. We'll have a long day tomorrow."

"I can help you watch."

"Okay, I'll wake you at midnight." Reed agreed readily. He had been awake for two whole days and could use some sleep.

Only a few frogs croaking around the water hole and the singing of night birds sounded as Reed settled in a few feet away, beside a large oak. The night was pitch black. He could see the silhouette of the horses and hear their large molars crunching on grass, but everything else was lost in the darkness. His sharp senses were strained as he sat back against the tree, staring off into the dark night. Tonight, he knew he wouldn't sleep as he could smell danger so thick he could cut it with a knife.

Only once during the night, did the horses alert, as a coyote came to drink unaware of the humans sleeping nearby. Reed could barely make out the animal as he lapped up the water, then slunk off to the north. As the sun started to shed its light in the east, Reed stood up and slipped through the trees surrounding the water hole. After carefully scouting out the trees, he turned back to where the girl had slept when her scream came from the water hole. Racing back, he found Lee standing beside the sandy bank looking down at a set of tracks.

"He was here, Reed." She pointed at the tracks of an Indian's moccasin. "Look!"

Reed looked at the tracks and shook his head. There was no way the Indian had not known they were nearby. The horses were hobbled less than thirty feet from where the Comanche had made the tracks. Why hadn't he slipped in for the kill? Maybe, he was just toying with them. Reed was slightly shaken. He hadn't slept but the Comanche had slipped in for water without alerting him or the horses. Lone Bear had been right about the Comanche warrior. Hawk was an extremely dangerous enemy.

With Lee following close behind him, Reed carefully retraced the tracks back to the west, almost a half mile. Finally, he found where Hawk had left his horse so the animal wouldn't alert the other horses. He studied the signs where the animal waited. The Comanche had watched them for some time as several piles of droppings laid about the place where the horse had been hobbled. Scouting out the area as he had seen Bannock and Lone Bear do, he found the tracks of the lone horse that led to the south. Reed studied the flat grasslands to the south, and he knew by now, the Comanche could be anywhere in this vast sea of grass. Hawk could have circled and be ahead of them just waiting. He didn't know where the Indian was, but one thing was certain, the Comanche knew where they were.

Returning to the horses, Reed thought out his options. He could take the girl and go back to Amarillo. He didn't think the Comanche would figure they would return, but then he would endanger the town by leading Hawk back to Amarillo. He knew their best chance was to stay in the tall grass and try to elude the Comanche.

"What will we do, Reed?" Lee asked shakily.

The signs were plain and the tracks were left to instill fear in the two young people. Hawk was a hunter and tracker, so there was no way he would have left tracks by accident.

Taking her by the shoulders, Reed looked down into the upturned face. "He's only one man, Lee. We're riding on to the herd."

"Only one man? No, he's Hawk the Comanche." Lee shook her head. "I've seen him, and he's a devil."

"He's just a man." Reed smiled. "Now, get a hold of yourself and help me watch for him."

"You haven't seen his hideous, scarred-up face and his snakelike eyes."

"Well, he knows we're here so we might as well have a fire, some coffee, and a hot breakfast before we head out." Reed wanted to change the subject and get her mind off the Indian.

"I think we should return to Amarillo." The girl looked around slowly. "He could be anywhere."

Reed nodded. "Yes, ma'am, he could, but we're going east to the crossing on the Red. You wouldn't want to set this killer loose on your friends back there in Amarillo would you?"

"I'm sorry, you're right. Wherever we go, this killer will go." Lee shook her head. "But, he's like a ghost that we can't see or fight."

"Don't worry, Lee. When the time comes, I'll fight him."

"Alright then, I'll fry us up some side meat."

After finishing a hot breakfast, Reed refilled his canteens and saddled their horses. Somewhere out there in the vastness of the prairie, he knew

Hawk was waiting and would set an ambush for them. He could wait and travel after dark, but the Comanche had already shown he was at home in the dark hours of the night. Helping Lee into the saddle, he handed her the pistol he had taken from Bodie's dead body, then led her to the east following the dusty road.

Suddenly on impulse, Reed turned the horses due south, away from the trail, pushing through the tall grass that grew belly deep on their horses. To stay on the road would give the Comanche the advantage, where he could set a trap anywhere he wished. By moving into the tall grass, he could keep the warrior guessing and maybe make a mistake. He was leaving a broad trail for Hawk to follow, but perhaps he wasn't riding into an ambush. Watching every blade of grass that moved, Reed kept his mind focused on his surroundings. His nerves were taught as a fiddle string, and again he turned back east to intersect the road. Somewhere ahead, before darkness came again, he had to find water and a safe place for them to hole up for the night.

The Comanche was smart and as cunning as a wolf. Reed knew their only chance was if the Comanche became overconfident, too sure of himself, and rode into the sights of his weapons. Reining in at the dusty road, Reed dismounted and studied the ground for tracks. No sign of the Comanche could be seen on the soft ground.

"He hasn't been down this road." Reed pointed. "Unless he's circled off to the side, far out in the grass. I believe we may be ahead of him."

"And if he has circled ahead of us?"

"That's a chance we'll have to take." Reed stepped up on his horse. "We're gonna gamble and ride hard to stay ahead of Hawk until dark."

"Then what?"

"Then, Miss Hargrove, I'm going to kill me an Indian."

"You hope." Lee surveyed the tall grass. "That killer could pop out anywhere in this jungle."

"He could alright, but I believe we fooled him by turning south. He may think we're running for Amarillo and safety. One thing's for certain, now he'll have to track us for a ways."

Reed kicked the horses into a high lope down the road. He knew if their luck didn't hold, Hawk could ambush them anywhere along this road, but that was the chance they had to take. In the deep grass and the wilds of the Llano, Reed had no doubt the Comanche was the better man. However, face-to-face with any type of weapon, Reed knew his odds were better. Almost at dusk, Reed reined in and stared down into a deep wallow made by herds of buffalo moving across the Llano. Water still puddled in the bottom of the wash which was good enough for their horses.

"We'll stay here tonight." Reed led the horses down into the wallow. "We'll sit back under that overhang and hopefully he'll show himself."

"But, if he doesn't come after us, he could be waiting on top in the morning." Lee dreaded going down into the wallow. She felt the wash was a trap.

"That's the chance we have to take." Reed looked at the disheveled girl. "He's already proven we're no match for him out in the open at night."

Again, total darkness covered the flat plains as Reed and Lee sat back against the cool ground of the wallow. There was no grass for the horses in the sandy wash. Water would have to suffice for the night. Reed hadn't unsaddled the horses in case they were needed in a hurry. He was forced to hold onto the lead ropes as there was no way to tie off the horses. Why the Indian hadn't taken their horses before, he had no way of knowing, but now he wouldn't get another chance. From where they sat, underneath the hangover, it would be impossible for Hawk to get a shot at them. Reed knew for now, they would be safe as long as he didn't sleep.

"You sleep and I'll watch for a while." Lee leaned up against his shoulder.

"I doubt I could."

"You scared?" She whispered.

"I'm scared alright." Reed wasn't lying. They were holed up like a prairie dog hiding from a coyote down there, and unable to see a thing was eerie. "If you shoot, don't shoot one of the horses."

Despite not wanting to sleep, Reed was exhausted from no sleep the night before and slept fitfully until Lee nudged him gently awake. Blinking to clear his eyes, Reed could smell the girl as she leaned close to him to whisper.

"Something is out there." Lee almost touched his cheek as she moved against him. "I heard something."

"Flatten yourself out, as flat as you can get, and keep that horse pistol ready." Reed pushed the girl down quietly.

"Don't you go out there." Lee grasped his sleeve and held on. "Stay here with me."

"I'm not going far." Sliding on his belly, Reed crawled between the horses and listened. Finally, he heard the lapping of an animal drinking water from the wallow. Sweat started forming on his forehead as he let his muscles relax, then he moved back beside the girl.

"It's only a coyote getting himself a drink." Reed pulled her back beside him. "Now, you get yourself some sleep."

Daylight started to settle over the sandy wallow as Reed stood up stiffly and studied what little ground he could see from down in the wash. Lee had been right, they had been safe under the overhang, but now he had to go back up the small trail to check out the surrounding grounds. Looking down at the water as he moved toward the horses, he saw the tracks of several night animals that had come in for water. Fox, coyote, and even a track of a large ridge running coon showed where they drank. Down in the wash, it had been pitch black and he hadn't been able to see any of the animals that had come to drink. He knew once again, they had been lucky making it unharmed through the night.

"I'm going out. You bring the horses up quick when I holler."

"Be careful, Reed." Lee touched his arm. "He could be up there, just waiting."

Smiling, he touched the girl's dirty cheek. "I s'pect I'll be as careful as he lets me be."

"I'm not joking, Mister Slocum."

"Neither am I." Reed smiled. "You just be ready."

Reed hardly started out of the wash when the heavy discharge of a rifle sent dirt flying into his face. Crouching back down under the bank, he moved back to where Lee stood shaking. Pushing her behind him, he studied the far bank, waiting for another shot.

"You, white man, send out squaw and I will let you live." The coarse voice of an Indian sounded from directly above the overhang they were under.

"Is that you, Hawk?"

"You know me then, white man?" The voice came again. "Yes, it is me, Hawk. You send out woman now."

"I can't do that."

"She is just one woman." The voice rang down. "You can get another in your village."

"So can you, Comanche."

"She is not for me, young one." Hawk snickered. "Señor Valdez will pay me many horses and money for the yellow-haired one."

Now, Reed had his answer to why the Comanche risked his life riding this far east into white man's land. Valdez had offered Hawk a big reward for the girl's return. Reed knew Comanches or any tribe put a high value on horses.

"You sure you're gonna live to collect all them horses?" Reed studied the rim of the wash. "They ain't gonna do you any good, if you're dead."

"Here, white man, you do not have rocks to hide behind." Hawk hissed. "I will wait up here until the thirst and hunger drives you from your place in the ground."

"We've got water down here, Hawk. Do you?"

"A Comanche drinks very little." Hawk laughed. "If you try for that dirty water, I can shoot you as easily as I can shoot your horses now."

"But you want the horses for yourself, right?"

"And the woman."

Reed shook his head. Lee had been right, coming down into the wash might have been a mistake. The wallow had served its purpose protecting them through the night. However, now having to ride out put them in a precarious position. All the Comanche had to do was sit up there and wait for them to show themselves. At this range, his rifle or even his bow couldn't miss. Sooner or later they would run out of food and what little water they had left in their canteens, then they would be forced from the wash right into his sights.

Leaning back against the cool wall of the cut bank, Reed eyed the trail out of the deep wash carefully. "He's got us trapped like a holed up coon."

"What are we gonna do?"

"We're gonna stay alive, Lee." Reed studied the overhang. "At least now we know where the devil is."

"Yes, we know where he is alright." Lee looked around the wash. "But even so, how are we going to get past him?"

"Hold the horses tight, real tight." Patting her arm, Reed rolled from under the overhang and fired several times at where he had thought the voice had sounded from. Throwing himself back under the embankment, Reed felt a bullet tug at his boot. "Look at that, he done shot off my boot heel."

"You're lucky it wasn't your head." Lee pulled him deeper under the cut bank. "That was a very stupid thing to do."

"I had to give it a try." Reed examined his boot. "I might have got lucky."

"Well, don't do it again."

"You very foolish, white man." The voice came again from above. "I almost got you."

"Well, you missed." Reed swore. "My boot will survive, Indian."

Hawk laughed cruelly. "Valdez offered many horses for your scalp, white man."

Hawk looked down at his torn sleeve. The young white's last bullet had almost hit him. This one was fast and dangerous with his small gun. Still, he knew there was only one way out, up the small animal trail that led down into the wash. He would wait them out. He had time on his side. Soon, hunger and thirst would force them from the protection of their hole in the ground.

"We're almost out of water, Reed." Lee shook her canteen and listened to the sloshing sound. "Maybe three swallows left."

"I have a little more left."

"What are we gonna do?" Lee asked nervously. "We're trapped."

"After dark, I'm going out there and kill me an Indian."

"He's a devil, Reed. He can see in the dark and you can't." Lee shook her head. "You can't go out there alone. I won't let you."

"We can't stay down here another day." Reed smiled over at her. "Without food and water, we'll just weaken with every passing day."

"I know."

"I'm going and you're staying here with your pistol ready." Reed ordered. "Do you hear me?"

"I hear what you're saying, but I don't have to like it."

Watching the shadows shift in the wash, Reed figured it was midafternoon. Only a few hours remained until it would turn dark. He knew the wallow would be covered in darkness at least until the moon showed its face overhead. Hopefully, he would be out of the hole and on equal ground with Hawk before the moon lit up the wash. Looking at her worried face, he knew she was scared. He was scared too. He would have to leave her alone down here while he went after the Comanche. If he failed, Lee would be helpless against the Indian and she knew it. The girl was terrified of the warrior, thinking him a devil of some kind.

"It'll be alright, Lee." Reed tried to reassure her. "I'll kill him."

"I know you will." She tried to smile. "You just make sure you sing out before you start back down here."

"I will."

Reed had just checked his pistol and started to remove his boots when the Comanche leapt down into the wash less than ten feet in front of them. Reed's pistol roared twice as the body fell in a heap at their feet. Lee screamed as the smoke and noise filtered around inside the cutbank. Blinking his eyes, Reed stared at the arrow sticking out of Hawk's back. The Indian had been hit before Reed pumped the two bullets into his body.

"Do not shoot, young one." A deep voice came from above. "It is me, Bannock. I come down."

Relief flushed through his body as Reed watched the stocky Kiowa slip noiselessly down the narrow trail. The warrior was a welcome sight as he walked to where they stood over the dead body.

"Bannock, oh thank goodness." Lee leaned up against the warrior shakily.

"What are you doing here?" Reed looked at the warrior and smiled. "How did you find us?"

"Me follow this one after he wounded Lone Bear back on the Llano." Bannock turned the bloody body over and smiled. "Young Slocum made sure Hawk was dead."

"Is Lone Bear dead?" Lee shuddered.

"No, him no dead, just hurt a little." Bannock jerked the Comanche necklace from around Hawk's neck. "I take this, no take scalp."

"You got any water? She's thirsty." Reed nodded at Lee.

"Come, we leave this place pronto… find camp." Bannock led the way out of the wash. "Water, hang on horse."

Reed never felt anything as comforting as the small fire Bannock had started when they reached a small stream. After their ordeal with the Comanche, both he and Lee were physically and mentally exhausted. Three rabbits laid spitted over the bright blaze. Reed knew Bannock had again saved their lives. His chances of getting out of the wash and killing the Comanche had been slim to none. He and Lee would be forever in the Kiowa's debt.

Bannock held up the heavy necklace as his strong white teeth bit deep into the rabbit leg. "Hawk, him heap strong warrior like Lone Bear say. Now, him dead strong warrior."

"Why did you follow us here, Bannock?" Reed was curious.

The warrior looked at the necklace, then back at Reed. "Young Slocum brave, strong warrior, but you still young, not ready to fight with Comanche."

"So you rode all this way?"

"Lone Bear and Nakima say for me to do this." The Kiowa nodded. "We give word to protect you."

"I wish I had something to give you, my friend." Reed replied.

"You give friendship, that is enough."

"Thank you." Reed smiled. "How did you get close enough to kill Hawk without him sensing you were there?"

"Hawk's rifle shoot, then he call down to you." Bannock grinned. "Comanche have much fun. No watch for enemy at his back."

"Why did you use your bow and not the rifle?"

Bannock shrugged. "Comanche stand over you, look down. I know he fall in hole with you. You see arrow, you no shoot Bannock."

"Well, we seen the arrow okay and it was a beautiful sight." Lee smiled.

Bannock nodded. "What will my young nephew and girl do now?"

Reed was surprised the warrior had called him nephew. Looking over to where Lee chewed on a piece of rabbit, he leaned forward. "I'll ride on to the herd. What do you wish to do, Lee?"

The small shoulders shrugged tiredly. "What choices do I have?"

"You can ride on with me or Bannock can return you to Amarillo."

"No, I can't do that. If anyone sees me with Bannock, they would shoot him first, then ask questions." Lee explained.

"If you wish to go to white village, I take you. No one see us." Bannock assured her.

"Thank you, Bannock, but I will continue on with Reed to the herd."

"This good. With the new sun, maybe I ride back to Nakima and Lone Bear. You tell Tall Pine, we wait for him there."

"We'll be safe enough now." Reed nodded. "Thank you, Bannock."

The warrior nodded solemnly. "Something happen back in big village of Amarillo when I passed through, following Hawk's trail."

"What?" Lee asked, alarmed.

"I do not know this thing, but I see old scout McKay and marshal try to follow Comanche's trail."

"What happened?" Reed was curious.

"Badge man, him go back to village. Old tracker, McKay, him ride for his lodge, I think."

Reed laughed. "The fishing marshal?"

"What's so funny?"

"Nothing Lee, only the thought of that marshal tracking Hawk hit me funny is all."

Bannock nodded. "Man carry badge looked scared, but McKay, him brave man. Years ago, him best tracker for blue coats."

As the sun started to peek out of the eastern horizon, and after a quick meal of biscuits and side meat, Reed and Lee waved good-bye and watched as Bannock passed from their sight. They both knew he had saved their lives and they would never be able to repay him.

"Thank you, Uncle." Reed held out his hand. "For everything."

Bannock nodded slowly. "You ride safely, Reed Slocum. Maybe, we meet again soon."

Tolman eased his horse slowly through the dark night as a slow rain fell, soaking him and his animal. Sun Boy, the young Kiowa Chief who visited Doan's Crossing regularly, had kept his promise. He had met with Tolman and informed him that Johnson and his men had just passed by Doan's, heading north after the herd. Now, he was scouting several miles behind the herd, following Watt Slocum's orders to search out and locate Rail Johnson and the riders. Tolman knew they would be coming along the herd's trail soon, and all he had to do was wait and listen.

Six days north, after crossing the Red, Watt figured Johnson could strike anytime now and not have to worry about any law interfering. He didn't know if Johnson would lead his men personally this time or have someone else do his killing for him. He figured Johnson would want to keep his status in the community as an honest rancher. Still, after the disgraceful routing of the first bunch of riders he had sent after the herd, Watt figured this time Johnson would probably lead the attack himself. The rancher didn't want any mistakes this time. He wanted the Bar S, Wes and Watt Slocum, to lose everything they owned. No, this time he would lead the attack personally so there would be no mistakes.

Crossing a small creek, the men had jokingly called Clear Creek, as its waters were so muddy, Tolman reined in his horse. His nose had briefly smelled the tantalizing aroma of a cook fire and bacon frying. Tying his gelding to a small post oak, he slipped silently upstream, moving into the slight breeze. The cold rain and wet footing covered any sound his moccasins made as he moved toward the sound of men talking. Out of the dark night, the glow of a fire, with several riders huddled around it, materialized.

Watching from under the dripping branches, Tolman thought he counted at least twenty riders sitting around with ponchos draped over their shoulders. The laughing voices carried to where he knelt, huddled under some deep foliage. There was no chuck wagon in sight so this was no trail herd. Tolman knew this had to be Johnson's gun hands. Fighting down the urge to slip in and release the picket line horses, Tolman took one last look at the camp, then retreated to where he had left his horse. The young Kiowa shook his head, thinking these men were foolish. Out in this vast land to kill and steal cattle, the white men sat around their fire talking foolishly without a night guard standing watch. Even the big man who sat by himself, alone in the rain, seemed to be asleep.

The night was wet and shrouded with a heavy fog as Tolman made his way slowly back to the Bar S herd. In the dark, the trail was dangerous as bog holes, prairie dog holes, drop-offs, and many other dangers riddled the land that could cripple a horse. He rode slowly through the night, keeping his horse in a slow walk. He figured the riders behind him would not move until daylight showed them the way. There was no hurry, since the herd couldn't move fast enough to get away, and out there in the Nations, they had plenty of miles to cover.

Daylight found Watt already had the herd pointed north and moving as Tolman caught up with the drag. Nodding, as the drag rider, Shorty Burch, pointed to the front. Tolman kicked his tired horse into a slow lope, keeping way off to the side, away from the cattle. The Bar S herd had been on the trail for several days and were trail broke and settled. Still a running horse near them could send the herd into a panic. Longhorn cattle were a curious proposition at best, as anything could put them on the prod or send them running all over creation. Normally, the trail boss would use an old calm lead steer to lead the herd north, pointing them across the rivers. Some called this animal a Judas steer, but a good lead steer made a herd of cattle so much easier to handle.

As Tolman reined in beside Watt, he noticed an old blue and white brindle steer slowly plodding at the head of the herd. For the many miles that still lay north to the cattle pens in Sedalia, the old steer would keep the same slow methodical pace, never slowing or moving faster. To the riders riding swing and drag it was boring, dusty, and slow, but they knew eventually Old Blue would get them there.

"He leads them to their death." Tolman nodded at the old blue steer.

Watt studied the disheveled youngster and the worn out horse. "Yes, he does. Tabor says this is about his seventh time down the trail."

Tolman was shocked. He studied the slow pace of the animal. "You mean you will bring him back to Texas after the drive is finished?"

"I reckon we will." Watt nodded. "A solid leader like him is valuable on a drive. He will keep us from losing many head when we cross the rivers."

"You place much value on him then?"

"My brother does." Watt nodded slowly. "You find anything behind us?"

"Yes, a big man almost as tall as you, Tall Pine, camps with about twenty riders. They follow the herd."

"I reckon that'd be Rail Johnson himself." Watt nodded slowly. "How far back are they?"

"It depends, maybe five or six miles if they haven't moved from where I saw them in camp last night." Tolman shrugged. "Maybe less now."

"And?"

"If they rode out before light, they could be close."

"You say they're twenty riders in the bunch?"

"Roughly, the fog was heavy, but I counted at least twenty."

"Ride to the chuck wagon and get some food in you." Watt looked at the youngster. "Grab some shut eye and then catch up a fresh horse."

"What will my father do?"

"I'm probably gonna kill me some cow thieves." Watt frowned. "Send Emmet Tabor up here when you pass him."

"I will get a horse and some food." Tolman smiled slightly. "I do not need any sleep."

Watt watched as the dark-skinned youngster rode back down the line of cattle. He was proud of his son. No one stood as straight or carried himself with as much pride as Tolman did. He had kept the youngster away from towns, very seldom letting him ride with him into Dade or any other white man's town. Very few knew the lad was his son, and Watt wanted it that way. He had ridden roughshod over many a man on the Llano, had killed some and beaten others senseless. He didn't want his problems falling back on the youngster. Out here, any Indian wasn't thought much of and a half breed even less, especially if he was the son of Watt Slocum. No, he didn't want his enemies to know about Tolman.

Watt knew the youngster was fearless, proud of his Kiowa ancestry, and he would back down from no man. Proud as Tolman was, only the slightest of insults could cause bad trouble. Watt just didn't want the youngster put in any danger. Watching, as Tabor loped his horse toward him, Watt thought of his other son Reed. He wondered how he was faring against Keeler and his bunch of cutthroats. He barely knew Reed, but in their brief encounter back at his camp, he could sense his older son was every bit as proud as Tolman. Now, he had two sons to worry about. He had sent Bannock and Lone Bear to watch over the boy, and he knew they would do their best to keep him as safe as they possibly could.

"You want me, boss?" The tall foreman reined his horse in, breaking into Watt's thoughts.

Nodding, Watt jabbed his finger back to the south. "We've got trouble coming at us pretty quick."

"Johnson's caught up with us, huh?" Tabor automatically turned in his saddle. "Well, at least we know where he is."

"I reckon. Tolman says maybe five miles back a big man is leading about twenty hands this way." Watt nodded. "It has to be Johnson and his bunch.

"That's bad, Watt." Tabor frowned. "You figure they'll hit us when we bed the herd down tonight?"

"I don't see any reason for them to hold back." Watt looked around and shook his head. "Sure ain't no law out here to prevent them from doing as they please."

"Nope, there's not much law out here in the Nations." Tabor agreed. "All he has to do is pick a few of us off, steal the herd, and take it on to Sedalia."

"This time, Emmet, there ain't gonna be no whippings or sending them off scot free."

"Yeah, I know what you're saying, boss."

"These men with Rail are hard cases, killers." Watt nodded. "You tell the men to shoot to kill."

"I'll pass the word."

"I'm gonna ride ahead and find us a better place to make a stand and hold the herd."

"We'll be ready."

"Tell Tolman to stay at the rear of the herd and keep us posted."

"Yes, sir. I'll tell him."

Watt kicked his sorrel into a short, ground-eating lope, covering the flat grass covered plains as he rode north. He needed a valley or some lowlands where he could keep the herd from being stampeded and fight off Rail Johnson's killers at the same time. He knew this time, with Johnson leading them, it would be a hard fight. Many would be killed, but he also knew the men that rode for the Bar S were good men who were willing to protect the herd with their lives.

Reining in at a high swell in the land, Watt looked down on a broad sandy river. He guessed it was the Canadian, a river covered in quicksand and boggy sandy banks. He'd been across the Canadian before, but it had been several years earlier when he had returned from the war. He remembered the old-timers, hanging around Amarillo, talking about how dangerous the river was to cross in places. It wasn't that the river was deep or had powerful currents, he worried about the quicksand and bog holes.

If he could cross the herd here, the other bank with its trees and small valley would be the perfect place to hold the herd and wait on Johnson and his riders. Watt meant to catch the men with Johnson in a cross fire as they crossed the broad river, and he didn't plan on giving them any warning. There was only one reason they were following the Bar S herd and he meant to stop them here on the Canadian. Any of his riders that didn't have the stomach for killing could stay back and guard the herd.

Reining the sorrel around, Watt hit a high lope back to the herd. Pulling his blowing horse in beside Tabor, he pointed back over his shoulder. "About five miles north, we'll hit the Canadian."

"The Canadian?" Tabor asked. "We must be making good time. I figured it'd be a mite farther."

"Near as I can figure it's the Canadian alright." Watt shrugged. "Ain't no other river that size north of us in the Nations."

"It's a mean river to cross unless you have time to mark the quicksand and bog holes."

"That's why we gotta get across before Johnson and his riders put in an appearance."

Tabor squinted off into the bright sunlight. "You figuring we'll have a better chance on the north bank?"

"I know we will. There's a small wooded area to hold them in." Watt frowned. "Johnson will follow us right down to where we cross the herd and when they start across, that'll be that."

"Cold-blooded killing, Watt?" Tabor looked at the big man. "Is that the way it's gonna be?"

"Well, Emmet, we've got fewer men than Johnson and most have never pointed a gun at another man, much less killed a man. You got any better ideas?"

"No, I reckon you're right." Tabor agreed. "But, most of our boys have fought Comanches a few times."

"These ain't Indians yelling and screaming. These men are hired killers and they are deadly."

"Alright, you've convinced me." Tabor nodded. "How you want to handle it?"

"I'll ride back to the remuda and get me a fresh animal." Watt nodded at the old steer. "You see if we might get a little extra speed out of Old Blue."

Tabor laughed. "He's kinda like me, old and lazy, but I'll try to move him along faster."

Reining in at the chuck wagon, Watt looked around for Tolman, then turned his attention on the head wrangler. "Slim, you seen Tolman?"

"Yes, sir. He rode out a couple hours ago." The skinny rider pointed to the south. "Caught up a fresh mount and headed out. I ain't seen hide nor hair of him since."

"Catch me up a fresh horse, will you?" Watt started unsaddling his tired sorrel. "One with a lot of bottom."

"You betcha, boss." Slim nodded. "You fixing to do some hard riding?"

"We all are, if I don't miss my guess."

Watt grabbed the braided, hemp lead rope of the hammer-headed roan that the wrangler had brought out and swung his saddle on the powerful animal. Quickly letting out his bridle to accommodate the long head, he buckled the cheek strap and rechecked his cinch.

"He sure has a big head, don't he, boss?"

"He does for a fact, but just look at all the brains it takes to fill that head." Watt patted the ugly-headed horse. "He'll do."

"Yeah." Slim laughed. "If it wasn't for that long, sad face, he'd be the best looking animal in the remuda."

"You're right about that, he's a looker for sure." Finished checking his saddle, Watt backed the big horse a few steps, then looked up at Slim. "Ride out and send about five of the boys with fresh horses to the drag."

"I'm on my way." Slim started to turn his horse, then stopped. "You watch him when you mount up, he can get a little salty at times."

"So can I, Slim." Swinging upon the roan, Watt cut him hard across the right ear with his reins as he felt the horse start to hump up to buck. Twice the big horse lunged hard, bawling out his anger as the heavy rein cracked down on his tender ear. Shaking his long head from the stinging blow, he lined out, deciding to give up any intentions of serious bucking.

Slim watched in anticipation of the coming wreck, but only laughed when he saw the show was over. "I reckon he ain't used to being treated like that. You must have hurt his feelings."

"I never seen a roan horse yet that wouldn't try you once." Watt eased up on the reins. "But, I've never seen one that wasn't a good horse either."

"True enough. I'll go get the men rounded up."

Turning for the rear of the herd, where he told Slim to send the men, Watt swung wide, trying to pick up any sign of a single horse. With all the cattle and horse tracks everywhere tearing up the ground it was hopeless. There was no way of knowing which track was the youngster's.

Watching, as the five riders rode in, Watt nodded in greeting. "Okay boys, this is where we cut out the men from the boys."

"What's on your mind, boss?"

"The Rafter J riders are just a short ways behind us." Watt nodded off to the south. "We're gonna cross the river ahead and make our stand on the other side."

"How many you figure there is of them?"

"Enough to go around." Watt looked over at the man. "Maybe, twenty or so."

"Yeah, and if I know Rail Johnson, they're all gun hands and killers." A rider named Hack Colby spoke up.

"You scared, Hack?" Another of the five laughed.

The curly-haired Colby nodded slowly. "Only a fool wouldn't be, Ned."

"Too scared to fight?" Watt studied the rider.

"I said I was scared, Mister Slocum. I didn't say I wouldn't fight."

Watt smiled. "Ain't no shame in being scared, Mister Colby. It's how you handle fear is what counts."

"I'll fight."

"What about the rest of you?"

Ned Baker spoke up. "We'll all fight. We've come too far to back out now."

"Okay, then." Watt laid out what he had planned for Johnson and his men. "It may seem like cold-blooded murder to you boys, but that's what they have planned for us."

As the afternoon wore on, Watt talked to all his riders. All had the same answer, they would fight. The ones that were fair gun hands, he put back at the rear of the herd where he expected the attack to come first. The younger men, who were least experienced with handling guns, he wanted them to stay on the flanks of the herd and help keep them running straight if gunfire erupted.

Chapter 13

Reed kept the horses in a hard walk to the north, alternating into a slow trot at times. He didn't know where the stableman in Dade had acquired the mare Lee rode, but she was a sure'nuff gaited saddle animal. The sorrel mare had a fox-trot that could burn a hole in the wind and keep it up for hours without tiring. With Hawk dead, Reed had returned to the dusty road where they could make better time without being afraid of an ambush. With the Comanche out of the way, all he had to worry about now was the outlaws and wild ones that traveled the road to Amarillo, preying on any unfortunate traveler they could find. Compared to the Comanche, Hawk, they were all amateur killers. They had been on the trail for almost six days since Bannock had returned to the south. If he had understood Uncle Wes' directions, the Red River crossing at Doan's was only a few miles further.

Lee had said very little in the last few days. Even riding the smooth-gaited horse, he knew she had to be exhausted. Hopefully, he could let her rest a day at Doan's Trading Post and get some good food in her. In their long days on the road, not once had the little woman spoken a word in complaint. Still, with all the hard traveling and miles they had put behind them, she looked worn out.

For the last few miles, the road had turned to the northeast and more trees started to crop out along the once grassy plains. In the distance, Reed could see what looked like a long tree line running north and south.

"Unless I miss my guess, Lee, we'll have a hot supper and soft bed to sleep in come nightfall." Reed pointed to the tree line.

"Will it be safe?"

"Safe enough, I reckon." Reed smiled, taping his pistol butt. "If not, I reckon this will take care of any problems."

Lee studied the strong face of the young Slocum. Since meeting him at the store for the first time, he had changed. After killing the Burden brothers and even when Hawk had them cornered down in the wash, he had showed no fear. Maybe, he had become more confident and reassured, or even cocky. Whatever it was, Reed Slocum was not the same young man she had first met in her father's store.

The trading post at Doan's Crossing was just a few ramshackle buildings formed into a small compound that smelled of cattle and hogs. Indians lined the porches of the trading post, smoking their pipes or sitting sullenly, waiting for any handouts the Doan's would offer. The Doan's were smart traders and they kept the Indians happy with their small trinkets of beads, stale crackers or other bits of cheap trade goods while trading for their hides. They had learned from other crooked traders, it was not good for business to cheat the Indian or short them on beef, and it was far better to keep them happy and returning each year.

With the passing of the trail herds and the heavy trading of guns, shells, and supplies, Doan's Store had become a very lucrative business. Tons of supplies crossed the river as Doan's Crossing was becoming the most traveled cattle trail coming from Deep South Texas. Foodstuff, rifles, and shells were sold by the cases to the herds heading on their long march north to the stock pens.

Dark, solemn eyes stared at Reed and the girl as they dismounted and tied up at the hitch rack outside of Doan's Trading Post. Reed heard a whistle or two come from across the street at what he figured was the local saloon and drinking establishment. Ignoring the men lining the porches, gawking at the girl, Reed pushed Lee ahead of him into the store. Walking up to the counter, he nodded at the tall, dark-haired man studying them.

"Howdy, folks. Welcome to Doan's."

"Howdy. We're looking to stable our horses, and get a hot meal and soft bed for the night."

"Joe will put up your horses for the night." The post trader nodded at a man standing nearby. "That'll cost you two dollars for the horses."

"Alright." Reed laid out two silver dollars on the counter. "And the food and room?"

"You'll have to go to the restaurant across from the saloon to eat, and see Beulah for a bed for the night."

"I'll need four boxes of forty-fours and three boxes for my Henry." Reed laid the rifle across the bar.

"You planning on a shooting war, mister?" The trader laughed.

"You never know." Reed stared at the man. "Have my horses saddled and ready at daybreak."

"Will there be anything else, young man?" Doan looked at the hard face, as Reed laid out the money for the ammunition.

"I'll pick up a few supplies before I ride out in the morning."

"That'll be just fine." The storekeeper looked over at Lee as he leaned across the counter, closer to Reed. "You be careful over there, young man. She's a mighty pretty young lady, and let's say some of those boys ain't exactly civilized."

"Yes, she is pretty. Maybe your boys need a little civilizing." Reed nodded. "How many days has it been since the Bar S herd passed through?"

Doan looked closely at the tall youngster. "Maybe, a week now. Wouldn't you say, Jack?"

"Give or take a day or two, I reckon."

"In the morning then." Reed waved his hand as he watched the hostler lead his horses to the back of the trading post. "Treat them good."

What the clerk at the trading post had called a restaurant was merely a box thrown together with hewed planks, and shingles pretending to be a roof. Still, the little eatery was waterproof and snug, and the food smelled wonderful to the hungry travelers. Sitting down at one of the small tables, Reed hoped the food would taste as good as it smelled. Windows with wooden shutters were open, letting flies, wasps, and anything else with wings come through. From behind the plank bar, a big rotund woman wearing a dirty apron and a tobacco-stained chin moved over to their table.

"What'll it be, young fella, steak and potatoes, or potatoes and steak?"

Reed smiled up at the woman and nodded. "About the same, ain't they?"

"Nope, sonny, they ain't." The woman wiped her mouth with a grimy sleeve. "One is buffalo steak and the other is beef steak."

"Well, tell me, ma'am, which is fresher?"

"Well, sir, 'twas me, I'd have the beef steak." The woman seemed to smile a little. "The beef may have to be stabbed again. The buffalo, well, sir, I don't think a knife would pierce it."

"Well, can you chew it?" Reed quipped. He liked the woman.

"Reckon y'all can, if your teeth are still in good shape."

"I reckon they are. Bring us two plates." Reed noticed the big woman looking sideways at Lee.

"Is something wrong, ma'am?"

"Quit calling me ma'am, name's Beulah."

"Yes, ma'am, I mean Beulah." Reed looked up at the big woman. "Is something wrong?"

"You planning on getting a room over at the Swede's for tonight?"

"She needs rest. We've been a long ways." Reed nodded. "I was hoping to get one here."

"Your lady is a beautiful little filly." Beulah poured some hot coffee. "I doubt the boys around here have ever seen a blond-headed girl like her before."

"So I've been told."

"Like I said, young man." Beulah turned to the cookstove. "Look across at that drooling bunch of misfits. If it were me, I'd ride on out tonight."

"Like I said, she's completely give out." Reed looked out through an open window at the men bunched together on the saloon porch, staring at the restaurant. "She hasn't got much more go in her tonight."

"You stay here tonight and she's liable to be worse than that, come morning." Beulah turned as the wooden door squeaked open and two foul smelling buffalo hunters strode in grinning from ear to ear. "Herb, you and Bee get on back over to the saloon."

"Oh Beulah, we just came in for some coffee." The bigger of the men grinned, showing a row of filthy, decayed, and rotting teeth.

Glaring at the men, she motioned to a far table. "Well, get yourselves over there and sit down."

Beulah's restaurant was just a hole-in-the-wall, but Reed had to admit the steaks and potatoes were about the best he had ever bitten into. Watching the two hunters out of the corner of his eye, Reed noticed the bigger one, called Herb, winked at the smaller man several times. Slipping the thong from his pistol, he cut his steak into pieces, then acted as if he was oblivious to everything but his supper.

"You boys wanting your supper?" Beulah looked at the two men as they downed another swallow of whiskey from the jug they had hidden in their coat.

The larger hunter smiled over at the one called Bee and grinned. "Yeah, Beulah, we sure would."

"Then put that bottle away and I'll get you some." Beulah pointed a finger at the two. "We've got us a lady here tonight. You'll treat her with respect. You hear?"

"Yes, ma'am. We sure will."

"I'll get you boys your vittles."

"The supper we're wanting is not what you're serving tonight." Herb elbowed the smaller hunter and chuckled.

"That'll be enough of that." Beulah glared at the two men. "Now, do you want supper or not?"

"Not from you tonight." Bee laughed again, then looked over at Lee.

Beulah's hand came from beneath the long counter holding a double-barreled shotgun. Pointing the shotgun at the pair, she motioned toward the door.

"Now, Beulah, don't get your dander up." Herb held up his hands. "We were just funning with you."

The café room was so quiet, you could hear a fly snoring.

"You boys know I don't allow anyone in my place to be rousted. Especially a lady, like she is."

"We were just funning, Beulah." Bee looked into the open barrels. "Can't you take a joke?"

The sound of both hammers being cocked back could be heard all over the room. "Why, boys, I'm just funning too. If you ain't out of my establishment by the time I blink, I'll blow you out!"

Both men lunged backward from their seats and headed for the door. "We're going, woman, take it easy."

"You tell the boys over there this shotgun will be waiting on anybody that thinks about getting out of the way with this lady. You hear me, Herb?"

"Yeah, we hear you, Beulah." Herb frowned as he turned toward the door. "You know, we could take this personal."

The big woman grinned slowly and raised the gun. "You sure will take it personal if this buckshot hits you in the rear. Now get!"

Reed shook his head and grinned as the big woman uncocked the shotgun. "You probably lost a couple customers, Miss Beulah, but we're thanking you."

"They'll be back. They like to eat." Beulah laughed. "Those boys are mostly alright, it's just the whiskey talking."

"Whiskey will always cause trouble alright." Reed remembered the usual fun loving riders on the Bar S and how a few shots of whiskey in town could turn them ornery. Many times, he had to ride herd on the men to get them home to the Bar S after a night of merry making.

"It does, but then again so do beautiful women." She smiled over at Lee. "I'll give you some advice, no charge."

"And just what would that be?"

"Finish your meal, saddle your horses, and ride on right now."

Reed looked over to where Lee's fork hesitated as she looked at the big woman. He stood and looked out the window. "Sounds like good advice to me."

"You mean those men would…?" Lee looked at Reed.

"The longer the whiskey runs, the longer they'll ogle you." Beulah shrugged. "Yes, ma'am, there could be trouble alright."

"These are white men. Aren't they civilized?"

Beulah laughed. "This is the Nations, honey. You left civilization about two miles south across the Red."

"You up to riding on tonight, Lee?" Reed knew she was tired. "It's your choice."

"She ain't got no choice, mister." Beulah shrugged. "Y'all either ride or you'll wind up killing someone, or getting yourself killed trying to protect her."

"What about Doan?" Reed looked at the woman. "He lets this sort of thing go on around here?"

"He's only one man and it doesn't go on all the time." Beulah looked again at Lee. "We don't have her kind here all the time."

Reed glared at the woman. "And just what kind is she?"

"The beautiful kind, young man, and sometimes that's the worst kind."

"We'll ride, Miss Beulah." Lee nodded over at Reed. "I don't want any more trouble."

"It's not you personally, honey, it's just men and whiskey." Beulah shrugged and smiled at Lee. "They'll insist you dance with every one of them several times, then this young man will get jealous and someone probably will get hurt."

"We have to get out of here." Reed stood by the door listening to the boisterous hunters in front of the saloon. "Sure can't go out the front door."

"I'll send the boy out the back and have the hostler saddle your horses." Beulah turned for the backroom. "And I'll put you up some bread and meat for the trail."

"I'm thanking you, ma'am." Reed smiled at the big woman.

"Don't thank me yet. You folks ain't clear of this place yet."

"We're clear, Beulah." Reed touched his forty-four. "It just depends on how much clearing or killing I'll have to do to get out of here."

"You a killer, young man?" The quiet laugh coming from the woman's mouth made Reed blush slightly. "I thought not."

"You thought what, Miss Beulah?"

"What's that, young man?"

"We won't be needing them horses till daybreak." Reed looked over to where Lee sat slumped in a chair. "She's exhausted. If you've got an extra bed, I'll pay good money for it for the night."

"I wouldn't advise it, sonny." Beulah pointed her chin to the window. "You see what you're up against."

Reed shrugged. "I don't see much out there."

"Well, it's your funeral. I do have a clean bed back there for the girl."

"Thank you, ma'am. You get Miss Hargrove settled and I'll see if I can get them boys across the street to change their minds about things."

"Miss Hargrove?" The woman turned to look at Reed.

"Yes, ma'am, she's my sister."

"Oh." Beulah smiled. "Your sister, huh?"

Reed pulled the door closed behind him as he started across the street to the porch of the saloon. At least eight men stood lounging along the boardwalk with drinks in their hands. The ones from the café, Herb and Bee, stood out in front of the others.

"Your young man is fixing to get himself hurt bad, honey. I'll guarantee you one thing; no one will bother you in here." Beulah reached for the shotgun.

Lee nodded tiredly as she moved to the window. "You asked if he was a killer. Yes, Beulah, he is. He's a very dangerous man."

"But, he's just a youngster."

"That youngster, as you call him, has killed two white men and probably twenty Comancheros and Comanches in the last three weeks."

"What?" Beulah blinked as she took in the words. "That polite young man?"

"He rescued me from them, then had to kill many Comancheros to keep me safe."

Beulah blinked as she looked out the window. "Do tell."

Stepping up on the board sidewalk, Reed came within two feet of Herb and Bee. Only the sound of a hardened fist crushing into the men's soft faces was heard as Reed dropped both men from the porch, out onto the street. Looking over at the others as they gawked down unbelieving at the two unconscious men, Reed smiled coldly. The forty-four came out so fast they didn't see the movement until they were looking into the large bore of the weapon.

"Anyone else got any ideas about my sister? If so, speak up now, and let's start this dance a going."

Not a word was uttered as the men filed back inside the saloon without looking back.

Toeing Bee over as he tried to rise, Reed pushed the barrel of his pistol into the hunter's mouth. "I see either of you before I pull out in the morning, you're both dead men. You understand me?"

Only a muffled sound came from Bee's mouth as he tried to answer. Holstering the pistol, Reed pulled the man to a sitting position, then slugged him unconscious again.

"Never did like to hit a man when he was down." Reed spoke quietly to Beulah as he entered the café. "Now, I believe I'll finish my supper."

Looking over to where Lee was standing, Beulah shook her head and smiled. "I believe it's time for you to get some rest, young lady."

"Tell the boy to have our horses fed and saddled at sunup." Reed bit into his steak. "We'll be pulling out, right after breakfast."

"Yes, sir, they'll be here."

Reed felt he had hardly closed his eyes when Beulah's banging on the wood stove brought him awake. He could smell the coffee boiling and the side meat sizzling in the cast iron skillet. Rising from the hard pallet, he had slept on, Reed looked around for Lee.

"Don't get nervous, young man. She's in the back freshening up."

Nodding, Reed walked to where the woman had set him out a hot cup of coffee. "I'm much obliged, Beulah. You sure done us a good turn last night."

"That girl is pretty and maybe a lot of things, but there's one thing she's not."

"What's that?"

"Your sister. I've never seen a sister look at her brother the way that girl looks at you." Beulah laughed good-naturedly. "No, sir. Those big blue eyes look at you like they were dripping molasses.

Reed looked up over his coffee and shook his head. "I wouldn't know what you're talking about, Beulah."

"I suppose not, you're still young and you're a man." Beulah laughed again. "But, Lee might have spilled the beans last night about not being your sister."

"What's being young and a man have to do with the way she looks at me?"

"Inexperience is what it's called." Beulah shook her head. "In case you don't know, sonny, and it seems you don't, that girl's in love with you."

"In love!" Reed almost spilled his coffee.

"That's what it's called around here." Beulah flipped the side meat and shook her head. "Course these wild men we have around here are in love with anything wearing a skirt."

"You married?" Reed's face was beet red and he wanted to change the subject.

The woman looked up from her cooking and smiled. "Was, several times."

"What happened?"

"Lost them all."

Reed looked over at the stove curiously. "Lost them all? How do you lose a husband?"

"Well, let's see, sonny." The big woman smiled. "The first one, Elmer, my favorite of the whole lot, he just up and died one night. Injuns got a couple of the others. One was killed in a knife fight and one ran off with a floozy from Amarillo."

"In a knife fight… what over?"

"Now, it sure weren't me. I'm telling you." Beulah acted like she was remembering. "Old Dexter was my husband, but he up and got himself killed over another woman."

"And the one that ran off with the Amarillo woman?" Reed didn't want to use the name Beulah had used for the woman.

"Yep, old Pike, he sure'nuff liked the skinny women and she sure was skinny. Beulah laughed. "Why that woman could slip through a keyhole if she had a mind to."

"Pike?" Reed thought of the old stableman back in Amarillo.

"Yep, that were his name."

The bedroom door opened and Lee came into the warm kitchen. "Good morning, everyone."

Reed could hardly meet her eyes as Beulah greeted her. "My, you're all cleaned up and you look rested."

"I feel much better now. Thank you, Miss Beulah."

"Me and your brother have been having us a good talk."

"Miss Beulah, you know Reed isn't my brother." Lee laughed. "I told you so last night."

Reed shook his head, realizing Lee had told Beulah she wasn't his sister. "Beulah's been telling me about her husbands, Lee."

"Husbands?"

"How many did you say you've had, Beulah?"

"Six, but I ain't quite through yet." The woman carried two platters of steaming food to the table. "Old Pike, he up and set me back for a spell, took me out of the marrying idea. But, I'm about in the mood for another one now."

At the mention of Pike's name, Lee looked at Reed with a shocked look on her face. "Beulah was married to a horse trader named Pike."

"What happened to him?" Lee asked.

"Like I done told Reed, the dang fool ran off with a skinny woman from Amarillo. Last I heard the fool was running a stable there and the floozy had done skipped town with a cardsharp." Beulah wiped her hands. "Serves the old reprobate right."

"Well, doesn't that beat all." A small smile came to Lee's face as she sipped on her coffee and winked at Reed.

"I'll bet you one thing though."

"What's that, Miss Beulah?"

"He'll never find another cook like me."

"No, ma'am, he sure won't." Reed agreed, and he wasn't lying, Beulah could cook. "You, my lady, are a fine cook, the best."

Several miles from Doan's Crossing, Reed was surprised when Lee broke out in uncontrollable laughter. Staring over at her as she shook, he knew she couldn't help herself.

"What's so funny?"

"Mister Pike. He never told us he had a wife." Lee shook her head. "I would have never figured he'd been married."

"And that's funny?"

Lee finally composed herself and looked over at him. "It would be funny to you too, if you had heard all your life, how he hated women, any woman."

"He did?" Reed shook his head. "He told you he hated women?"

"Many, many times I've heard Mister Pike say how he hated women." Lee shook her head, then wiped the grin from her face. "I believe Mister Pike has been lying to us, all this time."

Reed grinned. "Apparently, he has at that."

As Lee started to laugh again, Reed kicked his horse into a slow lope down the road. He was amazed how easily the little mare kept up beside him. He had never seen a horse that could single foot as fast as the little mare could and use very little energy. Back on the Bar S, the horse herd only had a few horses with a good running walk or foxtrot, but he had never seen one with the smooth action of her single-foot. The little mare was sure enough gaited with a running walk, fox trot, and a single-foot.

"She's something." Reed admired the mare. "That horse has more gaits than a spider has legs."

Lee patted the smooth neck. "Yes, she's worth her weight in gold."

If the herd traveled for five days from Doan's, at their steady plodding pace, Reed figured they could be at least fifty or sixty miles north. They would take two maybe three days traveling on fresh horses to catch up with the herd, depending on how fast he wanted to move. Fortunately, the torn up ground from the passing herd would be easy to follow even at night, providing he wanted to ride in the dark.

"I figure we'll catch up, maybe day after tomorrow." Reed looked back toward Doan's.

Following his gaze, Lee studied the flat ground behind them. "What's wrong, Reed?"

"The way this horse is flicking his ears, I believe our hunter friends from Doan's may be following us."

"Oh no!" Lee looked over at Reed. "Not again."

"I ain't sure who it could be, but somebody is following us."

"What will we do?"

"Hopefully, we'll catch up to the herd before our friends back there catch up to us."

"Let's hurry, Reed. I don't want you in any more danger."

Hearing her words, Reed remembered what Beulah had said when he last talked with her. The woman had said Lee cared for him deeply. He hadn't really believed her then, but now with Lee's words, maybe the woman had been right.

"Old Hawk's dead. We'll be alright." Reed smiled at her. "Don't worry."

Reed kept the horses traveling hard, only stopping to let them water and grab a few bites of the heavy grass covering the landscape. For two days, he had followed the gouged up trail, cut up with horse and cattle tracks. He was worried, there were too many horse tracks overlaying the cattle tracks. Possibly, Johnson and his men were following the herd.

"We've got to hurry, Lee." Reed nodded down at the tracks. "I think Rail Johnson and his men may be following the herd.

"Listen." Lee silenced him with her hand. "That sounded like a shot."

"I didn't hear it."

"It was a gunshot, but it was far away."

Reed kept the horses moving forward. "That may be a hunter. It can't be the herd or there would be more firing."

"What can we do?"

"We've got to keep after the herd." Reed nodded. "There's safety for you there."

Tolman had watched as Watt and Emmet started the herd north pushing them hard, trying to reach the river and put the water between the herd and Johnson's men. He figured Tall Pine was trying to move the herd somewhere ahead, where he could hold them if they were attacked. Turning his horse, he rode back to the south to find the Rafter J crew. The land through this part of the Nations was rolling hills covered in places with live oak and scrub timber. He knew he had to be cautious and not ride head on into Johnson or his riders.

Sitting his horse, down in a small draw, Tolman studied the hard-looking riders as they approached. He had finally found Rail Johnson and his men as they followed the herd north in a slow trot. As the riders passed his place of concealment, Tolman counted twenty-seven riders, all heavily armed. The grim-looking men followed the same large man Tolman had told Watt about. The man, Tall Pine called Rail Johnson.

With his attention focused on the passing riders, Tolman didn't see the lone horseman as the man rode up behind him. Only the blast from the rider's pistol warned him anyone was near, but it was too late. Tolman tried his best to hang onto his plunging horse as he shied from the gunfire.

Several men rode up on the lip of the deep draw, looking down at the fallen body. "It's just an Injun, boss. He's been watching you." The man who had shot Tolman hollered over to where Johnson was looking down at him.

"He dead?"

Without dismounting or riding down into the gully, the rider nodded. "Deader than a gut shot possum, Mister Johnson."

"Then let's ride, we ain't got time to worry over an Injun." Johnson whirled his horse around. "We've got more important fish to fry."

Tolman groaned and turned over slowly, then looked about the draw as he tried to clear his head. Blood covered his left arm where the bullet had ripped a deep furrow. He had heard the men talking as they looked down where he lay. Luckily, they hadn't come down to make sure he was dead. Staying still, he listened as the horses faded into the distance before trying to move. Packing the wound with sand, Tolman stopped the bleeding, then regained his feet. The wound wasn't serious, but his head had slammed hard against the packed ground as he was flung from the spooked horse. His head was spinning, making his legs feel rubbery from the heavy blow to his head. Worse, the horse had run off, leaving Tolman afoot at least five miles behind the herd and unable to warn Tall Pine. Climbing out of the gorge, Tolman started after the riders afoot.

Joe Casper whipped his dun horse hard, racing to catch up to the front of the herd, then reining up beside Slocum and Tabor. Stopping their horses, the two men looked over as the cowhand reined in.

"Boss, we've got a problem."

"What is it, Joe?" Watt looked over at the worried rider. "Has Johnson caught up with the herd?"

"No, sir, not Johnson." The redhead shook his head. "It's Tolman, boss."

"Tolman?" Watt looked at the rider. "What happened?"

"His horse just came running into the remuda covered in sweat." Casper added. "And worse, his saddle has blood on it."

Tabor looked back over the herd, then back at Slocum. "I'm sorry, boss. What do you want to do?"

Watt shook his head. "Let's get the herd across the river."

"What about Tolman?"

Watt looked at Tabor. "If he's alive, we'll find him, but first we've got to get the herd taken care of."

"But, he's your son, Watt."

"Yes, Emmet, he's my son. If he's alive, I'll find him." Watt looked hard at the two men. "But, not until the herd is secured."

"Yes, sir."

The voice went cold. "If he's dead, I'll hunt down and skin every mother's son that's riding with Rail Johnson."

"We could send a couple riders to look for him." Tabor suggested.

"You'll send one man back a mile and watch for Johnson and his crew, and that's all. We're already outnumbered and outgunned without sending any more men out."

"Okay, Watt." Tabor shrugged. "I just thought…"

"I know what you thought, Emmet. If Tolman's alive, he'll get back to us. If not, well, we can't help him. Now, let's get this herd moving toward the river."

"You're the boss."

Watt nodded sadly. "Thank you, Emmet."

The old brindle lead steer sniffed at the river's edge. With a little prodding from Tabor, the steer waded into the river and started across the wide Canadian. The water wasn't deep where Slocum had told the point riders to start them across, but still there was the danger of quicksand and bog holes. Wading almost halfway across before hitting swimming water and a slight current, the old steer led the front of the herd straight across.

"How long you figure it will take to get them all across, Watt?" Tabor watched the herd as they strung out across the muddy river. "I'm figuring we don't have much time."

"I don't know, Emmet. Hopefully, we'll be across before Johnson and his bunch catch us in the middle of the river." Watt shrugged. "But, we've got to hurry. They catch us out there and we're all goners for sure."

"The rest of the herd is strung out about a half mile back."

"Our rider seen anything of Johnson and his men?"

Tabor shook his head. "No, sir, haven't heard a word from him, nary a thing yet."

Watt nodded. "Let's cross back over and get the men set for Johnson and his bunch."

Johnson was taking his time. He was a cautious man and wanted to make sure everything was on his side. He had sent a rider ahead to spot the herd and Slocum's riders while he and the rest of his riders kept lagging behind, out of sight. Out here in the Nations, he knew he had plenty of time to take the herd since there was no one to stop him. He didn't care about a few of his hired hands getting shot, maybe even killed, but he wanted to be sure he had enough men left to trail the herd on to Sedalia. He also knew they weren't the only band of rustlers watching the Bar S Herd. No, he knew he had to take the herd without losing too many of his hired guns.

The lanky rider, Johnson had sent out, came loping back to the riders. "They're moving faster, picking up speed, Mister Johnson. They're about two miles ahead."

"Anything else?"

"Well, yes sir." The rider wiped his face. "A riderless horse came by me running hard, then in a few minutes, that's when the drag riders of the herd started hollering and pushing the herd into a fast trot."

Johnson looked over at the rider who had shot Tolman. "You sure that man you shot was an Indian?"

"Positive."

"His horse wouldn't run to the herd unless he worked for Slocum."

"I don't know, Mister Johnson."

Boone Hames pushed his horse closer to Johnson. "It must have been the Indian's horse. The one that shot Gage with an arrow."

"Yeah, I forgot about you telling me of him. All right, let's get to it. The fat's in the fire now." Johnson looked up at the sky. "Let's ride! Hit 'em hard boys and try not to leave any survivors!"

With a chorus of yells, the riders spurred their horses and followed Johnson toward the herd in a hard run. Each man was a gunman and a killer, and out there, no one would stop them. With the money, Johnson had promised, each man was eager to follow the rancher against the herd. The flat lands of the territory and the turned up sod from the large herd made it easy for the horses to run the herd down. Johnson waved his men on as the rear of the herd was spotted.

Chapter 14

Reed reined in the horse as he watched several mounted warriors emerge from their hiding place behind a stand of live oak and blackjack trees. At least fifteen warriors, all carrying rifles, sat their horses in a semicircle in front of them. Watching as a lone rider rode forward to within feet of where he and Lee sat their horses.

"He's Kiowa." Reed studied the bronze face and dark eyes.

"What you do here, white man?" The voice came out hard. "Why you in our lands?"

"I'm riding to catch up with the cattle herd ahead."

"You are foolish to travel alone with woman." The warrior looked over at Lee. "These are dangerous lands."

"She is my woman. We ride to catch up with my father."

"Who is your father?"

"Watt Slocum, the Kiowa call him Tall Pine." Jed hoped the warrior would know the name.

"Tall Pine." The warrior nodded. "I have heard of this one."

"He is a blood brother to the Kiowa."

Suddenly, several warriors pointed behind Reed at an oncoming rider. Relief covered Reed's face as he recognized Bannock riding slowly toward them. He had no idea the warrior still followed them. It had been Bannock following them, not the buffalo hunters from Doan's. Nodding solemnly, the rider reined in his tired horse beside him.

Reed greeted the warrior. "Bannock, I'm sure glad you have come. It is good you are here."

"Does Bannock know this one?" The warrior looked at Bannock, then pointed at Reed.

"Him my nephew, son of Tall Pine." Bannock nodded at Reed. "What does my brother, Sun Boy, wish of this one?"

"We have come to meet Tall Pine's other son Tolman." Sun Boy studied Reed and Lee. "Tolman promised many cows if we help Tall Pine get herd across river."

"Have you seen Johnson and his men?"

"We see many whites." Sun Boy nodded to the north. "They ahead, follow herd."

Sun Boy turned as another warrior reined in beside him and whispered. Looking at Bannock, the warrior nodded. "My uncle is far from the Llano."

"It is good to see, Young Deer." Bannock kicked his horse beside the young warrior and shook his hand. "You have grown since we last met."

"Young Deer says Tolman was shot by men following herd." Sun Boy pointed at Reed. "He say this one fight with buffalo hunters back at Doan's."

"Tolman… is he dead?" Reed kicked his horse forward.

"Tolman no dead, him just shot a little in arm." Young Deer touched his arm. "Two warriors stay with him until we get back to where he rests."

Sun Boy looked curiously at Reed. "Young Deer say you kill two bad men at Doan's with your hands."

"I didn't kill them, just knocked them senseless."

Bannock nodded and laughed. "He looks young, my brother, but this one a great warrior."

"He must be. These tough white men." Sun Boy laughed. "I would like to have seen him hit them."

"Let's get to Tolman and the herd." Reed kicked his horse as Sun Boy and the Kiowas turned north.

Lee dismounted and knelt beside Tolman, who laid back weakly in the shade of a small blackjack tree. Quickly washing the blood from his arm, Lee bound the wound with clean cloth from her saddlebags.

After taking a few sips of water, Tolman nodded at her. "Thank you."

"You okay, Tolman?" Reed was watching as Lee cleaned the nasty tear, then bathed the youngster's head with water.

"I am okay. I got careless and let one of Johnson's men slip up behind me." Tolman moved his head. "Stupid of me."

Bannock nodded. "You were taught better."

"I know, Uncle."

"Good, you stay here and watch after Lee. I've got to get to the herd." Reed turned for his horse.

"No, I ride with you. Tall Pine need us all." Tolman stood up slowly.

"I can't let her ride with us. There's gonna be a lot of hard riding and shooting. I can't leave her here unprotected." Reed looked down at Lee.

"I stay with Little Missy. Tolman ride my horse. His place is with you and Tall PIne." Bannock replied.

Nodding, Reed swung onto his horse. "If you're up to it, Tolman."

"Yes, it is my place to go."

"Will Sun Boy and his warriors fight with us?" Reed asked the chief.

"You give many cow, we fight." Sun Boy understood Reed's words.

"Chief, if you help us out of this mess, you'll get your cows." Reed laughed.

"Then we fight." Laughing, Sun Boy raised his rifle and yelled a war cry. "We would fight for Tall Pine for nothing, but since you offer cows…"

Reed looked at Lee. "Bannock will bring you to the herd if we win."

"You'll win." Lee smiled. "I know it."

"You ready, Brother?" Reed looked over at Tolman.

"I'm ready."

Reed could see the dust, from the fast moving herd, when he heard the sound of gunfire. Kicking his horse into a hard run, Reed charged forward until he could make out the forms of Johnson's men, firing at a few men at the tail end of the running herd. Several dead steers lay where stray bullets had killed them. Waving Sun Boy and his warriors to the right side of the herd, Reed and Tolman raced up behind Johnson's men.

With the dust from two thousand heavy steers beating the ground as they panicked, cattle bawling in fear, and the continuous roaring of guns made the scene complete pandemonium.

Reining in, trying to locate Johnson's riders through the thick dust, Reed looked at Tolman and grinned. "Sun Boy is on the herd's flank. Let's hit them hard from behind."

Reed spurred his horse hard, charging at the fleeing figures. Losing sight of Tolman, as he raced into the melee with his forty-four blazing away at the closest riders, Reed emptied two saddles. He wasn't worried about hitting the Bar S crew since they were further ahead, making a stand behind the herd. Several of Johnson's men fell before they discovered they had enemies behind them.

"Boss!" Boone Hames reined his excited horse in beside Johnson. "We've got riders shooting at us from behind and on our flank."

Johnson could hear the steady blast of rifles as he sat choking back the dust and chaos of the running fight. Cussing, he shook his head as he wondered where the riders came from. "Who are they?"

Hames shrugged as he tried to control of his excited horse. "From what I can see through all this dust and dirt, they're Indians mostly."

"How many men have we lost?"

"Several, I seen three shot out of their saddles by one rider." Hames whirled his horse. "I don't know how many the Indians killed."

"Let's ride out of here, Boone." Johnson turned his horse. "Come on, we're whipped."

"What about our men?"

"They're on their own. They'll pull out if they can." Johnson swore again. "I figure most of them are dead already."

Hames shook his head. Abandoning his own riders and running away went against his grain. To run out and leave their own men to be killed, seemed cowardice to him. Seeing Johnson's broad back as he started to disappear in the dust and haze, Hames kicked his horse just as a figure appeared before him. He recognized him as the same rider who had killed the other three men. Both pistols discharged at the same time and Hames slowly fell sideways from his saddle. Trying to raise his heavy pistol, he lurched on his side as another heavy slug finished him off.

Tolman reined in beside Reed as Hames rolled over and breathed his last breath. The herd had raced to the north, letting the dust from their passing slowly clear. An occasional discharge of a pistol sounded, then as the two brothers looked down at the dead bodies, suddenly everything became quiet.

"The big man, Tall Pine calls Johnson, rode alone in that direction." Tolman pointed with his rifle. "He must not get away."

"You ride to Bannock and check on the girl, and I'll go after him."

"You know this one Johnson?" Tolman asked.

"I know him." Reed looked to where Tolman had pointed. "He's not getting back to the Brazos to cause any more trouble for the Bar S."

"Be careful, my brother." Tolman spoke tiredly. "I believe him to be a dangerous man."

Reed looked over at the dark face, then glanced down at his bloody side. "You're wounded again, Tolman."

The white teeth showed as the warrior smiled. "Again, I was lucky. It is just a scratch."

"Enough scratches like that and you'll bleed to death." Reed nodded. "I want to get to know you a whole lot better."

"You must ride before the big man gets too far." Tolman motioned with his head. "I will tell our father where you go."

Reed hesitated. "You sure you're alright?"

"Your woman will bind my wounds." Tolman grinned.

"My woman?" Reed's face turned red.

"Are you blind, Brother?"

Reed kicked the dust-covered sorrel horse toward Doan's Post. Reloading his forty-four, he followed the beaten trail to the south in a hard lope. Studying the ground as he rode, Reed finally found what he was looking for. A single horse had passed in a hard run, heading south before him. The rider had to be Johnson fleeing back to his own grounds, knowing Watt Slocum would surely be following him. All of Johnson's hired guns were dead or running for their lives, and his only hope was to get back to his ranch. Slowing his tired animal to a short lope, Reed kept his eyes glued ahead of him. He hoped to catch Johnson before he crossed the Red. If he killed the rancher in Texas, he'd have to answer to the Rangers.

His horse was done in, and he couldn't push him any faster. Reed knew he would never catch Johnson north of the river. If he was lucky, he might pick up a fresh horse at Doan's to continue the chase. He wasn't giving up, even if he had to follow Johnson all the way back to the Rafter J ranch. Reining in at the hitch post, in front of Beulah's Café, Reed dismounted and tied the exhausted horse. Stepping into the small frame room, he took a seat at the counter and nodded at the big woman.

"Howdy, ma'am."

"Young fellow, you look like you've been in a war."

"Reckon I have at that." Reed smiled as she placed a cup of coffee on the bar. "Thank you. I could sure use a big drink of water."

"We already heard about the fight." Beulah poured Reed a large glass of water. "One man, then two others, came flying through here like their pants were on fire. Never stopped, waved, or nothing."

"I expect they're across the river by now."

"Yep, didn't even stop to eat." Beulah looked at the hole in Reed's shirt. "That bullet get any of your hide?"

Reed hadn't noticed the bullet hole in his shirt. "No, reckon not. Tell me, Beulah, was one of them men a big man?"

"Yep, some of the young bucks that hang around here said he was the leader of the ones that hit your herd."

Back on the trail, when Reed had followed Johnson's tracks, he had spotted two other sets of horse prints heading south. He had picked up another two sets of tracks probably ridden by Indians. All riders heading for Doan's in a big hurry.

"These warriors probably were some of Sun Boy's warriors." Reed wolfed down the dinner that Beulah placed before him. "I need a fresh horse. Can you send your boy over to the stable and get me one and have him take care of my horse outside?"

"I can do that." Beulah hollered out the back door for her swamper.

"Tell the stableman, I need one with plenty of bottom and I'll settle up with him when I get back." Reed hollered at the broad back as she turned.

Beulah stopped and turned. "You going after them all by yourself?"

"Unless you want to go help me?" Reed grinned.

"Is that a proposal, sonny?"

"Yes, ma'am, it just might be."

"Well, I know it's just because of my cooking, but I'm gonna have to turn you down all the same."

"Why, Miss Beulah, why would you do that?"

"You're just too old for me, that's why." Beulah winked, but then grew serious. "You gonna kill all three of them?"

"Just the big one. He's the one I want."

"Where's the girl?"

"She's safe, in good hands."

"She'll be in safe hands after you marry up with her, maybe."

"I've got to ride, Beulah. Thanks for everything."

"Thank you, youngster, for the proposal." The big woman grinned from ear to ear.

Reed waved at Beulah, then turned the powerful black horse toward the Red. He could feel the power under him as the black hit a hard lope. The chunky horse had a rough gait, not as smooth riding as the sorrel. However, Reed could tell the animal had a lot of power and endurance which was exactly what he needed. Beulah had said the three fleeing riders hadn't changed horses at Doan's which was a mistake they were going to regret when their horses played out. He intended to run Rail Johnson to the ground before he rode too far into Texas.

Wading out of the muddy Red River, Reed studied the tracks in front of him. Two riders had ridden south, while the third turned east, following the river. He wasn't interested in the lone rider so he kicked the black horse to the south. The deep prints in the soft sandy bank showed one of the horses carried a heavy load and it had to be Rail Johnson, the only one he wanted. Johnson and whoever rode with him hadn't tried to hide their tracks, anyone could easily follow the sandy trail.

Reed wanted Johnson bad. He knew the rancher would return to the Rafter J and cause more trouble for the Bar S, even if the herd was sold and the note was paid off. Rail Johnson hated the Slocum name and he would do everything in his power to bankrupt the ranch. Everything that happened over the last month, Reed laid at the doorstep of the Rafter J owner. Kicking the black into a faster gait, Reed pushed the horse hard to the south.

Bannock and Lee watched and listened to the gun battle from a small knoll, a mile behind the running herd. They saw a big man suddenly emerge from the dust and noise below them, then he raced to the south. Only minutes passed when two other riders followed him. Staring down from the knoll, the warrior watched as seconds passed, then Reed Slocum came riding from the haze, following the first three riders.

"It's Reed." Lee pointed down at the flats. "He's chasing those men."

Bannock cocked his head. "Fight over. No more shooting."

"What happened? Is the herd safe?"

"Tall Pine win. If him lose, young one not chase these men and these bad men not run south." Bannock nodded.

"Isn't anyone going to help him?" Lee asked worriedly.

"Come, we go find Tall Pine, see what happened." Bannock kicked his sorrel mare.

Bannock and Lee had hardly dropped from the knoll when they met Tolman coming toward them, out of the veil of dust and bawling cattle. Everything was in turmoil as the Bar S riders started rounding up strays, pushing the herd back together while searching out any more of Johnson's riders. With all the noise, part of the herd hadn't crossed the Canadian yet and stampeded away from the river in every direction.

"Him wounded again." Bannock quickly noticed how the youngster was sitting his horse. "His body shows blood."

Bannock helped Tolman from his horse to a small shade tree. Examining the side wound, Lee found a small bluish bump under Tolman's skin.

"The bullet's still in him." Lee held her canteen for Tolman to drink. "Bannock, get some bandages from my saddlebags, and hurry."

"Have you seen my brother?" Tolman gritted his teeth in pain. "He goes after the ones that attacked the herd."

"He passed below us, following some men just before we met you." Lee took the bag from Bannock. "Who were those men?"

"The big one is enemy of our father Tall Pine." Tolman studied the small knife. "My brother will kill Johnson or die trying. I was riding to find you."

"Bannock, please start a small fire and sterilize this knife." Lee looked into Tolman's eyes. "This is gonna hurt."

"You have done this before?" The dark eyes watched her every move.

"Yes, I even removed a bullet from Tall Pine twice."

"I must go help my brother." Tolman tried to rise.

"You just lie still while I take care of your wound.

"Who shot my father?"

"Two white trappers fighting over hunting rights on Grant Range."

"I did not hear of this." Tolman watched as Lee took the knife from Bannock. "We hunt there now. I guess Tall Pine won?"

"Yes, he won." Lee nodded. "Bannock take hold of Tolman's arms."

"No, I take care of my own arms."

"It will hurt, young one." Bannock stepped back.

"Cut it out. I am not a woman to be held down." Tolman tensed.

As Lee made her first cut above the purplish lump, just under the skin on Tolman's side, she heard several horses approaching. Absorbed in her work, she didn't have time to see who the riders were. Blood flowed down the young one's side as he gritted his teeth. Not a whimper came from him nor did he move a muscle as she dug out the bullet. Tolman's eyes were closed as she took the hot knife from Bannock.

Watt Slocum knelt beside his son and studied the red-hot knife. "Get ahold of yourself, son, this is gonna really bite." Watt smiled down at Lee and Tolman. "I know."

Only a nod and a hard jerk of his body as it tensed from the searing iron came from Tolman, and no other sound was uttered. Quickly applying grease and binding the wound with clean bandages, Lee looked at the arm wound she had doctored earlier. Redressing the arm, Lee smiled and stood up tiredly to face Slocum.

"Reed has ridden after Rail Johnson alone." The blue eyes looked up at the tall man.

"The young one, him follow three men south." Bannock nodded.

"Why would he do that? We whipped Johnson. The fighting's over, and I figure he's headed south as fast as his horse can run." Watt shook his head and cussed. "The herd's got a clear trail now, straight to Sedalia."

"You're right, boss." Tabor looked at Slocum. "But, we might run into other cattle rustlers ahead."

"Nothing you and the boys can't handle, Emmet." Watt looked down at Tolman, then led Lee a few feet away. "How are his wounds?"

"He'll be alright in a few days. Sore, but he'll recover." Lee smiled tiredly. "The bullet entered his back but didn't exit. I don't think it hit anything vital. I had to cut it out."

"Again, I'm thanking you, Lee."

"You must go help your other son Reed."

"I'm riding. You and Tabor get Tolman back to the chuck wagon and make him stay in it until he's strong again."

"We'll see to it." Tabor nodded. "You just hurry back."

"You worried about what's ahead, Emmet?"

"Dang right I am, we don't know what's out there." Tabor grinned. "You scared of the dark?"

Tabor frowned at Watt. "This isn't a joking matter."

Watt looked down at Tolman and nodded. "You're right, Emmet. I'll get back as quick as I can. Keep him still."

"We'll take care of Tolman and the herd, boss."

"I know you will." Watt nodded again at Tolman. "I'll be back, boy."

Only a slight nod came from the wounded youngster as he watched Slocum follow Bannock to the south.

"Bring him back safe, Mister Slocum."

Hearing the urgency in her voice, Watt smiled. He could feel the deep worry in her voice, and there was no doubt, her face and pleading voice spoke volumes. Lee Hargrove was in love with Reed. He knew it wasn't just fear he was hearing in her voice, she was deeply smitten with Reed. He smiled to himself as he rode away. He liked Lee Hargrove. She would make a wonderful wife and daughter-in-law.

Rail Johnson reined in his horse and looked at Cole Sanders as he rode up next to him. The gunman finally caught up with Johnson after chasing him for almost a whole day from Doan's. Johnson thought someone was following him, but he didn't know it was one of his riders.

"You've been riding hard, Mister Johnson."

"We need to get back to the ranch fast, Cole." Johnson shrugged tiredly. "We've got to hire more men."

"That's a fact, we sure got ourselves shot to pieces back there." The lanky gunman nodded. "We're gonna need more men, a lot more men."

"I reckon the ones that aren't dead scattered to the winds." Johnson cussed. "They won't be back."

"The ones I seen still alive were riding hell-bent for leather out of there alright." Sanders nodded. "Cleve left me and headed east after we crossed the Red."

"No matter, I'll hire more men. Better men this time."

"We won't make it back if we don't rest the horses." Sanders looked at the sweating horses. "I wore mine out trying to catch up with you."

Johnson knew he was a better horseman than to misuse his horse like he had as he ran from the carnage behind him. He was ashamed since he knew fear had fueled his running the horse so hard. He looked over at Sanders, hoping the tall man wasn't seeing the fear in his face.

"You're right, Cole." Johnson agreed. "We'll rest the animals for the night."

Sanders nodded. "You take the horses on up the trail and find a good campsite. I'll be along directly."

"What are you gonna do?"

"I'll find me a good place to sit awhile. I'm gonna watch our back trail for a spell." The gunman looked back the way they had ridden. "Someone just might be following us."

"I'll be up the trail."

"If nothing shows, I'll be along." Sanders handed Johnson his reins. "Here, take my horse and find some water for him."

The trail of two horses heading south was plain to follow. Crossing a small stream of water, Reed reined in and let the horse water as he studied the tracks. He figured Johnson and whoever rode with him had crossed the small stream less than an hour ahead of him. Water still puddled in the deep tracks where they exited the water. Now, he would have to ride with caution.

Two hours later, riding slow and cautious, Reed reined in his horse as a figure stepped from behind an oak tree, less than fifty feet in front of him. Studying the surrounding grounds, Reed couldn't see anyone else. Nudging the horse forward a few feet, Reed reined in again and watched the tall man. By the look of the man's low-slung holster and the clothes he wore, this one was no cowpuncher. Reed knew he was looking at a gunfighter. Most of the men he had shot from their horses, back at the herd, weren't cowhands either. The tall figure standing before him was no doubt one of Johnson's hired killers.

"Where you headed, boy?" The voice was low.

"South, mister. I'm in a hurry." Reed answered the tall man.

"You ain't in that big a rush, youngster." The man smiled coldly. "You're after Rail Johnson, I reckon."

"I am." Reed nodded. "Are you the man riding with him?"

"Well, now, I reckon I am that man."

"I'm not after you, mister. Step aside and I'll ride on." Reed studied the man's eyes. "Get out of my way now."

"Nope, can't let you kill my golden goose as they say." Sanders smiled. "Besides, I watched you kill many of my friends back at the herd."

"You didn't see me do anything." Reed's voice became hard. "Mister, if you don't step aside, you won't need a golden goose or anything else."

"That's big talk from a kid still wet behind the ears." Sanders grinned. "Step down, boy, I need your horse."

"It's your funeral, mister." Reed turned the horse, putting the animal between him and Sanders as he dismounted. Looking over the saddle, he watched as the man set himself, placing his feet wide apart.

Stepping from behind the horse, Reed looked at the gunman and waited, watching the cold eyes narrow into slits. Watching as the man's right hand opened and closed, Reed sensed he was fixing to draw. Only the man's eyes gave him away as he blinked, just before he made his move for his pistol. Both guns roared almost at the same time, sending their deadly lead flying across the short space that separated the two combatants.

From where he stood, feeding a small fire, Rail Johnson lurched and whirled around at the sound of gunshots. Sweat popped out on his forehead as fear grabbed at his heart. Johnson knew the shots had been fired almost simultaneously. One of the shots had to have been Sanders, but who was the other shooter and who won? Quickly saddling his horse, Johnson whipped the animal hard, racing away to the south, leaving Sander's horse tied where he was. He was in a panic and for the first time, he was alone. He had no way of knowing if Sanders had been killed or had done the killing. Fear gripped the big man. He couldn't control himself, and never in all his life had he felt the fear that consumed him now. Never before had he been alone, without his riders to back him up. He felt shame for his cowardice, but he was alive. The last few days, everything seemed to have gone wrong.

Keeler looked at Valdez and shook his head. The Mexican had picked up pistoleros at the Comanchero camp and without rest had turned back to the east. Keeler couldn't believe the Comanchero Chief was riding east to look for the young Slocum without so much as a little rest. Keeler knew it was the blond-headed woman that Valdez really wanted. With all the women at the Comanchero Camp, he couldn't understand how the Mexican could be so infatuated with one woman. Worse, Valdez was making him lead them to the east, straight back into danger just to show him where the man who had taken the woman lived. Keeler knew this whole disaster had been his fault and that he had been foolish and greedy. He should have listened to Hawk and Bodie Paul and turned the woman loose. Now, he was deep in northeast Texas again, leaving the Llano Estacado and the safety the deep prairies provided.

Looking around at the men surrounding him, Keeler swore. Valdez had only brought five Mexican riders and three Comanche warriors on this raid. Even Pedro Garcia had tried in vain to talk Valdez out of this foolish chase after the woman. Keeler shook his head as he looked over at Garcia, the man thought Valdez was wrong, but he was loyal to Valdez as a pet dog. He didn't like it, but he would follow Valdez to hell, even if it meant death to himself. Valdez had tried to say that he wanted Reed Slocum, but everyone knew he wanted the woman back.

Riding back into the Brazos River country, Keeler wondered what had become of Hawk. He knew the Comanche was a great warrior, but the young Slocum had proven many times he could kill great warriors easily. He figured Hawk was probably dead, because if he still lived, he would have returned to the Comanchero Camp already.

It had taken the hard-riding Comancheros several days to reach far east Texas. The riders were all tired and wanted to stop to rest, but Valdez wanted to catch up with the young Slocum so he urged them on. Two hours after crossing the Bosque River, the riders sat looking at the Bar S ranch house from a grove of trees. Everything about the ranch yard seemed quiet and peaceful from where they waited and watched. Keeler studied the ranch house and surrounding barns, and they were exactly as Bodie had described them. The outlaw leader didn't like riding in on the ranch, but Valdez wasn't giving him any choice. If he didn't ride forward, he knew the Mexican would kill him.

"This is the home of the young one you seek."

"You are sure this is the killer's hacienda?" Valdez glared at Keeler.

"I am sure." Keeler nodded. "Bodie Paul, the short one who rode with me, worked here. He told me about this place many times."

"I do not see any activity around the barns except for one old man." Valdez studied the layout of the ranch. "Where are all the riders that work here?"

Keeler shrugged. "That, I couldn't tell you."

Motioning in sign language, Valdez sent a Comanche to slip silently through the early morning toward the ranch. Keeler shook his head as the Indian was in plain sight. Nevertheless, he blended in so well with the tall grass and foliage, making him hard to pick out as he moved toward the ranch buildings. The riders sat patiently, waiting until the warrior returned. Suddenly, he reappeared right in front of them.

Looking up at Valdez, the warrior pointed back at the house. "Only one old one, a woman, and a hurt man stay at lodge."

"You sure?" Valdez asked. "Did the woman have yellow hair?"

"No, her hair same as Comanche, black."

"Let's go." Valdez motioned the riders to spread out around the house. "Kill anyone who comes out at us."

Pointing at the barn, Valdez watched the three Comanche warriors attack the old man as he walked from the barn. Dismounting at the hitch rail, he pushed through the door without knocking, coming face-to-face with the woman. Quickly clasping his hand over her mouth, Valdez shoved the woman to Garcia, then eased quietly into the bedroom where the injured man was resting. The blue eyes opened with a start to find Valdez and Keeler standing in the doorway.

"What do you men want?" Wes tried to rise, but fell back on the bed.

Seeing the pain-racked face, Valdez grinned and holstered his pistol. Stepping closer to the bed, he stared down into the man's face. He could see the resemblance with the young one who had killed so many of his men. Rage filled his heart as he held back from killing Wes Slocum.

"I come looking for, I believe your nephew, señor." Valdez smiled a veiled smile. "You two have the same looks."

"If you're talking about Reed Slocum, yes, he's my nephew." Wes looked up at the Mexican. "What do you want with Reed?"

"He has a blond-headed woman with him." Valdez's voice became hard. "She belongs to me. I want her back."

Watt had already told his brother about Lee Hargrove and her father, and about Keeler, his men, and the Comancheros. Looking at the

Mexican, Wes shrugged slightly. Apparently with these men here, Reed had been successful in his attempt to free the captured woman. Also, he was still alive and unharmed.

"He's not here. Hasn't been here for over a month."

"Where is he, señor?" Valdez touched the pistol butt threateningly.

"I wouldn't know, mister." Wes spit the words out. "Your threats mean nothing here, Mexican."

"You are a brave man, señor." Turning to where Garcia held the woman, Valdez motioned at him. "Bring the woman over here, Garcia."

Pushing Jeanne into the room, Valdez held her in front of Wes. "Now, señor, I will ask you only once more."

"I already told you." Wes looked worriedly at the woman. "I've been in this bed for almost three weeks. I have no idea where he may be."

Speaking rapidly in Spanish, Valdez sent one of his riders outside. Minutes later one of the Comanches returned to the room, brandishing the bloody scalp of the old horse wrangler. Grabbing the face of the woman viciously, Valdez grinned as he pressed the scalp against her terrified face.

"She has a pretty face. I wonder what it would look like with no hair." Valdez handed Garcia his knife. "I will only ask you one more time."

Looking at the frightened woman, then at the scalp, Wes nodded slightly. "He's probably taken the woman to join up with the herd headed north to Sedalia. He means to keep her out of your ugly grasp."

"So, you deceive me." Valdez clicked his tongue. "You already know about the woman."

Nodding, Wes looked up at the tall Mexican. "I know. My brother stopped by here before he headed north after the herd."

"Your brother, is he the one the Kiowa call Tall Pine?"

'That is what they call Watt Slocum alright." Wes looked into the dark eyes of Valdez. "Any harm comes to her or the boy, he'll follow you to hell and back."

"But, señor, this is Texas, and some already call it hell." Valdez smiled and shrugged.

Spitting into the tall Mexican's face, Wes laid back weakly. "Go to hell, Mex."

Taking his knife back from Garcia, Valdez stared down at the hurt man. "I do not like for anyone to lie to me."

"I told you, go to hell, Mexican."

"You first, señor. Enjoy your trip." The blade plunged deep into Wes' chest.

Dragging the sobbing woman from the bedroom, Valdez held the bloody knife to her face. "How many days will it take me to catch up with the cattle, señorita?"

Scared out of her wits, Jeanne mumbled several words before she was understood.

"She's saying maybe ten days, Jefe."

Turning, Valdez walked to the stove and poured himself a cup of coffee. "You will fix my men some food, señorita."

Nodding dumbly, Jeanne stumbled to the stove and started cooking as Valdez and his men loitered around the kitchen and sitting room.

"Jefe, what will you do?"

"We'll ride north after the woman and the young killer." Valdez looked about the room. "Muy pronto."

Keeler's head jerked sideways to look at the Mexican. To follow the herd north could be sure death for all of them. Shaking his head slowly, he knew Valdez had lost his mind for sure. The Mexican was obsessed with Lee Hargrove. The man had only met the girl once. He couldn't believe they had lost thirty men, ridden hundreds of miles chasing Reed Slocum, and all for one blond-headed girl. Seeing all of this, Valdez still persisted in his idiotic quest to regain the girl.

"She's not worth it, señor." Keeler dropped his eyes to the floor. "We'll all be killed if we go after Reed Slocum and the girl."

The glazed eyes turned on Keeler with a coldness that chilled the man. "We could leave you in there with the other gringo. Is that what you wish?"

Looking over at Garcia, who avoided his eyes, Keeler nodded. "I'll ride with you, señor."

Garcia knew Valdez and his moods, and he wasn't about to say anything more on the subject until his leader cooled his temper. Pointing at the girl, Garcia raised his shoulders questioningly, then pulled his blade when Valdez nodded.

Chapter 15

Watt Slocum and Bannock exchanged horses at Doan's and crossed the Red to follow the tracks of four horses. Exactly as Reed had found, one horse turned to the east after crossing the river while the other three kept their horses heading south. Bannock knew one of the horses belonged to Reed, leaving only two men ahead of him. Pointing out the horse tracks heading east, Watt stayed south on the heels of the southbound horses. Ten miles from the river, Bannock reined in and pointed to what looked like a body, lying far ahead of them on the trail.

"Ride in slow, Bannock. It could be an ambush." Watt kicked his gelding forward. "Be careful."

"Could be the young one, Tall Pine." The words only brought a frown from the big man as they rode to the body. "No, not your son. This one has black hair."

Waiting for Bannock to sort out the tracks to figure out what happened, Watt sat his horse, thankful it wasn't Reed. He watched as Bannock sniffed around the body like a bloodhound on a trail. Watt was a fair tracker, but compared to the Kiowa, he was a novice and he knew it. Bannock could read a track like a white man could read a book.

Waiting and watching until the warrior approached him, Watt spoke up. "What happened?"

Bannock pointed across the trail at a large cedar. "That one wait until young one come very close, then stepped into road and stopped him."

"Reed killed him?"

"This one foolish." The black head nodded. "Yes, young Slocum kill, then ride away."

"You think Reed was hurt?"

"No, young one not hurt. Dead one fired weapon once, but I not find any blood." Bannock swung up on his horse. "Young one not hurt."

"Let's ride."

Arriving at Johnson's camp, Bannock again examined the ground closely for any tracks. Pointing at the tracks of a fast running horse heading south, Bannock swung back on his horse. Two other horses followed the first at a slower speed.

"The one he follows is scared. Him a fool and push horse too hard." Bannock shook his head. "The young one has two horses now, run down the one ahead, and kill him before next new sun comes again."

Watt looked over at the warrior and nodded. "He may be scared, alright, but Rail Johnson, if cornered, will still be a dangerous man."

"No, Tall Pine. No man can stand against the young one." Bannock grinned. "This one has become a killer of men. Him very dangerous, my brother."

Watt frowned. He knew what the Kiowa spoke was true. "I am sorry it has come to this."

"Your son alive. You should be happy."

"I'm happy he is alive, but I'm not happy what all this killing has taught him."

Bannock nodded, knowing how Tall Pine felt. Still, he knew Reed Slocum was one of the bravest and greatest fighters he had ever known, and he was proud. Anyone would be proud of such a son.

Reed couldn't understand why Sanders had given him a fair chance and hadn't ambushed him from behind the large oak. He could only figure, the gunfighter was too sure of his own proficiency with a gun. He never expected the youngster he was facing could be so fast. The disbelief on his face as he crumpled onto the sandy road spoke volumes.

Kicking the black, he loped down the road until he found the small fire Johnson had started just before he heard the gunshots. Quickly studying the tracks, he took Sander's horse and continued to the south. Switching horses without dismounting, Reed urged the horse into a fast pace. He would save the black for the final run against Johnson. Now he knew, he had the man ahead. There was no way the horse, carrying the heavy weight of the man, could run much further. The horse had come a long way from where Johnson had attacked the herd. He had to be about played out. All he ever heard of Rail Johnson's hardness had been a lie. The rancher was a coward, leaving his men and running away from the fight he had started. Now, he showed himself to be a fool as well, pushing his horse so hard.

Reed's figuring had been right. Less than five miles ahead, he found the wind-broke horse lying on his side in the road. Reed swore as he looked down at the tortured animal. Johnson had run the poor thing into the ground and didn't have the decency to finish the pain-racked heaving horse. Pulling his heavy forty-four, Reed fired one shot. He knew wherever Johnson was, he would hear the shot. Rage and hate filled Reed's head. He wanted the rancher to know death followed close behind him and there was no escape.

The Comanche scouts riding point for Valdez heard the gun blast, then pointed to where a figure was weaving toward them through the thin line of oak and mesquite trees. Johnson had no idea he was running straight into the guns of the Comancheros. Exhausted as he was, not used to running on foot, plus being overweight and out of shape, his eyes remained focused mostly on the ground. Only pure fear kept him in a staggering run this far.

Pulling up short, as he came face-to-face with the Mexicans, the big rancher looked up into the faces of Valdez and his curious riders. As he ran through the jumble of oak and mesquite, he had lost his hat somewhere and his once warm overcoat had become ripped into threads by the mesquite thorns. Looking up at the dark riders, he took a step back in surprise.

"You have run far, señor." Valdez looked down at the exhausted man. "Who do you run from?"

"Slocum and his men." The voice was raspy, parched dry. "Water… please."

Nodding, Valdez waited as the big man guzzled at the canteen Keeler had handed him. "You say the one called Slocum follows you?"

"I believe he just killed one of my men back there a piece." Johnson raised the canteen greedily, letting water splash down his chin. "You must have heard the shot."

"We heard a shot." Looking down at the panting ragged man, Valdez smiled. "The herd is close then?"

"No, the herd is across the Red River, maybe sixty miles or more." Johnson finally caught his breath. "But, Slocum is near, real close."

"Then you have run far from the one who pursues you?"

"My horse died a few miles back."

"A man that runs his horse to death, is not much of a man, señor." Valdez looked down at Johnson with contempt. "You are a coward."

"You'd run too if the devil himself was chasing you."

"What devil? I see nothing." Valdez looked at the tree line.

"Slocum is following." Johnson looked behind him. "He's killed all my men."

"Which Slocum, mister?" Keeler spoke up. "The young one or the old one?"

"There's only one Watt Slocum and he's come for me." Johnson looked nervously at the tree line. "I'm a dead man as sure as I'm standing here."

"We're looking for Reed Slocum."

"That's Watt's son, but I haven't seen him for some time." Johnson seemed puzzled. "Maybe two months or more."

"And a young blond-headed woman, have you seen her?" Valdez asked about Lee.

"Blond-headed woman?" Johnson shrugged. "No, I've seen no one like that."

"Señor, where do you run to?"

"To my ranch, if I can get there." Johnson knew he was looking straight at Comancheros, the deadliest killers on the Llano, but couldn't understand what they were doing this far north of the great grasslands. "If you men will get me there safely, there'll be a big reward in it for you. Mucho dinero, señor."

"We will get you to your rancho, but first you will lead us to this Slocum, who is following you." Valdez nodded slowly.

"He's back there." Johnson's knees seemed to shake at the thought. "He's a killer. I told you, he's already killed all of my men."

"We will kill this gringo. We will do the fighting, and then we will take you to your rancho." Valdez shook his head. "But first, you must take us to where he killed your man."

Handing Keeler back the canteen, Johnson's hands shook. "I'm done in. I can't walk back that far."

"Bring this gentleman a horse, Garcia." Valdez smiled. "Make him comfortable."

"Sí, Jefe."

Several saddled horses were being led by Valdez's riders, taken from the Bar S just in case they ran into trouble and needed fresh animals. Saddlebags, filled to capacity with food and shells, bulged the heavy bags. Keeler knew by Valdez's tone, he wouldn't be taking Johnson anywhere but to an early grave. If the one behind was Reed Slocum, the rancher was as good as dead.

"What do you think, Señor Keeler?" Valdez whispered. "Which Slocum will we run into ahead?"

"First, we've got to be careful." Keeler was worried. "We don't know which Slocum is ahead or how many men he has with him, and there's always the rangers."

"The rangers are not here." Valdez shook his head. "We have seen no signs of the rangers."

"Not right now, but you never know when they're liable to show up." Keeler nodded worriedly. "They ride patrol through here quite often, looking for Comanches out on a raid."

Valdez shrugged. "I will not leave here without the woman and the young killer's hair. You must know that by now, señor."

"You heard the man, señor. He said he hadn't seen Reed Slocum."

"He will be ahead of us or with the herd, and the girl will be close." Valdez frowned at Keeler.

"You ain't forgetting Watt Slocum?"

"The one the Comanche and Kiowa call Tall Pine?"

"He's the father of Reed Slocum, the one who killed your men." Keeler shook his head. "The father is much more dangerous than the son."

"I do not believe anyone is as dangerous as the young Slocum." Valdez disagreed. "Do not believe everything you hear."

Keeler knew they were all crazy men, riding foolishly to their deaths. Still, he knew better than to try to argue Valdez out of this madness. The man had completely lost his senses. Thoughts of the blond-headed girl drove the Mexican forward like a madness. Keeler wanted to ride away from this stupidity, but he knew if he tried to escape, Valdez would send his Comanche trackers on his trail. One lone man against three Comanche warriors in their environment would be suicide.

Keeler couldn't understand Valdez, since the man was normally a rational and cautious leader. The Valdez he had traded with would never do what he was doing now. Surely, the blond-headed woman hadn't cast a spell over the man after only one dinner with her. Valdez was infatuated with the woman and would not quit his search for her. In the end, he believed Valdez's obsession with the girl was going to get them all killed.

Keeler knew Garcia was dedicated to Valdez. However, the young Comanche bucks only followed him for the horses, loot, and glory they would carry back to their village. He couldn't understand the other Valdez riders. They all knew the others that followed Valdez on his first chase, after the young Slocum, had been killed trying to take back the girl. He wondered why they still followed Valdez, but Keeler knew the answer. Their fathers had followed Valdez's father so they would follow Valdez blindly. Their lives were his, and without his leadership, they would be lost.

Bannock reined in as he heard the far-off sound of a gunshot as Reed put the horse out of its misery. "Maybe, they try to ambush the young one again?"

"Let's ride." Watt kicked his horse into a hard lope.

Thirty minutes later after a hard run, Watt looked down at the dead horse, then over at Bannock. "Looks like Rail Johnson is afoot now."

"The big man running from fight, him too big to run far on foot." Bannock nodded. "Young one catch him pretty quick, I think."

"It'll be dark in an hour or so." Watt looked up at the sky. "Let's ride."

"The big man will be dead before night comes." Bannock shook his head and kicked his horse into a lope. "We go, but I think we will find big man dead."

"Follow him, Bannock." Watt ordered the Kiowa. He was worried. Johnson might be on foot, but he was scared and still dangerous. "You track and I'll watch ahead. We've got to find him before dark."

"I have faith in young warrior. Him mighty in war. Fat man, no kill this one." Bannock turned and followed Johnson's tracks.

"Find him, Bannock."

Valdez had sent the Comanche with Garcia to scout the trail ahead. He knew if Slocum was following Johnson's tracks, he would ride right into them. He wanted Garcia to identify the rider coming after Johnson. Either the young killer or his father Tall Pine, but it really didn't matter to the Mexican leader, knowing both would have to die before he could retake the woman. Still, he wanted to know which Slocum, he was up against this time. He knew as a leader of the Comancheros, he was finished. Comanches wouldn't follow a leader that had failed as miserably as he had. He had been a fool and so many fighters were killed, Comanche and Mexican, over his fanatical chase after a mere squaw. There was even a possibility that Lobo Cayuse, because of his brother Wild Horse's death, might set his warriors against the few Mexican fighters he had left. If Lobo Cayuse turned on him, the stronghold would be destroyed and looted, and the Mexicans left behind massacred.

Still, the picture of the blond-headed woman seared his mind almost to madness. She was the most picturesque thing of beauty he had ever seen. He would kill the Slocums, recapture the woman, then he and Garcia, along with the woman, would ride for his hacienda deep in Mexico. Before riding out of the stronghold, he had stuffed three saddlebags with American greenbacks and gold, enough for him to live in royalty the rest of his days. His plan was good this time. First, he would have to ambush the young gringo killer coming toward them, and then he would torture the young one and make him tell where the blond-headed woman was.

Reed dismounted and led his horses while following Johnson's footsteps. Lower on the ground, he wouldn't be as easy a target as he would be riding horseback. The signs revealed where the big man had fallen several times on his flight to the south as he tried to get away from his pursuers. He found the man's hat, and even his pistol had been dropped in his haste to flee. Bits of Johnson's overcoat were left hanging where the mesquite thorns had ripped at the coat. Reed was amazed how the big man had run all this way after abandoning his ruined horse. Several times, Bodie had told him as they worked with the forty-four that fear could actually work for a man, making him even harder to kill. He had said a coward, when cornered, was ten times more dangerous than a brave man.

Only the slightest of movement caught his eye as he eased along the trail through the heavy mesquite flats. Something moved, off to his right. Turning away from Johnson's trail to see who had been watching his approach, Reed found signs of two horses turning south. Someone else was now out there with Johnson and they had been scouting him out. Now, they had withdrawn for some reason instead of waiting to ambush him. Maybe they were Johnson's men who somehow had gotten by him and rejoined the rancher with news they had found him.

There were so many questions and so little time to get answers. In the jumble of mesquite thickets and scrub oak there were no rock barriers for him to hide behind, only flat open spaces with few large trees. He had to decide quickly, either mount his horses and make a run for the Red or fight whatever unknown force was before him.

He wanted Johnson, but the tracks could have been only a couple of Kiowa bucks out hunting who had ridden off after seeing him. Veering back to the east, Reed again quickly picked up Johnson's staggering tracks, revealing the man didn't have anything left. Somewhere, close ahead, he would be waiting. Checking his rifle and pistol, he mounted and rode forward with his eyes keenly watching the trees ahead. Too late, he finally saw ten mounted men waiting behind a line of mesquite trees. Johnson stood before them, a beaten man with his eyes wild with fear.

Valdez grinned, less than a hundred feet separated them from Reed. "Ola, young one. You have finally come out where I can see you."

Reed nodded slightly. He was shocked as he gazed about the area. "You're a long way from home, Valdez."

"I follow you here, señor." Valdez smiled happily. "You have something that belongs to me, and I want her very badly."

"The girl?"

"That is correct, the girl." Valdez dropped his smile and became serious. "You give her to me, and perhaps, I will let you live."

"You're gonna let me live?" Reed laughed. "That's funny."

"I do not see the humor, señor. You gave me my life back once." Valdez shrugged. "Your life for the girl is not anything funny."

"You came all this way to get killed over one little old girl?" Reed laughed. "Are more of your men willing to die just to get you a woman?"

"My men do as they are told. Now, where is the blond-headed woman?"

"I expect she's in Missouri by now, Señor Valdez. Far out of your heathen grasp." Reed shrugged. "Now, why don't you and your men just turn around and ride back to your hole in the ground."

"Just like that, huh?" Valdez frowned. "You are very rude, Señor Slocum."

"I probably am rude. I didn't have a very good upbringing as a child." Reed smiled. "But, it could make a man rude to have his woman stole, then be chased halfway across Texas by a bunch of horse thieves."

Valdez snapped his fingers. "So you want us to turn and leave just like that."

"No, not just like that." Reed spat on the ground and pointed at Johnson. "You'll leave that coward here. He's mine."

"What will you do with him?" Valdez looked down at Johnson. "He is nothing."

Reed noticed the Comanche bucks were trying to move their horses and spread apart. "Tell your Indians to sit still or start shooting."

Raising his hand, Valdez spoke to the Comanche. "Stay where you are."

"Now, to answer your question, I aim to kill him." Reed swore and pointed. "I will nail his hide to that tree."

"We will ride, but not until after you are dead." Valdez shrugged. "If you manage to kill all of us, then you can have this coward."

"Turn your dogs loose and quit yapping, Mexican."

Valdez stood slightly up in his stirrups. "First, you take a look at the manes of the Comanche horses." The Mexican nodded at the horses. "Do you recognize the scalps hanging from them?"

Reed quickly looked the Comanches over. Three scalps hung from their manes. Two were the scalps of men, but the third was a long dark scalp of a woman.

"You tell me, Valdez." Reed shrugged. "Who are they?"

Valdez laughed and looked over at Keeler. "Tell the young one who the scalps used to belong to, señor."

Keeler dropped his eyes slightly as if he was ashamed. "They are your uncle's scalp and two from his hired people."

"You lie." Reed kicked his horse slowly forward. "You killed a hurt man and two helpless ones?"

"Stay back, Reed." Johnson held up his hand. "That's your uncle's scalp alright along with Jeanne Long and his horse wrangler old Henry."

"Uncle Wes!" The forty-four materialized before Valdez could blink, then a shrill cry came from Reed as he spurred the black and charged forward.

Bannock had led Watt to within hearing distance as they watched and listened as Valdez and Reed exchanged words. Slipping forward slowly, they waited and listened from behind a row of densely populated cedar trees.

"I told you, the young one is a mighty warrior." Bannock smiled and nodded. "He has no fear."

Watt shook his head as he listened to Reed talk with Valdez. The Mexican was enjoying himself as he led ten riders against the lone young man. "He's gonna get himself killed for sure, bucking that many men."

"Him no get killed. Him great warrior." Bannock grinned. "Him make fool of Valdez, you see, by and by."

"Yeah, you said that already." Watt slipped from his horse, hoping he would be in time to help Reed. "Slip off to their left and I'll go right."

Bannock slid from his horse and looked over at Watt. "Him charging ahead. Him no want help."

"Git!

Valdez froze and stared in shock as the young horseman spurred his black horse straight at them. Charging them was the last thing he thought Reed would do. The young gringo was very foolish, but Valdez had to admit he was a brave man. Riding straight at them, outnumbered ten to one, and screaming like a banshee, the young one started his gun blazing. Valdez hated him, but he had to admire a man with that kind of guts.

Reed watched as two riders fell from their horses from his first shots. Then, he felt the pull of a bullet tugging at his shoulder. Suddenly, before he could find another target, two more men fell from their saddles. Seeing the riders falling about them, the Comanche hesitated, looking for more of the enemy. Almost atop of Valdez and his men, Reed fired into the Comanche warriors who were turning to flee. Valdez sighted down his barrel at Reed as he turned his pistol on the last Comanche. Seeing his chance, as Valdez's attention was on the young fighter, Keeler fired point-blank at Valdez, hitting him in the chest and knocking him from his horse. Lying on the ground, Garcia took one shot at Keeler as he had seen the man who had ruined everything for Valdez, turn to flee after shooting his leader.

Flinging his arms out, Keeler fell sideways from his plunging horse and rolled across the sandy ground. With no time to reload his pistol, Reed jerked his rifle and rode into the remaining Mexicans, firing steadily. A wild shot from the dying Garcia, knocked Reed's saddle horn from his saddle. With his last rifle shot, Reed dispatched the Mexican with a shot to the head. Ejecting the spent shell, Reed snapped the hammer on an empty chamber.

"Well now, Mister Slocum." Johnson rose from the ground where he had been cowering. "It's just you and me now, boy."

Reed looked into the huge rifle bore that was trained on him. "You're a sniveling coward, Johnson."

"I reckon I am at that, but now, there's gonna be no one that knows it but me." The big rancher took a deep breath.

Bannock and Watt had watched as the last of the Mexicans and Comanche had fallen. However, from where they raced toward the scene, neither could get a good shot at Johnson. Both could hear Johnson and Reed talking, but there was nothing they could do as Johnson raised his rifle. Johnson had never looked their way and didn't even realize they were anywhere near.

Grinning, Johnson raised his rifle to bear on Reed's chest. "Good-bye, boy. It's been good knowing you."

Only the click of the misfiring rifle sounded as Reed threw himself from the saddle and landed on top of the big rancher. The slashing blade, of his skinning knife, flashed before the terrified man felt the blade's searing fire as it cut deep into his innards.

Sinking slowly to his knees as Reed withdrew the bloody knife, Johnson shook his head slowly. "You've done killed me, boy."

"For what you have done, I sure hope so." Reed started to reload his pistol as Watt and Bannock raced up. "Now, I aim to hang your miserable bones to the nearest tree."

Holding his stomach, Johnson slowly shook his head. "You wouldn't do that, Reed. It's not civilized."

"I'll do it, Johnson, and I never said I was civilized." Reed looked around. "You want to pick the tree?"

Slowly, the big rancher sank to the ground.

Reed stood over the body, looking down at the dead man. "You made me what I am. You started this whole mess with your hatred."

Watt noticed the blood all over Reed's shoulder and down his arm. "You okay, son?"

"Lost a little blood is all." Reed walked to where Valdez lay crumpled, studying him. "Was it worth it, señor?"

"She would have been, I think." Valdez nodded. "Would you light me a cigarette, young one? In my pocket."

"Why should I?" Reed looked down into the dark eyes. "You have killed my people."

"We are enemies, señor. Yes, I have killed your people, but you have also killed mine." Valdez smiled as a trickle of blood ran down his chin. "But, we still respect each other. Por favor, señor. Will you not give a man his last request?"

Reaching inside the fine embroidered vest-pocket, Reed pulled out the makings and tried to roll a cigarette. I'm not much good at this."

"It is okay, young one." Valdez smiled. "Just a puff."

Lighting the cigarette, Reed placed it in the man's mouth. "Here."

Looking up to where the towering figure of Watt looked down at him, the Mexican smiled and slowly nodded. "Your son here is muy hombre, Señor Slocum. You should be proud."

"How do you know who I am?" Watt was curious.

"Everyone on the Llano knows of you, Señor." Valdez nodded. "You look like this one."

"I am proud of both my sons." Watt nodded.

"Gracias, Reed Slo…" The last words were cut off and the dark head rolled sideways as smoke slowly drifted from his mouth.

"Him should have stayed in his canyon." Bannock knelt beside Valdez. "Him safe there, deep in the Llano Estacado."

"You knew him well, Bannock?"

"Yes, me and him small boys together many moons ago." Bannock nodded. "A very long time ago."

"Well, he's a goner now, for sure." Watt spoke up.

Bannock nodded. "I told Tall Pine, young one is a mighty warrior. You believe me now."

Watt looked over to where Reed was tying a rope to Rail Johnson's feet. "Yes, I believe you, Bannock. I feel sad that he has killed so many."

"What does he do, Tall Pine?"

Watt had heard Reed's threat to nail Johnson to a tree. "I reckon what he said he was going to do."

"Will you stop him?"

Watt shook his head. "No, Bannock. I don't think anyone could stop him, even if they wanted to."

Reed turned back and looked around at all the carnage covering the ground. Nine dead bodies lay within a small perimeter of one another, including men and horses. Two of the Mexican riders had managed to escape, retreating out of danger before they were shot.

"If you two hadn't showed up, I might have been alright, probably mighty dead."

"Bannock, kick a fire together away from this mess, and let's get your mighty warrior's shoulder fixed up."

A mile away from the battlefield, Bannock built a fire alongside a clear stream and helped Watt wrap up the bleeding shoulder where the bullet had entered Reed's upper arm. The wound was painful, but not dangerous. Bannock fixed food from the saddlebags Valdez had brought. Sitting around the fire eating, Reed leaned back against his saddle.

Watt tied several of the captured horses to oak trees scattered about. While unsaddling one of the horses, Watt found one of the bags filled full of greenbacks and silver. He didn't know how much the bag held, but it was a lot. Smiling, he carried it to the fire.

"Valdez has given us a gift."

"What him give?" Bannock looked at the saddlebags.

"Three bags chocked full of money." Watt smiled.

Reed looked over at the bulging bags. "We gonna keep it?"

"Unless you can prove who it belongs to I am."

"Is it honest money?"

"We've all earned it, boy." Watt shook his head. "We've fought and bled for it, and I aim to keep it. Besides, I figure some of it came from Wes' safe."

"He didn't have a safe."

"His desk drawer." Watt nodded. "Old Valdez stole it and now we've taken it back."

Daylight broke from the east, bringing the first hot rays of sunshine as Reed sat stiffly beside the small fire, sipping on coffee Bannock had boiled. Watt saddled and haltered all the Mexican horses. Removing the scalps from the Comanche horses, he placed them in a leather pouch to be taken back to the Bar S for burial.

Handing the reins of three horses to Bannock, he nodded slowly. "These are yours, my brother. Plus, all the others not carrying the Bar S brand."

"Thank you, my brother." Bannock took the ropes. "These three will do. Getting them back safe to camp might be hard."

"I'll keep the others for you at the ranch then."

"That is good." Bannock nodded. "What will Tall Pine do now?"

"If Reed is well enough to ride, I'll head back to the Bar S and see to things there."

"I can ride, but where?" Reed spoke up.

"You'll catch up to the herd and ramrod them on to Sedalia." Watt nodded over to where Reed sat. "Think you can do that?"

"Yes, sir." Reed nodded. "But, I figured you'd want to lead the herd north yourself."

"No, I've got more important things to see to back at the ranch." Watt seemed sad as he looked into the small fire. "Burying and such."

"I'm sorry about Uncle Wes. He was a good man."

"I am too, Reed." Watt nodded his huge head. "Me and him missed so much time together over this Johnson business."

"So did we, Pa."

"Yes, son. I reckon we did."

"You gonna be at the ranch when I return or are you riding back to Dade?" Reed pulled on his coffee.

"I'll be there, boy." Watt nodded slowly. "I'm sending Bannock after Nakima and any of the Kiowa that want to live at the ranch."

"That sound's fine to me." Reed smiled. "They will be welcome and that'll give me and Tolman plenty of time to get acquainted."

Watt laughed. "We may have to bash a few hard heads around that country to make them understand."

"Probably." Reed agreed. "Indians aren't too well thought of in those parts."

"Well, if you're sure you're up to it, we'll all ride out after we eat."

"Sounds good."

"And Reed, you bring that girl back here with you." Watt raised his hand. "But, you marry her in Sedalia first."

"You sure she wants to marry up with someone like me?" Reed looked over at the big man. "She's seen my bad side."

"Boy, the way she looks at you with them big cow eyes…" Watt shrugged at Bannock. "What do you think, brother-in-law."

"Lodge needs woman. You marry yellow-haired woman before someone run off with her again." Bannock shook his head. "I grow old chasing after you and woman."

"We are indebted to you, Uncle." Reed nodded. "Tell me, why did you follow us into these parts?"

"Me lonely." Both Watt and Reed laughed at that remark.

Watt was surprised when Reed called Bannock uncle, but he was proud at the same time. All his life, Reed had been taught to hate Indians out on the prairie, but now he had put that prejudice behind him.

"If you need bride price, I give you these three horses."

Reed knew Bannock was serious about the horses. "Her father is dead. Who would I pay?"

The warrior laughed. "My nephew is right."

"Tell me, Tall Pine." Reed looked over at Watt. "Do I inherit all the Kiowa as relatives?"

"They are if you want them for relatives, son." Watt smiled. "And I'd like for you to call me pa or father."

"I do, Pa." Reed looked at Bannock. "I would be proud to have them for relatives."

The next morning, Reed waved as Watt and Bannock rode out of sight. Reed stopped only long enough at Doan's Crossing to switch the black for his rested sorrel horse, and pay the hostler. He also had one of Beulah's good meals, and then with a nod, he mounted and turned north.

"You marry that girl, Reed Slocum, and you take good care of her." Beulah spoke the words as she watched his broad back fade in the distance, knowing he hadn't heard her. "And take care of that shoulder."

Reed had offered her a job as cook at the Bar S if she wanted to sell her small café and quit Doan's. She hadn't said no, but she hadn't said yes. She liked the wildness of the trading post with all the hunters and Indians moving about. Then again, a safe easy life, living on the ranch and cooking sure had its merits. And with all the hands riding for the ranch, there may be a new husband.

Reed had only been gone a few hours when two Kiowa youths rode in telling of the fight and all the bodies lying about in the mesquite thickets. Fear showed on their faces when they told about one body, standing alone upright against a tree.

Beulah looked to the north where she had last seen Reed as he rode away. "Lee was right, you are a dangerous young man."

Reed wondered what he was going to say to Lee as he neared the herd on his fifth day of travel. His shoulder had stiffened up on him, causing him to keep the sorrel to a slow trot. Looking ahead, he could finally see the dust of the drag. The nearness of the chuck wagon made his heart race. Soon, he would come face-to-face with the girl that he knew would be there. Telling her of the feelings he held for her would be harder than facing the likes of Valdez.

The herd was bedding down for the evening as Reed rode to the chuck wagon and slowly dismounted. Seeing him, Lee rushed to his side and hugged him.

"Reed, you're back." Lee stepped back and took in the haggard face and the bloody shirt. "And you're hurt."

"I'm back, that's the important thing."

Tabor walked up and took the worn out sorrel. "You best get some grub in him and a clean shirt."

As Tabor led the horse away, Lee took Reed by the arm, turning him to the fire where several punchers and Tolman sat eating their evening meal.

"Wait, Lee." Reed held her back. "I want to ask you a question before we join the others."

"Yes." Lee smiled.

"I know this is kinda sudden." Hesitating as his face turned red, Reed finally blurted out the words. "Will you marry me?"

"Yes, Reed Slocum." She smiled. "I will marry you."

"Yes." His face broke into a grin.

Lee laughed. "If you hadn't asked me, Mister Slocum, I was fixing to ask you."

The End

9 781942 869337